A gli... of g... ... ...e
and stopped ...

No. That had been the dream. It *had* to be.

She went ove... ... memories, ... the spot, staring at the ring, t... ... ... wh... was dream and what was re... A... ... ours travelling, and many more ... ... t... enty-four hours barely felt re... Images and memories ... played through her mind as i... ... ... omebody else.

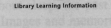
The thrumm... ... ... e gig last night. That had bee... ... he music capt... ing her senses, hijacking he... ... emot... ... ... e... ... ng her full of adrenaline. R... ...

Hot and swe... ... cares... ... before d... wn. Dream.

Dancing with ... Joe in the... ... trying to talk business, shouting in his ear. Moving so closely with him that they'd felt like one body. Feeling the music play between them like a language only they spoke. Maybe that was real.

The slide of his bare skin against hers. So, so dreamy.

Him talking softly, trading tracks, sharing a pair of headphones, until one and then both of them fell asleep. God, she wished she knew.

But as she raised her left hand and examined the demure gold band on her third finger she was certain of one thing.

Las Vegas chapel wedding. *Real.*

FALLING FOR THE REBEL PRINCESS

BY
ELLIE DARKINS

MILLS & BOON

First Published in Great Britain 2017
By Mills & Boon, an imprint of HarperCollins*Publishers*
1 London Bridge Street, London, SE1 9GF

© 2017 Ellie Darkins

ISBN: 978-0-263-92297-4

23-0517

Our p... e
proc... ging and
man... tions of
the c...

Prin...
by C...

Ellie Darkins spent her formative years devouring romance novels, and after completing her English degree decided to make a living from her love of books. As a writer and editor, she finds her work now entails dreaming up romantic proposals, hot dates with alpha males and trips to the past with dashing heroes. When she's not working she can usually be found running around after her toddler, volunteering at her local library or escaping all the above with a good book and a vanilla latte.

For Mike and Matilda

CHAPTER ONE

'NOT YET!' CHARLIE GASPED, willing herself to be dragged back under.

In her dream her skin was hot and damp, on fire from his touch.

Awake, her tongue felt furry.

In her dream her body hummed, desperate for the feel of him.

Awake, her eyes stung as she peeled them open.

In her dream she begged for more, and got everything she didn't even know she needed.

Awake, she needed to pee.

She admitted defeat and stretched herself properly alive, wincing at the harsh Nevada sunlight assaulting her in the hotel room. As her toes encountered skin she flinched back, realising that she did have this one, small reminder of her dream. The man who'd taken the starring role was beside her on the mattress, his face turned away from her, his arms and legs sprawled and caught in the sheets. She looked away. She couldn't think about him. Not yet.

Easing herself out of bed, she willed him not to wake. And worked her thumb into her waistband, rubbing at her skin where her jeans had left a tight red line. The T-shirt she'd slept in was twisted and creased, and she glanced around the room, wondering whether her luggage had been transferred when the hotel had upgraded them to a luxury suite. She shuddered when she caught sight of herself in the mirror and tried to pull her hair up into some sort of order.

It had started out backcombed and messy, and her eyeliner had never been subtle in her life—but a couple of hours' sleep had taken the look from grunge to tragic. She wiped under her eyes with a finger, and the tacky drag of her skin made her shudder. And desperate to shower.

A glint of gold caught her eye and stopped her dead.

No. That had been the dream. It had to be.

She went over her memories, rooted to the spot, staring at the ring, trying to pull apart what was dream and what was real. After eighteen hours travelling and many more without sleep, the past twenty-four hours barely felt real, images and memories played through her mind as if they had happened to somebody else.

The thrumming, heaving energy of the gig last night. That was real. The music capturing her senses, hijacking her emotions and pumping her full of adrenaline. Real.

Hot and sweaty caresses just before dawn. Dream.

Dancing with Joe in the club, trying to talk business, shouting in his ear. Moving so closely with him that they felt like one body. Feeling the music play between them like a language only they spoke. Maybe that was real.

The slide of his bare skin against hers. So, so dreamy.

Him talking softly as they lay on the bed, trading playlists on their phones, sharing a pair of headphones, until one and then both of them fell asleep. God, she wished she knew.

But as she raised her left hand and examined the demure gold band on her third finger, she was certain of one thing.

Vegas chapel wedding. Real.

She banged her head back against the wall. Why did she always do this? She was losing count of the number of times she'd looked over the wreckage of her life after one stupid, impulsive move after another and wished that she could turn back time. If she had the balls to go home and tell her parents that she didn't want their royal way of life and everything that came with it, maybe she'd stop hitting the self-destruct button. But starting that conversation would lead to questions that she'd never be prepared to answer.

Thinking back to the night before, she tried to remember what had triggered her reaction. And then she caught sight of the newspaper, abandoned beside the bed. The slip of the paper under her fingertips made her shiver with the memory of being handed one like it backstage in the club last night, and she let out a low groan. It had been the headline on the front page: Duke Philippe bragging about his forthcoming engagement to Princess Caroline Mary Beatrice of Afland, otherwise known as Charlie. It was the sort of match her parents had been not so subtly pushing on her for years, the one she was hoping that would go away if she ignored it for long enough. She knew unequivocally that she would never marry, and especially not someone like Duke Philippe.

She'd left the cold, rocky, North Sea island of Afland nearly ten years ago, when she'd headed to London determined to make her own way in the music business. Her parents had given her ten years to pursue her rebellion—as they put it. But they all knew what was expected after that: a return to Afland, official royal duties, and a practical and sensible engagement to a practical, sensible aristocrat.

So there was nothing but disappointment in store for her family, and for her.

She shrank into the bathroom and hid the newspaper as she heard stirring from the bed. Perhaps if she hid for long enough it just wouldn't be true—Joe Kavanagh and their marriage would fade away as the figment of her imagination that she knew they must be.

Marriage. She scoffed. This wasn't a marriage. It was a mistake.

But it seemed as if her body didn't care which bits of last night were real and which were imagined. The hair on her arms was standing on end, her heart had started to race, and she felt a yearning deep in her stomach that seemed somehow familiar.

'Morning,' she heard Joe call from the bedroom, and she wondered if he'd guessed that she was hiding out in there. 'I know you're in there.'

The sound of his voice sent another shiver of recognition. British, and educated. But there was also a burr of something rugged about it, part of his northern upbringing that felt exotically 'authentic', when compared to the marble halls and polished accents of her childhood.

She risked peeking round the bathroom door and mumbled a good morning, wondering why she hadn't just left the minute that she'd woken up—running has always worked for her before. She'd been running from one catastrophe to another for as long as she could remember. Because this was her suite, she reminded herself. They'd been upgraded when the manager of the hotel had heard about their impromptu wedding, and realised that he had royalty and music royalty spending their wedding night in his hotel.

The only constant in her life since she'd left the palace in Afland had been her job. She'd worked from the bottom of the career ladder up to her position as an A&R executive, signing bands for an independent record label, Avalon. And that was the reason she had to get herself out of this room and face her new husband. Because not only was he a veritable rock god, he was also the artist that she'd been flown out here to charm, persuade and impress with her consummate professionalism in a last-ditch bid to get him to sign with her company.

She held her head high as she walked back into the bedroom, determined not to show him her feelings. The sun was coming in strong through the windows, and the backlighting meant that she couldn't quite see his expression.

'How's the head?' he asked, his expression changing to concerned.

She wondered whether she should tell him that she'd only had a couple of beers at most last night. That her recklessness hadn't come from alcohol, it had been fuelled by adrenaline and something more dangerous—the destructive path she found herself on all too often whenever marriage and family and the future entered the conversation.

Had Joe been drunk last night? She didn't think so. He'd seemed high when he'd come off stage, but she had been at enough gigs to know the difference between adrenaline and something less legal. She remembered him necking a beer, but that was it. So he didn't have that excuse either.

Why in God's name had this ever seemed like a good idea—to either of them?

'I've felt better,' she admitted, crossing the room to perch on the edge of the bed.

Up close, she decided that it really wasn't fair that he looked like this. His hair was artfully mussed by the pillows, his shirt was rumpled, and his tiny hint of eyeliner had smudged, but the whole look was so unforgivably sexy she almost forgot that whatever had happened the night before had been a huge mistake.

But sexy wasn't why she'd married him. Or maybe it was. When she went into reckless self-destruction mode, who was to say why she did anything?

Even in this oasis in the middle of the desert, she hadn't been able to escape the baggage that came with being a member of the royal family. The media obsession with royal women marrying and reproducing. Someone had raised a toast when they had seen her, to her impending marriage, asked her if she was up the duff and handed her a bottle of champagne. She'd been tempted to down the whole thing without taking a breath, determined to silence the voices in her head.

'So,' she said. 'I guess we're in trouble.'

Trouble? She was right about that. Everything about this woman said trouble. He had known it the minute that he had set eyes on her, all attitude and eyeliner.

He had known it for sure when they'd started dancing, her body moving in time with his. So at what point last night had trouble seemed like such a good idea?

When they'd left the dance floor, in that last club, their bodies hot and sticky. When she'd been trying to talk business but he'd been distracted by the humming of his skin and the sparks that leapt from his body to hers whenever she was near. When Ricky, the drummer in his band, had joked that he needed to show some real rock-star behaviour if they were going to sell the new album, and Joe had dropped to one knee and proposed.

He hadn't thought for a second that she would go along with it.

But Charlie had stopped for a moment as their eyes had met, and as everyone had laughed around them he had been able to see that she wasn't laughing, and neither was he. The club had stilled and quietened, or maybe it was just his mind that had, but suddenly there had been just the two of them, connected through something bigger than either of their bodies could contain. Something he couldn't pretend to comprehend, but that he knew meant that they understood each other.

And then she had nodded, thrown back her head and laughed along with everyone else, and they had been carried on a wave of adrenaline, bonhomie and contagious intoxication into a cab and up the steps of the courthouse. Somehow, still high from their performance and bewitched by the Princess, he hadn't stepped out of their fantasy and broken the spell.

They'd been cocooned in that buzz, carrying them straight through the ceremony. Such a laugh as they'd toppled out of the chapel. Right up until that kiss. Then it had all felt very real.

Did she remember that feeling as they had kissed for the first time? He knew in his bones that he could never forget it, as they were pronounced husband and wife.

'Are you going to hide in there all morning?' he asked.

In the daylight, she didn't look like a princess any more than she had the night before. Maybe that was how he'd found himself here. He'd expected to be on edge around her, but as soon as he had met her... Not that he was relaxed—no, there was too much going on, too much churning and yearning and *desire* to call it relaxed. But he'd been... He wasn't sure of the word. Her boss had sent her out here to convince him that their label was a good fit—and he'd been right. They had... Maybe fit was the right world. They'd just understood each other. She understood the music. Understood him. And when they had started dancing, there had been no question in his mind that this was important. He didn't know what it was, but he knew that he wanted more.

And marrying her—it had been a good move for the band. You couldn't buy publicity like that. He must have been thinking about that, must have calculated this as a business move. It was the only thing that made sense.

But was she expecting a marriage?

Because she came with a hell of a lot of baggage. Oh, he knew which fork to use, and how to spot the nasty ones in a room of over-privileged Henrys. He'd learned that much at his exclusive public school, where his music scholarship had taken him fee-free. But the most important part of his education had been the invaluable lesson he'd got in his last year—everyone was out to get something, so you'd better work out what you wanted in return.

The only place he felt relaxed these days was on the road, with his band. They moved from city to city, sometimes settling for a few weeks if they could hire some studio space, otherwise going from gig to gig, and woman to woman, without looking back. Everyone knowing exactly what they wanted, and taking what was on offer with no strings attached.

'Come on,' he said, reaching for her hand. As his fingertips touched hers he had another flash of that feeling from last night. The electric current that had joined them together as they had danced; that had woven such a spell around them that even a visit to a courthouse hadn't broken it.

'I can't believe we got married. This was your fault. Your idea.'

Was she for real? He shrugged and reminded her of the details. 'No one forced you. You seemed to think it was a great idea last night.'

So why was she looking at her ring as if it were burning her?

'Wh…?'

He waited to see which question was burning uppermost in her mind.

'Why? Why in God's name did I think it was a great idea?'

'How am I supposed to know if you don't? Maybe

you were thinking it would be good publicity for the album.'

He looked at her carefully. Yes, that was why they had done it. But also…no. There was more to it. He couldn't believe that she was such a stranger this morning. When they'd laughed about this last night, it hadn't just been a publicity stunt—that sounded too cold. It had been a joke, a deal, between friends. A publicity stunt was business, but last night, as they'd laughed together on the way to the courthouse, it had been more than that.

And maybe that was where he had gone wrong, because he knew how this worked. He knew that all relationships were deals, with each partner out to get what they wanted. He had no reason to be offended that she was acting like that this morning.

'I'm not sure why you're mad at me. You thought it was a great idea last night.'

'I hadn't slept for thirty-six hours, Joe. I think we can say that I wasn't doing my best reasoning. We have to undo this. What are my parents going to say?'

Her parents, the Queen of Afland and her husband. He groaned inwardly.

'Last night you said, and I quote, "They're going to go mental." As far as I could work out, that was a point in the plan's favour.'

In the cold light of morning—not such a good idea. Bad, in fact. Very bad.

He had married a princess—an actual blue-blooded, heir-to-the-throne, her-mother's-a-queen *princess*.

He was royally screwed.

'Look,' Joe said. 'I'm hungry, too hungry to talk

about this now. How about we go out for breakfast
and discuss this with coffee and as much protein as
they can cram on a plate?'

CHAPTER TWO

CHARLIE GAZED INTO her black coffee, hoping that it would supply answers. Her memories had started to filter back in as she'd sipped her first cup; shame had started creeping in with her second. She hoped that this cup, her third, would be the one that made her feel human again.

'So how do we undo this?' she said bluntly. 'This is Vegas. They must annul almost as many marriages as they make here. Do we need to go back to the courthouse?'

She looked up and met Joe's eye. He was watching her intently as he took a bite of another slice of toast. 'We could,' he said. 'If we want an annulment, I guess that's how we go about it.'

'If?' She nearly spat out her coffee. 'I don't think you understand, Joe. We got *married*.'

'I know: I was there.'

'Am I missing something? The way I see things, we were joking around, we thought it would be hil*ar*ious to have a Vegas wedding, and we've woken up this morning to a major disaster. Aren't you interested in damage limitation?'

'Of course I am, but, unlike you, I think the reasons we got married were sound. Not necessarily the *best* reasons to enter into a legally binding personal commitment, but sound nonetheless.'

She raised her eyebrows. 'Remind me.'

'Okay, obvious ones first. Publicity. The band needs it. The album is almost finished, we're looking for a new label, and there is no such thing as bad publicity, right?'

'Mercenary much?'

'Look, this isn't my fault. You were good with mercenary last night.'

She snorted. 'Fine, publicity is one reason. Give me another.'

'It shows you're serious about the band.'

She crossed her arms and sat back in her seat, fixing him with a glare. 'I've signed plenty of bands before without marrying the lead singer. They signed with me because they trust that I'm bloody good at my job. Are you seriously telling me that whether or not I would marry you was going to be a deal-breaker?'

He leaned forward, not put off by her death stare. In fact, his eyes softened as he reached for her hand, pulling her back towards him. She went with it, not wanting to look childish by batting him away.

'Of course it wasn't,' he said gently. 'But breaking the marriage now? I'm not sure how that's going to play out. I'm not sure what our working relationship could look like with that all over the papers.'

She shook her head, looking back into the depths of her coffee, still begging it for answers.

'All of which I have to weigh against the heartbreak of my family if we don't bury this right now.'

She avoided eye contact as she tried to stop the

tears from escaping. But she took a deep breath and when she looked up they were gone. 'Do you think anyone knows already? The press?'

'We weren't exactly discreet,' he said, with a sympathetic smile. 'I'd think it's likely.'

'And that can't be undone, annulment or not.'

He leaned back and took a long drink of his orange juice. 'So let's control the narrative.'

'What do you mean?'

'What story would hurt your family more—a whirlwind romance and hasty Vegas marriage, or a drunken publicity stunt to further your career? Because that's how the tabloids are going to want to spin it.'

'What's your point, Joe?' She'd taken her hand back and crossed her arms again, sure that this conversation was taking a turn that she wasn't going to like.

'All I'm saying is that we can't go back in time. We can't get unmarried, whether we get an annulment or not. So we either dissolve the marriage today and deal with the fallout to our reputations…'

'Or…?'

'Or we stay married.'

Her breathing caught as just for a second she considered what that might mean, to be this man's wife.

'But we're not in love. Anyone's going to be able to see that.'

He scrutinised her from under his lashes, which were truly longer and thicker than any man's had a right to be. 'So we're going to have to work hard to convince them. You can't deny that it's a better story.'

'And you can't deny that it means lying to my family. Ruining all the plans they were making for my life.

I don't know what your relationship with your family is like, but I'm not sure that I can pull it off. I'm not sure that I want to. Things are diffi—'

She stopped before she revealed too much. Joe raised an eyebrow, obviously curious about why she had cut herself off, but he didn't push her on it.

'Would you rather they knew the truth?'

Of course not. She had been hiding the truth from them for years, ever since she'd found out that she could never be the daughter or the Princess that they needed her to be.

'Are we seriously having this conversation? You want to stay married? You do know that you're a rock star, right? If you were that desperate for publicity you could have found a hundred girls who actually *wanted* to be your wife.'

'Wow, you're quite something for a guy's ego. For the record, this isn't some elaborate ruse to get myself a woman. I don't have any problems on that score. All I'm doing is making the best of a situation. That's all.'

Charlie took a big bite of pie, hoping that the sugar would succeed where the coffee hadn't. 'Well, I'm glad to hear that you're not remotely interested in me as a woman.'

He fixed her with a meaningful stare, the intensity of his expression making it impossible for her to look away.

'I never said that.'

Heat rose in her belly as he held the eye contact, leaving her in no doubt about how he thought of her. She shook her head as he finally broke the contact. 'I can't believe that I'm even considering this. You're crazy. There's no way we can keep this up. What happens if we slip? What happens when someone finds out it's not for real? What happens when one of us meets someone and this marriage of convenience isn't so convenient any more?'

He reached for her hand across the table, and once again there was that crackle, that spark that she remembered from the night before. She saw him in the chapel, eyes creased in laughter, as he leaned in to kiss her. Those eyes were still in front of her, concerned now though, rather than amused.

'It doesn't have to be for ever. Just long enough that it doesn't look like a stunt when we split. You weren't planning on marrying someone else any time soon, were you?'

'Never.' Her coffee cup rattled onto the saucer with a clash, liquid spilling over the top.

'Wow—that really was a no.'

She locked her gaze on his—he had to understand this if they were going to go on. 'I mean it, Joe. I didn't want to get married. Ever. I'm not wife material.'

'And yet here I am, married to you.'

He held her gaze and there was something familiar there. Something that made her stomach tighten in a knot and her skin prickle in awareness. With all the unexpected drama of finding themselves married, it seemed as if they'd both temporarily forgotten that they had also found themselves in bed together that morning.

Perhaps he was remembering something similar, because all of a sudden there was a new fire in his eyes, a new heat in the way that he was looking at her.

Her memory might be a bit ropey, but between the caffeine and the sugar her brain had been pretty much put back together, and there was one image of the night before that she couldn't get from her mind.

You may now kiss the bride.

They'd all burst out laughing, finding the whole thing hilarious. But as soon as Joe's hand had brushed against her cheek, cupping her jaw to turn her face up to him, the laughs had died in her throat. He'd been looking down at her as if he were only just seeing her for the first time, as if she had been made to look different by their marriage. His lush eyelashes had swept shut as he'd leaned towards her, and she'd had just a second to catch her breath before his lips had touched hers. They had been impossibly soft, and to start with had just pressed dry and chaste against hers. She'd reached up as he had and touched his cheek, just a gentle, friendly caress of her finger against his stubbled skin. But it had seemed to snap something within him; a gasp had escaped his lips, been swallowed by hers. His mouth had parted, and heat had flared between them.

She'd closed her eyes, understood that she was giving herself up to something more powerful than the simple actions of two individuals. As her eyes had shut her mouth had opened and her body had bowed towards her husband. Her hips had met his, and instantly sparks had crackled. His hands had left her face to lock around her waist, dragging her in tight and holding her against him. His tongue had been hot and hungry in her mouth; her hands frenzied, exploring the contours of his chest, his back, his butt.

And then the applause of their audience had broken into her consciousness, and she'd remembered where they were. What they were doing.

Blood had rushed to her cheeks and she could feel them glow as she'd broken away from Joe, acknowledging the whoops with an ironic wave.

'All right, all right,' she'd said, a sip of champagne helping with the brazen nonchalance; she'd hoped that she was successfully hiding the shake in her voice. 'Hope you enjoyed the show, people.'

She'd looked up at Joe to see whether she had imagined the connection between them, whether he'd still felt it buzzing and humming and trying to pull their bodies back together. By the heated, haunted look in his eyes, she wasn't alone in this.

He was worried, and he should be, because this marriage of convenience had just got a whole lot more complicated, for both of them. It had been a laugh, a joke, until their lips had met and they had both realised, simultaneously, that the flirting and banter that had provided an edge of excitement to their dancing that night would be a dangerous force unless they got a lid on it.

In the cold light of the morning after, she knew that they needed to face the problem head-on. She broke her gaze away from him, trying to cover what they had both clearly been remembering.

'Ground rules,' she said firmly, distracting herself by taking another bite of pie. 'If we do this, there have to be ground rules to stop it getting complicated.' He nodded in agreement, and she kept talking. 'First of all, we keep this strictly business. We both need to keep our heads and be able to walk away when the time is right. Let's acknowledge that there is chemistry between us, but if we let that lead us, we're not going to be objective and make smart decisions. And I think we both agree that we need to be smart.'

'People will talk if we don't make this look good. It has to be convincing.'

'Well, duh.' She waved to the waitress for a coffee refill. 'You're really trying to teach me how to handle the press? Obviously, in public we behave as if we're so madly in love that we couldn't wait a single minute longer to get married. We sell the hell out of it and make sure that no one has a choice *but* to believe us. But that's in public. In private, we're respectful colleagues.'

He snorted. 'Colleagues? You think we can do that? You were there, weren't you, last night? You do remember?'

Did she remember the kiss? The shivers? The way that she could still feel the imprint of his mouth on hers, as if the touch of skin on skin had permanently altered the cells? Yeah, she remembered, but that wasn't what was important here.

'And that's why we need the rules, Joe. If you want to stay married to me, you'd better listen up and pay attention.'

'Oh, I'm listening, and you're very clear. In public, I'm madly in love with you. Behind closed doors I'm at arm's length. Got it. So what are your other rules?'

She resurrected the death stare. 'No cheating. Ever. If we're going to make people believe this, they have to really believe it. We can't risk the story being hijacked. Doesn't matter how discreet you think you're being, it's never enough.'

'I get it. You don't share. Goes without saying.'

She dropped her cup back onto her saucer a little

heavier than she had planned, and the hot, bitter liquid slopped over the side again. 'This isn't about me, Joe. Don't pretend to know me. This is about appearances. I've already told you, this isn't personal.'

'Fine, well, if you're all done then I've got a rule of my own.'

'Go on, then.' She raised an eyebrow in anticipation.

'You move in with me.'

This time, the whole cup went over, coffee sloshing over the side of the table and onto her faded black jeans. At least she'd managed to miss her white shirt, she thought, thanking whoever was responsible for small mercies. She mopped hastily with a handful of napkins, buying her precious moments to regain her composure and think about what he had said. Of course she understood deep down that they would have to live together. But somehow, until he'd said it out loud, she hadn't believed it.

They would be alone together. *Living* alone together. No one to chaperone or keep them to their 'this is just business' word. Watching him across a diner table this morning, it wasn't exactly easy to keep her hands off him, so how were they meant to do that living alone together?

But she knew better than anyone that they had to make this look good. If her parents knew that she'd only done this to get out of the marriage to Philippe they would be so disappointed, and she didn't know that she could take doing that to them again.

Separate flats weren't going to cut it. By the time she looked back up, she knew that she seemed calm, regardless of what was going on underneath.

'Of course, that makes sense. Are you going to insist on your place rather than mine?'

'I'll need my recording studio.'

She nodded. 'Fine. So that's it, then? Three ground rules and we're just going to do this?'

'Well, if you're going to chicken out, you need to do it now.'

'I'm not eight years old, Joe. I'm not going to go through with this because you call me chicken.'

'Fine, why *are* you going to do it?' Nice use of psychology there, she thought. Act as though I've already agreed. He really did want this publicity. But it didn't matter, because she'd already made up her mind.

'I'm doing it because I don't want to hurt my family any more than I have to, and because I think it'll be good for my career.' And because it would save her from being talked into a real marriage, one which she knew she could never deserve.

'As long as you're doing it, your reasons are your own business,' Joe replied. She felt a little sting at that, like a brush of nettles against bare skin. Her own business. Damn right it was, but the way he said it, as if there really were nothing more than that between them… It didn't make sense. She didn't want it to make sense. She just knew that she didn't want it to hurt.

'So what are we going to tell people?' she asked after a long, awkward silence. 'I guess we need to get our stories straight.'

He nodded, and sipped at his coffee. 'We just keep it simple. We were swept away when we met each other yesterday, knew right away that it was love and decided we needed to be married. The guys in the

band will go along with it. You don't have to worry
about that.' Somehow she'd forgotten that they'd been
there, egging them on, bundling them in the cab to the
courthouse. When she thought back to last night, she
remembered watching Joe on stage, sweat dripping
from his forehead as he sang and rocked around the
stage. Him grabbing her hand and pulling her to the
dance floor when they'd gone on to a club after the
gig, when he hadn't wanted to talk business.

She remembered the touch of his mouth on hers, as
they were pronounced husband and wife.

But of course there had been witnesses, people who
knew as well as she did that this was all a sham.

'What if they say something? They could go to
the press.'

'They won't. Anyway, to everyone else it was just
a laugh. And if anyone did say something, it'd be up
to us to look so convincingly in love that no one could
possibly believe them.'

'Ah, easy as that, huh.'

As they sat in the diner she realised how little
thought they'd actually given this. She didn't even
know when she would see him again. Her flight was
booked back to London that night. She'd only been
in Vegas to take this meeting. Her boss had sent her
on a flying visit, instructed to try anything to get him
to sign. She'd given her word that she wouldn't leave
without the deal done. Would he see through them
when they got back? Would he realise how far she
had gone to keep to her promise?

'I'm flying home tonight,' she said.

He raised an eyebrow. 'You were pretty sure you'd

get me to sign, then. Didn't think you'd have to stick around to convince me?'

'I thought you'd be on the move, actually. I was told that you were only in Vegas for one night.' She knew that the band were renowned for their work ethic and their packed tour schedule, moving from city to city and gig to gig night after night. This had been her only chance for a meeting, her boss had told her as he'd instructed her to book a flight.

If he was always on the move like that, perhaps this would be easier than she thought. It could be weeks, months, before they actually had to live together. And by then, maybe… Maybe what. Maybe things would be different? There was no point pretending to be married at all if she thought that they would have changed their minds in a few weeks. They had to stick it out longer than that. If they were going to do this, they had to do it properly.

'I am, as it happens. I'm flying back to London tonight too.'

Why had he said that? They were meant to be in the States for two more weeks. Their manager had booked them into a retreat so that he could finish writing the new album. It should have been just a case of putting the finishing touches to a few songs, but he had an uneasy feeling about it this morning. He needed to go back and look at it again. There were a few decent tracks there, he was sure. But a niggling voice in his head was telling him that he still hadn't got the big hitters. The singles that would propel the album up the streaming charts and across the radio waves.

There was studio space booked for them in London in two weeks' time and it had to be fixed before then.

Their manager was going to kill him when he told him he wouldn't be showing up.

He could write in London; he had written the last album in London. It had nothing to do with Charlie. Nothing to do with her feelings, anyway. As she kept saying, this was just business. But it would look better for them to arrive home together.

Nothing to do with their feelings. Right. He would make her believe that today. Because her memory might be fuzzy but he could remember everything. Including the moment that they'd been on the dance floor, him still buzzing from the adrenaline of being on stage, her from the dancing and the music and the day and a half without sleep.

They'd moved together as the music had coursed through him, the bass vibrating his skin. She'd been trying to talk business, shouting in his ear. Contracts and terms, and commitment. But he hadn't been able to see past her. To feel anything more than the skin of her shoulder under his hand as he'd leaned in to speak in her ear. The soft slide of her hair as he'd brushed it off her face. 'Let's do this,' she'd said. 'We'd be a great team. I know that we can create something amazing together.'

She'd reached up then, making sure she had his attention—as if it would ever be anywhere but on her again. And then Ricky had said those idiotic words, the ones that no judge could take back this morning.

She'd laughed, at first, when he had proposed, assuming that he was joking. It had had nothing to do with the way she'd felt when his arm was around her. The way that that had made him feel. As if he wanted to protect her and challenge her and be challenged by her all at once.

He could never let her know how he had felt last night.

It was much better, much safer that they kept this as business. He knew what happened when you went into a relationship without any calculation. When you jumped in with your heart on the line and no defences. He wouldn't be doing it again.

And then there were the differences between them. Sure, it hadn't seemed to matter in that moment that he'd asked her to marry him, or when they were dancing and laughing and joking together, but a gig and a nightclub and beer were great levellers. When you were having to scream above the music then your accent didn't matter. But in the diner this morning there was no hiding her carefully Londonised RP that one could only acquire with decades of very expensive schooling, and learning to speak in the echoey ballrooms of city palaces and country piles.

He'd learnt that when he'd joined one of those expensive schools at the age of eleven, courtesy of his music scholarship free ride. His Bolton accent had been smoothed slightly by years away from home, first at school, and then on the road, but it would always be there. And he knew that, like the difference in their backgrounds, it would eventually come between them.

His experiences at school had made it clear that he didn't belong there.

And when he'd returned home to his parents, and

their comfy semi-detached in the suburbs, he had realised that he didn't belong there any more either. He
was caught between two worlds, not able to settle
in either. So the last thing that he needed was to be
paraded in front of the royal family, no doubt coming into contact with the Ruperts and Sebastians and
Hugos from his school days.

And what about his family? Was Charlie going to
come round for a Sunday roast? Make small talk with
his mum with Radio 2 playing in the background? He
couldn't picture it.

But he would have to, he realised. Because it didn't
matter what they were doing in private. It didn't matter that he had told himself that he absolutely had to
get these feelings under control, their worlds were
about to collide.

It wasn't permanent. That was what he had to remind himself. It wasn't for ever. They were going to
end this once a decent amount of time had passed,
and in the meantime they would just have to fit into
each other's lives as best they could.

Just think of the publicity. A whirlwind romance
was a good story. No doubt a better one than a drunken
mistake. But since when had he allowed the papers
to rule on what was and wasn't a good idea for him?
No, there was more to it than that. Something about
waking up beside her in bed that he wasn't ready to
let go of yet.

'I have an album launch party to go to first,
though,' he said at last. 'What do you say to making
our first appearance as husband and wife?'

CHAPTER THREE

CHARLIE ADJUSTED THE strap on her spike heels and straightened the seam of her leather leggings. As soon as the car door opened, she knew there would be a tsunami of flashes from the assembled press hordes. She was considered fair game at the best of times, and if news of the wedding had got out by now, the scrum would be worse than usual.

These shots needed to be perfect. She wasn't having her big moment hijacked by a red circle of shame.

It was funny, she thought, that neither she nor Joe had called his manager, or her boss yet, and told them about what had happened. Not the best start to a publicity campaign, which was, after all, what they had agreed this marriage was. It was more natural, this way, she thought. If there was a big announcement, it would look too fake. Much better for them to let the story grow organically.

As the limo pulled up outside the club she realised that no announcement was necessary anyway. Word had obviously got around. The hotel had arranged for them to be picked up from a discreet back door, an old habit, so she hadn't been sure whether there had been photographers waiting for her there. If there had, they'd taken a shortcut to beat them here. There were definitely more press here than a simple album launch warranted. The story was out, then.

Without thinking, she slipped her hand into Joe's, sliding her fingers between his. The sight of so many photographers still made her nervous. It didn't matter how many times she had faced them. It reminded her of those times in her childhood when she'd been pulled from the protective privacy of her family home and paraded in front of the world's press, all looking for that perfect picture of the perfect Princess. As a child she had smiled until her cheeks had ached, dressed in her prettiest pink dress, turning this way and that as her name was shouted. It had been a small price to pay, her parents had explained, to make sure that the rest of their lives were private. But as she'd got older she'd resented those days more and more, and her childish rictus grin had turned into a sullen teen grimace.

And then, when she was nineteen, and had realised that she would never be the Princess that her family and her country wanted her to be, she'd stopped smiling altogether. She remembered sitting in the doctor's office as he explained what he'd found: inflammation, scar tissue, her ovaries affected. Possible problems conceiving.

She might never have a baby, no chubby little princes or princesses to parade in front of an adoring public, and no hope of making the sort of dynastic match that would make her parents happy.

Her most important duty as a royal female was to continue her family's line. It had been drummed into her from school history lessons to formal state occasions from as far back as she could remember. Queens who had done their duty and provided little princes and princesses to continue the family line.

And things hadn't changed as much as we would all like to think, she knew. The country had liked her mother when she was a shining twenty-something. But it was when she'd given the country three beautiful royal children that they'd really fallen in love with her, when she had won their loyalty. And that was something that Charlie might never be able to do. She might never feel the delicious weight of her child in her arms. Never breathe in the smell of a new baby knowing that it was all hers.

What if she never made her parents grandparents, and saw the pride and love in their eyes that she knew they were reserving for that occasion?

And as soon as she'd realised that, she had realised that she could never make them truly proud of her, somehow the weight of responsibility had fallen from her shoulders and she'd decided that she was never going back. If she wanted to roll out of a nightclub drunk—okay. If she wanted to disappear for three days, without letting anyone know where she was going—fine. If she wanted to skip a family event to go and listen to a new band—who cared?

Her mother insisted on a security detail, and Charlie had given up arguing that one. Her only demand was that they were invisible—she never looked for the smartly dressed man she knew must be on the row behind her on the plane, and so she never saw him. And the officers didn't report back to her mother. If she thought for a second that they would, she would have pulled the plug on the whole arrangement. That was why they'd not intervened last night: they knew she had a zero-tolerance approach to them interfering with anything that didn't affect her physical safety.

She was never going to be the perfect Princess, so why build her family's hopes up? She could let them down now, get it out of the way, in her own way, and not have to worry with blindsiding them with disappointment later.

Except it hurt to disappoint them, and it didn't seem to matter how many times that she did it. Every time, the look on their faces was as bad as the time before.

What would they say this time, she wondered, when they realised that she had married someone she had just met—so obviously to scupper the sensible match that they were trying to make for her? And she had married a rock star at that, someone who couldn't be further from the nice reliable boys that they enjoyed steering her towards at private family functions. What was the point of going along with that? she'd always thought. Entertaining the Lord Sebastians and Duc Philippes and Count Henris who were probably distant cousins, and who all—to a man—would run a mile as soon as they found out that they might not be needing that place at Eton or Charterhouse, or wherever they'd put their future son's name down for school before they had even bagged the ultimate trophy wife.

Joe leaned past her to look out of the window, and then gave her a pointed look. 'I guess our happy news is out.'

'Looks that way,' she said, with a hesitant smile. 'Ready to face the hordes?'

'As I'll ever be.' He looked confident, though, and relaxed. As if he'd been born to a life in front of the cameras, whereas she, who had attended her first photo call at a little under a day old, still came out in a sweat at the sight of a paparazzo.

But she stuck on what she'd come to think of as her Princess Scowl, in the style of a London supermodel, and pressed her knees and ankles together. It was second nature, after so many hours of etiquette lessons. Even in skin-tight leather, where there was no chance of an accidental underwear flash. She ran a hand through her hair, messing up the backcombed waves and dragging it over to one side in her trademark style. A glance in the rear-view mirror told her that her red lip stain was still good to go, managing to look just bitten and just kissed. She took a deep breath and reached for the door handle.

Joe stopped her with the touch of his fingertips on her knee. 'Wait.'

It was as if the leather melted away and those fingertips were burning straight into her skin. Wait? For ever, if she had to.

But before she could say, or do, anything, they were gone, as was Joe. Out of the door and into the bear pit. Then her door was wrenched open and his hand was there, waiting to pull her out into the bright desert sunshine. She gripped his hand as he helped her from the car, and the flashbulbs were going off before she was even on her feet.

Shouts reached her from every direction.

'When was the wedding?'

'Was Elvis there?'

'Were you drunk?'

And then there it was, the question that she'd never

anticipated but that she realised now had been inevitable from the first.

'Are you pregnant?'

She stumbled, and it was only Joe's arm clamping round her waist and pulling her tight that stopped her falling on her face in front of the world's press. And then she was falling anyway, because Joe's lips were on hers, and her heart was racing and her legs were jelly and her lips…her lips were on fire. One of his hands had bunched in her hair, and she realised that this, this look, this feeling, was what she'd been cultivating in front of the mirror for more years than she cared to think about. Just been kissed, just been ravished. Just had Joe's tongue in her mouth and hands on her body. Just had images of hot and sweaty and naked racing through her mind. He broke away and gave her a conspiratorial smile. She bit her lip, her mouth still just an inch from his, wondering how she was meant to resist going back for more.

And then the shouts broke back into her consciousness. 'Go on—one more, Charlie!'

And the spell was broken. She wasn't going to give them what they wanted. She turned to them, scowl back in place, though there was a glow now in the middle of her chest, something that they couldn't see, something that they couldn't try and own, to sell for profit.

She grabbed Joe's hand and pulled him towards the door of the venue, ignoring the shouts from the photographers.

She dragged him through the door and into a quiet corner.

'So I guess we survived our first photo call.'

She had hoped the relative seclusion of this dark corner would give her a chance to settle her nerves, for her heartbeat to slow and her hands to stop shaking. But as Joe took another step closer to her and blocked everything else from her vision, she felt anything but relaxed.

'Are you okay? You look kind of flushed,' he asked.

'I'm fine. I just hate…never mind.' Her voice dropped away as her gaze fixed on his lips and she couldn't break it away. This wasn't the time to think about what she hated, not when she was so fixed on what she loved, what she couldn't get enough of. Like the feeling of his lips on hers.

'Joe, I thought I saw you come in. And the new missus!'

Ricky, the drummer from Joe's band, Charlie recognised with a jolt.

More flashbacks of the night before: the band laughing with them in the taxi cab to the courthouse, joking about how they were going to have to sign with her now she'd done this. She had to convince them that they'd been mistaken last night. That she'd married Joe for love at first sight, before they started talking to journalists. If it wasn't already too late.

She reached for Joe's hand and gripped it tightly in hers, hoping that it communicated everything that she needed it to.

'Hi, Ricky,' she said, plastering on a smile that she hoped broadcast newly wedded bliss and contentment.

'So your first day as husband and wife, eh. How's it working out for you?'

She tried to read into his smile what he was really saying. If only she could fake a blush, or a morning-after glow. But in the absence of that, she'd have to go on the offensive.

'Pretty bloody amazingly, actually,' she said, leaning into Joe and hoping that he'd run with this, with her.

'Really?'

Ricky gave Joe a pointed look, and it told Charlie everything that she needed to know. He had thought last night that this was all a publicity stunt, and nothing that he had seen yet had changed his mind.

'Well, I'm just glad that you both decided to take one for the team.' He grinned. 'It was a brilliant idea. I wish I'd thought of it first.'

She opened her mouth to speak, but Joe got there first.

'I'm not sure what you mean, Ricky. We're not doing this for the team. I admit it was a bit hasty, but we really meant it last night. We wanted to get married.'

'Because you're both so madly in love?'

She felt Joe's hand twitch in hers and tried not to read too much into it.

'Because it was the only thing we *could* do,' he said. 'I don't care what we call it. Love at first sight. Or lust. Whatever. I just knew that once I had Charlie in my arms there was no way I was going to let her go. And if that meant marriage, then that's what I wanted.'

Bloody hell, maybe he should have been an actor rather than a singer. He certainly gave that little speech more than a little authenticity. She leaned into him again, and this time he dropped her hand and wrapped his arm around her shoulders. She looked up at him, and there was something about the expression in his face that forced her up onto her tiptoes to kiss him gently on the lips.

'Wow, okay,' Ricky said as she broke away. 'I guess I missed something last night. So, someone wants to chat with us about the new album, if you've got a minute.'

'Okay,' Joe replied, 'but you do remember what we decided last night. We're going to say yes to Charlie's label. I'm not going back on my word.'

'A bit early in the marriage for those sorts of ructions, is it?' Ricky looked at them carefully, and Charlie knew that they hadn't dispelled all of his doubts, regardless of how good an actor Joe was. 'Either way, we still need to speak to them. Until this deal is signed, we schmooze everyone, as far as I'm concerned. I know the others feel the same.'

She *had* to call her boss. She couldn't think why she hadn't done it before now. She'd do it on the way to the plane. She glanced at her watch. They couldn't stay long if they were going to make the flight. For a second she thought wistfully of her family's private plane, and how much easier life had been when she'd been happy to go along with that lifestyle, to take what she didn't feel she had earned. But it had got to the point where she simply couldn't do it any more. If she was never going to be able to pay her parents back with the one thing that everyone wanted from her, she couldn't use their money or their privilege any more.

She had some money left to her by her grandparents—despite her protestations, the lawyers had told her that it belonged to her and there was nothing that she could do about it—and her salary from the record label.

'I'm sorry, do you mind if I talk to them?' Joe asked, turning to her.

'Of course not.' She forced a smile, trying to live in the moment and forget all of the very good reasons she should be freaking out right now. 'Go on.'

But Joe turned to Ricky. 'You go ahead,' he said. 'I'll be there in a second.'

'You all right?' he asked, when they were alone. 'Still happy with everything? Because if you're going to change your mind, now's the time...'

She drew away from him and folded her arms. 'Why would I have changed my mind?'

She didn't understand what had happened to cause this change in mood. His shoulders were tense, she could see that.

Was it because he'd just reminded Ricky of their deal to sign with her the night before? The thought made her feel slightly sick, reminded her that whatever they might say to his band, whatever story they might spin for the papers, when it came down to it, this really *was* just a publicity stunt, or a business arrangement or...whatever. Whatever it was, she knew what it wasn't. It hadn't been love at first sight. It wasn't a grand romance. It wasn't a fairy tale, and there was going to be no happy ending for her. Well, fine, it wasn't like she deserved one anyway.

But now that they were married, they had to make it work. They had to appear to be intoxicated with one another. Luckily, intoxicated was one of her fortes. She forced herself to unfold her arms and smile. 'Of course I'm all right.'

Taking a deep breath, she stepped towards him, and with a questioning look in her eye snaked her arms around those tense shoulders. She placed another chaste peck on his lips, and smiled as she drew away. 'See? Picture perfect. Everything's as we agreed. Let's go say hi to everyone.'

Under the pressure of her arms, she felt his shoulders relax and his face melted into a smile. 'Well, we could give them something to talk about first.'

His arms wrapped around her waist, and she was reminded of the rush of adrenaline and hormones that she had felt outside when he had kissed her in front of the cameras. Her breath caught as her body softened into his hold. This time when his lips met hers, there was nothing chaste about it. Her arms tightened around him as he lifted her just ever so slightly, rubbing her hips against his as she slid up his body. His arms wrapped her completely, so that her ribs were bracketed with muscular forearms, and his hands met the indents of her waist. She was surrounded by him. Overwhelmed by the dominance of his body over hers.

His mouth dominated her too, demanding everything that she could give, and it was only with the touch of his tongue that she remembered where they were. She pushed both hands on his chest, forcing him to give her space, to unwind his arms from around her waist.

She smiled as she looked at him, both of them still dazed from the effect of the kiss. 'Do you think they bought it?' she asked, remembering that just a few moments ago they had been discussing the fact that this relationship was just a business deal—that the purpose of the kiss had been to keep up appearances. But Joe's face fell, and she knew that she had said the wrong thing.

'I think they bought it fine,' he said. 'It was a winning performance.'

Through the bite of his teeth, she knew that it wasn't a compliment.

She shook her head, then reached up and pecked him one last time on the cheek. 'Whatever it was, it blew my mind.' She met his eyes, and she knew that he saw that she was genuine. Whatever else might be going on, there was no denying the chemistry between them. It would be stupid to even try.

But beyond that, beyond the crazy hormones that made her body ache to be near his, was there something else too? A reason that the disappointment in his eyes made some part of her body hurt? She slipped her fingers between his and they walked over to where Ricky was holding court with a woman that she recognised from another record label, her competition, and a music journalist.

'So here's the happy couple,' the hack said with a smile, raising her glass to toast them. Charlie spotted a waiter passing with a tray of champagne and grabbed a flute for herself and one for Joe. She saw off half the glass with her first sip, until she felt she could stare down the journalist with impunity.

She watched Joe as they chatted, her hand trapped within his, and tried not to think about whether the warm glow of possessiveness she felt was because she'd bagged him as an artist, or a husband.

As they walked through Arrivals at Heathrow Airport, Joe felt suddenly hesitant at the thought of taking Charlie back to his apartment, definitely not something he was used to. It wasn't as if he were a stranger to taking girls home. Though in fairness home was more usually a hotel room or their place. But now that he and Charlie were back on British soil, he realised how little they'd talked about how this was going to work.

'So we said we'd stay at my place,' he reminded her as they headed towards the end of another endlessly long corridor.

'We did,' she agreed, and he looked at her closely, trying to see if there was more he could glean from these two words. But he had forgotten that his new wife was a pro at hiding her feelings—she'd had a lifetime of practice. Charlie offered nothing else, so he pushed, wanting the matter settled before they had to face the press, who were no doubt waiting for them again at the exit of the airport. Airport security did what they could to push them back, but couldn't keep them away completely. Not that he should want that, he reminded himself. They wanted the publicity. It was good for the band. It was the whole reason they were still married.

But even good publicity wasn't as important as finishing a new album would be—that thought hadn't been far from his mind the last few days. He couldn't understand how he had thought that it was nearly finished. He'd played the demo tracks over and over on the plane, and somehow the songs that he'd fine-tuned and polished so carefully no longer worked when he listened to them. They didn't make him *feel*. They had a veneer of artifice that seemed to get worse, rather than better, the more that he heard them.

His first album had come from the heart. He shuddered inwardly at the cliché. It was years' worth of pent-up emotion and truths not said, filtered through his guitar and piano. It was honest. It was him. This latest attempt… It was okay. A half-dozen of the tracks he would happily listen to in the background of a bar. But it was clean and safe and careful, and lacking the winners. The grandstanding, show-stopping singles that took an album from good to legendary.

He was still writing. Still trying. But he was out of material and out of inspiration. His adolescent experiences, his adult life of running from them had fed his imagination and his muse for one bestselling album. But he couldn't mine the same stuff for a second. It needed something new. So what was he meant to write about—how ten years on the road made relationships impossible? How his parents kept up with his news by reading whatever the tabloids had made up that week? That his only good friends had spent most of that time trapped with him in some mode of transport or another for the last decade? It was hardly rousing stuff.

'Do you want to go back there now, then?' he asked Charlie.

How was this so difficult? Was she making it that way on purpose?

She looked down at her carry-on bag. 'This is all I have with me.'

'We can send someone for your stuff.'

'No.' She didn't want anyone riffling through her things. Occasionally she missed the discreet staff from her childhood home in the private apartments of the palace, who had disappeared the dirty clothes from her bedroom floor before it had had a chance to become a proper teenage dive, but she loved the freedom of her home being truly private. That the leather jacket that she dropped by the door when she got home would still be right there when she was heading out the next morning.

She stopped walking and looked up at him. 'Okay, so we go back to yours tonight. Tomorrow we go to my place and pack some stuff. Does that work for you? Or I could go back to my place tonight. Sleep there, if we don't want to rush into—'

'You sleep with me.'

He couldn't explain the shot of old-fashioned possessiveness that he had felt when she suggested that they sleep apart. Except... The bed share of the previous night. That was a one-off, wasn't it? He supposed they'd find out later, when she realised that his apartment's second bedroom had been converted to a recording studio. Leaving them with one king-sized bed and one very stylish but supremely uncomfortable couch to fight over. He was many things, but chivalrous about sleeping arrangements wasn't one of them. He couldn't remember the last time that he had slept eight hours in a bed that wasn't hurtling along a motorway or through the clouds. So he could promise her a chivalrous pillow barrier if she absolutely insisted, but there was no way he was forgoing his bed. Not even for her.

'For appearances' sake,' he added to his earlier comment. 'What would it look like if we spent our first night back apart?'

CHAPTER FOUR

'WHEN ARE WE going to tell our families?' Joe asked as the driver slid the car away from the kerb, and the throng of photographers who had been waiting for them grew distant in the rear window.

He was probably just hoping to fill the awkward silence, Charlie thought, rather than trying to bait her. But the niggle of guilt that had been eating away at her turned into a full-on stab. She really should have called her parents before she had left the States, but she had just kept thinking about how disappointed they were going to be in her—again—and she couldn't bring herself to do it.

But now they had another load of morning editions of the tabloids to worry about, full of their red-carpet kisses from the night before. Or was it two nights? Losing a day to the time difference when they were in the air hadn't helped her jet lag, or her sense of dis-location from the world. Whenever it was that those kisses had taken place, somehow, she didn't think that they were going to help matters.

'When we get home,' she said, cracking open a bottle of mineral water and leaning back against the leather headrest. In theory she had just had a eleven-hour flight with nothing to do but catch up on missed sleep. And it wasn't even as if she and Joe had spent the time chatting and getting to know one another. He had pulled out noise-cancelling headphones as soon as he was on board and she'd barely heard a word from him after that.

She'd shut her eyes too, pulled on a sleep mask and tried to drift off. But sleep had been impossible. First her mind had run round in circles with recriminations and criticisms; then slowly, something else had crept in. The scent of Joe's aftershave, the drumming of his fingers on the armrest as he got into whatever he was listening to. Her body remembered how she had felt that morning waking up next to him, after her dream filled with hot, sticky caresses. Before her memory returned and she remembered the idiotic thing that they had done. When he was just a hot guy in her head and not the man she had married in a fit of self-sabotage. Lust, pure and simple.

Things were anything but simple now. Attraction could be simple. A marriage of convenience could be simple too, she supposed. She was the product of generations of them. But she and Joe had gone and mixed the two, and now they were paying the price. As Joe shifted on the seat beside her she opened her eyes and watched him for a few moments.

Their late night followed by a long, sleepless flight had left him with a shadow on his jaw that was more midnight than five o'clock. She could almost feel the scratch of it against her cheek if she shut her eyes again and concentrated. She snapped herself out of it. Too dangerous. *Far* too dangerous to be having those sorts of feelings about this man. They had made this arrangement complicated enough as it was. Attraction made it more complicated still. Acting on that attraction anywhere but in the safety of the public gaze was complete madness. No, they were just going to have to get really, really good at self-restraint. She was so looking forward to shutting her bedroom door on Joe and the rest of the world and finally being able to relax and sleep off the jet lag.

Their driver hauled their bags up the stairs to his first-floor warehouse conversion, and Charlie breathed a sigh of relief when they shut the door on him. Home and private at last, all she wanted to do was sleep.

'Do you mind if I just crash?' she asked Joe. 'Which is my room?'

He looked suddenly uncomfortable. 'About that, there's actually only one bedroom.'

Determined not to lose her cool in front of him, she forced the words to come out calmly. 'What do you mean there's only one?'

She crossed the huge open living space and stood on the threshold of Joe's bedroom, her mouth gaping at what he had just told her. He was the one who had suggested they live at his apartment. He couldn't have mentioned he didn't have a guest room?

'You can't think that I'm going to sleep with you.'

'As if, Princess. You're not that irresistible, you know.' Way to kill an ego. Not that she cared right now. All she wanted was to sleep. No, she corrected herself. She needed privacy to call her parents and let them know that she'd messed up—again. And then she needed to sleep. Probably for about three days straight.

'Look, Charlie. I'm tired, I'm grouchy. I have to go call my mum and explain why I decided to get married without her there, and then I'm sleeping. The mattress is big enough for us both to starfish without getting tangled. So you do what you like, but I'm going to bed.

He was tired? *He* was grouchy?

She stood for a moment in the doorway, and could almost feel the delicious relief of slamming it shut with her on the inside. Instead, she pulled herself up to her full five feet ten inches, turned on the spot and stalked off with a grace that her deportment coach had spent months all but beating into her.

Charlie plopped down onto the couch with significantly less grace—no way was she contorting on there to sleep—and pulled out her mobile. She dialled her mum's private number, and heard her voice after a single ring. She could picture so clearly the way the Queen would be working at her desk with her phone beside her blotter, just waiting for her to call.

'Caroline.'

So much said in just one word. She'd been worried about disapproval, disappointment. But the heartfelt, unreserved concern in her mother's voice was the killer.

'Hi, Mum.'

'Charlie, are you okay?'

She dropped her forehead into her hands and wished for the first time that she had gone to do this in person. Surely it was the least her mother deserved. But—like so many of her other mistakes—it was done now, and couldn't be undone.

'I'm fine, Mum. I'm sorry, I know I should have called earlier…' Her voice tailed off and she held her breath, waiting for forgiveness.

'I'm just glad to hear from you. Are you going to tell me what happened?'

She wanted to tell the truth. To confess and tell her that she had messed up again. Her mum would forgive her...eventually. But that wouldn't stop her being disappointed. Nothing could do that. So she steeled herself to lie, to trying to cover up just how stupid she had been this time.

'I met a guy, Mum, and I don't know what happened, but we just clicked. It was love at first sight, and we wanted to get married right away.'

The long pause told her everything she needed to know about how much her mum believed that story.

'If you've made a— I mean if you've changed your mind, Charlie, we can take care of this, you know.'

It was the air of resignation that did it—the knowledge that her mother had been anticipating yet another catastrophe that strengthened her resolve.

'It wasn't a mistake, Mum. It's what I wanted. What we both wanted.' Another long pause, followed by the inevitable.

'So when do we get to meet this young man and his family?'

Her heart kicked into a higher gear as she worried what her mother was expecting—how formal and official was this going to get?

'I was thinking family dinner this weekend. Fly in and stay Friday night—how long you stay is up to you. I've already told your brother and sister. My secretary will ring with the details.'

Charlie couldn't speak. So this was real. She was going to bring Joe to meet her family, pretend that they were crazy in love. She nodded, then realised what she was doing. 'Okay, Mum, we'll be there.' Because when your mum was the Queen it was hard to say no, even more so when you had just done something you knew must have bruised her heart, if not broken it completely.

'I can't wait, darling.' The truth she could hear in her mum's voice broke her own heart in return.

She hung up and for a second let the tears that had been threatening fall onto her cheeks. Just three. Then she drew a deep breath, wiped her eyes and set her shoulders. She had, once again, got herself into an unholy mess and—once again—she would dig herself out of it. There was one other call that she knew she had to make—to her boss, Rich. But she had just disappointed one person whose approval she actually cared about. She didn't have it in her to do the double. She'd need at least a couple of hours' sleep before she could think about that.

She scrubbed under her eyes with a finger, determined to show no signs of weakness to her new husband. This was a professional arrangement and she had no business forgetting that.

As she opened the bedroom door she squared her shoulders. For just a few more hours it was just her and Joe, before the lawyers and managers and accountants wanted to start formalising everything at work. Damned right she was going to enjoy the calm before the storm.

The door opened and she looked over to the bed. *Holy cra—*

She was never going to be able to sleep again. At least not while she was pretending to be married to this man. He hadn't been lying when he'd said that there was room for the two of them to sleep side by side. It was an enormous bed. But the man she had decided to marry had chosen to starfish across it diagonally. There was barely room for a sardine either side of him, never mind anyone else.

And space wasn't the only issue. She'd assumed no naked sleeping, but maybe this was worse. The white T-shirt he must have pulled on before climbing between the sheets hugged tight around his biceps, revealing tattoos that swirled and snaked beneath the fabric, tempting her to follow their lines up his arms. The hem of the shirt had ridden up, showcasing a strip of flawlessly tanned skin across his toned back. And, just to torture her, the sheets had been kicked down to below his tight black boxers—the stretch of the fabric leaving nothing to the imagination. For half a second she thought about sleeping on that back-breaking couch. Or even calling a cab back to her own flat. But the lure of a feather mattress topper was more than she could resist. She kicked off her jeans, noting that her black boy shorts underwear was more than a little similar to her husband's. Luckily *her* white shirt covered her butt.

She crawled onto the mattress beside Joe, trying to keep her movements contained and controlled. Waking him would open the door to a host of possibilities that she didn't want to—couldn't—contemplate right now. Lying on her side on the edge of the bed, she tried to ignore the gentle rhythm of Joe's breathing beside her. She balanced on her hip, the edge of the bed just a couple of inches in front of her. So much for a deep, relaxing sleep. There was no way that was going to happen with her frightened of hitting the floor on one side or Joe on the other. No, she had to start as she meant to go on, and there was no way she was enduring marriage to a man who thought she would perch on the edge of the bed.

She snuck out an experimental toe and aimed at the vicinity of Joe's legs. When her skin met taut, toned muscle, she wasn't prepared for the flash of warmth that came with it. For the memory of the night that flashed back with it. Of her and Joe heading for the bed in their suite, high from champagne, the roulette wheel and the new and exciting gleam on the third fingers of their left hands.

She'd jumped back onto the mattress, the bemused bellboy still standing watching them from the doorway. As Joe had approached her, the look in his eyes like a panther stalking its prey, the bellboy had withdrawn. Her eyes had locked on Joe's, then, and her breath had caught at the intensity in his gaze. And then he had tripped on the rug and fallen towards the bed headfirst, breaking the spell. She'd collapsed back in a fit of giggles, and as her eyes had closed she had been overtaken by a yawn.

She'd fallen asleep so easily the night before. Maybe she could kick him out completely. That might be the only way she was going to get to relax enough to fall asleep. She remembered the look on his face, though, when he'd told her he wasn't giving up his bed for her. She didn't think he'd take crashing to the floor well. And, really, they had enough troubles at the moment without him being any more annoyed with her. She braced herself for the heat that she knew now would come and pushed at his leg again. Success. He shifted behind her and she shuffled back a few inches on the bed. She could hear Joe still moving, but she lay stiff and still, determined not to give up her hard-won territory.

With a great roll Joe turned over, and their safe, back-to-back stand-off was broken. His breath tickled at the back of her neck, setting off a chain reaction of goosebumps from her nape to the bottom of her spine. Maybe she had been better off on the edge of the bed, because her body was starting to hum with anticipation. Her brain—unhelpful as ever—was reminding her of how good it felt to kiss him. How her body had thrummed and softened in his arms. She reached down for the duvet and tucked it tightly around her, though she didn't really need its warmth. But with her body trapped tight beneath it she felt a little more secure. As a final defence, she shoved in her earphones and found something soothing to block out the subtle sounds of a shared bed, and shut her eyes tight.

Joe stood in the bedroom doorway, surveying the scene in front of him. A pair of black skinny jeans had been abandoned by the bed, and silver jewellery was scattered on the bedside table. Dark brown hair was strewn across the pillow and one long, lean calf had snaked out from beneath the duvet. Along with the jeans on the floor, it answered a question that he'd been tempted but too much of a gentleman to find out for himself.

His wife. He had to shake his head in wonderment of how that had happened. A simple kiss from her did things to his body that he had never experienced before. He'd woken with his arms aching to pull her close and give her a proper good morning. And she was the one woman he absolutely couldn't, shouldn't fall for. They had gone into this marriage with ground rules for a good reason. They couldn't risk their careers by giving in to some stupid chemical attraction, or, worse still, by getting emotionally involved.

He'd made the mistake before of giving his heart to someone who was only out to get what she wanted. He'd learnt his lesson, and he wouldn't be making the same mistake again. And of all the women he could have married, it had to be her, didn't it? One who would throw him back into that world of privilege and wealth.

He'd spent just about every day since he was eleven years old feeling like the outsider. And now he had gone and hitched himself to the ultimate in exclusive circles. Once he and Charlie were married, there was no way of getting away from them. But he had learned how to deal with it a long time ago. Keep his distance, keep himself apart, to prevent the sting of rejection when he tried to fit in. The same rule had to apply to Charlie. It didn't matter what she had told her parents, how real they were going to make this thing look—he couldn't let himself forget that it was all for show.

He placed a cup of coffee down among her earrings and bracelets, and from this vantage point he could see the chaos emerging from her suitcase, where more shirts were spilling from the sides.

Charlie jerked suddenly upright, knocking his arm and sending the coffee hurtling to the floor.

'Crap!'

He jumped back as the scalding liquid headed for his shins. Charlie was scrambling out of bed, and grabbed her jeans from the floor to start mopping up the coffee from the floorboards. 'What the hell?' she asked, crouching over the abandoned coffee.

'I thought I'd bring you a cup of coffee in bed, you ungrateful brat.' She sat back at the insult and crossed her arms across her chest. 'I suppose I ought to expect the spoilt little princess routine,' he continued, and they both flinched at the harsh tone in his voice. 'Sorry. Look, you wait there. I'll grab a towel.'

He retreated to the kitchen and took a deep breath, both hands braced palms-down on the worktop; then grabbed some kitchen roll and headed back to the bedroom. Charlie was crouched like a toddler, feet flat on the floor, attacking the coffee with a hand towel from the bathroom. She took a slurp from the cup as she worked, swishing the towel around ineffectually, and chasing streams of coffee along the waxed floorboards and under the bed.

'Here,' he said, taking the sopping towel from her and holding out a hand to pull her up. 'I'll finish up. You drink your coffee.'

'Thanks,' she said, relinquishing the towel with a look of relief. 'And for the coffee. Sorry, I was just a bit disorientated.'

'Forgot you picked yourself up a husband in Vegas?'

'Something like that.' She grabbed her watch from the bedside table and shook off the coffee, leaving flecks of brown on the snowy white duvet cover.

'Ugh. I've got to be at work in an hour.'

She walked over to the bathroom, and he directed his gaze pointedly away from the endlessly long legs emerging from beneath that butt-skimming shirt. He had no desire to make this arrangement any more difficult than it undoubtedly was. Keeping it strictly business was the only way that it was going to work. She eyed her suitcase uncertainly. 'I've got more jeans, but I'm all out of clean tops. Can I raid your wardrobe?'

'Go for it. I'm jumping in the shower. We'll need to leave at quarter to if we're going to walk.'

She stopped riffling through the rails in his dressing room for a second.

'We?'

'I think I'd better come talk to Rich. There's a lot to go through before we can sign anything.'

Of course she hadn't forgotten that Rich had sent her out to Vegas with a job to do. So why wasn't she exactly thrilled about the prospect of going in and seeing him this morning? Because this hadn't been what he'd meant, she knew. It hadn't been what she'd wanted either. If this was a casting-couch situation she wasn't sure which of them had been lying back and thinking of the job, but she knew that she was good at what she did. She knew that she could have bagged this signing without bringing her personal life or family into the picture. But who was going to believe that now?

Her face fell, and somehow he knew exactly what she was thinking.

'You think he's going to be pissed at you?'

'Why would he be? He sent me out there to close this deal. Job done, mission complete. He's going to be thrilled.'

'Really? So why don't you look happy about it?'

'It's nothing.'

'It's clearly something.'

He sat on the edge of the bed as she turned back to

the wardrobe and started looking through his shirts again. Sliding them across the rail without paying much attention.

'I'm just not sure how he's going to react to…this.' She waved a hand between them so he understood exactly what 'this' was. His hackles rose.

'You told me you weren't involved with anyone. Are you telling me you and he are…a thing? Because that would be a major problem. I can't believe you'd—'

'It's nothing like that.' She grabbed hold of a shirt and pulled it from the hanger. 'God, why does everyone assume that any professional relationship I have is based on sex?' He lifted one eyebrow as he took in her half-dressed form and the unmade bed.

'Oh, get lost, Joe. This is nothing to do with sex. This was *your* idea. I'd have got you to sign anyway.'

'Really? Why did you say yes, then?' She had been starting off to the bathroom, but she stopped halfway across the room, his shirt screwed up and crumpled in her hand.

'Oh, why does a party girl do anything, Joe?' Her smile was all public, showing nothing of the real woman he had spent the last couple of days with. 'I'm an idiot. I was drunk. It was a laugh.' It was what everyone would assume, there was no doubt about that—but what was most shocking to him was that she didn't believe that any of those statements were true. So if it hadn't been just for a laugh, and it wasn't about her job either, then why had she done it?

He waited for the water to shut off and for Charlie to emerge from the bathroom before he grabbed his wash bag from his suitcase. She kept her back to him as she emerged and headed straight into the dressing room. Respecting her obvious need for privacy, and reluctant to continue their argument, he went straight into the bathroom and locked the door.

So what was the deal with her boss if she wasn't sleeping with him? Why was she so bothered about what he would think about their marriage? Their reasons for staying together were still good. The papers had been full of stories about the two of them, and there had been talk about the anticipation of their new album. It was exactly the sort of coverage that you couldn't buy. Her boss would be able to see that. He should be pleased that she'd got the job done and with a publicity angle to boot.

He stepped under the spray of the shower and let the water massage his shoulders. Maybe he should let her go and deal with her boss on her own. But he was keen to get this contract signed. He had meant what he had said. He'd been impressed with what the label had pitched to him—he would have signed even without Charlie turning up in Las Vegas.

He followed in her footsteps to the dressing room and wasn't sure whether to be disappointed or relieved that the towel had been discarded on the floor and she was fully dressed. One of his shirts was cinched in at the waist with a wide belt of studded black leather. A pair of black leather leggings ended in spike-heeled boots and she was currently grimacing into the mirror as she applied a feline ring of heavy black eyeliner.

'Walk of shame chic,' she said as she met his eye in the mirror. 'What do you think?'

'I think that now you're a married woman we can't call it the walk of shame. This is home. If you want it to be.' He leaned back against the wall as she paused with a tube of something shiny and gold in her hand. His eyes met hers in the mirror, and he gave a small smile. Relaxing in that moment, he enjoyed their connection—the first since they had woken up that morning. And he remembered again that feeling when he had first met her. When he had glanced across the stage and seen her in the wings, watching him. How they had danced and felt so in tune, so together, that the idea of marriage had seemed inevitable, rather than idiotic.

He laughed as she broke their eye contact to apply a coat of mascara, complete with wide open mouth.

'Come on,' he said, heading to the kitchen. 'I'll make another coffee.'

She glanced at her watch, returning his smile.

'We might have to drink on the go.'

He couldn't deny that he was startled. Princess Caroline all worried about being late for work the morning after bagging the biggest signing of her career. She was just full of surprises.

In the kitchen he set the coffee machine going and grabbed his only travel mug from a cabinet. 'Okay, but we're sharing, then,' he shouted back to her as he added frothy steamed milk.

By the door, he grabbed wallet and keys from the tray on the console where he'd dropped them the night before. Waiting for Charlie, he had an unimpeded view of her kicking her coffee-stained jeans towards her suitcase, and swiping some of the jewellery from the bedside table, but knocking the rest of it under the bed. Spot the girl who'd grown up with staff, he thought again to himself. They were going to have to talk about this at some point, he realised. He wasn't going to pick up after her like some sort of valet.

Was that how she saw him, he wondered—on a par with the staff? Barely visible in a room? She swept past him and out of the door; then drew up short in the corridor, clearly surprised that he wasn't just following in her wake.

'Are you coming?' she asked over her shoulder.

Slowly, Joe turned his key in the lock and then walked towards her. He took a long sip of coffee from the travel mug and then met her eye.

'You're not a princess here, sweetheart,' he told her gently. 'Home means you do your own fetching and carrying.'

Her brows drew together and he knew he'd pissed her off. 'I'll start by carrying this, then, shall I?' She took the coffee from him and walked into the lift, letting the door close in his face behind her.

Charlie swiped them into the office with her key card and waved at the receptionist on her way past. Avalon Records was based in a rundown old Regency villa on a once fashionable square. The grandeur of the high ceilings and sweeping staircases was in stark contrast to the workaday contents. Laminate wood desks had been packed into every corner of the building, and tattered swivel chairs fought for space with stacks of paper and laser printers.

She headed to her desk with eyes forward, intent on not letting anyone—especially Joe—see how nervous she was. Not that she needed to worry about that. She had been so keen to get into the office early that the place was practically deserted. She reached her desk and stashed her bag in a drawer, making herself busy for just a few more moments, turning on the computer and getting everything straight in her head so that the minute Rich arrived she could sell the hell out of this situation.

This was a good day, and there was no way she was leaving Rich's office until he agreed with her. Not only had she closed the deal that Rich had sent her out there to do, she had tied Joe and The Red Kites to their future in the closest way possible. Rich should—and he would—be eternally grateful. This was a massive coup for their indie label, tempting the hottest band of the year away from the big multinationals. She grabbed a couple of files and a notebook from under a pile of papers and then turned back to Joe.

He was staring at her desk with a mixture of shock and despair.

'What?' she asked, alarmed by his expression.

'Oh, my God. You're a slob.' He laughed as he spoke, his eyes wide. She leaned back against her desk and crossed her arms across her chest.

'I am so not.'

'You totally are. I thought maybe back at my place it was because we were both still living out of our cases. I need to clear you some space in the war…' His voice drifted and a shadow crossed his expression before he shook it off and got back to the point. 'But this proves it. I mean…how do you find anything?'

She waved the files in her hand at him.

'Because they're exactly where I left them.'

He shook his head again. 'But wouldn't they also be exactly where you left them if they were…say… filed neatly in a drawer?'

She raised her brows. 'You wouldn't by any chance be interfering, would you, Joe? Because this is my desk, and my office, and my job, and you don't get to boss me around here.'

He snorted out a breath. 'Oh, right, because at home you're so biddable and accommodating.' He laughed again, taking a step closer until she was trapped between him and the desk. She could smell his shower gel, the same one that she'd borrowed that morning, knowing even as she'd done it that she was going to be haunted by this reminder of him all day. She looked up at him, enjoying the novelty of a man who was still a smidge taller than her, even when she was in heels.

'I'm not interfering. I'm just getting to know you. We can talk about this more at home.' He took another half-step closer and she hitched a butt cheek onto her desk, looking for just a little more space, a little more safety. Breathing space for sensible, professional decision-making.

Then Joe lifted his hand and even without knowing where it was heading—hair, cheek, lips—she knew it would be more than her self-control could stand. She grabbed his hand mid-air, but that didn't help. It just pulled him closer as their linked hands landed on the desk by her hip. The front of his thighs pressed against hers, long and lean and matched so perfectly to her body he could have been made for her. She could feel the gentle pressure of his breath on her lips, and her eyes locked on his mouth as she remembered the times that they had pressed against hers. Her brain was desperately trying to catch up with the demands of her body. Remember the agreements they had made. They were meant to be madly in love in public. They were business associates when they were home. But what were they to each other here? In this public place, but with no one there to see them.

She dragged her gaze away for a moment, over Joe's shoulder to the still-deserted office. She had wanted to be in early. To show Rich that she was still as committed—as professional—as ever. But it had left her and Joe dangerously secluded.

His fingers untangled from hers, and she was hit with syncopated waves of regret then relief. But neither lasted long as his hand completed its original journey and landed this time on her cheek. His palm cupped her face as he tilted her head just a fraction. The sight of his tongue sneaking out to moisten his lips set off a chain reaction from the tight, hard knot low in her pelvis to the winding of her arms around his shoulders to the low sigh that escaped her throat as she closed her eyes and leaned in, waiting for the touch of his mouth.

A door slammed behind her and she jumped back, whacking her thighs against her desk in the process. She pushed at Joe's chest, knowing even before she turned to look at Rich's office what she was going to find.

Her boss was standing in front of the closed door to his office, leaning back against it with his arms crossed. Proof that the slam had been entirely for effect. Bloody drama queen, Charlie cursed him under her breath.

'The lovebirds return,' Rich said, leaning forwards and extending his arm to shake Joe's hand. 'It's good to see you again, Joe. We weren't expecting you. Are you just seeing the wife to work, or…?'

'Actually, Rich, we have good news.' Charlie

watched her boss's face closely, trying to judge his reaction. 'Joe and the rest of the guys are all in agreement. They want to sign with us. Joe wanted to come and give the good news in person this morning.'

Rich's professional smile didn't give anything away, but she knew him well enough to see the slight hint of tightness around his eyes that told her that this wasn't unmitigated pleasure.

'That is great news,' he said, clapping Joe on the back. 'I guess this is a pretty good week for us all, then. Congratulations to you both. Married? Love at first sight, the papers are saying. I have to admit, I was surprised not to hear it from the horse's mouth.' He gave Charlie a pointed look and she pulled herself up to her full height, determined not to act like a chastised teenager. She had every right to do just what she wanted. She didn't need Rich's permission, or his approval, to marry whomever she chose.

'You know how it is, Rich. The papers knew what was happening almost before we did. We didn't have a chance to tell people ourselves.'

'Funny how that happens, isn't it?' Rich said with a quirk of his eyebrow. So he definitely wasn't going to buy 'love at first sight' then. Time for Plan B.

Joe looked from her to Rich, and must have picked up on the atmosphere between them.

'Look, we just wanted to give you *this* news in person,' Joe said. 'I know that there's loads to work out with the lawyers and stuff so just let me know when you want to start.' He leaned forward to shake Rich's hand again before turning back to Charlie. She waited to hear Rich go back into his office, but the click of the door handle didn't come. Was this a test? Was he trying to see if this was all for show?

She didn't have time to worry about it as Joe's lips descended on hers. His hands framed her face, his fingertips just teasing at her hairline. His lips were warm and soft as they pressed against her mouth, full of promise and desire. But then his hands dropped to her shoulders as he broke away, and when she opened her eyes she was met by a twinkling expression in his. 'See you at home, love.'

He swept out of the office with a final wave at Rich, and she fought the urge to lean back against her desk to catch her breath.

Instead her hands found the files that she'd grabbed before Rich had arrived, and she stalked into his office with her head held high.

'Are you ready to get started? We've got a lot to cover.'

Rich stood in the doorway, not joining her at the table as she pulled out a chair and sat. Then shook his head as he took in her determined glare. 'I'll be with you in a second.'

Five minutes later he returned with two cups of coffee and a look of determination that matched her own.

She was reading through a boilerplate contract, making notes in the margin with a red pen, and Rich waited for her to finish scribbling before he sat.

'Here, have a caffeinated peace offering. Have you slept at all since you left for the airport? I'm betting your body has no idea what time zone it's in right now.'

'Thanks.' She took the coffee and realised that he was right. She should be exhausted, but she wasn't.

Something to do with having a brand-new husband she wasn't sure if she was meant to be keeping her hands off or not, she supposed.

'So are you going to tell me what happened?'

'I thought you said you already knew.'

'I told you I'd read the papers. I want the real story. From you, preferably. I think I deserve that. This affects us all. This is work. When I sent you out there to seal the deal, I didn't mean do *any*thing. I thought maybe… I don't know. The Princess thing: sometimes it works. I never expected you to… Just… What happened, Charlie?'

She looked him in the eye, still trying to work out her angle. How much she should share. How much she should hide. But Rich was right. This went beyond her personal life. She and Joe had made a calculated business decision—he couldn't expect her to keep it from the head of the business.

'We got carried away. Vegas, you know.' She gestured vaguely with her hands. 'We'd had too much to drink. We thought it would be funny. And that, you know, the publicity wouldn't be a bad thing for the band.'

'So it wasn't…' He hesitated, and Charlie just knew he was trying to find the right words. The ones that would annoy her the least. She prayed he wasn't about to ask the question she knew deep down was coming. 'It wasn't a quid pro quo deal. Nothing to do with the contract.'

She bristled, even though she'd been expecting it.

'What are you implying, Rich? Because if you think that I would do that—that I would need to… There's nothing I can say to that.'

Rich held out his hands for peace.

'I'm just trying to understand here, Charlie. I wasn't implying anything. So you thought it was a laugh, to celebrate the deal, and the publicity wouldn't exactly harm the band. But…now? What's going on now? You're living together?'

'We thought it would look better if it was love at first sight rather than a Vegas mistake. We're both committed to keeping up the pretence until the publicity won't be as harmful.'

'And it's all for show?' Rich asked. She nodded. 'So that little moment I walked in on earlier?'

'All part of the act.'

Rich sighed, non-committal. 'Okay, all of that aside, this is an amazing opportunity for us. Great job on getting the signing. I knew that I could trust you to take care of it.'

Charlie straightened the papers in front of her, enjoying the warm glow of Rich's praise for her work. She'd survived the first meeting: it could only get better from here.

'So how did it go with your boss after I left?' Joe asked when she arrived home that evening. 'It looked like things were about to get heated between you.'

She crossed to the fridge and surveyed the contents as she thought about it.

'It was a bit hairy at first,' she admitted as she grabbed a couple of beers and waved one in Joe's direction. He took them both from her and reached behind him into a drawer to find a bottle opener.

'Does he always get so involved in his staff's personal lives?'

'Only when they go around marrying potential clients.'

He raised his eyebrows in a 'fair enough' expression, pulling out the bar stool next to him at the kitchen island.

'Why do you care so much what he thinks anyway? If you're so adamant that there's nothing going on between you.'

'Jealous again, darling?' She threw him some serious shade while taking a sip of her beer and resting her hip on the stool. The hardness of his gaze drew her up short. 'Don't be an idiot, Joe. I'm not impressed or in the least turned on by the jealousy thing. Drop it.'

'Okay,' he conceded. 'So there's nothing romantic going on between you. Tell me what that weird vibe was, then. Why were you afraid of disappointing him?'

'He's my boss. I'd quite like to not get fired. Are you so much of a celeb these days that you don't remember what it's like to hold down a job?'

'Said the Princess.'

'You wanted to know why I don't want to disappoint Rich? Because he's the only one who doesn't call me Princess. Even when others aren't doing it to my face, they still treat me differently, and it drives me crazy. Rich is the only person who doesn't make exceptions or allowances. He's the one person who treats me like a normal goddamn human being and expects me to act like one. If I stepped out of line he'd fire me in a heartbeat.'

'And you'd walk straight into another job.'

She resisted the urge to throw her beer at him. 'Maybe I would. But not one that I deserve. Not one that I could do as well as the one I have now. Rich has made me work my arse off for every achievement. Every signing. Every bloody paycheque has been in exchange for my blood, sweat and tears. He's the only one who could see that I can do it. I work hard, I earn my keep. When I let him down, I'm proving them right. All the people who just expect the world to fall into my lap.'

Which was why there was no way that she was walking away from the life that she'd built for herself, just because she'd promised her parents she'd come home at some fixed point in time.

'I'm sorry, I didn't mean to.'

'It's a sore point, okay. Because I have let him down. This whole thing is stupid. It's beneath me. I messed up, and I don't like having it pointed out to me by the people whose opinion I value.'

He gave her a long, assessing look. 'We never talked about how it went with your parents, did we?'

She knocked back another long glug of beer.

'They want to meet you.'

'Mine too.'

She caught his eye, and managed a tentative smile. 'How do you reckon that's going to go?'

'My mum asked if she needed to wear a hat.'

Frothy beer hit her nose as she snorted with laughter.

'What did you tell her?'

'That I had no idea. I have no idea how this works.' The laughter died in his eyes and he looked suddenly solemn.

'Are you freaked out by it? The royalty thing? Because I thought you went to Northbridge School. My cousins are there. And you didn't seem all that impressed when I arrived in Vegas.'

He hesitated; the last thing that he wanted was to talk about his school days. He'd been awkward enough there, the scholarship kid from up north. And that was before the school's very own Princess—she didn't need the royal blood to call herself that—had used and humiliated him. 'Yeah, I knew your cousins at school,' Joe said, 'but we weren't friends. I didn't exactly click with my classmates.'

'School can be a cruel place.'

'I guess.' He took another swig of his beer and thought back. It had been a long time since he'd really thought about that part of his life. After he'd been ignominiously dumped in front of half his school year, he'd taken the lesson, moved on, and tried to forget about the humiliation. 'There wasn't any bullying or anything like that. The masters would never have stood for it. It's just, I didn't fit in, you know.' There was no need to tell her the whole ugly story. It had been embarrassing enough the first time around.

'And you're worried it's going to be like that with my family?' Charlie leaned forward and rested her elbow on the bar and her chin on her hand as she asked the question. 'They're really nice, you know,' she said earnestly. 'Well, my brother's an idiot, but every family has one of those.'

'I'm sure they are nice, Charlie. But they're different. We're different. And that's not something that we can change.' The last time that he'd been around people who moved in royal circles, the fact that he was different had become a currency in a market that he hadn't understood. Luckily, he was older and wiser now. He knew to look out for what people wanted from him, and to make sure he was getting a good deal out of it too. He also knew that no one was ever going to see their match as a marriage of equals.

'It's a good job that this is just all for show, then,' she added. 'So my family won't be making you uncomfortable for long.'

A look of pain flashed across her face, and he wondered what had caused it. It was too deep, too old to have been caused by this argument.

'It doesn't matter,' she said after a long pause, turning away from him almost imperceptibly. 'I'm never going to marry, so you don't have to worry about some future husband being trapped in that world.'

'I hate to break it to you, but it's a bit late for never.' He leaned in closer, nudging the footrest of her stool, trying to bridge the gulf that had suddenly appeared between them.

'Well, except this isn't real, is it?' she said.

He nodded, trying to hide his wince at the unexpected pain her statement had caused. Time for a change of subject, he thought. 'So why are you never getting married? Well, getting married again.'

'It's just not for me.' She shuffled to the back of her stool, reinstating the distance that he had tried to breach.

'Wow. That's enlightening.' She was hiding something from him, he knew it. Something big. And while she could keep her secrets if she wanted—it worried him. Because how was he meant to know how to handle this situation if he didn't have all the information? With all the women that had come before her, he knew exactly what they wanted, and they knew what he wanted in return.

With Charlie, despite their best efforts to keep this businesslike, he knew that everything she said carried shades of meaning that he didn't understand. It made him nervous, knowing that he was making calculations without all of the information he needed.

'Look, what does it matter, Joe? I wouldn't make a good wife, it wouldn't be fair for me to get married—not to someone who actually wanted to be my husband. But you'll have a chance to see them all for yourself. When I spoke to my mother yesterday she invited us over for dinner with the family on Friday. We'll need to stay. It's too far to fly there and back in an evening.'

'Yeah, great,' he said, though he knew that his lack of enthusiasm was more than clear.

'Anyway, I don't want to talk about this any more. How about we go out? I'm not sure what's going on with the jet lag, but I'm not sleeping any time soon. We could go get a drink—I know a place not far from here.'

'Like a date?' he asked, uncertainly. Had she suddenly decided that that was what she wanted?

'Like a chance for the press to see us as loved-up and glowing newly-weds.'

He nodded, trying to work out whether he was relieved or disappointed that it was all part of the act. 'Wouldn't newly-weds be more interested in staying home and getting to know one another?'

She spoke under her breath so quietly he could barely hear her reply: 'All the more reason to go out.'

CHAPTER FIVE

SHE PULLED THE front door closed behind them while she smudged on a bright red lip crayon. The bar was a ten-minute walk away. She'd been to their open mic night a few times, looking out for artists that she'd seen online but wanted to check out playing live before she decided if she was interested. As they turned the corner by the bar, though, she realised that this wasn't going to be one of those nights where she struck professional gold. And when they walked in and saw the screens showing lyrics, her worst fears were confirmed. It was no-holds-barred, no-talent-required, hen-parties-welcome karaoke. A trio of drunk students were belting out a rock classic, spilling pints of beer with their enthusiasm. Well, at least their taste in music couldn't be faulted, Charlie thought, boosting the roots of her hair with her fingers in honour of her spirit sister.

'Well, they're certainly going for it,' Joe said with a grin that slipped slightly as they hit a particularly painful note. 'This your usual kind of place?'

She looked around. The place itself was great: a shiny polished wood bar, real-ale pumps gleaming and—importantly—well stocked with decent beer.

Plus there was plenty of gin on the shelves, and good vodka on ice for later in the evening. But most importantly of all, the manager, Ruby, had her number and would call with any hot tips for new acts she might be interested in.

'Charlie!' Ruby greeted her with a smile. 'Don't usually see you here on a Tuesday. Don't tell me this is your honeymoon. That would be too tragic.'

Charlie forced a laugh at this reminder of her newly married status.

'I wish. No time for a honeymoon. But Joe—or we, now, I guess—live just round the corner and we fancied a quiet drink. I'd say you'd be seeing more of me, but…' She looked over at the singing students.

'Wanted to try something new. Don't worry, I won't be repeating the experiment.'

They all watched the tone-deaf trio with similar expressions of amusement.

'Sorry,' Charlie added, realising that she hadn't introduced Joe. 'Joe, this is Ruby, she runs this place. Ruby, this is Joe, my…er…'

'Her husband,' Joe filled in, sliding one arm around her waist and with the other leaning over the bar to shake Ruby's hand.

'I read about your news. Congrats! Vegas, huh. You guys have a wild time?'

'"Wild" is one word for it.'

'The best.'

Charlie, remembering her part, relaxed into Joe's arms. Ruby was watching them carefully, and Charlie wondered what she was thinking. Was she trying to judge whether they were for real? Were they going to face this scrutiny from everyone they met? She might not count Ruby as quite a friend, but Charlie would normally have at least considered her an ally. Well, they would just have to convince her, she decided. Because they were going to make this pretence of a marriage work. The alternative was to disappoint her family even more than she already had.

She just had to remember that it was all make-believe. She didn't get to be the glowing newly-wed in real life. Being a wife, like being a princess, came with certain responsibilities, certain expectations that she knew she couldn't fill. There was no point letting herself fall for a guy only to have him up and leave when he found out that she might not be a complete woman.

Charlie ordered a couple of beers and led Joe over to one of the booths in the back of the bar. It was comfy and private, upholstered in a deep red leather, and just the sort of spot that a loved-up couple would choose, she thought.

'They're really going for it, huh,' Joe said, indicating the girls on the karaoke, who had moved on from rock to an operatic power ballad. He took a swig of the ale, and Charlie watched as his throat moved. His head was thrown back, so he couldn't see her watching him. From inside the sleeve of his tight white T-shirt she could see half a tattoo, weaving and winding around his arm. She was concentrating so hard on trying to trace the pattern that she didn't notice at first that his eyes had dropped and she'd been totally busted.

'Looking at something you like?' It could have sounded cheesy. It *should* have sounded cheesy. But somehow the sincerity in his gaze saved it. 'You wanna see the rest of it?'

Okay, so that was definitely flirtatious. She looked around quickly to see if anyone was eavesdropping. Surely if they were already hitched she should know what his tats looked like.

Ruby was serving at the bar, the drunk girls were still singing enthusiastically, and most of the other customers had been scared off.

She slipped off her bench and darted round the table, sliding in beside Joe until her thigh was pressed against his.

'All yours,' he said, lifting his arm. Her fingertips brushed at the edge of the cotton T-shirt, which was warm and soft from contact with his skin. She traced the band that wound around his bicep, looking up and meeting his eye when he flinched away from her touch as she reached the sensitive skin near his underarm.

'Ticklish?'

'Maybe.' One side of his mouth quirked up in a half-smile, and she filed that information away, just in case she should ever need it.

She shouldn't ever need it, she reminded herself.

This was just an arrangement, and she had no business forgetting it. No business exploring his body, even something as seemingly innocent as an arm. Her body remembered being in bed with him. It remembered those kisses. The way that she had arched into him, desperate to be closer. She shot off the bench, diving for safety on the other side of the table.

'It's nice. I like it.' She tried to keep her voice level, to prevent it giving away how hard she was finding it to be indifferent to him.

'Well, there's plenty more. But maybe we should keep those under wraps for now.' She nodded. Not trusting herself to reply to that statement. She took a sip of beer, hoping the chilled amber liquid would cool her blazing face.

'So the open mic here's usually good?' Joe asked, and she jumped on the change of subject gratefully.

'It is,' she said. 'Very different from tonight. It's normally pretty professional. I've found a couple of great artists here.'

'You like to find them when they're still raw?'

'Of course. I mean a fully formed band with a track record is pretty great too.' She inclined her head towards him and he smiled. 'But there's something about finding raw talent and helping it to develop. It's… It's what gets me to work on a Monday morning when sometimes I'd rather drag the duvet over my head.'

'Must be tough to stay motivated when you don't really have to work.'

She dropped her bottle on the table a little harder than was strictly necessary. 'And why do you think I don't have to work?'

'Oh, I don't know, royal families are all taxpayer-funded, right?'

She placed both palms face down on the table, forcing herself to appear calm, not to slam them in a temper. 'The *working* royals are taxpayer-funded. Yes. And the key word there is "working". Do you know what the royal family is worth to my country's economy in terms of tourism alone? Not that it matters, because I opted out. I don't do official engagements and I don't take a penny.'

'Come on, though. You've never had to struggle.'

'Oh, because a wealthy family solves all problems. We all know that.'

She wished it were true. She had asked the doctor when she had first got her diagnosis whether there was anything that could be done, and the answer was a very equivocal 'maybe'.

Maybe if she threw enough money at the problem, there might be something they could do to give her a chance of conceiving. But it wouldn't take just money. It would take money and time and invasive procedures. Fertility drugs in the fridge and needles in her thighs. It could mean every chance of the world discovering she was a failure on the most basic level, and absolutely no guarantee that it would even work. No, it was simpler to accept now that marriage and a family weren't on the cards for her and move on.

'Where did you pick up this chip on your shoulder, anyway?' Charlie asked. 'I thought your education was every bit as expensive as mine.'

He looked her in the eye, and for a moment she could see vulnerability behind his rock-star cool.

'I had a full scholarship,' he said with a shrug.

'Impressive.' Charlie sat back against the padding of the bench. 'Northbridge don't just hand those out like sweeties. Was it for music?'

She was offended by his expression of surprise. What, did he expect her to recoil at the thought that he didn't pay his own school fees? God, he really did think that she was a snob. Well, it was high time she straightened that one out. Finishing her beer in one long gulp, she slid out of the booth and held out her hand to pull Joe up.

'Somehow,' she said, when he hesitated to follow

her, 'you seem to have got totally the wrong idea about what sort of princess I am. We're going to fix that. Now.'

His expression still showing his reluctance, he allowed her to pull him to standing, but leaned back against the table, arms folded over his chest.

'How exactly do you plan to do that?'

'We, darling husband, are going to sing.'

He eyed the karaoke screens with trepidation.

'Here?'

'Where else?' But he still didn't look convinced.

'Are you any good?'

'I'm no music scholar, but I hold my own. Now, are you going to choose something or am I?'

She grabbed the tablet with song choices from Ruby at the bar, who looked eternally grateful that someone would be breaking the students' residency.

'Are you going to help choose? Because I'm strongly considering something from the musical theatre oeuvre.'

That cracked his serious expression and he grinned, grabbing the back pocket of her jeans and pulling her back against the table with him, so they could look at the tablet side by side.

'As if you'd choose something that wasn't achingly cool.'

She swiped through the pages in demonstration.

'Hate to break it to you, but there's a distinct lack of "achingly cool". The only answer is to go as far as possible in the other direction. We go for maximum cheese.'

'I was so afraid you were going to say that.'

'Come on.' She swiped through another couple of

choices until she landed on a classic pop duet. 'It's got to be this one.' She hit the button that cued up the song and bought another round at the bar to tempt the drunk girls away from their microphones. With another couple of beers for her and Joe in hand, she stepped up onto the little stage.

She glanced around the bar—the girls had done a good job of emptying the place, but a few tables had stuck it out, like her and Joe, and now had all eyes on her. She could see the cogs whirring as they tried to place her face. Obviously not expecting to see a princess at the karaoke night. Even one with her reputation.

'It's a duet!' she shouted to him from the stage. 'Don't you dare leave me hanging!'

She held out her hand to him again and this time he grabbed it enthusiastically, pulled himself up to the stage beside her and planted a heavy kiss on her lips.

The surprise of it stole her reason for a moment, as her breath stopped and her world was reduced to the sensation of him on her. She lifted her hands to his arms, bracing herself against him, feeling unsteady on the little stage as one arm slid around her waist and his hand pressed firmly on the small of her back, pulling her in close.

Her fingers teased up his bicep; though her eyes were closed, her fingers traced the pattern of his tattoo from memory, nudging at the hem of his sleeve as they had earlier, keen to continue their exploration.

A wolf whistle from the crowd broke into their little reverie, and Charlie looked up, only to be greeted with the cameras of several phones pointing in her direction. Well, they'd be in the papers again. She shrugged mentally and reminded herself that that was the whole idea of this marriage.

That was why he'd kissed her.

It took a few moments for reality to break through. For her to remember that of course he'd only kissed her because they had an audience. This wasn't real—they just had to make it look that way. And just as her confidence wavered, and she wondered why that thought hurt so much, the music kicked in and Joe passed her a microphone.

'Come on then, love. Show me what you've got.'

She pulled her hair to one side, puckered up her finest pout and prepared to rock out.

They made it through the first verse without making eye contact, never mind anything more physical, but as they reached the chorus Joe reached around her waist and pulled her back, so her body was pressed against him from spike earrings to spike heels. She faltered on the lyrics, barely able to remember how to breathe, never mind sing.

She looked round at Joe to see if it had had the same effect on him, but when she saw his face she knew that he wasn't feeling what she was feeling. He was just feeling the music: every note of it. His throaty, husky voice giving the pop song a cool credibility it had never had before.

She pulled away to see him better, and though she picked up the words and joined in, it was only a token effort. Backing vocals to his masterful performance. This was why she'd agreed to marry him. The man Joe became on stage was impossible to refuse. She had kicked herself every minute since she'd woken up with a Vegas husband she no longer wanted, asking how she could have been so stupid.

But she hadn't been stupid, she realised now. It was just that they had been so magnetically drawn to one another because of his passion for music—any music—that it would have been pointless even trying to resist. Joe's eyes opened as the song slowed, and their gazes met, freezing them in the moment.

Does he feel it too? she wondered. Or had he just been so high on the adrenaline of performance that he would have agreed to marry anyone who had crossed his path?

She could see his adrenaline kicking up a notch now. His gestures growing more expansive, his grin wider, his eyes wilder.

She sang along, trying to keep pace with his enthusiasm, but whatever performance gene he'd been born with, she was clearly lacking.

The song finished with an air-guitar solo from Joe, and a roar of applause from the bar. She'd been so intent on watching him that she hadn't noticed the place fill up. From the many smartphones still clutched in hands, she guessed that they were about to go viral.

Joe grabbed her around the waist, and before she could stop him, before she could even think about whether she wanted to, his mouth was on hers, burning into her body, her mind, her soul, with his intensity. His hands were everywhere: on her butt, in her hair, gently traipsing up her upper arm. His lips were insistent against hers, demanding that she gave herself to him with equal passion. And his tongue caressed hers with such intimacy that it nearly broke her. Soft and hard, gentle and rough, he surprised her with every touch.

When, finally, he pulled away, they both gasped for air, and she was grateful his arms were still clamped around her waist, keeping her upright. And that she'd turned so that her back was to the bar, so no one would be able to see her flaming red cheeks or the confusion in her eyes.

'Uh-oh. Looks like we've got an audience,' Joe said, and Charlie registered that the surprise in his voice seemed genuine. Had he really not noticed that they were being watched? Because if not, that kiss needed an explanation. The knowledge that it was all for show had been the only thing keeping her from losing her mind. He couldn't go and change the rules now.

'Are you up for another?' Joe asked.

Another song? Another drink? Another kiss? None of the options seemed particularly safe after that performance.

'I think my singing days are done,' she said with a smile, jumping down from the stage and heading back to the relative safety of their booth.

'Where did they all come from?' Joe asked, drinking the beer he'd abandoned when he'd gone into performance mode.

'Happened quickly, huh.'

'So fast I didn't even notice.'

Then why did you kiss me? The question hung, loud and unspoken, in the air.

'So what's your family like?' Charlie asked, suddenly desperate for a change of subject. 'You're from up north, right?'

Joe nodded, and named a town near Manchester. Of course she already knew where he'd grown up from her research into the band, but small talk seemed the safest option open to them at the moment. 'They must have been proud of you. For the scholarship. For everything since.'

'Of course. They were chuffed when I got into the school. It was their idea, actually. My mum was a gifted pianist but never had the opportunity for a career in music. They wanted me to have the best.'

'Sounds like a lot of pressure.' If there was one thing she understood it was the heavy weight of family expectation. But Joe shrugged, non-committal.

'Their motives were good. Still are.'

'But you weren't happy?'

'It was an amazing opportunity.'

'That's not what I asked.'

He sighed and held up his palms. 'I don't like to sound ungrateful. I have no reason to complain. The school funded me. My parents made sacrifices.'

'You remember who you're talking to, right? I do understand that having the best of everything doesn't always make you happy. It doesn't make you a bad person to acknowledge that. It makes you human.'

He was quiet for a beat. 'So what's making you unhappy, Princess Caroline?'

'Oh, no. You are so not changing the subject like that. Come on. Mum and Dad. What are they like? How did they react to…' she searched for the words to describe what they were doing together '…to Vegas?'

He grimaced; she cringed. 'That bad?'

'They weren't best pleased that we did it without them there. They're hurt, but happy for me. I don't know, but I think that made me feel worse.' He was silent for a moment, fiddling with the label of his beer bottle. 'They want to meet you.'

And she was every bit as terrified of that as he was about meeting her family. She knew that she had a reputation that was about as far as you could get from ideal daughter-in-law. 'I could ask my mother to invite them this weekend? Face everyone at the same time?'

He choked on his beer, caught in a laugh.

'That's sweet, Charlie, but how about we start with introducing them to one royal and go from there. Not everyone is as super cool as me when it comes to meeting you and yours.'

'Oh, right,' she laughed. 'Because you were so ice-cool you practically dropped to one knee the night that we met.'

She wondered whether her tease had gone too far, but his mouth curved in a smile. 'What can I say? You give a whole new meaning to irresistible.'

She could feel herself blushing like a schoolgirl and incapable of stopping it. 'So we see my parents Friday night. Do you want to see yours this weekend too? If you wanted to go sooner I guess I could talk to Rich. Work remotely or something.'

He shook his head. 'Don't worry. I think this weekend will be plenty soon enough. We can fly into Manchester on Saturday. Be back home by Sunday night. No need to miss work.'

'Actually, I could do with stopping by a festival on Sunday, if you fancy it. There's a band I'd like to see perform, and try and catch them for a chat.'

He nodded, and then Charlie glanced at her watch, realising with surprise that over an hour had passed since they had left the stage. The bar had thinned out a little again, leaving the atmosphere verging dangerously on intimate.

'Speaking of work, I've a fair bit to catch up on. I need to be in the office early tomorrow. Mind if we call it a night?'

He swigged the last of his drink and stood, reaching for her hand as she slipped off the bench. 'I like that you're tall,' he said as they left the bar with a wave to Ruby. 'As tall as me in those shoes.'

'Random comment, but thanks,' she replied, trying to work out if there was a hidden message in there that she wasn't getting. 'Are you just thinking out loud? Is this going to be a list?'

'I'm just… I don't understand. You're right. I didn't play it cool, that night. I didn't play it cool on stage just now. I'm just trying to figure this out. Maybe it is the royal thing, but I didn't struggle not to kiss your cousins when I was at school with them.'

'So you think it's because I'm tall?' Really thinking: What are you saying? Are you saying you like me? That this is real for you?

'I'm thinking about everything. I just figure that if I can work out what it is…you know…that makes us crazy like that, we can avoid it. Stop it happening again. Keep things simple.'

Her ego deflated rapidly. So it didn't matter what he was feeling, because all he wanted was a way of not feeling it any more. After their madness on stage, they were back on earth with a crash, and she had the whiplash to prove it.

'Well, I'm sorry, darling, but I'm not losing the heels.'

'God, no. Don't,' he said with so much feeling it broke the tension between them. 'I love the heels.'

Which was meant to be a bad thing, she tried to remind herself, but the matching grins on their faces proved it would be a lie.

'Or maybe it's the hair,' he came up with as they walked back to his flat, their fingers still twined. 'There's so much of it. It's wild.'

She tried to laugh it off. 'So we've established you have a thing for tall women with messy hair. I guess I was just lucky I fit the bill.' She turned serious as they reached the front door of the warehouse and stepped into the privacy of the foyer. 'Are your parents going to hate me?'

'Why would they hate you?'

'Notorious party girl seduces lovely northern lad into hasty Vegas marriage. Am I not the girl that mothers have nightmares about?'

'Is that how you see what happened? You seduced me? Because I remember things differently…'

'It's not about what I remember. It's about what your mum will think.'

'My mum will think you're great.' But his tone told her that she wasn't the only one with reservations about the big introduction. 'You'll mainly be busy with dodging hints about grandchildren.'

Her stomach fell and she leaned back against the wall for support while the rushing in her ears stopped.

'She won't seriously be expecting that, will she?'

'She's been bugging me for years about settling down and giving her grandkids. Isn't that what all mums do?'

Apparently they did—that was why she made a point of seeing hers as little as possible.

She drew herself up to her full height again, not wanting Joe to see that there was anything wrong.

'Well, we'll just have to tell her that we don't have any plans.'

Joe was looking at her closely, and she wondered how much he had seen. Whether he had realised that she had just had a minor panic attack.

'It's fine; we'll fend her off together. Are you sure you're okay?'

So he had noticed. She pasted on a smile and pushed her shoulders back, determined to give him no reason to suspect what was on her mind. 'Of course. Just tired. That jet lag must be catching up with me after all.'

It wasn't until she reached his front door that she remembered the whole bed situation. How was she meant to sleep beside him after a kiss like that? After he'd all but told her that he was finding it as hard to resist her as she was to resist him.

She dived into the bathroom as soon as they got into the apartment, determined to be the first ready for bed, and to have her eyes closed and be pretending to sleep by the time that Joe came in. Or better still, actually *be* asleep, and not even know that he was there. She pulled a T-shirt over her head, still warm from the dryer, and gave herself a stern talking-to. She couldn't react like that every time someone mentioned babies or pregnancy. There were bound to be questions after the hasty way that they had got married, and she was going to have to learn to deal with them.

CHAPTER SIX

THERE WAS DEFINITELY something that she wasn't telling him. Something to do with the way that she'd reacted just now when he'd warned her that his mum would probably be hinting about grandchildren.

What, did she already have an illegitimate kid stashed away somewhere? No. It couldn't be that. There was no way that she'd be able to keep it out of the papers. What if she was already pregnant? That could be it. After all, she had accepted a completely idiotic proposal of marriage from a man that she barely knew. Was she looking for a baby daddy, as well as a husband?

And how would he feel if she was? That one was easy enough to answer: as if he was being used. Well, there was nothing new in that. He'd learnt at the age of eighteen, when it transpired that the girl he had been madly in love with at school was only with him for the thrill of sleeping with the poor northern scholarship kid, and bringing him home to upset her parents in front of all their friends, that women wanted him for *what* he was, not who.

And after years on the road, meeting women in every city, every country that he had visited, he knew that it was true. None of them wanted him. The real him. They wanted the singer, or the writer, or the rock star, or the rich guy.

Or—on one memorable occasion—they wanted the story to sell to the tabloids.

Not a single one of them knew who he really was. Not a single one of them had come home to meet his parents. And that was fine with him. Because he knew what he wanted now too. And more importantly he knew that relationships only worked if both of you knew what you wanted—and didn't let emotions in the way of getting it.

But it didn't mean anything, he told himself, Charlie coming home with him at the weekend. Like all the others, she was just using him. He provided a nice boost to her career, and a new way of causing friction with her family, though he couldn't pretend to know why she wanted that. And he was using her to get exposure for his band, and sales for his new album. If he ever finished it.

He tidied up the bedroom while he waited for her to finish in the bathroom, chucking dirty clothes in the laundry hamper and retrieving the rest of Charlie's jewellery from under the bed. They would have to pick up the rest of her stuff from her flat at some point. He'd clear her a space in the wardrobe. Of all the things that he'd thought about that night that they got married, how to manage living with a slob hadn't been one of them. He surveyed the carnage in his apartment, and shrugged. Lucky his housekeeper was going to be in tomorrow. He'd leave a note asking her to clear some space in the drawers and wardrobe.

The thought of it was oddly intimate. Strange,

when they were already having to share a bed. Sharing hanging space should have been the least of their worries. But there was something decidedly permanent, committed, about the thought of her clothes hanging alongside his.

It wasn't permanent.

They'd both known and agreed from the start that this wasn't real, and it wasn't going to last. They just had to ride out the next year or so. Let the press do their thing, and then decide how they were going to end things in a way that worked out for both of them. It was as simple as that.

Joe waited outside Charlie's office, wondering whether she'd be pleased or not if he went in. Somehow, over the past three days they'd barely seen each other. That night after the karaoke she'd been asleep by the time that he'd got out of the bathroom, lying on her side on the far side of the bed, so far away that they didn't even need a pillow barrier as a nod to decency. Then she'd been up before him the next morning, though she had said that she had a lot to catch up on. The pattern had stayed the same ever since. She was in the office before he'd had his breakfast every morning, and came home late, clutching bags and suitcases from her flat.

The only sign that they were living together at all was the increasing chaos in his apartment. His housekeeper did her best in the daytime, but once Charlie was home she was like a whirlwind, depositing clothes and hair grips and jewellery on every surface. Leaving crumbs and coffee rings all over the kitchen and the coffee table. He wasn't even mad: he was amused.

How had the prim and proper royal family produced such a slob?

It wasn't as if she were lazy. The woman never stopped. He knew that of her reputation at work. That she worked hard to find her artists, and then even harder to support them once they were signed. She was on the phone to lawyers, accountants, artists all day long, and then out at gigs in the evening, always looking for more talent, more opportunities.

Perhaps that was it, he thought. Why waste time picking up your dirty clothes when there was new music to be found?

The pavements started to fill with knackered-looking workers as the clock ticked towards six. As East London's hipster types exited office buildings and headed for the craft-beer-stocked pubs as if pulled by a magnet.

She'd told him she'd arranged for a car to collect her from work and swing by the apartment to pick him up, but as the hours after lunch had crawled by he'd realised that sitting and waiting for her was absolutely not his style.

He strode into the building, mind made up, and smiled at the receptionist.

'Hey, Vanessa. I'm Charlie's husband. Okay if I go straight through?' There. He made sure he sounded humble enough not to assume that she'd know who he was—though he would hope that the receptionist at his own label would recognise him—but confident enough to be assured that he wouldn't be stopped. He breezed past her, wondering why he felt so nervous. All right, he hadn't even visited Afland before, never mind the private apartments at the royal palace, but he had met a fair few royals, between his posh school and attending galas and stuff since his career took off. Deep down, he knew it wasn't who her family was that was making him nervous. It was the fact that he was meeting them at all.

He'd not been home to meet the family for a long time. Not since the disaster with Arabella.

That weekend when he was eighteen, he'd thought he had it made. His gorgeous girlfriend, one of the most popular girls in school, had invited him and a load of their friends to a weekend party at her parents' country house. For the first time since he had started at the school he had felt as if he had belonged. And more importantly had thought it meant that Arabella was as serious about him as he was about her. He'd been on the verge of telling her that he loved her. But as soon as he'd arrived, he'd realised that there was something wrong. She'd introduced him to her parents with a glint in her eye that he knew meant trouble, and had stropped off when they'd welcomed him with warm smiles and handshakes.

Turned out, he wasn't the ogre she'd been expecting them to see. And if he wasn't pissing off her parents, he was no use to her at all. So she'd broken it off, publicly and humiliatingly, in front of half the school and their parents.

Was Charlie doing the same thing? Perhaps marrying him was just one more way for her to stick her middle finger up at her family. Another way to distance herself from her royal blood. But instinctively he felt that wasn't true. Whenever they'd discussed her family, she'd made it clear that she didn't want to upset them. That had been the main thing on her mind that first morning in Vegas. But she hadn't been so concerned about it that she hadn't married him in the first place.

He showed himself through the office, over to where he remembered Charlie's desk was. She couldn't see him approach, her back to him, concentrating on her computer. Her hair was pulled into a knot on the top of her head, an up-do that could almost be described as sophisticated, and a delicate tattoo curled at the nape of her neck. He'd never noticed it before—and that knowledge sent a shudder of desire through him. How many inches of her body were a mystery to him? How many secrets could he uncover if they were to do the utterly stupid thing and give in to this mutual attraction?

They couldn't be that stupid. *He* wouldn't be so stupid. Opening up to a woman, especially a woman like Charlie, was like asking to get hurt.

By the time that he reached her desk, she still hadn't looked up. He couldn't resist that tattoo a moment longer. He could feel the eyes of her co-workers on him, and knew that they were watching, knew that they had read the gossip sites. It was all the excuse he needed, the reminder that he had a part to play.

He bent and pressed his lips to the black swirl of ink below her hairline.

The second that he met her skin a shot of pain seared through his nose and he jumped back, both hands pressed to his face.

'What the h—?'

'What the h—?'

They both cried out in unison.

'Joe?' Charlie said, one hand on the back of her

head as she spun round on her chair. 'What were you *thinking*?'

He gave her a loaded look. 'I was thinking that I wanted to kiss my wife. What I'm thinking now is that we might need a trip to A&E.' She looked up then, clocked the many pairs of eyes on them, and stood, remembering she needed to play her part too.

'Oh, my goodness, I'm sorry, darling.' She reached up and gently took hold of his hands, moving them away from his nose. 'Does it still hurt?'

She turned his head one way and then the other, examining him closely as she did so.

'Not so much now,' he admitted, finally making eye contact with her. It was the truth. With her hands gently cupping his face like that, he could barely feel his nose. Barely think about any part of his body that didn't have her soft skin against it.

'No blood anyway,' she added.

He smiled. 'Can't meet the in-laws with a bloody nose and a black eye,' he said. 'Not really the best first impression.'

'They'll love you whatever,' she said, returning his grin, but he suspected it was more for their audience than for him.

She was wearing a black dress, structured and tight, giving the illusion of curves that her tall, athletic figure usually hid. Was this what her parents wanted of her? he wondered. For her to tone herself down and wear something ladylike?

Her phone buzzed on the desk behind her, breaking the spell between them. 'That'll be the car,' she said, gathering up her stuff and shutting down her computer. As she grabbed her purse off the desk she sent a glass of water flying, soaking a stack of scrawled notes.

'Argh,' she groaned, reaching into a drawer for a roll of paper towels. 'Last thing we need.'

'It's fine,' he said, grabbing a handful of the towels. 'Here.' He mopped up the puddle heading towards the edge of the desk and spread out the soggy papers. 'They'll be dry before we're back on Monday. No harm done.'

She blotted at them some more with the paper, glancing at her phone, which was buzzing again on the desk.

'Is it time we were going?'

'Mmm,' she said, non-committal, silencing it. 'It's okay, we've got time.' She started straightening up another stack of papers, and throwing pens in a cup at the back of the desk.

'Wait a minute. Are you tidying?'

She shrugged. 'It's happened before, you know.'

'Maybe, but right now you're stalling, aren't you?'

She stopped what she was doing and looked him straight in the eye, leaning back against the desk with her arms crossing her chest. 'Says who?'

'Well, you just as good as admitted it, actually. What's going on? Ashamed to introduce me to your family?'

She started with surprise. 'Why would I be ashamed?'

'Because you're nervous. Why else would you be?'

'Maybe I'm desperate for them to fall in love with you.'

'Maybe.' He watched her with a wry smile. 'I guess we're going to find out. Are you ready?'

She sighed as she pulled on her jacket and swung her bag over her shoulders. 'Ready.'

As the car pulled through the gates at the back of the palace a few hours later, Joe took a deep breath. He might have been all blasé with Charlie, but now that he was here at the palace, with its two hundred and fifty bedrooms and uniformed guards and a million windows, perhaps he was feeling a little intimidated. Regardless of what he'd thought earlier, his brief brushes with royalty before he had met Charlie hadn't left him at all prepared for this.

Throughout the short flight to the island, he'd been making a determined effort not to feel nervous—forcing his pulse to be even and his palms dry.

And now, as they stepped out of the car and through the doors of the palace, perhaps if he closed his eyes, shut out the scale of the entrance gates, the uniformed staff in attendance, and the police officer stationed at the door, he could almost imagine that this was just any other dinner.

Eventually, following Charlie into the building and through a warren of corridors, he had to admit to himself that there was no escaping it. 'The private apartments are just up there,' Charlie told him as they rounded yet another corner.

He nodded, not sure what the appropriate response was when your wife was giving you the guided tour of the palace she had grown up in. In fact, he'd barely spoken a word, he realised, since the car had pulled through the gates.

The uniformed man who had met them at the door faded away as the policeman ahead of them opened the door. He nodded to them both as Charlie greeted him by name, and Joe followed her through the door. Unlike the corridors they'd followed so far, the interior of the private rooms was simple. Plush red carpets, gilt and chandeliers had fallen away, leaving smart, bright walls, soft wood flooring and recessed lighting.

'It's like another world in here,' Charlie said with a smile. 'My parents had it renovated when we were small. They were doing big repair work across the whole palace, so they took the opportunity to modernise a bit.'

'No chandeliers, then?'

'Not really my mother's style. They keep them in the state rooms for the visiting dignitaries and the tourists. But my parents have always preferred things simpler.'

He followed her down the corridor, and she paused in front of a closed door. 'Ready?' she asked.

He took her hand in his and squeezed. 'Let's do it.'

She opened the door into a light-flooded room.

Her parents were seated on a sofa to one side of a fireplace, what looked like gin and tonics on the coffee table in front of them.

'Oh, you caught us!' said Queen Adelaide, Charlie's mother. 'We started without you. I know, we're terrible.' She stood and kissed Charlie on the cheek.

Joe just had time to register the stiffness in Charlie's shoulders before her mother, Her Majesty Queen Adelaide of Afland, was stepping around her and holding out her hand.

He held his own out in return, but couldn't find his feet to step towards her. Was it because she was the head of state or the head of Charlie's family that was making him nervous?

'You must be Joe,' Queen Adelaide said, smiling and filling the silence that was threatening awkwardness. 'How do you do?'

Charlie's father stepped forward and shook his hand too, but he wasn't as skilled as his wife at hiding his feelings, he noted. And in his case, his feelings appeared to be decidedly frosty.

'Joe. How do you do?'

He wasn't the only frosty one, Joe realised, watching Charlie as they took a seat on the sofa opposite her parents. Her shoulders were as stiff as he had ever seen them, and her back was ramrod straight. She reached for one of the drinks that had appeared on the coffee table while they were getting the formalities out of the way.

They sipped their drinks as silence fell around them, definitely into awkward territory now. And still a distinct lack of congratulations. Perhaps they were waiting for the others to arrive.

Just as he was taking a deep breath, preparing to dive into small talk, he heard a door open, and the apartment filled with the noise of rambunctious children.

'Grandma! Grandpa!'

The kids barrelled into the room with squeals of excitement. The tense atmosphere was broken, and Queen Adelaide and Prince Gerald beamed with proud smiles and stood to scoop up their grandchildren. But Charlie stayed seated; though she smiled, the expression seemed forced.

Three adults followed the kids into the room. Joe recognised Charlie's sister and brother-in-law, and a second woman who he guessed must be the nanny.

She drifted out of the room after seeing the children settled with book and toys, and Joe shook hands with his new in-laws.

'So, Vegas!' Charlie's brother-in-law said as they all sat down. 'Wish we could have done that. Would have given anything to avoid the circus that we had to endure.'

'Endure?' Charlie's sister, Verity, slapped her husband's leg playfully. 'If that was a circus, I don't know how you'd describe our life now, chasing after these two.' But she smiled indulgently as she said it. Charlie leaned forward and helped herself to her sister's drink, uncharacteristically quiet.

'It was definitely low-key,' Joe said. 'Just us and a couple of friends.' He took hold of Charlie's hand, wondering whether she was planning on checking back in to this conversation again at any point. He withheld the details of the kitschy chapel they had chosen: it had seemed so funny at the time, but less so now that they were facing the consequences of their actions. He looked across at Charlie, and saw the tension in her expression that revealed how uncomfortable she was.

Isn't that what I'm meant to be feeling? he thought. You're back in the bosom of your family. This is meant to be your home, so why are you so uncomfortable?

He was so distracted by wondering what was preoccupying her that he forgot that he had been nervous about meeting the family. Her family were half of the reason he was so sure that this relationship wouldn't work so if it wasn't her family causing the problems, then where did that leave them?

Using one another—that was it. And he knew that

he had to keep his head if he was going to stay ahead of the game, make sure that she was never in a position to hurt him.

His thoughts were interrupted by the arrival of Charlie's brother, Miles, who bowled into the room wearing an air of privilege that outshone his exquisitely tailored suit. He greeted Charlie's brother-in-law with hearty slaps on the back—they'd been friends at school, Joe seemed to remember—and then doled out kisses on the cheek to his female relatives.

'So you're the guy who seduced my sister,' he said when he reached Joe.

He gave Miles a shrewd look. Was he trying to get a rise out of him? Well, he'd have to try harder than that.

'I'm Joe,' he said, standing to shake his hand. 'It's good to meet you.'

Charlie had risen beside him and he wrapped an arm around her waist. She seemed calmer with her brother than with her sister. Interesting, Joe thought. Because so far, her brother seemed like a bit of an ass. But families were strange, he knew. Maybe she'd always been closer to her brother. He tried to push it from his mind as they all sat down again. The nanny came back in, then, and the room was suddenly in chaos as toys were put away, negotiations for 'just five more minutes' were shut down and a pair of desultory kids doled out goodnight kisses.

When they got to Charlie, that stiffness came back to her shoulders, and she straightened her spine, sitting beside Joe on the sofa as if she were in a job interview. She sat deadly still as the children climbed up onto the couch, still offering kisses and messing around.

In contrast to all of the other adults in the room, who were joining in with the kids' silliness, Charlie pretty much just patted them on the head and dodged their kisses.

What was her issue with the kids?

There was no getting away from the fact that there *was* something going on. Joe looked over at Charlie's mum and sister to see if they had noticed—looking for any clues to what was going on—but their attention was completely on the children. Joe's earlier suspicion came back to him. Could she be pregnant? Did that even fit with what he was witnessing?

It did if she was in denial, he supposed. If she was pregnant and didn't want to be. Or didn't want to be found out.

Finally, the kids were bundled out of the room by the nanny, and a member of staff appeared with a silver tray bearing champagne flutes and an ice bucket.

'Ah, perfect timing,' Adelaide declared as the glasses were handed round and champagne poured.

The tone of her voice shifted ever so subtly, from relaxed and convivial to something more formal. Maybe more rehearsed. Charlie was close by Joe's side still, and this time it was she who took his hand, and ducked her head under his arm as she wrapped it around her shoulders and turned in towards him, until she was almost surrounded by his body. He tried to meet her eyes, but she evaded him. He couldn't be sure with her avoiding eye contact, but if he didn't know better he'd say that she wanted him to protect her. From her own family? Who seemed—to his surprise—a bunch of genuinely nice people who cared about one another. Her slightly annoying brother aside. It just didn't make any sense. Not unless she was keeping all of them—him included—in the dark about something.

'Joe and Charlie,' Adelaide began, 'I'm so pleased that we are all together this evening. While we can't say that we weren't surprised by your news...' her raised eyebrows spoke volumes about how restrained she felt she was being '...your father and I are delighted you have found someone you want to spend your life with. Now we didn't get to do this on your wedding day, so I'm going to propose the traditional toast. If you could all charge your glasses to the bride and groom. To Charlie and Joe.'

Queen Adelaide took a ladylike sip, while Charlie polished off half her glass and pulled Joe's arm tighter around her.

'Joe, we're absolutely delighted to meet the man who wants to take on, not only our wonderfully wild Caroline, but also her family, with everything that entails. We're always so happy to see our family grow, and, who knows, perhaps over the next few years it might be growing even further.'

From the corner of his eye he saw Charlie flinch, and he knew exactly how she had taken that comment of her mother's, whether it had been meant as a jibe about grandchildren or not. He sipped at his champagne, having smiled and nodded in the right places during Queen Adelaide's speech.

'Are you okay?' he whispered in Charlie's ear when the toasts were done and attention had drifted away from them.

She nodded stiffly, telling him louder than words that she absolutely wasn't.

'Want to try and make a break for it?'

She cracked half a smile. 'We'd better stay. I'd never hear the end of it.'

He wondered if that were true. Charlie's parents looked delighted to have her home. But were they really the types to nag and criticise if she left? They'd welcomed him with good grace in trying circumstances. Perhaps they deserved more credit than Charlie was giving them.

But there was no getting around the fact that she was still on edge, even after all the introductions were out of the way and they were all getting on fine. Which meant there was more to this than just her worrying whether they were going to buy their story.

What if he was right? What if she was pregnant, and was using him? Would he walk away from her? From their agreement? How would that look to the press…?

He suspected there was nothing worse as far as the tabloids were concerned than walking away from a pregnant royal wife.

He still had his arm around Charlie's waist, but he could feel a killer grip closing around him, making it hard to breathe. He'd thought that he'd gone into this with his eyes open. He'd thought he'd known what she wanted from him. Had he been duped again? Was he being used again, without him realising it?

'So, Joe, you were at school with Hugo and Seb, is that right? At Northbridge?' Charlie's brother had come to sit beside them, dragging his thoughts away from his wife.

'Yeah, they were a year or two ahead of me though. You know what it's like at school. A different year could be a different planet.'

'They remembered you, though.'

He heard Charlie move beside him, and, when he glanced across at her, she looked interested in the conversation for the first time since they'd arrived.

'What did they tell you?' she asked, a glint in her eye. 'You have to share. Don't you dare hold out on me, big brother.'

'Oh, you know, the usual. Ex-girlfriends and kiss-and-tells. God, you've let your standards slip, getting yourself hitched to this one.'

'Standards? Really? Who did he date at school?'

'You really want to know?' Miles laughed and rolled his eyes. 'Masochist. Fine, it was Arabella Barclay,' Miles said.

He watched Charlie's reaction from the corner of his eye. It was clear that she knew her, or knew of her.

'Wow. Miles is right, Joe. Blonde, skinny, horsey. If you've got a type, I'm definitely not it.'

Her brother laughed, and Joe resisted the urge to use his fists to shut his mouth.

'Thank God I came to my senses and left all that schoolboy rubbish behind,' he said. Trying not to think of that leggy, horsey girl. Or maybe he *should* be thinking about her. Really, looking back, he owed Arabella a big thank you. She'd done him a favour, teaching him about how relationships *really* worked, rather than the schoolboy idealism he'd had at eighteen.

'Trust me,' Joe said, dropping his arm from Charlie's shoulders to her waist, 'you were everything I didn't know I was looking for.' He closed his eyes and leaned in for a kiss, thinking that a peck on the lips would finish off their picture of newly wedded romance nicely. And banish bitter memories of Arabella into the bargain.

How could he have forgotten? Perhaps his brain erased it on purpose, in an attempt to protect him? The second his lips met Charlie's a rush of desire flooded his blood, and he clenched his fists, trying to control it. To control himself. Was this normal? This overwhelming passion from the most innocent of kisses? He pulled away as Charlie's lips pouted, knowing that another second would lead them to more trouble than he could reasonably be expected to deal with.

Her eyes were still closed, and for the first time since they'd arrived at the palace her features were relaxed. A hint of a smile curved one corner of her lips, and the urge to press just one more kiss there was almost overwhelming.

'Okay, you've proved your point.' Miles laughed. 'I will never mention Arabella again. Or the fact that she's still single and still smoking hot.'

Charlie opened her eyes to roll them at her brother.

'Do you think we can stop trying to set my husband up with his ex?'

Miles held up his hands. 'You're the newly-weds. Your marriage is your own business. I was just providing the facts,'

'Well, as helpful as that is, darling,' Charlie's mother interjected, 'I think we can leave gossip about school friends for another time.'

Joe glanced at Adelaide, and as she met his eye he realised that he had an unexpected ally. He smiled back, curious. Charlie had been so worried about how her parents were going to react that it had never occurred to him that they'd actually be pleased to meet him.

They sat down for dinner in one of the semi-state-rooms, and Joe looked around him in awe. Away from the modest private apartments, it struck him for the first time that this really was Charlie's life. She'd grown up here, in this home within a palace. Her life had been crystal and champagne, gilt and marble and staff and state apartments. Carriages and press calls, church at Christmas and official photographs on her birthdays. And she'd walked away from all of that.

She'd chosen a warehouse apartment in East London. A job that demanded she work hard. A 'floor-drobe' rather than a maid. A real life with normal responsibilities. It occurred to him that he'd never asked her why. He'd mocked the privileges that she'd been born with, but he'd never asked her about the choices that she'd made.

As the wine flowed and they settled in to what to Joe seemed like a banquet of never-ending courses, Charlie relaxed more. He watched her banter with her brother and sister, and marvelled at the change in her since they had first arrived. When her hand landed on his thigh, he knew that it was all for show. Part of appearing like the loved-up new couple they were meant to be. But that didn't stop the heat radiating from the palm of her hand, or the awareness of every movement of her body beside him.

It didn't stop his imagination, the tumble of images that fell through his mind, the endless possibilities, if this thing weren't so damned complicated.

He wanted her. Could he have her? Could they go to bed, and wake up the next morning and *not* turn the whole thing into a string of complications? Could they both just demand what they wanted, take it, and then agree when it needed to be over?

They shouldn't risk it. He looked down at her hand again and caught sight of the gold of her wedding ring. It would never be that simple between them. They were married. They worked together. There was unbelievable chemistry between them, but that didn't mean that a simple night in bed together could ever be on the cards. They'd acted impulsively once, when they'd decided to get married, and that meant that the stakes were too high for any further slips on the self-control front.

Work. That was what he should be concentrating on. Like the fact that he still hadn't managed to write anything new for the album. He'd told Charlie and her boss that it was practically finished when he'd agreed to sign the contract. It *had* been finished. It still was, he supposed, if he was prepared to release it knowing that it wasn't his best work. What he really needed was to lock himself in his studio for a month with no distractions. Unfortunately, the biggest distraction in his life right now was living with him. And then there was the fact that if he was holed up in his studio, then where was the inspiration supposed to come from? What he'd end up with was an album about staring at the same four walls. What he needed was a muse. A reason to write.

Taking Charlie to bed would give him all the material he needed. He was sure of that. But at too high a cost.

They left the drawing room that night and headed to bed with handshakes and kisses from Charlie's family. Charlie stiffly accepted the kisses from her mother, and she climbed the stairs stiff and formal with him.

Joe watched her carefully as she led them down corridor after corridor, low lit with bulbs that wouldn't damage the artworks. He was vaguely aware of passing masterpieces on his left and right, but his attention was all on Charlie.

'Did you have a good time?' he asked. 'I thought it went pretty well; I liked your family.'

She nodded, staring straight ahead instead of at him. 'They liked you. Even Miles.'

'That's how he acts when he likes someone?'

She huffed an affectionate laugh, and turned to face him. 'I know. He's an idiot. We keep hoping he'll grow out of it.'

'Do you think they bought our story?' he asked. Her eyes seemed to turn darker as she looked ahead again. The sparsely spaced lights strobed her expressions, yellow and dark, yellow, dark.

'I'm not sure,' she admitted. 'But I don't think they're going to call us out on it. My mum already—'

She stopped herself, but he needed to know. 'What?' he asked.

'When I first called and told her what we'd done, she told me that she'd take care of it. If we wanted this marriage to go away.'

'And you didn't take her up on it?'

'We'd already talked about why that would be a bad idea. We made an agreement and I'm sticking to it.'

Her face was still a mystery. She was hiding something else. He knew that she was. Something that meant she was happy with their lie of a marriage rather than the real thing. Maybe he'd shock it out of her with some brutal home truths.

'Charlie, I want you. I know we said that sleeping together would be a disaster. But what if it wasn't?'

She turned to him properly now, her eyes wide with surprise. 'And where the hell did that come from?'

'It needed saying. Or the question needed asking. Maybe it could work. Maybe we could give it a go. I mean, we're acting out this whole relationship, so why not make it that bit more believable?'

'Why not? Do you really need me to list the million reasons it's a horrendous idea? As if our lives weren't complicated enough—you want to add sex to the mix?'

'But that's what I'm saying. Maybe it doesn't have to complicate things. Maybe it would simplify them. We're living together. We're married. We're making everyone believe that we're a couple. I mean, how would sex make any of that more complicated?'

'Because you forgot the most important thing—we're pretending. Yes, we had a wedding, but this isn't a marriage. We're not a couple. We're doing this for a limited time only, and mixing sex in with that would just be crazy.'

'So you don't want to. Fine, I just thought I'd ask the question. Clear the air.'

'Whether I want to or not isn't the issue, Joe.'

'So you do.'

'Urgh.' She threw her head back in frustration. '*Totally* not the point. And to be honest I'm surprised you're asking, because we both know that there's some crazy chemistry between us. We've talked about it before. And at no point has either of us thought that doing something about it was in any way a good idea. I don't know why we can't just drop it.'

'Maybe I don't want to.'

They stopped outside a door and Charlie hesitated with her hand on the doorknob, a frosty silence growing between them. Joe decided to take a punt, knowing that he could be about to set a bomb under their little arrangement. But if she wasn't going to volunteer all the facts, he had to get them out of her somehow. A pregnancy wasn't the sort of thing you could ignore for ever.

'How are you planning on passing me off as your baby daddy, then, if we're not sleeping together?'

Charlie took in a gasp of a breath, and as he watched her straighten her spine he realised that he'd been right about one thing—this was going to be explosive. But a shiver ran through him as Charlie walked into the room and he wondered whether he had just made an enormous mistake.

CHAPTER SEVEN

CHARLIE KEPT WALKING, calm and controlled, past the four-poster bed, trying to cover the typhoon of emotions roiling through her. She stopped when she reached the bathroom, an island of cool white marble after the richness of the bedroom.

'What are you talking about, Joe?'

Her teeth were practically grinding against one another, and she didn't seem to be able to unclench her fists.

'You're pregnant, aren't you?' His voice faded towards the end of the sentence, as if he were already regretting asking. But she didn't care about that, because the grief and pain that she had been holding at bay all night, seeing her sister's happiness with her children, her easy contentment, broke through the dam and flooded her. Winded, as if she'd been punched in the gut, she turned. She retched into the sink, as a week of new pain caught up with her. This had been building since she'd seen the newspaper headline announcing her own imminent engagement. She'd held it at bay, distracted herself with her stupid Vegas wedding and then burying herself in her work. But with Joe's crazy, heartless words—his absolutely baseless accusation—the pain had gripped her and wouldn't let her go.

Joe caught up with her and leaned against the bathroom door frame as she retched, hoping that she wasn't going to get a second look at her dinner.

'Are you okay?'

She threw him the dirtiest look that she could muster before hanging her head over the sink.

'Is it morning sickness?'

It took every ounce of self-control she possessed not to howl like a dog and collapse in a heap on the floor. Instead she forced herself upright, regaining control over her body.

'I. Am. Not. Pregnant.'

She forced the words out as evenly as she could, determined not to give him the satisfaction of seeing how he was hurting her, driving the knife deeper and twisting it with everything that he said.

'Are you sure? Because—'

She broke.

'I'm infertile, Joe. Is that sure enough for you?'

Her spine sagged and her legs turned to jelly as she spoke the words that she'd buried for so many years. She didn't even put out her hands to break her fall. There was no point—what could hurt more than this?

But instead of hitting cold marble, she landed on soft cotton, hard muscle. Joe's arms surrounded her, and her vision was clouded by snowy white shirt. She pushed away, not wanting him here, wanting no witnesses to her despair. But his arms were clamped around her, his lips were on her temple and his voice was soft in her ear.

'God, Charlie, I'm so sorry. I never would have said that if… I didn't know. I'm sorry.'

More murmurs followed, but she'd stopped listening. The tears had arrived. The ones that she'd kept at bay since she was a teenager. That she'd forced down somewhere deep inside her.

They tipped off the mascaraed ends of her lashes, streaking her cheeks, painting tracks down Joe's shirt as he held her tight and refused to let go, even as she struggled against him. Eventually, she stopped fighting, and accepted the tight clamp of his arms around her and the weight of his head resting against hers. She listened to the pulse at the base of his throat, heard it racing in time with her own. And then, as her heaving sobs petered out to cries, and then sniffs, she heard it slow. A gentle, rhythmic thud that pulled her towards calm. They'd slumped back against the claw-footed bath, her legs dragged across Joe's when he'd pulled her close and she'd fought to get free. The shoulder of his shirt was damp, and no doubt ruined by her charcoaled tears.

'You know,' he said eventually, 'we'd be more comfortable in the other room.' Their conversation in the corridor, when he'd oh-so-casually asked if she wanted to sleep with him, felt like a lifetime ago. Surely he couldn't be suggesting…

But he was right. The floor was unforgiving against her butt, and as comfortable as the bath probably was once you were in it, it didn't make for a great back rest.

She stood, pulling her dress straight and attempting something close to dignity.

'Let's just forget this whole conversation. Please,'

she added, when he stood behind her and met her gaze in the mirror.

He crossed his arms.

'I'm not sure that I can.'

'Well, I'm sure that if I can manage not to think about it, you can too.' She didn't care that he'd just been gentle and caring with her. Spiky was all she had right now, so that was what he was going to get. She walked through to the bedroom, her arms crossed across her chest and her hands rubbing at her biceps. She was cold, suddenly. Something to do with sitting on a marble floor perhaps. She climbed under the crisply ironed sheets and heavy embroidered eider-down, pulling it up around her shoulders in a search for warmth. She figured she didn't need to worry about Joe's suggestion about sleeping together. There was no way that he was going to be interested in her now, with her messed-up mascara and malfunction-ing uterus. When she looked up he was still standing in the doorway of the bathroom, watching her. She pulled the sheets a little tighter and sank back against the padded headboard, wondering if he was going to drop the subject.

'So how's that going for you?' he asked eventually. 'Not thinking about it, I mean.'

She shut her eyes tight, trying to block him out. She didn't need him judging her on top of everything else. But he wasn't done yet. 'Because it looks to me like burying your feelings isn't exactly working.'

Throwing the sheets down, she sat up, and met Joe's interested gaze with an angry stare. 'Just because you catch the one time in goodness knows how many years that I let myself think about it and get upset—all of a sudden you're a bloody expert on my feelings.'

'You might not think about it, but that doesn't mean that it's not hurting you.' His voice was infuriatingly calm, just highlighting how hard she was finding it to keep something remotely close to cool. If she didn't get a handle on her feelings, she was heading for another breakdown, and that little scene in the bathroom did not bear repeating.

'God, Joe. Stop talking as if you know me. You know *nothing* about this.'

He came to sit beside her on the bed, and his fingertips found the back of her hand, playing, tracing the length of her fingers, turning them over to find the lines of her palm. 'I know that it's getting between you and your family,' he said at last. 'I know that it hurts you every time you see your niece and nephew. Every time your mother casually mentions grandchildren.'

She looked up from their joined hands to meet his eye. He'd seen all that? 'You think you're so insightful, but an hour ago you thought that I was pregnant,' she reminded him.

He boosted himself up on the bed, and with a huff she scooched over, making room between her and the edge of the bed. He picked up her hand again, and focussed intently on it as he spoke. 'So I misinterpreted the reason you were acting funny. That doesn't mean I didn't see it. That I don't understand.'

'You don't. How could you?' She tipped her head back against the headboard and closed her eyes, wishing that he would just drop this. It wasn't as if it really affected him. He had no vested interest in whether she could procreate. It wasn't fair that he was pushing this when she so obviously didn't want to talk about it.

But if she could admit it to herself, perhaps talking felt almost...good. She realised that there had been a heavy weight in her stomach, sitting there so long that she'd forgotten how hard it had been to carry at first. Over time, she had got so used to the pain that she had lost sight of how it had felt not to have it there.

'I know that you let it push you into doing stuff that you regret. What happened that night in Vegas. Was it something to do with this?'

'I was just letting off steam. Having fun.'

'I don't believe you. I've not known you long, Charlie, but I can see straight through you. If I'd known you better that night I'd never have gone through with it. If I'd been able to see how you were hurting.'

'Hurting? I was enjoying myself. I got carried away.'

'For God's sake. Can you still not be honest with me, even now? I'm trying to tell you that you don't have to bury this any more. That if you want, we can talk about it. But you're trying to tell me you don't even care and I know that that isn't true. This is why you said you never wanted to get married, isn't it?'

She rolled her eyes, and tried to fake a snort of laughter. 'As if I even have to worry about that. Who would marry me if they knew?'

'Is that really what you think?' Pulling back, he put some distance between them so he could look her in the eye.

'It doesn't matter, Joe. I came to terms with it a long time ago. But yes, it's what I think. What would be the point of getting married?'

'I don't know. Speaking hypothetically here…isn't it usually something to do with spending your life with someone that you love?'

She snorted. 'Who knew you were such a romantic? But in a real marriage, sooner or later, kids always come up. Everyone's expecting it. Everyone's waiting for it. When you come from my family, especially.'

'And you're going to let that dictate what you do—who you date. What the great unwashed masses expect of you?'

'It's not just them, though. You don't understand. You don't understand my family. It only exists to perpetuate itself. To provide the next generation.'

'And that's the sort of person you'd want to marry, is it? The sort of person who sees you as a vessel for the next generation? If someone's looking at you like that, Charlie, you need to run, as fast as you can, and find someone who deserves you.'

The fire in his voice and in his expression was disconcerting, so much so that she found that she didn't have a counter argument. Because how could she argue with that? Of course she wanted someone who saw her as more than just a royal baby maker, but that didn't mean that he existed.

Joe's arm came around her shoulders, and she turned in to him, accepting comfort from the one person who could truly offer it. The one person who knew what she was going through—even if he couldn't really understand.

Listening to the rhythmic in–out of his breathing, she gradually felt her muscles start to relax. First her shoulders dropped away from her ears as her own breaths deepened to match Joe's. Then her fingers unclenched from their fists, her back gave out as she let Joe's side take her weight, and then her legs, bent at the knee and pulled up to her chest, tipped into Joe's lap, and were secured by the presence of his hand tucked in behind her knee.

With everything that had been said and revealed in the course of a night, there was no danger of things turning sexy. Charlie could feel that her eyes were swollen, and her skin felt red and tight from tear tracks. She felt anything but desirable. Burying her face in Joe's shirt, she tried to decide what she *did* feel.

Secure.

Anchored.

Not that long ago, an emotional night like this one would have seen her out on the town, running from her problems, looking for a distraction. But tonight, with Joe's solid presence beside her, she was exhausted. And where had running got her over the years anyway? Right back here in the palace, with her problems exactly where she'd left them.

She took a deep breath in, and as she let it go she released the remaining tension in her arms and legs, concentrating on loosening her fingers and toes. Her eyelids started to droop, and she knew that there was no point fighting it. She was going under, and she didn't want to go alone.

CHAPTER EIGHT

CHARLIE SNORED.

As in she was a serious snorer.

As in it sounded as if he were sharing a bed with a blowing exhaust pipe.

It seemed there was no end to the ways that this woman kept on surprising him.

Not that the snoring was bothering him, particularly. After all, there was no way that he was ever going to be able to get back to sleep. Not with the way that she had turned her back to him and scooted in, tucked inside the circle of his arms, and pressing back against him. Every time that he moved away, she scooted again, fidgeting and squirming in a way that was just…too good. So he'd stopped fighting it and pulled her in close, where at least she kept still, and his self-control had half a chance of winning out over his libido.

When they had fallen asleep last night they had been sitting against the headboard, one of his arms draped loosely around her shoulders. She had been curled up and guarded. Forcing herself into the relaxed state that she couldn't find naturally. He'd felt protective. As if he wanted his arms to keep out all the hurts that seemed to be circling her, waiting to strike. And he'd wanted to get into her head, to show her that the way she saw herself wasn't the way the rest of the world saw her. He certainly didn't see her as damaged goods. As being less than a woman whose insides happened to work differently. But he knew she wouldn't believe him if he told her that.

And more to the point, he didn't want her to think that he had some vested interest in the matter. He'd crossed a line yesterday by suggesting that they sleep together, and, now that he knew how narrow a tight-rope she was walking, he felt like kicking himself for adding more uncertainty and confusion into the mix. They weren't going to sleep together. She had been right—it would make an impossibly complicated situation even worse. He didn't want to lead her on. This was a limited-time deal, and it would end when they thought the timing was right for both of their ca-reers. He wasn't getting involved emotionally—he had known all his adult life that relationships worked best when both parties knew exactly where the boundaries were, exactly what they wanted to get out of it. They would be crazy to go back on those agreements now.

He just had to remind himself that she didn't want that either. She wanted this marriage for what it could do for her career. For the ructions it would cause with her family. And, in light of recent revelations, perhaps she wanted it as a hide-out. An excuse not to meet some suitable guy who might have marriage and ba-bies on his mind.

But that was last night. This morning, 'protective' had well and truly taken a back seat. There were more pressing things on his mind, like the way that her legs fitted so perfectly against his: from ankle to hip they were perfectly matched. Or the way that his arm fitted into the indent of her waist.

Or the fact that if she were to wake up this minute, she'd know exactly how turned on he was, just by sharing a bed fully clothed.

How had his life got so complicated? In bed with a woman he wanted desperately—whom he had already married—but whom he knew he absolutely couldn't have. He cursed quietly, trying to pull his arm out from under her. If he wasn't getting back to sleep, he could be doing something useful, like taking a cold shower and then trying to write.

They were due to fly back to the UK and be up at his parents' house by tea time—they'd made no plans for the rest of the day, and he wondered whether he might be able to find some time alone to work. Last night, Charlie had promised to show him the music room, and the urge to feel the keys of a beautiful grand piano beneath the pads of his fingers had been niggling him since he'd woken. But every time he'd tried to make his escape, Charlie had pressed back against him again and he'd thought...not yet. Just another few minutes.

When she settled, he went for it again, this time pulling his arm out firm and fast, determined not to be seduced into laziness another time. His arm was free at last, and Charlie rolled onto her front, a frown on her face as she turned her head on the pillow first one way and then the other. He felt bad, seeing her restless like that. She had had too little sleep since her overnight stop in Las Vegas, and he knew that for once the black rings under her eyes had nothing to do with eyeliner. He stood watching her for a moment, reminded of that first morning, another night where they had collapsed into bed fully clothed.

He pulled off his T-shirt as he headed for the bathroom, and turned on the shower. He let it run cool before he climbed underneath, concentrating on the sensation of the water hitting his head and shoulders, trying not to think of the beautiful woman lying in his bed.

He wished that they could get out of their second trip this weekend. He wasn't sure that there was a good time to introduce your parents to your fake wife, but he guessed that the morning after a huge row and a heartfelt confession was pretty low on the list. Would Charlie be funny with him this morning? He tried to guess how she would act—whether she'd want to talk more, or pretend that it had never happened and she had never said anything—but had to admit to himself that he didn't even know her well enough to predict that.

By the time that he got out of the shower, she was sitting on the edge of the bed, rubbing at her eyes. So much for some alone time. He secured his towel firmly around his waist before he called out to her.

'Morning.'

Really, was that the best he could come up with? he asked himself.

'Hey,' she said back, tying up her hair and stretching her arms up overhead. 'Have you been up long?'

'Just long enough to shower. I was going to take you up on the offer to play in the music room. Have you got stuff you need to do this morning?'

She frowned, and he realised how that had come

across. But was it really so unreasonable of him to tell her that he needed some space? She had no problem with staying at the office late when she didn't want to see him—this was practically the same thing.

'I was just going to chill. Maybe hang out with Miles for a bit. I've not had a chance to do that since we got back.'

He nodded, trying not to show how claustrophobic he was starting to feel. Was this a normal part of newly married life? he wondered. This discomfort with sharing your personal space?

He crossed to the bureau, where he'd discovered their clothes had been unpacked, and pulled on a T-shirt and a pair of jeans. He'd wondered when he first woke up that morning whether she'd be uncomfortable with him today, he'd not expected when he'd been lying next to her that he would be the one trying to put space between them.

But it wasn't about her, or even about him. It was about feeling inspired to write for the first time all week, and wanting to make the most of it before the motivation deserted him again.

'You don't mind, do you, if I go?'

He was already halfway out of the door as he asked the rhetorical question, hoping that he remembered how to find his way back to the room she'd pointed out to him the day before.

When he eventually saw the piano in front of him, he let out a long sigh of relief. Then sat on the stool and let his fingertips gently caress the keys, pressing first one, then another, and listening to the beautiful tone of the instrument. One to one with a beauty like this, he could forget that he had a wife somewhere in this maze of a palace. Forget all of the complications that she had brought into his life.

He ran up and down a few scales, warming up his hands and fingers, trusting muscle memory to conjure up the long-memorised patterns. He'd been no more than a baby the first time he'd played the piano, he knew. Remembering family photos with him perched on his mother's knee as they picked out a nursery rhyme together.

These scales and arpeggios had taken him through recitals and grade exams. From his perfectly average primary school to the most influential and exclusive private school in the country.

They never changed, and he never faltered when he played them. From the final note of a simple arpeggio, his fingers automatically tipped into a Beethoven piece. His mother's favourite. The one that he'd practised and practised until his hands were so sore they could barely move, and he could see the notes dancing before his eyes as he tried to get to sleep. It was the piece that he'd perfected for his scholarship interview. The one that had opened up a new world of possibilities in his career—and had eventually taught him the truth about human relationships. Okay, so he wasn't writing any new material. Not yet. He let the thought go; saw it carried away by the music. Because this was important too, these building blocks of his art and his craft.

He let his hands pick through a few more pieces, and he stretched his fingers, feeling the suppleness and strength in them now that they were warmed up. He placed his tablet on the music stand, flicked through folders, looking for where he'd jotted down ideas for new lyrics and melodies, stored away for future development.

There'd been nothing new added for a while. Lately, when he'd been working on songs for the album, he'd been much further down the line than this. It was ages since he'd been at square one with a song.

He listened to a few snippets of audio that he'd recorded. A few odd words and phrases that had struck him. None of it was working. He'd been right the first time around when he'd chosen other ideas over these. He shut off his tablet and returned his fingers to the keys. It was only since he'd met Charlie that he'd been so dissatisfied with the songs that he'd written before. Why should that be? He tried to reason it out logically. Because maybe if he could work out why he suddenly hated those songs, he could work out how to write something better. He let his fingers lead, picking out individual notes, and then chords, moving tentatively across the keyboard as he experimented with a few riffs.

A combination of chords caught his ear, and he played them back, listening, seeing where his fingers wanted to trip to next. Maybe that was something…it was something for now, at least. He grabbed a guitar from beside the piano and tried out the same chords. Then picked a melody around them. He turned on the recorder on his iPad. He wasn't in a position to risk losing anything that might be any good. He turned back to the piano and tried the melody again, tried transposing it down an octave, shifting it into another key. He crashed his fingers onto the keyboard harder. There was something there, he knew it. Some potential. He just couldn't crack it. He needed to get through to the nub of the idea to find out what made it good. How to work with it to make it great.

He'd just picked up his guitar again, determined to at least make a start on something good, when the door opened behind him. He spun round on the stool and threw an automatic glare at the door.

Charlie drew up short on the threshold.

'S-sorry,' she stammered, and he knew his annoyance at being disturbed must have shown on his face. 'I brought you a coffee.'

He noticed the tray in her hands and thought twice about his initial instinct to kick her straight out. Maybe he could do with the caffeine, something to get his brain in gear.

'Thanks,' he said grudgingly. 'You can come in—you don't have to stay in the doorway.'

He set the guitar down and turned back to the piano, hoping that she would get the hint, but, instead of hearing the door shut behind him, he was being not so gently nudged to the side of his stool while Charlie held two cups of coffee precariously over the keyboard.

'That sounded interesting,' she said. 'What was it?'

He fidgeted beside her, wishing she'd just go and leave him to it.

'It's nothing. Just playing around with a few ideas. Trying to generate some inspiration.'

She plonked herself down beside him and he held a breath as the hot dark liquid sloshed dangerously close to the piano. Somehow, miraculously, the coffee didn't spill. 'What for?' she asked. 'I thought the songs for the album were all done.'

He shrugged. He really didn't want to go into this now. 'They were.'

'Were?' She finally placed the drinks down on the top of the piano and turned towards him, trying to catch his eye. 'Are they not any more? What happened to them?'

He kept his eyes on the keyboard, his fingers tracing soundless patterns in black and ivory. 'Nothing happened to them. I'm just not sure that I want to include all of them. There's one or two I'm looking at rotating out.' He kept his voice casual, trying not to show the fear and concern behind this simple statement. It didn't work. Charlie's back was suddenly ramrod straight.

'And you're telling me this now? How long have you been thinking this?'

'Are you asking as my wife or as a representative of Avalon?'

'I thought they were the same thing.' The monosyllables were spoken with a false calm, giving them a staccato rhythm. But then she softened, leaned forward and sipped at her coffee, looking unusually thoughtful before she spoke.

'What can I do to help?'

His first instinct was to tell her to leave him in peace—that was the best thing she could do for him. But the timing of this creative crisis suggested that she was in some way to blame for his current dissatisfaction with his work. So maybe she could be the solution too. 'What about a co-writer? I can call a couple of people. Maybe someone to bounce ideas off.'

'I'm not sure,' he said eventually. 'I was happy with

everything before we went to Vegas. I didn't feel like I had to do anything more to it.'

'And now?'

'I don't know. I listened to the demo when we were on the plane. I reckon half the tracks need to go.'

She visibly paled. But to her credit she clearly tempered her response. Regardless of the fact that losing half the tracks would throw a complete spanner into the plan that she and Rich had been working on for recording and releasing the album.

'Can we listen together?' she asked. 'You can talk me through what you're worried about.'

He hesitated. No one outside the band had heard the new tracks. The record companies that had been so keen to fight over them had taken their history of big sellers, and not insisted on listening to the new material. Letting his songs loose on the world was hard enough when he was happy with his work. Letting someone listen to something he knew wasn't right… It was like revealing the ugliest part of his body for close inspection.

But this was what Charlie did. He knew her reputation. He knew the artists and albums that she had worked on. She got results, and her artists trusted her. Maybe he should as well. He'd spent the last week with his head buried in the sand, trying to ignore the problem. It was time to try something different.

He reached for the tablet, ready to cue up the demo, but Charlie stopped him with a hand on his arm.

'Why don't you play?' she asked, nodding at the piano keyboard in front of them. 'One-man show.'

He shrugged. It didn't make much difference to

him. The songs weren't good enough, and it wouldn't matter how she heard them.

He rattled through the first bars of a track he picked at random. Trying to show her with his clumsy hands on the keys how far from good the song was.

She didn't say a word as he played, but her knee jigged in time with the music, and as he reached the middle eight her head nodded too.

He reached the end and looked over at her—ready for the verdict. 'I don't hate it,' she said equivocally. 'Are there lyrics?'

'The chorus maybe. The verses are definitely going.'

She nodded thoughtfully.

'Well, let's hear it before we do anything drastic.'

He returned his hands to the keys and took a deep breath, straightening his back until his posture rivalled hers. He'd been taught to sing classically at school, and there was a lot to be said for getting the basics right.

It had been a long time since he'd sung to someone one-to-one, with just a piano for company. In fact, he couldn't remember ever sitting like this with someone. With so much intimacy.

A lump lodged itself in his throat. Was he really nervous? He'd sung to her the first night that he'd met her. Spotted her on the side of the stage halfway through the gig and made eye contact. Had that been it? The moment that everything had changed for them?

There had been thousands in the audience that night. He'd played at festivals where the audience stretched further than he could see. Just a couple of days ago he'd sung with her in front of a growing crowd of Londoners. It hadn't occurred to him that day to be nervous.

But the thought of singing with her sitting beside him at the piano was bringing him out in a sweat.

She waited, letting the silence grow. Waiting for him to fill it. He pressed a couple of keys experimentally then worked his way into the intro.

Her thigh was pressed against his leg; he felt the pressure of it as he worked the piano pedal. He closed his eyes, hoping that banishing her from at least one of his senses would get his focus back where it needed to be.

He took a deep breath and half sang the first words of the verse. His hands moved without hesitation and he felt his voice grow stronger as he moved from verse to chorus and back again. He winced as he sang the second verse, aware that the lyrics were trite and clichéd.

He'd written about love. Or what he thought love might feel like as a thirty-something. The more he thought about the only time he'd thought he'd been in love, the more uncertain he was that that was what he had really felt for Arabella. Sure, it had been intense at the time. There were songs that he'd written then that still tugged at the heart strings. But something told him that love was meant to be…bigger than that. The connection he felt with Charlie right this second, for example. That was big. In fact, he couldn't quite decide if it was warm and enveloping big, or heavy and suffocating big. All he knew was that it was scary big. And a million miles from what he had felt for Arabella when he was eighteen.

And of course all that was seriously bad news—

because big scary feelings did not make for a happy marriage of convenience. He tackled the middle eight with energy, abandoning his original lyrics, and just singing what came into his head. Trying to lose himself in the notes and not overthink.

He sang the last chorus as if there were no one else listening, new lyrics streaming through him as if he were a vessel for something greater than him.

He let his hands rest on the keyboard when he finished, and kept his eyes locked on them as well. He couldn't let her see. It was too dangerous. Too risky to the arrangement that they had both agreed to. He waited until he could be sure his expression was neutral before he picked up his mug from the table beside the piano and took a sip.

'So?' he asked, not sure that he wanted to know what she thought of it.

'Please, please tell me that's not on the cull list.'

He took a second to really look at her. Her eyes were wide, almost surprised. Her bottom lip was redder and fuller than the top, as if she had been biting on it and had only just let it go. He imagined that if he looked hard enough he would be able to see the shadowed indentation of her top teeth still there. That if he leaned down and brushed his own lips against it it would be hot and welcoming.

'I'm not sure about the first half,' she went on at last, 'but the lyrics in the second? The bridge? That last chorus. That's winning stuff, Joe. That's straight to number one and stay there. That's break the internet stuff. I can't believe you were going to toss that.'

'The first half though.'

'The first half we can fix. Anyone who can write the second half can fix the first, I promise you that.'

He stayed quiet for a long moment. He could ask himself what had just happened, but the truth was that he already knew. She had happened. She was what was different about his writing. He finally had the inspiration that he needed.

He had no doubt that he still had a lot of work to do, but maybe working with Charlie would be a good thing. It had certainly helped with these lyrics; they'd worked their way into his brain as he was singing, reaching his lips as if he were channelling them, not writing them.

He launched into the opening chords of another song. One he was more sure of. He tweaked the words as he sang, reaching for more unusual choices, to pinpoint emotions he'd only been able to sketch before.

He glanced across at Charlie and she was smiling. A weight of pressure lifted slightly; a measure of dread fell away. They could fix this. Together.

More than anything, this was what really brought it home to him what they'd done. They had tied themselves together in every possible way. His career and his personal life were indivisible now.

For so long 'personal life' had been synonymous with 'sex life'. When Charlie had stipulated *no cheating* he'd known that it was a no brainer. Of course he wouldn't sleep with anyone else. But had he really thought it through? He'd voluntarily signed up for months of celibacy. Maybe years. Perhaps he had assumed unconsciously that 'no cheating' and celibacy weren't necessarily the same thing.

Everything seemed to keep coming back to that

question—even though they had agreed right from the start that that wasn't going to happen. And now he had acknowledged that his feelings for her were so much more serious than he had originally thought. Had he really thought the word 'love' earlier?

He finished the song on autopilot and knew from Charlie's expression that she could feel the difference. Her smile was more polite and that sparkle had gone from her eyes.

'Lots of potential in that one,' she said diplomatically. 'Definitely one we can work on.' She glanced at her watch and had a final sip of her coffee.

'I should let you work. Are you sure I've packed the right stuff for your parents' house? Because I can go out and pick something up if I need to.'

'Well, you probably can leave your tiara here,' he said with a smile, so she knew it wasn't a dig. 'Just something for dinner tonight. Doesn't need to be as fancy as at your place.'

Had he really just referred to the palace they were sitting in as 'your place'? Perhaps he was getting more used to this royal thing than he had thought. Getting used to her.

It was getting harder and harder to remember they were only in this to forward both of their careers. The lines between business and personal were blurring to the point that he couldn't see them any more. And that was dangerous, because the further they moved away from that simple transactional relationship, the more at risk his heart and his feelings would be.

'And make sure you've got something you don't

mind getting dirty if we're going to that festival. I'm not going to spend the whole time in VIP.'

She rolled her eyes.

'You so don't need to worry about that.'

CHAPTER NINE

CHARLIE CRAWLED UNDER the duvet and across the tiny double bed until she was almost pressed against the wall. Really, the sleeping arrangements in this marriage kept going from bad to worse.

'Do you think they liked me?' she whispered as Joe unbuttoned his shirt and pulled it back over his shoulders, revealing those tattoos she was still getting to know. He pulled a T-shirt from his bag, and then they were covered again. She almost spoke up and asked him not to, but stopped herself. Cosy sleeping arrangements or not, she had no rights over his body. No authority to ask for a few more minutes to look at his skin.

'They loved you,' he replied, sitting on the side of the bed and pulling off his jeans. 'Of course they did. What did you expect?'

'You know what I expected,' she said, tucking her hand under her pillow and turning on her side to face him. He slid between the sheets and lay beside her, mirroring her posture until they were almost nose to nose in the bed.

'And I told you that you didn't have to worry,' he said, though she didn't quite remember it that way.

Why should she care anyway? In a few months these would be her ex in-laws. She wouldn't ever see them again.

He wondered whether his parents had suspected that there was something off about their relationship. But they had been so distracted by Charlie, and protocol and the whole Princess thing that they hadn't seemed to notice anything.

He could feel the warmth of her under the cool sheets, and for a second was flooded by the memory of waking up with her that morning, with her legs fitting so closely to his. Did she even know what she had done?

'Did you know you're an aggressive spooner?' The question just slipped out of him. She looked shocked for a second, but then had to stifle a laugh.

'What's that meant to mean?'

'It means you were grinding into me like a horny teenager this morning. I didn't know where to put my hands.'

Her mouth fell open. 'I did not.'

He couldn't resist smiling. 'You so did. Forced me out of bed.'

Not strictly the truth, of course. He'd lain there so much longer than was a good idea, just soaking up the feel of her.

'A gentleman would have moved away,' she said.

'A lady wouldn't have reversed straight back in again every time I did.'

She kicked out at his leg. 'You're totally making this up.'

'Why would I do that?' he asked.

'I don't know. Maybe you want me to do it again.'

'Would you?' The very air around them seemed to be heavy with anticipation as he waited for her to answer.

'I asked first,' she said at last, deliberately not answering his question.

Was she serious? Were they really talking about this as if it might happen? She looked as if she wanted it. Her eyes were wide, her lips moist and slightly parted. One hand was tucked under her cheek and the other below her pillow. He didn't dare look any further down. He'd seen her pull on a pyjama top and shorts earlier, and he knew that gravity would be making the view south of her throat way too distracting. Too tempting.

'Maybe,' he replied at last.

Such a simple word. Tonight, such a dangerous one.

She turned her back to him but didn't make any effort to come closer. Was she testing him? Seeing if she came halfway whether he would come forward the other half.

With her back to him it was safe at last to look down. From where she'd tied her hair in a messy knot, the ink at the nape of her neck, down the length of her long, elegant spine. The tapering of her waist disappeared into the shadows under the sheets.

If he reached for her, would that be the point of no return?

Would the touch of his hand on her waist be the same as telling her that he wanted a relationship? That he loved her?

Were those statements true?

He wanted her. He knew that. That was the easy question. But how many times did he have to tell himself that having sex with the woman pretending to be his wife was a bad idea? That it could never be just sex, because it was already so much more than that.

What would she want from him in return? More than sex meant thinking with his heart, rather than his head, and that had got him badly hurt—and embarrassed—before.

He had tried his hardest to learn his lesson after Arabella, but even that humiliation hadn't been enough for him to spot the woman who was only with him so she could sell his secrets to the highest bidder.

Could Charlie really want him for who he was, rather than what he could do for her?

He couldn't remember ever being more turned on, more tempted than he was right now, but he had to be smarter than that.

Taking what he wanted came with a price tag. But tonight he couldn't be certain what the price was, or whether he would be willing to pay. And so as much as it killed him to do it, he turned over, pulled the duvet high on his chest and squeezed his eyes shut.

He heard a rustle behind him and tried not to imagine Charlie lifting her head from the pillow and looking over at him, wondering what had happened. He didn't want to see her confusion as he cut dead their flirtation. Her head hit the pillow hard, and the duvet pulled across to her side of the bed.

'Night, then,' she said, nicking territory and duvet as she spread out her limbs.

He was so tempted to retaliate. Almost as tempted as he had been to kiss her. To be pulled back into their banter. But he kept silent and still, feigning sleep.

* * *

Had she imagined it, last night? she wondered, trying to decide if she should be blaming Joe or her over-active imagination for what had happened. Why, oh, why had she had to be so insistent that they didn't have sex? Because that was where this relationship had been heading, before they were so stupid as to get married.

If they'd done the sensible thing and had a one-night stand that first night, like any self-respecting party girl meeting a rock star, they could be thousands of miles apart and a week into forgetting it all by now. Instead she had been shacked up at her new in-laws', trapped in the world's smallest double bed and ready to explode from frustration.

Surely her imagination wasn't good enough to have imagined that flirtation last night. Joe was the one who had brought up the subject of spooning, and when she'd decided she was so goddamned turned on that she didn't care any more whether it was a good idea or not, and all but wiggled her arse at him, he'd literally turned his back on her—the body-language equivalent of 'thanks, but no thanks'. Only less polite.

So when she'd woken first this morning, there was no way she was going to hang around for him to wake up and rehash the whole thing. One rejection was plenty, thanks. She'd known as soon as she told him about her infertility that she was taking herself well and truly off the market as far as he was concerned. It had been stupid to expect any other reaction to her advances than the one that she had got.

So she'd got up and found Joe's mum already in the kitchen, and before she quite knew what was happen-

ing there was a cup of strong tea in front of her and
the smell of bacon coming from the stove.

'Did you sleep well, then, love? Oh, I shouldn't
ask that really, should I? Not to a newly-wed. And
that bed in there's so small. Not even a proper double.
Hardly room to—'

'Shall I put the kettle on?'

Charlie breathed a deep sigh of relief—not the emotion she'd expected to feel when setting eyes on Joe
that morning. He leaned in the kitchen doorway, co-
lour high on his cheeks as he crossed his arms and
gave his mum a look.

'No need, love.' His mum bustled round, pouring
another cup from the pot and setting it on the table
for Joe.

'I was just saying to Charlie—you are sure it's okay
for me to call you Charlie?' She didn't stop for an answer. 'I was just saying that the bed in your room.
It's hardly big enough for you on your own, never
mind for the two of you great tall things. We'll have
to do something about that. Maybe you should have
our room.'

Joe kissed his mum on the cheek and extracted the
tongs from her clasped fist.

'You're babbling, Mum. Sit down and drink your
tea.'

His mum sat and he shot a glance over her head to
Charlie, who smiled conspiratorially in return.

'You sure you don't want to come with us today,
Mum?' Joe asked as he served up the bacon sarnies.

'Me in all that mud? You must be mad, love.'

'Mud? It's twenty-five degrees outside. Not every
festival is Glastonbury in the rain, you know.'

'I've seen these things on the telly, love. Maybe if you were playing, but I'll give it a miss. You two love birds don't want me and your father there playing gooseberry anyway.'

Joe rolled his eyes as he picked up a sandwich, 'Mum, there'll be thousands of people there. It's not like we're expecting to be alone.'

'Don't be obtuse, Joe. You know full well it's not the same.'

'I feel awful shooting off like this,' Charlie said. They'd sat down to dinner barely an hour after they had arrived last night, and she'd been so beat after four courses and dessert wine that they'd retreated to bed long before midnight.

'Don't be daft, love. You young people are so busy, and Joe's already told me how hard you work.' Interesting…when had he told her that? 'It's been lovely that you made it up here with everything that you've both got going on. Don't go and spoil it by overstaying your welcome.'

Charlie smiled, surprised by how at home she felt with Joe's parents already. As if she really were becoming part of the family. Probably best that they were leaving this afternoon, then. Before this became another reminder of how hard it was becoming to keep reality and pretence straight in her head.

They climbed into Joe's car, chased by kisses and offers of baked goods for the journey. The festival was out in the countryside, about half an hour from his parents' house. Thank God it was no further, Charlie thought, twenty minutes of isolated confinement later. There was a limit to the tension that her body could take, and she was rapidly approaching it.

They were going to have to talk about what had happened last night. She'd hoped that maybe they could just ignore it—forget it had happened. And then his mum had been so funny with her babbling that she'd thought that they'd taken a shortcut and moved past it. But after breakfast they had been back in Joe's tiny bedroom, trying to pack their bags without touching. Moving around each other as if they were magnets with poles pointing towards one another. And she knew it would take next to nothing for those poles to flip and they would be back where they had been last night, drawn together, with only their self-control and better judgement fighting against the inevitability of the laws of nature.

She rested her chin on her hand; her elbow propped on the door as she gazed out of the window. They had barely spoken a word since they'd climbed into the car.

'Have you played here?' Charlie asked, needing the tension broken—before it broke them. The question counted as work. Talking about the band and work was safe. It was the only safe zone they had.

'Two years ago,' Joe replied, his eyes still locked on the road. They hadn't left it for a second since they'd left his parents' driveway. 'Were you here?' he asked.

'Yeah, with one of my artists. I didn't see you.'

'I wonder how many times that's happened,' he said, and for the first time he glanced over at her.

She furrowed her brow. 'That what's happened?'

'That our paths have crossed and we've not seen each other.' His eyes were back on the road now, but he looked different somehow, as if he was having to work harder to keep them there.

She tried to keep her voice casual, not wanting to

acknowledge the way the tension had just ratcheted up another notch. 'I don't know. Must be loads if you think about it.'

'I can't believe it,' he said.

She looked over at him again, to find him watching her. They'd pulled up at a junction, but his attention was all on her, rather than looking for a gap in the traffic crossing their path.

'Why?'

'Because...*this*. Because of the atmosphere in this car for the last twenty minutes. Because of how it felt in Vegas, knowing that you were watching me. I just can't imagine being in a room with you and not feeling that you were there.'

How *what* had felt in Vegas? She thought back to that moment when she was watching him from the side of the stage and their eyes had met. He had felt that too?

He reached for her hand. She considered for a split second whether she should pull away. It was what he'd done last night. She'd reached out to him, and he'd known it was too dangerous. A bad idea.

Could she be as strong as he had been?

His hand cupped her cheek, and she knew she could. She could be strong and resist, as he had. But maybe she could be a different kind of strong. Maybe looking at all the reasons this was a bad idea, all the reasons it was a terrifying choice, and *still* choosing it, maybe that was strong too.

She leaned forward across the centre console, sliding her hands into his hair and bringing their mouths together.

Her body sighed in relief and desire as his tongue

met hers, simultaneously relaxed and energised by this feeling of...perfection. This was it. This sense of fitting together.

A horn blared behind them and she sprang back, reeling from her realisation.

He grimaced as he slid the car into gear and pulled away, with just a slight lurch as the clutch found its biting point. This was what she'd been waiting for; and it was what she'd been dreading. She'd been running from it her whole adult life. She didn't want to be completed. She didn't want to belong with someone. Her one-off dates and casual boyfriends—she never had to tell them she was infertile. Never had to spell out the future that they would never have. Never had to explain that if she shacked up with someone long-term and the babies didn't come that they'd be hounded by the press and his virility would be called into question. Their bins would be searched and their doctors harassed. Her body had been public property since before she was born. Anyone who wanted to spend their life with her would be volunteering for the same deal—who in their right mind would do that?

Ten more minutes. She had to survive just ten more minutes in this space with a man she was finding it impossible to remember to resist. They showed their passes at the gate and, in silence, Joe directed the car through the gates and down a rucked track towards the VIP parking, waved along by marshals. When they arrived, Joe pulled on the handbrake and opened the door, while she gathered her things from the footwell. Her door opened, and Joe was there, holding out his hand like a cartoon prince.

'Very gallant,' she said lightly, knowing that her

confusion was causing a line to appear between her eyebrows.

He handed her down from the car, and as her feet reached the ground he pressed her back against the rear door, one of his knees nudging between hers. His hand caught at the ends of her hair and he pulled gently, bringing a gasp of pleasure and anticipation to her lips. She tilted her head to one side as she met his eyes, and saw passion and desire. Another inch closer and she was trapped. Car behind, hard body in front, and still that hand in her hair, pulling to one side now, exposing the pulse of her throat. She licked her lips in anticipation and closed her eyes as Joe moved closer. First cool lips descended and then a flicker of warm tongue in a spot that made her shudder. The butterfly caresses of his mouth traced up the side of her neck, then suddenly down to her shoulder, where her shirt had slipped, exposing her collarbone. The sharp clamp of his teeth on her sensitive skin made her gasp in shock. But the noise was lost as his lips were suddenly on her mouth, and his tongue was tangling with hers.

She wound her fingers in his hair, levering herself a little higher, desperate to bring their bodies in line. Cursing her decision to wear flat biker boots instead of her usual heels. Who cared about practicalities when there was a man like this to kiss?

Joe pressed into her with an urgency she'd not felt from him before. An urgency that made her wonder how spacious the back of his car was, and how much faith they wanted to put in the tinted windows.

It was as his lips left hers, to dip again to her neck, that she heard it.

Click.

Her eyes snapped open and she pushed at Joe's chest. She didn't have to look far over his shoulder to see the photographer. She took a second, breathing heavily and trying to remember that she was meant to be pleased about the press involvement in her life for once, before she spoke.

'You knew he was there?' she asked quietly, her lips touching Joe's ear. Her calves burned as she stretched up on tiptoes, but she wasn't ready to back down, back away, just yet.

'Spotted him as I got out of the car,' Joe whispered back.

Which explained the little display he'd just put on, then. Thank God she hadn't suggested taking the party back into the car.

'You okay?' he asked, and she forced a smile, pushing slightly on his chest and trying to regain her equilibrium. Desperate for a balance between trying to convince the photographer that that kiss had rocked her world, and not letting Joe see the truth of it.

'I'm fine.'

Their encounter with photographers at the airport seemed a long time ago and a long way away. She'd barely noticed over the past week that they hadn't been harassed by the paparazzi as much as she'd thought they might be—perhaps her mother had had a discreet hand in that. But there was no way that even her mother could keep them away here. The reality of the situation struck her—something she'd not counted on when she and Joe had been making plans for seeing family and work: they were going to be on display, all day. They couldn't afford to slip up. She closed her eyes and kissed Joe lightly on the mouth, telling herself it was just her way of warming up for the performance she knew that they had to nail.

'Want to go listen to some music?' she asked.

'No,' he said with a smile. 'I want to stay here and kiss you.'

She couldn't help grinning in return, not even trying to work out if it was for real or for show. Leaning back against this car in the sunshine, kissing a super-hot guy—that sounded pretty good to her too. But the moment was gone, and she couldn't lose the photographer from the corner of her eye.

'You're so going to get me fired,' she said. 'I'm meant to be working.'

'Well, then, jump to it, slacker. I'm not going to be one of those husbands who expects you to stay home and play house. Get out there and earn your keep.' He took a step back from her, and she slid her hands behind her butt. She knew real life was waiting for them, but what was just a few more minutes?

'I'd make a lousy housewife.'

'Oh, I don't know,' he said with a laugh. 'Some people like the hovel look. I hear it's big this year.'

She poked him in the ribs and laughed back.

'I'm not that bad.'

'You're worse.' He turned and stood beside her, draping a casual arm around her shoulder and pressing a kiss to her temple.

It would be too easy to take this little scene at face value, she knew. A week ago she'd be giving herself a stern talking-to. That all this was for the benefit of the photographers and the eager public. But today... today the line was more blurred. Her first thought had been that Joe was just putting on a show, but they had been moving so much closer for the last few days that she knew that some part of it was real. Their performance, it didn't feel like some random invention—it was more… Maybe it was what their relationship might have been if their lives were simpler. If she weren't a princess with a wonky reproductive system. If he formed actual emotional relationships rather than using women to get what he needed. Would it work? she couldn't help but wonder. If they had been two ordinary people, with ordinary lives, would they have been happy together?

'Come on, then,' she said at last, pushing herself away from the car, trying to shake the thought from her mind. It didn't matter if it would work that way, because they weren't those people, and never could be. Joe moved with her, his arm still around her shoulders as they made their way into the festival.

As Joe had promised, they were in the VIP zone for no more than half an hour before she was dragging him through a dusty field of festivalgoers, littered with abandoned plastic cups. She refused to watch the band from the side of the stage—she wanted the full experience, to see what she would be working with if she ever got this band to agree to sign with her.

The Sunday afternoon vibe was chilled and relaxed, with families dancing to the music, kids on shoulders, or eating on picnic rugs on the ground. Groups of people sat on the floor, passing round cigarettes and bottles of drink.

The sun was hot on her back, and she was pleased she'd pulled on one of Joe's long-sleeved shirts with her denim shorts, protecting her shoulders from burning.

For a while they just wandered, soaking up the at-mosphere of a group of people united by a passion for music. Joe's fingers were loosely wound between hers, keeping her anchored to him. To their story. The impression of that kiss was still on her lips, and had been refreshed every now and again with a brief re-enactment. They couldn't just keep an eye out for cam-eras and people watching. For the first time since they had arrived back in the UK, they were truly having to live out their fake marriage in full view of the public.

And the weirdest part…it wasn't weird at all. In fact, it felt completely natural to be walking round with her hand in his. The way he threw an arm over her shoulders if they stopped to talk to someone. For once, she decided she actually liked being in flat shoes. Liked that his extra height meant that she was tucked into his body when he pulled her to him. It felt good—warm, safe, protected. Everything she'd been telling herself she didn't want to be.

'Want to find something to eat?' Joe asked when the band they had been watching finished.

'Dirty burger?' she asked, with a quirk of her brow.

'Whatever turns you on.'

You know what turns me on. The response was right there on the tip of her tongue, but she held it back, not trusting where it might lead them.

'Come on,' she said, pulling him towards a van selling virtuous-looking flatbreads and falafel. 'These look amazing. I'm having a healthy lunch, then I'm going in search of cider.'

With lunches in hand, they picked their way across to another stage, where Casual Glory, the band Charlie wanted to see, were just warming up at the start of their set.

'I saw these guys in a pub last year,' she told Joe. 'I wanted to sign them then and there. But then all the suits got involved and… I don't know, maybe they got spooked but somehow it didn't come off. I don't want to let them out of my grasp again.'

'They're still not signed?' Joe asked.

She dropped to the floor and sat cross-legged, watching the band while she ate.

'Free spirits. Didn't like the corporate stuff. And I'm not sure what I do about that, to be honest, because the music business doesn't really get much more laid-back than with Avalon.'

'You think you can get them to change their minds?'

Charlie nodded. 'I'm going to. I'm just not sure how yet.'

'You're not going to marry him, right?'

She laughed under her breath.

'One husband's already too many, thanks.'

He wound an arm around her neck, pulling her close and planting a kiss on her shoulder.

'You're right: they're good,' Joe said after they finished another song. 'Loads of potential. You should bag them.'

'Yeah, well, try telling them that,' she joked.

'I will, if you want. Are we going to say hi when they're done?'

'That's the plan.'

She leaned against his shoulder, soaking up the sun warming the white cotton of her shirt. Her head fell to rest against Joe's and she shut her eyes so she could appreciate the music more.

'Tired?' Joe asked in her ear, and she 'mmm'ed in response. She couldn't remember the last time she'd had a properly restful night's sleep. Turned out being married was more likely to give you black bags than a newly-wed glow.

'Come here, then.'

Joe pushed her away for a moment, then slung his leg around until she was sitting between his thighs, her back pulled in against his front. She relaxed into him, shutting out all thoughts of whether this was a good idea or not. Just letting the music wash through her. Soak into her skin and her brain.

'Comfortable?' Joe whispered in her ear.

'Too comfortable.'

She felt more than heard him chuckle behind her as his arms tightened. A press of lips behind her ear. A kiss on the side of her neck. A tingle and a clench low in her abdomen: a silent request for more and a warning of danger ahead.

Instead of heeding it, she let her head fall to one side, just as she had done by his car. They were in public, she reasoned with herself. There was only so far this could go. It was all a part of their performance.

'How about now?' he asked, pulling her hair over to her other shoulder. 'Feeling sleepy still?'

God, he was driving her insane.

'Like I could drop off at any moment.'

He growled behind her and she smiled, revelling in the way she was learning to push the boundaries of his self-control. His hand in her hair was tough and uncompromising now, and she let out a gasp as he pulled her back slowly, steadily, never so hard that it hurt. Making her choose to come with him rather than forcing. She opened her mouth to him without question. The hand still round her waist flattened on her belly, pressing her closer still.

She let out a low sigh of desire and her arm lifted to wind round his neck, opening her body. Was Joe controlling her without her realising? She didn't remember meaning to do it. Then his hand dropped from her hair and cupped her jaw: the kiss gentler now, sweeter.

She opened her eyes and smiled back at him, and she knew her eyes must look glazed, dopey. 'All right, I'm not likely to sleep in the next year. Is that what you wanted?'

'I'll take it,' he said with a smug smile. She leaned back into him again, languor and desire fighting to control her limbs.

CHAPTER TEN

'I WISH WE didn't have to go back tonight,' Joe said, stretching out his legs and leaning back on his elbows. Maybe it was the sun making him lazy, making him feel that he never wanted to leave this place. Charlie moved so she was lying to one side of him, her head propped on her hand.

'I thought you'd be dying to get back in your studio,' she said. 'You seemed all…inspired and stuff yesterday.'

'I am. I do want to write.' He'd had ideas swirling round his brain for two days; when they'd been at his parents' house he'd been desperate for a bit of space and time to try and get them down on paper, or recorded on his phone. But since they had arrived at the festival, since that kiss, everything felt different. 'I can't remember the last time that I was relaxed like this. The last time I felt still. I like it.'

'You can be still in London,' Charlie said.

He shrugged—or as best he could with his body weight resting on his elbows. 'I don't know if I can. Or maybe it's that I know that I won't.'

She sat up and gave him a serious look. 'Not every day can be Sunday afternoon at a festival. Real life is still out there, you know.' Of course he knew, but somehow he was managing not to care.

'I do know. But it feels that it can't get us here.'

'What are you worried about "getting us"?' she asked.

Why did they have to think about that now? Why couldn't they just enjoy this? He wished he knew. He'd just told her he felt still—what he'd wanted to say was that he felt happy. Content. He'd wanted to say that he'd stopped trying to work out if what she was saying was loaded. A way to get something more than they'd agreed from their arrangement.

Here at the festival, life was simpler. He could kiss and touch her. Laugh with her. Treat her as the woman he was in love with. No holding back.

Was that really it? Was that what was making him feel so…serene? Because he didn't have to pretend not to love her?

His phone chirped and he fished it out of his pocket, grateful for the distraction from his own thoughts.

'Amazing, they're here. Some friends of mine have stopped by,' he told Charlie. 'Want to say hi after you've done your work stuff?'

'Sure, why not? Who are they?'

'Owen's band supported us at a couple of gigs a few years ago. We hung out a bit. His wife's lovely too. You'll like them.'

He stood and pulled her up as Casual Glory finished their final number. His arm fell round her shoulders in that way that felt so completely natural. Perhaps it was just their height, he thought. He'd told her that he'd liked that she was so tall, but her flat biker boots today meant that he was a few inches

taller than her. Or maybe it was something else—
something to do with escaping their real lives and real
pressures. They were meant to be putting on a show
to the public today—but in reality it had given them
permission to stop pretending for the first time since
they had woken up married.

They passed through security to the VIP area,
and Charlie headed straight for the lead singer of
Casual Glory and gave him a hug. Joe hung back a
little, watching her work, impressed. She didn't just
schmooze—though she did compliment them on
their awesome set. She also challenged them, asked
them about their goals and their hopes for the future.
Showed them subtly that she would be their ally if
they wanted to make that a reality. And she made sure
that each member of the band left with her business
card in their pocket and some serious thinking to do.

Charlie cut the conversation short before they out-
stayed their welcome, and they headed over towards
the bar. He surveyed the room once he had a jar of
craft cider in hand—it was full of people resting their
feet, snatching glasses of free champagne, and trying
to get a sneaky snap of the VVIP whose hen do was
in full drunken flow in the corner.

He tapped the side of his glass, wondering whether
he had missed his friend, and whether they should
commandeer one of the golf buggies to go in search
of him when he recognised Owen's shaggy, shoulder-
length hair and waved at him from across the crowd,
squeezing Charlie's hand at the same time. He wondered for a split second whether he had done the right
thing in looking Owen up, but it was too late to back

out now. Owen turned and saw him, waving from across the tent.

'Hey,' Joe called out, making a move towards his friend.

Charlie followed the direction of Joe's wave and saw Owen—she recognised him from a gig she'd been to last year. And then a blonde woman—polished and beautiful—stepped from behind him, a chubby baby settled on her hip. Charlie's stomach lurched and she felt bile rise in her throat. Joe should have warned her.

He was the one who had called her out on how uncomfortable she had been acting around her sister and her kids. He had to know just how hard this would be for her. Especially with the way that talking about everything had been tearing open old wounds recently.

She realised that she'd come to a halt, and only Joe's hold on her hand pulled her forwards.

'Owen, hey, man. Alice, you look gorgeous.' Joe shook his friend's hand and kissed Alice's cheek. 'Guys, this is Charlie.' He'd pulled her to him and wrapped his arm around her waist. He was putting her through this and he didn't even care—didn't even think to try and understand how much this was hurting her.

Alice leaned in and kissed her cheek and Owen shook her hand.

'Congratulations, you two!' Alice said with a friendly smile. 'I can't believe someone's tied this guy down. You deserve a medal, Charlie. I can't wait to hear all the details.'

Charlie tried to return her smile, but felt her facial muscles stiffen into a grimace.

'And who's this?' Joe asked, chucking the baby's cheek and being rewarded by a belly laugh. 'Looks like we should be the ones saying congrats.' Charlie sensed something slightly forced in his cheerful tone. What was he up to?

'This is Lucy,' Alice said, and shifted the baby to hold her out to Joe. 'Want to hold her?'

'Are you sure?' He took the baby awkwardly and held her up to his face, pulling funny faces. Joe with a baby. Charlie watched him closely, trying to work out what he was feeling. His smile was open and straight-forward, and she envied him for it. She wished she could enjoy the sweet, heavy weight of a baby in her arms without being haunted by the inevitable regret and sadness.

'That must have moved quickly, then,' Joe was say-ing. She struggled to follow the conversation—feeling as if she had missed some vital part. 'The last time I saw you, you were still mired in bureaucracy trying to bring this one home.'

'Our social worker was awesome,' Alice replied. She turned to Lucy with another megawatt smile. 'We've adopted Lucy,' she said.

And the bottom fell out of Charlie's stomach. She stumbled, and the only thing to grab hold of to stop her falling was Joe. Again, goddamn him.

Had he planned this? Manipulated her into meet-ing this gorgeous family, with their beautiful baby?

Of course he had—that was what she'd heard in his voice. He'd been planning this behind her back. So after everything he had said about her being enough for any man just as she was, and it didn't matter if she could have children or not, here was the proof that he felt otherwise. She'd always known that it was always going to be true in the end.

It was as if he'd not listened to a word she'd said since they'd met. As if he didn't know her.

'L-lovely to meet you,' Charlie managed to stammer, and then she turned and started walking. She didn't even care where she was going. She just had to get out of there. Away from Alice and her gorgeous baby. Away from Joe and his lies and manipulations.

She reached sunshine and fresh air but kept walking, wanting as much distance as she could get between her and Joe. She couldn't remember where the car was so she just walked out. Out as far as she could. Tears threatened at the edges of her eyeliner, but she knew that she must not let them fall. Even now, they had to make this deception work, or what had been the point of any of it? She spotted the VIP car park and headed towards Joe's car. She just wanted to not be here.

The keys. Damn it. Well, maybe there would be someone else leaving and she could hitch a ride—

'Charlie!'

She recognised Joe's voice, her body responded to it—to him—immediately, but she fought it and kept walking. He couldn't possibly have anything to say to her that she would want to hear.

'Charlie, stop. Please!'

Ahead of her, someone was staring at them. She wanted so much not to care. To be a nobody—unrecognisable in a crowd. Someone no one knew or cared about. But she stopped, because she wasn't that person. She could never be that person.

Joe caught up with her, rested his forearms on her

shoulders. God, if he asked her what was wrong, that was it. She was running and crying and she didn't care who saw.

'I'm sorry,' he said. 'I should have warned you that they have a baby.'

She shrugged his arms off her shoulders. He was trying, but he still didn't get it. 'I'm not angry about the baby, Joe. Babies don't make me mad. I'm angry because you tried to manipulate me.'

'Manipulate you? How?'

He'd raised his voice, but then looked around. Remembered where they were.

'Maybe we should talk about this in the car.'

She narrowed her eyes. Right—they needed to protect their secret. He climbed into the car and she sat on the passenger seat, looking straight out ahead, not able to face looking at him properly.

'I should have warned you about the baby,' he said again. 'But I thought I was doing something good. I thought seeing how happy they are to have her would help. That they're a family, even if not by conventional means.'

'So what are you telling me—you want to adopt a kid? Is that your next big idea? Your next publicity campaign? It doesn't matter that I'm damaged goods, because you can always stick a plaster on that?'

'Don't be ridiculous, Charlie. This isn't about me and you know it.'

'Oh, of course, because all this is just for show. It's all about your career.'

'Yours too,' he bit back. 'You make me out to be mercenary, but don't pretend that you're not using me every bit as much as I'm using you.'

He was using her.

Of course he was, she had known that from the start. But to hear him say it like that—no sugar coating—it winded her. And he thought that she was just as bad as him. That she had made a cold, calculated decision to use him. Well, she couldn't let him go on believing that. She wasn't that much of a bitch.

'My career? You know that that wasn't why I married you. Unlike you, I'm not that mercenary. I saw a headline in the news, that night. My parents trying to marry me off to one of those suitable husbands who'd be waiting for his heir and spare. I married you because my family were trying to force me into being the happy wife that I knew I never could be. When I have reminders of my infertility thrust in my face, Joe, I have been known to go a little crazy and act out. I could see the life I had built for myself slipping away and I was so heartbroken I couldn't think straight. That doesn't make us the same.'

CHAPTER ELEVEN

'You were still using me,' Joe said. Charlie rolled her eyes at him, but he was still reeling.

'Oh, because you're such a goddamn expert, are you?' she said. 'Is it all women that you know so well, or is it just me? Because I've been on your telly and in your newspapers my whole life you think you know what I'm feeling.'

'I never said I think I know you—but I think I know something about women. About relationships. I do have some experience of this.'

'Oh, so we're finally going to get to the bottom of this. Good. It was Arabella, I assume, who broke your heart.'

'Nobody said my heart was broken.'

'You scream it without saying a word, Joe. You with your trust issues and fear of commitment. You've already seen every article of my dirty laundry. Are you going to tell me what went on to make you such a cynical son of a b—? Or are we going to carry on trying to work out what's going on with us while having to avoid stepping on the elephant in the room?'

He slapped the steering wheel. Why was she so determined to make this about him—to make him the bad guy? He had been trying to help, and now she wanted to drag up his past as if that had anything to do with what they were arguing about. 'There is no elephant. Arabella and me—it wasn't a big deal. I wasn't heartbroken. If anything I'm grateful to her. She taught me a lot.'

'Like what?'

'Like how relationships actually work—and I don't mean the hearts and flowers rubbish. I'm talking about real adult relationships where both partners are upfront and honest about what they expect.'

'And let me guess, what Arabella expected wasn't just to enjoy your company. What else did she want?'

He tried to wave her off, but he knew that she wasn't going to let this drop. The fastest way out of this argument was just going to be to tell her the truth. Then she'd see that Arabella had nothing to do with any of this.

'She wanted to piss off her parents. She thought that taking me home to meet them would do that.'

Charlie raised her brows. 'And when did you find this out?'

'When we turned up at her house for the weekend. They were perfectly nice to me and Arabella was furious. I think that she thought that one whiff of my accent and they'd be threatening to disinherit her. She'd read too much D H Lawrence.'

'And before that… Were you in love with her?'

He shrugged, because what did it matter how he had felt when he was a naïve eighteen-year-old?

'Before that, I thought things were as simple as being in love with someone. I know better now.'

'That's a pretty cynical way to go through life.'

'Is it? Are you telling me that if you meet a guy you love you'll just marry him—no thinking about real life, your family, your career? Children?'

'I married you, didn't I?'

He didn't know what he could say to that. She had just told him that she hadn't been thinking straight. Surely she couldn't be saying that she loved him. But she didn't deny it either. He shook his head—he had to try and make Charlie understand how Arabella had helped him. That he was happy with his life as it was. Or he had been, until he had met her.

'All I know is that since Arabella, I've not been hurt,' he said. 'Someone tried. Pretended that she wanted me, when all she wanted was something she could sell to the papers. If I'd not learnt my lesson after Arabella, maybe that would have affected my heart too. But I'm a quick study.'

Charlie reached for his hand and absent-mindedly traced the lines of the bones beneath the skin. He tried not to notice, tried not to feel that caress in the pit of his stomach. She was still looking out of the window, and he was cowardly grateful that she wasn't making him do this eye to eye.

'And is that what you want from life?' she asked. 'From the women in your life—just to not get hurt? Or, one day, are you going to want more than that? Are you going to want to risk going all-in? Risk your heart, and see what you get back.'

He let his head fall back against the head rest, and let out a long, slow breath. 'I don't know, Charlie. What could be worth that?'

She turned to face him, and he knew that she was not going to put up with his evasion any more. That all pretence that they were not talking about them now was flying out of the window.

'Are you serious?' she said, her eyes blazing. 'Don't you think that this could be worth it? That *I* could be?'

Her expression was wide open—she was holding nothing back, now. No more secrets. Nowhere left to hide.

'This was meant to be all for show,' he said.

'And yet here we are. We both know we didn't go in to this for the right reasons, Joe. But the more time we spend together, the more I feel this…this pull between us that I've never felt before. And I don't know what to call it. I'm scared to call it love, but nothing else seems to fit.'

'But what do you *want*, Charlie?'

'For God's sake. Why do I have to want anything, Joe, other than you? Why can't you believe that that's enough? I want what we had last night, whispering and laughing in bed together. I want yesterday, at the piano, feeling like I can see into your soul when you play and sing just for me. I want this afternoon, sitting in the sun with my eyes closed and your arms around me, not able to imagine feeling more complete. But what about you? Do you want a string of girls who will give you what you ask for and nothing more, or do you want a relationship? A connection. Something *real*.'

He opened his mouth to speak, but she held up a hand to stop him. He wanted to tell her that of course he wanted all that, but how was he meant to know if that was what she really wanted too? That laying his heart out there in the open felt like asking to have someone come and smash it until there was nothing left.

'I don't want your knee-jerk reaction,' she told him. 'Whatever the answer is going to be, I need to know that you've thought about it. That you mean it.'

They sat in silence for a long minute.

'I think we both need some time,' he said eventually. 'And some space. I don't think you should come back to London,' Joe said. 'Not yet.'

Her face dropped instantly, and he knew that he had hurt her. He reached out to her and softened his expression. 'Go back to your mum. Tell her what you've told me, and make your peace with her. Make your peace with what your parents want for you, and decide, with all your cards on the table, whether it's what you want too. If it is, we'll find a way to get it for you. I'll disappear from your life if that's what you need from me.

'But if you don't…even if, with no secrets, you still want to be married to me? Come home to me, Charlie.'

CHAPTER TWELVE

CHARLIE SAT IN silence as the car sped along the roads that were so familiar to her from her childhood. She had spoken to her mother as soon as she had set off for the airport, and sensed that she wasn't entirely surprised that she was on her way back already.

She still hadn't decided what she wanted to say to her. How she would explain that she loved her parents, all her family, but that she didn't want the life that they had decided on for her.

Now the heat of the argument had faded, she could see that Joe hadn't been cruel to introduce her to his friends. The opposite, in fact. He'd shown her what she should have seen all along. Her ability to bear children or not had never been the problem—if she couldn't have kids naturally that was something that might be sad, and difficult for her and a husband to overcome. But it didn't mean that she could never have a family on her own, and it definitely wasn't a reason not to marry at all.

No, her reason for not marrying the men that her parents had introduced to her was much simpler—she didn't want them.

She didn't want the men, or the families, or the life that they represented.

She didn't want to give up her home in London, or her job, or the pride that she had built in herself and her abilities since she had left home.

She didn't want to go back to Afland just because of a promise she had made when she was eighteen and wanting to leave. Didn't want the life that she had made for herself to be over just because the date on the calendar ticked over and she was twenty-eight years old instead of twenty-seven.

Charlie bit at a nail as the car pulled through the gates of the palace and her hand barely moved from her mouth until she was in her mother's study, sitting on the other side of her expansive desk, feeling more like a job candidate than a daughter. And then she remembered that she was the one who had stalked in here and sat, leaving her mother standing on the other side of the desk, arms raised in greeting.

'So, was there something in particular you needed to talk about, sweetheart?' Adelaide asked, drawing her chair around the desk to sit beside her daughter.

Charlie felt her spine stiffen as she thought about all the things that she'd not said to her mother over the past ten years, not knowing where to start.

'I don't want to come back, Mother. After my birthday. I know I promised I would—'

'That was a long time ago,' her mother interrupted gently. 'I'd hoped that you would want to come back to live here, that your father and I might see a little more of you. But I'm not going to force you. I don't think I could if I wanted to. Now, are you going to tell me what this is really about? Is it Joe? Because we never really had a chance to talk properly before. I thought when you called after the wedding, maybe you had done something that you regretted, but then when you were here…honestly, darling, the atmosphere between you.'

Charlie couldn't help but smile when she thought of him.

'So I'm right,' her mother continued. 'You two are crazy about each other.'

'It's complicated,' Charlie said with a sigh.

'Well, I think it often is.' Her mother gave her an encouraging smile. 'Maybe if you tell me everything, it would help.'

'I wish it would, Mum. But the thing is…' She couldn't believe that she was about to volunteer the information that she'd held secret for so long, that she'd had nightmares about her mother finding out. What if she did react as she had in her dreams? Pushing her out of the family, banishing her from the island of Afland for ever? But wasn't that what Charlie had done to herself? She'd all but cut herself off from her family—her mother couldn't do any worse than that. She took a deep breath, squeezed her fingernails into her palms and spoke.

'The thing is, I might not be able to have children.' The words tumbled from her mouth in a hurry, and she kept her gaze locked on the surface of the desk, unable to meet her mother's eye.

Adelaide reached for her hand, and held it softly in her lap. 'I'm so sorry, darling. That must be terribly hard for you. And is having children important to Joe?'

'No.' She shook her head, and finally lifted her

gaze to meet her mum's eyes. The gentle kindness and love on her face made a sob rise in her throat, but she forced it down, wanting to finish what she'd started. Wanting, more than anything, her mum's advice. 'He says… It doesn't matter, does it? It's not about Joe. It's about me, it's about the fact that I'm never going to be who you want me to be.'

'I just want you to be *you*, darling. And more than that, I just want you to be happy.'

But that was crap, because she'd seen for herself what her mum wanted for her. A suitable husband, marriage, babies. 'Then what was all that with Philippe?' she asked, an edge to her voice. 'Why was he talking about engagements and moving to Afland with your blessing? Why did I have to read about it in the paper?'

'Honestly, Charlie, after all this time how can you believe anything that you read? Philippe came for dinner with his parents and he asked if you were still single. You know that he'd always had a soft spot for you. Then his father asked if you were planning on moving back to Afland. I don't know where he got the rest of it from. If I know his father as well as I think I do, the story probably came directly from him. I'm sorry that the press team weren't able to keep his mouth under control. I'm not going to lie and say that I haven't thought that you might be happier if you moved home and made a good match. It's kept your father and I happy for thirty-odd years, and your sister fairly blissful for the last seven. But we were never going to force you. Did you really think that we would?'

Yes, she had. She'd thought that there was only

one way that she could make her parents happy and proud of her, but she could see from her mum's face that she'd got it wrong.

'No, I don't think you'd force me, Mum.' She stayed silent for a moment. 'I'm sorry that I've not been home much.' Her mum wrapped an arm around her shoulders. 'But seeing Verity, and the children…'

'That must have been hard.'

'I just knew that that might never happen for me, and if it doesn't then where do I fit in this family?'

Adelaide squeezed her shoulders and reached for a tissue from the silver dispenser on her desk. 'You're my little girl, Charlie. That's where you fit. Where you'll always fit. But maybe things aren't as bad as they seem. Have you seen a doctor about it?'

'Not since I first found out. I didn't want to talk about it, didn't want the press getting hold of anything.'

'Well,' Adelaide said. 'How about I set up an appointment with my personal doctor, and you can have some tests? At least then you might know where you stand. If you knew the secrets that man had kept for me…well, let's just say I know that he can be discreet.'

'And if I definitely can't have children?' Charlie asked, a shake in her voice.

'Then it won't change the way I feel about you even a tiny bit, Charlie. Surely you know that. I just want you to be happy. Is Joe making you happy?'

'He's trying. I'm trying.'

'That's good. Keep trying, both of you.'

Charlie looked up and smiled at her mum, and could see from her expression that they weren't finished yet.

'What, Mum? I know there's something else you want to say.'

'I just… I'd like to see you at home more, darling. I know that you want to stay in London. I know how important your career is. But it doesn't have to be all or nothing. You could come back to visit more. We'd love to see you. And maybe you could do a few official engagements. I can't tell you how much I've missed you.'

Charlie plugged in her headphones as she climbed into the car and cued up the tracks that Joe had sent her. They had only been apart for a night—nothing in the grand scheme of things—but the already so familiar resonance and tone of his voice managed to relax her muscles in a way she didn't know was possible. She closed her eyes as the car crept along the London streets from the airport, drumming her fingers in time to the music in her ears, remembering the morning they'd been in the music room, sitting at the piano where she'd taken lessons as a girl, next to a man who made her skin sing.

Was it pathetic that she'd broken into a smile as soon as she'd seen his name on her phone?

She tapped at the screen to bring the message up again.

Call me when you get in.

Did he mean it? Or was it just a pleasantry? Like, *Call me when you get in, but obviously not if it's late, or inconvenient. Maybe just leave it till morning.*

Ugh. She was irritating herself, sounding like one

of those pink glitter princesses she'd tried all her life not to be.

She shot off a text, the traditional middle ground between calling and not calling, telling him she'd landed and was heading back to her place. It was too much to just turn up on his doorstep, especially when she wasn't even sure that he wanted her there.

The car twisted through the darkened streets of the city, over brightly lit dual carriageways, past the twisted metal of the helter-skelter sculpture in Stratford, and on towards her flat.

Her stomach sank at the thought of another night sleeping without Joe. She told herself that a month ago she'd been perfectly happy barely aware that he existed. But that had all changed the minute that she had set eyes on him, and they couldn't change that now. Somehow, she knew that without him her flat would feel empty, even though he'd never set foot there before.

As the car approached the stuccoed, pillared front of her apartment building, she spotted a dark shadow on the front steps and her stomach lurched. She glanced back through the windshield, checking that the police officers she knew should be on her tail were there, and breathed a sigh of relief when she saw one of the officers speaking into a radio.

Just as the driver asked her over the intercom whether she wanted him to drive on, the headlights illuminated the steps, throwing light onto Joe's face, and shadows into the space behind him. She let out the breath she had been holding, and told the driver that it was fine, he could stop. She took a moment before she opened the door to gather herself, prepare for what might come with Joe.

Had he come to tell her that he wanted her? That he wanted to make this a real marriage, or that he wanted out?

'Hi,' she said as she stepped out of the car and up the steps.

'Hey,' Joe replied, giving nothing away.

She grabbed her bag from the driver and stepped past Joe, unlocking the door and pushing it open.

She reached down to grab the mail and then dumped it on the hallway table, glancing round and trying to remember what state she'd left the place in. She didn't normally care about the condition of the flat, as long as it was warm and watertight. She had spent her whole childhood and adolescence looking forward to the freedom of space that was entirely her own. But there was something selfish and lonely about that, about the fact that she didn't have to consider a single person's feelings except her own. Maybe that was why she felt irrationally pleased that the worst of the mess had been bundled into bags and carted over to Joe's place. Her flat was usually her sanctuary but today it felt cold and unloved, and for a second she thought about the warm exposed brick and softly waxed wood of Joe's warehouse and felt a pull of something like homesickness.

She shook herself as she crossed to the windows and pulled back the curtains and blinds and opened a window. It was just feeling a bit neglected in here, because she hadn't been home for a few days, she reasoned. It was nothing a bit of fresh air and the warm light of a few lamps wouldn't fix.

'Want a drink?' she called out to Joe—anything

to stall actual, meaningful conversation. She grabbed them both a beer from the fridge and handed one to him.

'Nice place,' Joe said. Small talk. Good—she could handle small talk. She had plenty of formal training. Or maybe it had been bred into her. Either way, she grabbed his opening gambit and held onto it like a raft.

She chatted about the flat. How she'd chosen it for the big south-facing windows. The French doors out into the shared garden. The view of the park and lack of traffic noise from the front. She sounded like a desperate estate agent trying to close a sale.

Opening the French doors, she took her beer out to the patio, dropping onto one of the chairs and propping her knees against the edge of the little bistro table. The fairy lights her upstairs neighbour had threaded through the boughs of the trees twinkled at them, creating a scene she could have found in a fairy tale.

Shivering, she wished she'd grabbed her jacket, but she was too bone-tired to move.

'You're right, it's quiet out here,' Joe said, following her. 'Peaceful, and pretty. I can see why you like it so much.'

She looked up and met his eye, trying to judge if he was being sarcastic. But he looked genuine. He sat in the seat beside her, his thighs spread wide as he leaned back and let out a sigh.

'Long trip back,' he commented. 'For both of us.'

She 'hmm-ed' in agreement.

'Lots of time to think,' he added.

She looked up at him, wondering if this was it. When all their tiptoeing finally stopped and they decided if they wanted to run from the relationship they'd both been fighting from the first.

'Come to any conclusions?' she asked.

She wasn't sure she even wanted to know, because, whatever the answer, she knew that they still had a lot of work to do. He could declare his undying love for her this minute and that wouldn't remove a single one of the obstacles in their way. Still, even the thought of it made the hairs on her arms stand up.

'You're cold,' Joe said, stripping off his jacket and handing it to her. She draped it round her shoulders, refusing to acknowledge how delicious it felt to be wrapped in the warm, supple leather that smelt of him.

'I care about you, Charlie. I think you know that I do. But it's not as simple as that, is it?'

'I don't think that it ever is.'

'Honestly, after Arabella, and then the kiss and tell, when I'd picked myself up and convinced myself it hadn't been that bad, I thought I'd cracked it. That I'd finally figured out how these things work. And I've had no reason to doubt that I was right. What I was doing—it was working for me. Honestly, I've had no complaints.'

'So that's what—'

'Please, let me finish,' he said with a gentle smile. 'It was great, until I saw you watching me from the side of the stage in Las Vegas, and I felt something so overwhelming I still don't have the words to describe it. And I told myself that getting married was a great joke, or a killer career move or... I don't know. I told myself it was about anything except falling in love with you before I'd even said hello.'

Her heart pounded. She was desperate to say something, to ask if that was what he felt now—love. But he'd asked her for space to talk, and he deserved that.

'But I was kidding myself. I love you, Charlie. I think you knew that before I did.'

She let out the breath she had been holding, her thoughts whizzing by so fast it was impossible to concentrate on just one of them.

He sat watching her for a moment, and then grinned. 'That's it. I'm done,' he said. 'Twenty-four hours' thinking and that's all I've worked out. Say anything you like.

'Did you speak to your mum?' he asked eventually, his face falling when she couldn't think of what to say in response.

She nodded, still searching for the words. 'It was good,' she said eventually. 'I think… I think I got a lot of things wrong.'

'About me?'

She smiled, tempted to call him out on his self-centredness that only a rock star could get away with.

'About family, about children, about myself.' She looked up and met his eye. 'Yes, probably a few things wrong about you too.' She sighed, knowing that she was going to have to dig deeper than that. For so long, she'd kept as much as she could get away with to herself, but Joe deserved more than that from her.

'I'm not going back, to Afland. Well, not properly. I told my mum I'd take on some official duties, but my life will be here, Joe. I'm staying in London. And I hope to God that it's with you, because I've missed you like… I don't know. Like I suddenly lost my hearing and there was no music in the world.'

Now it was her turn to squirm, looking into her

man's eyes as she waited for him to reply. 'Is that what you want, Joe?'

'I want you, Charlie. Any way I can have you. Is that enough?'

She leaned forwards and pressed a hard kiss against his lips, gasping with pleasure as his hands wound around her waist under the warm leather of his jacket. 'It's enough,' she managed to whisper between kisses. 'We can make it enough—if we both want it.' His arms pulled tighter around her waist and she moved away from him for just a split second, and then she was sitting on top of him, her legs straddled around him and the chair. He leaned back, meeting her eyes as she settled on top of him. 'We're doing this?' he asked.

She answered him with a kiss.

EPILOGUE

'YOU KNOW, YOU HAVEN'T said it,' Joe said sleepily, brushing a strand of her hair back from her shoulder. He pulled the duvet up around them and Charlie in close, settling her in the crook of his arm as he laid his head on the pillow.

'Said what?'

Her eyes were shut, her body loose and languid, and her voice so sleepy she barely formed words.

'You know what.'

She opened her eyes and looked up at him, a teasing smile on her lips. 'I can't say it now that you've asked.'

Joe pressed a kiss into her hair. 'I don't need you to. But, you know, tomorrow, if you happened to feel the urge…'

'I predict lots of urges, tomorrow.' She smiled wickedly. 'It's a long, long list. But if that's the one that you want to put at the top…'

If he'd had any energy left, he would have rolled on top of her and taken care of a few of those urges right now. But instead he pinched her waist. 'Give me an hour's sleep and I'll put myself entirely in your hands.'

'Good. Exactly where I want you. Later,' she said,

with another kiss against his chest. 'I think there's something we need to talk about first.'

He sighed sleepily. 'I thought we were done talking.'

She shuffled away from him on the bed, pulling up the sheets to try and find some modesty.

'It's important, Joe,' she said, and he opened his eyes properly at the serious tone of her voice. 'There's a lot we didn't talk about. Children for one. It's not a fun conversation, but we have to have it. I'm going to see my mum's doctor, but there are no guarantees. What if it never happens for us?'

He rubbed his face and sat up. 'If it comes to that, Charlie, we'll deal with it. Together. There are other ways to have a family.'

'Is it what you want?' she asked, a wobble in her voice. 'Because I don't know if adoption is something that I could take on. With my family, the succession, it's complicated.'

He kissed her on the forehead, smoothing a hand down her spine. 'I know that. But no, it doesn't matter to me. You're what matters to me.'

'But I might never have a family, Joe. And there's no point taking this any further if that's not something that you can live with. If you're always going to want more.'

He stopped her with a kiss on the lips. 'The only thing I want in my future is you,' he said, between kisses. 'We're going to travel the world. We're going to make beautiful music. We're going to party until we can't take any more. If children come along, the more the merrier. But nothing, *nothing* is going to make me a happier man than knowing that you will come home with me every night, and wake up with me every morning.'

'I love you,' she whispered, and he smiled as he squeezed her tight and pressed a kiss against her hair. She ran her hands over his chest, and he stretched, bringing their bodies into contact from where she had propped herself on his chest right down to their toes.

'And I love you too. Now, are we making a start on that list of yours?'

* * * * *

If you really enjoyed this story, check out
NEWBORN ON HER DOORSTEP
by Ellie Darkins.
Available now!

If you're looking forward to another
royal romance read, you won't want to miss
MARRIED FOR HIS SECRET HEIR
by Jennifer Faye.

The inadvertent contact made him groan.

Tristyn backed up. "You're in my space." When Josh didn't step away, she said, "Could you please get out of my space?"

"I could…" Instead, he stepped forward, breaching the distance between them.

"Twelve years," he murmured as he caught her chin in his hand. "It's a long time to wonder, don't you think?"

"I guess that depends on what you're wondering." Her tone was neutral but he caught her breathlessness.

"The same thing you are."

She was trembling. Not with fear, she realized. With desire. But going down that path with Josh now would be dangerous. Still, she played along.

"And what is that?" she asked.

He didn't say the words. He simply brushed her lips with his.

And with that kiss, any thought of resistance fizzled away. In that moment there was only Josh. And the intoxicating sensation of his kiss.

Twelve years ago she would've given anything to experience this. Twelve years ago she'd been totally unprepared for this. Even now, she wasn't sure what to do with the desire that pulsed through her veins.

All she knew was that if she touched him now, she wouldn't be able to stop.

* * *

Those Engaging Garretts!—
The Carolina Cousins

THE LAST SINGLE GARRETT

BY
BRENDA HARLEN

First Published in Great Britain 2017
By Mills & Boon, an imprint of HarperCollins*Publishers*
1 London Bridge Street, London, SE1 9GF

© 2017 Brenda Harlen

ISBN: 978-0-263-92297-4

23-0517

Our policy is to use papers that are natural, renewable and recyclable products and made from wood grown in sustainable forests. The logging and manufacturing processes conform to the legal environmental regulations of the country of origin.

Printed and bound in Spain
by CPI, Barcelona

Brenda Harlen is a former attorney who once had the privilege of appearing before the Supreme Court of Canada. The practice of law taught her a lot about the world and reinforced her determination to become a writer—because in fiction, she could promise a happy ending! Now she is an award-winning, national best-selling author of more than thirty titles for Mills & Boon. You can keep up-to-date with Brenda on Facebook and Twitter or through her website, www.brendaharlen.com.

For my readers—thank you!
XO

Chapter One

Tristyn Garrett didn't get paid to keep tabs on Josh Slater. Though her responsibilities at Garrett/Slater Racing seemed ever growing and changing, that wasn't one of them. So when Dave Barkov came into the building for his nine-thirty meeting with her too-sexy-for-his-own-good boss, she buzzed Josh's office. As a co-owner of the race team, Josh didn't always keep regular hours, but he was always there when he needed to be.

So why wasn't he there now?

"Excuse me for a minute," she said to Mr. Barkov, and made her way down the hall to Josh's office. The door was open, but the lights were off and the chair behind his desk was empty. His computer, which was always on, was flashing a reminder of the meeting with Dave Barkov, which Josh wasn't there to see.

Across the hall, her cousin's office was also empty, but she knew that Daniel was at the wind tunnel with Ren D'Alesio and his crew chief. She had received no communication from Josh to explain his absence.

Ordinarily she wouldn't worry about where he was, what he was doing or even who he was with, but Mr. Barkov was a potential new sponsor and this tour of the facilities in Charisma, North Carolina, had been set up weeks ago. She knew because she'd set it up, after ensuring that the date and time worked for Josh. Right now, she was silently cursing the fact that she worked for him.

Their relationship was a mostly, if not strictly, professional one. Josh had been friends with her cousin Daniel for as long as she could remember, and over the past several years, he'd become a regular fixture at family events. He was, in many ways, like another cousin to her, except that she got along really well with all her cousins and her relationship with Josh wasn't always so amicable.

At the shop, they worked well together because each was focused on the performance of their respective duties. But away from GSR, there was often an uncomfortable… friction…between them.

She blamed Josh for that friction. He seemed to enjoy saying and doing things for the sole purpose of riling her, and even aware of that fact, she couldn't always control her reactions. Her sisters liked to tease that it was sexual tension and suggested that Tristyn could alleviate the problem by getting naked with Josh, but that wasn't going to happen—no way, no how, not ever.

But his failure to show up for a scheduled meeting with a new sponsor was completely out of character. Because as much as she occasionally accused him of being immature and unreliable, when it came to the business aspects of GSR, he was the poster boy for responsibility. Of course, he'd sunk a large portion of his own money—courtesy of his interest in Slater Industries, the company owned and operated by his parents—into the business and had convinced her cousin to do the same.

While Mr. Barkov waited, Tristyn called Josh's cell phone. She also sent a text message and an email, but he didn't respond to any of her attempts at communication. So she put a smile on her face and apologized to the sponsor, explaining that both the team's owners were tied up in a meeting elsewhere and offering to either reschedule or give him the promised tour of the facilities herself.

Mr. Barkov opted for the tour.

Two hours later, when he had finally gone and Daniel had returned from his meeting, she gave a perfunctory knock on her cousin's open door before she stepped through it and into his office. "Where the hell is he?"

Daniel looked up from his computer screen, his dark brows drawing together. "Who?"

She rolled her eyes. "The Slater half of Garrett/Slater Racing."

"I haven't seen him yet this morning," Daniel admitted.

"Because he's AWOL," Tristyn said, not even trying to hide her irritation.

"A few hours late is hardly AWOL," he chided.

"It's not a few hours," she argued. "Nobody has heard a single word from him since he left the track Saturday afternoon."

"He said something about having to deal with a family crisis," her cousin told her.

Concern immediately edged aside her irritation. "What kind of family crisis?"

Daniel shrugged. "I didn't ask. I figured that came under the heading of 'personal' business, which means it's none of mine—and none of yours, either."

Tristyn considered that for a minute before nodding in acknowledgment of the point. "Okay—it's none of my business," she agreed. "But I think you should call him."

"Why?"

"Because I've tried calling, texting and emailing, with no response, so I'm wondering if there's a reason that he's ignoring me."

Her cousin's brows winged up. "Is there?"

"Not that I'm aware of," she said. "But he's never ignored my communications or been out of touch for so long before."

Daniel hit the speakerphone button, then punched in his friend's number. The call went immediately to voice mail—as each of hers had done.

You've reached Josh Slater. Please leave a message and I'll get back to you.

The beep sounded, then Daniel began to speak. "Hey, Josh. Give me a call when you get this message. I've got Tris in my office with a worried look on her face because she can't get in touch with you."

"I'm only worried that I'll have to cover for him when Dave Barkov shows up to meet the crew and tour the facilities," she interjected. "Oh, wait—I already did."

Daniel disconnected the call and slid her a look. "And you wonder why he might be ignoring you," he noted drily.

"He blew off a meeting with a potential sponsor," she said again.

"He'll check in soon," her cousin assured her, but she suspected he was trying to convince himself as much as her.

"Let me know when he does," she suggested.

Tristyn went back to her desk. As the administrative assistant and head of PR for the team, she had more than enough work to keep herself busy for the rest of the day. By three o'clock, when Josh hadn't checked in with her or returned Daniel's call, she picked up her purse and stopped by her cousin's office again.

"I'm going to detour past his place on my way home," she said.

Daniel glanced at his watch, frowned. "You're really worried about him, aren't you?"

Maybe she was a little concerned, because it wasn't like Josh to be out of touch. The man practically lived with his phone in his hand, answering calls when they came in and responding to emails and text messages right away. But she wasn't going to admit her concern to her cousin.

"I'm annoyed," she said, because that was true, too. "I had to work through my lunch today to make up for the time I spent with your sponsor because Josh was a no-show."

"I'm sure Dave Barkov was more grateful than annoyed," her cousin said. "After all, you're a lot prettier than Josh is."

She kissed his cheek. "I'll see you tomorrow."

As she drove toward Josh's condo, she thought about her cousin's parting remark. While it was true that no one would ever apply the "pretty" label to Josh Slater, there were several others that came to mind. At six feet two inches, with dark blond hair, smoky gray eyes and a mouth that promised all kinds of wicked pleasure, he was tempting. Tantalizing. Hot.

Oh, yes, he was very definitely hot.

And she'd already been burned.

Josh Slater stared at the disaster zone that used to be his kitchen and tried to decide if he should wade into the mess or call a hazmat team. In addition to the pile of dishes from breakfast and lunch, there was a long drip of dried pancake batter on the oven door, toast crumbs on the counter, Cheerios on the floor and a pot with the congealed remnants of mac and cheese stuck to the bottom. He waded into the mess and had just filled the sink with soapy water when a knock sounded at the door.

He wasn't expecting any more visitors—he'd already had more than he'd anticipated this weekend and wasn't eager to add to the number. He decided to ignore the summons and pretend he wasn't home.

The knock sounded again, louder and more insistent this time. He frowned, thinking that if a knock could exhibit personality traits, this one was brisk and impatient, very much like...Tristyn Garrett.

Because she was on his mind, he wasn't the least bit surprised to hear her voice come through the door. "If you're in there, Josh, you better open this door before I call 911 and have the fire department break it down."

Since she didn't usually issue idle threats, he wiped his hands on a towel and opened the door. "What are you doing here, Tristyn?"

"Nice greeting." Her deep green eyes narrowed as they skimmed over him, silently assessing. "You look like hell."

He scrubbed a hand over his face, felt the rasp of stubble on his jaw. Apparently he'd forgotten to shave this morning. But at least he'd showered. He was pretty sure he'd showered.

Tristyn, by contrast, looked stunning. With her slender build, deep green eyes and perfectly shaped mouth, she could easily have made a fortune in front of a camera. Of course, as a Garrett, she was already heir to a fortune. Still, she worked as hard as anyone else at GSR, often exceeding even his expectations—as she'd done again by showing up at his door.

"I didn't get much sleep last night," he finally responded to her comment.

He saw the cool derision in her eyes fade. "Are you sick?" She took a step forward and lifted her hand as if to check his temperature.

He stepped back, forcing her to drop her hand. Since she'd been enticed by her cousin Daniel to work for Garrett/Slater Racing two years earlier, he'd been forced to acknowledge that his best friend's little cousin was all grown up. But she was still his best friend's cousin, which meant that even if she looked like every man's fantasy, she was off-limits to him.

That knowledge hadn't stopped him from dreaming of

her hands on him—frequent and explicit dreams. But he didn't want her touching him because she felt sorry for him. It was much better if they both respected the walls she'd built between them.

"No, I'm not sick," he told her. "I'm just exhausted from trying to keep up with three very demanding females."

As he'd expected, the casual—and yes, deliberately provocative—words erased any hint of sympathy from her pretty green eyes. Now they glittered like emeralds—hard and sharp. "Seriously? You blew off a scheduled meeting with a sponsor because you're recovering from a weekend orgy?"

Before he could respond, a tiny voice piped up to ask, "Whatsa orgy?"

Ah, hell.

Josh cringed at the sound of the adult word coming out of the little girl's mouth as he turned to face his five-year-old niece. "I thought you were watching a movie in the bedroom," he said.

Emily shook her head. "I don't like the movie—it's scary."

"It's a princess movie," he pointed out. "How scary can it be?" Although he'd never seen it himself, he'd found it in one of the half dozen suitcases his sister had dumped in his foyer along with her three daughters, so he'd assumed it was suitable for the kids.

"It's scary," she insisted.

"This is my niece Emily," Josh said. "Emily, this is Tristyn."

"Hi," the little girl said shyly.

Tristyn crouched down so that she was at eye level with the little girl—inadvertently providing him with a perfect view down the open vee of her blouse. And the view was perfect: sweetly rounded curves peeking over the edge of delicate white lace. He didn't look away until the lower part of his anatomy began to stir with appreciation.

"What movie are you watching?" Tristyn asked.

"*The Princess and the Frog.*"

"Are you at the part where the prince goes to see the witch doctor?" she asked.

Emily nodded solemnly, her big blue eyes wide and worried.

"That is a scary part," Tristyn admitted. "But I watched the movie just a couple of weeks ago with my niece, so I can tell you that the scary part will be over soon, then there are some funny parts and the movie has a happy ending."

Emily chewed on her lower lip. "For real?"

"For real," Tristyn promised.

"You wanna watch the movie?" the little girl asked.

"I would love to watch the movie," she said. "But I need to talk to your uncle for a little bit first, okay?"

"Okay," Emily agreed, and reluctantly headed back to the bedroom where the "scary" movie was playing.

Tristyn stood up again, tugging down the hem of the short skirt that had ridden up her thighs. She had spectacular legs to go with her tempting feminine curves—an almost irresistible package.

"Is she one of the females who kept you up all night?" she asked him now.

"Yeah," he admitted, with obvious reluctance. "Emily is my sister's middle daughter. She has two sisters, Charlotte, who is a couple years older, and Hanna, who is younger."

Tristyn curled her hand into a fist and punched him in the arm. She put some force behind the motion, but her effort glanced off his biceps.

He lifted a brow. "What was that for?"

"Because you're an idiot." She opened her hand, flexed her fingers. "Jeez—your arm is as hard as your head."

"You've often accused me of being an idiot," he pointed

out, ignoring her latter comment. "But it's never driven you to violence before."

She just shook her head. "What is wrong with you that you would rather let me believe you spent the weekend participating in an orgy than admit you were taking care of your sister's kids?"

"Maybe I didn't want to disillusion you."

"Into thinking that you had a heart in addition to your hormones?"

He shrugged. "We both know that our relationship is… safer—" he decided "—when you don't have any illusions about me being a nice guy."

"Don't worry—discovering that you spent a weekend with your nieces isn't going to change my opinion of you."

"Good to know," he said.

"Although I am curious about why they're here—and where your sister is."

"Long story."

"And why haven't you been answering your phone?" she asked.

"Because I can't find it," he admitted.

"You're kidding."

He shook his head. "I remember answering a text message when I was scooping up ice cream for the girls last night, but I haven't seen it since then."

"I assume you've looked in the kitchen?"

He hesitated, just a fraction of a second. "Yeah."

"That didn't sound very convincing."

"The kitchen is a bit of a mess right now," he admitted. "But I'm hoping the phone will turn up as I clear things away."

"I'll give you a hand," she offered, already moving toward the kitchen.

Josh followed, enjoying the sexy sway of her hips—

and nearly ran right into the back of her when she halted abruptly in the doorway.

She slowly turned to face him. "This is a *bit* of a mess?"

"I didn't have a chance to clear away breakfast dishes before it was time for lunch," he admitted.

"But you have a dishwasher," she pointed out.

"Still filled with clean dishes from yesterday."

She shook her head despairingly. "I'll put those away while you get the rest of this chaos organized."

He should have refused her offer of help, but the truth was, he was grateful. He was also appreciative of the fact that every time she bent forward, he could see down her top. Because Tristyn Garrett might be a pain in his ass a lot of the time, but she had a body that seemed to have been designed to fuel male fantasies.

She removed the cutlery basket and set it on the counter, then paused. He gestured to the drawer on the other side of the dishwasher, assuming that she didn't know where to put the clean forks and knives. But she made no move to open it.

"Um…Josh."

He immediately shifted his gaze from the nicely rounded curve of her butt to her face, hoping like hell she hadn't seen him looking where he had no business looking. "What?"

She lifted something out of the basket and held it up. "I found your phone."

Chapter Two

While his response was a harshly muttered four-letter expletive, Tristyn had to press her lips together so that she didn't laugh. Because it wasn't funny.

Well, it was *kind of* funny.

Because Josh's phone was as essential to him as the air he breathed into his lungs and the blood that flowed through his veins. A fact that was evidenced by the apoplectic expression on his face.

He snatched the device out of her hand and marched purposefully down the hallway. Curious to see how he would handle this incident, Tristyn followed, her steps faltering when she realized she was in the doorway of the master bedroom.

Josh's bedroom.

Part of her wanted to turn away, to let his private sanctuary remain private. Another part urged her to take a peek. That part won.

Her gaze moved around the space, noting the enormous king-size platform bed centered on the far wall and flanked by a set of night tables that matched the wardrobe, long dresser and entertainment stand. She glanced up at the ceiling—nope, no mirrors. So maybe he wasn't quite the degenerate she'd always believed him to be.

And while there was no denying this room was a man's domain, the decor was simple but inviting. Walls painted in a pale neutral tone that reminded her of the sand on a pristine Caribbean beach; pale floors that she guessed were bamboo and that contrasted nicely with the dark walnut finish of the classic mission-style furniture she recognized from the Garrett catalog.

Usually a man's domain, she clarified, as her attention shifted to the three girls snuggled together on the bed, propped up on a mountain of pillows against the head-board. Emily—the one who hadn't wanted to watch the scary movie—was on the side closest to the door. In the middle was Hanna—a preschooler, Tristyn guessed, with big blue eyes focused on the screen and uneven blond pig-tails sprouting out of the sides of her head. On the far side was Charlotte—obviously the oldest sibling, also blond and blue-eyed, wearing ripped jeans and a black T-shirt with some kind of picture on the front that Tristyn couldn't see because the girl's arms were folded across her chest in a posture that she recognized as pure unhappy female attitude.

None of them paid any attention to their uncle. It was as if they weren't even aware that he was facing them from the foot of the bed. But that might be because they were all mesmerized by the animated feature playing on a tele-vision screen that was probably ten inches bigger than the one Tristyn had in her living room.

Josh scooped up the remote and thumbed a button to pause the movie, which finally succeeded in drawing the girls' eyes to him.

Charlotte opened her mouth as if to say something, then saw the phone in Josh's hand, slid a quick glance toward the sister snuggled up beside her and closed it again without saying a word.

"Anyone?" Josh prompted.

"I talk," Hanna offered, crawling to the end of the mattress and reaching her hand up for the phone.

"That would be great, wouldn't it?" he said, his gaze moving over each of them in turn. "But someone put it in the dishwasher."

His littlest niece nodded solemnly. "Make it c'ean."

Tristyn saw a muscle in his jaw flex. "It didn't need to go in the dishwasher to be cleaned," he said through gritted teeth. "It was already clean."

This time Hanna shook her head. "I dwop ice cweam on it."

Josh blew out a frustrated breath and scrubbed his free hand over his face.

"You did say that you didn't want to find sticky fingerprints on any of your things," Charlotte pointed out in defense of her sibling.

"Meaning that I didn't want any of you to touch any of my things," he clarified.

His eldest niece shrugged. "Hanna tends to take things literally."

"She killed my phone."

The little girl looked up at him. "I so-wee, Unca Josh." She reached up to take the phone, puckered her lips and kissed the screen before handing it back to him. "All better?"

He sighed again as he dropped the now useless device into the side pocket of his cargo shorts, but one side of his mouth curved in a half smile. "It's not that easy, kiddo." He tapped a finger to his cheek. "You have to give a kiss here to make it all better."

She smiled and held her arms in the air. He slid one of his around her torso, and the natural ease with which he lifted the little girl onto his hip made something inside Tristyn's chest flutter. She wasn't usually the type to get quivery over a man, but apparently seeing this strong, sexy male cuddle with a sweet little girl was all it took for her to feel warm and fuzzy inside.

Hanna wrapped both her arms around his neck and gave him a smacking kiss on the cheek. Then she drew her head back, her nose wrinkling with obvious displeasure. "You're scwatchy," she told him.

"Yeah, I forgot to shave this morning," he admitted, setting her on the bed again.

She immediately returned to the pile of pillows, then smiled at him again. "Movie?" she asked hopefully.

"After your movie is done and the kitchen is clean, we're going to have to go out so that I can buy a new phone," Josh told them, as he picked up the remote again.

Tristyn turned to follow him back down the hall. "If I hadn't seen it with my own eyes, I never would have believed it."

He glanced over his shoulder. "Believed what?"

"That you're a marshmallow."

He stopped then and turned to face her, his brows drawing together over smoke-colored eyes. "I am not."

"Yes, you are," she insisted. "You're all soft and squishy—like the Stay Puft Marshmallow Man."

Those eyes narrowed dangerously, the only warning she had before he took two slow and deliberate steps forward. She automatically took two steps back. He laid his palms flat on the wall on either side of her, then leaned in, so that his body brushed against hers. His undeniably lean and very hard body.

"Do I feel soft and squishy to you?" he asked, his mouth close to her ear.

She lifted her palms to his chest, where his heart was beating in a rhythm much steadier than her own, to hold him at a distance. She had to moisten her suddenly dry lips with her tongue before she could reply, but she managed to keep her tone light and casual when she said, "In here." And tapped her fingers against his rock hard chest. "Your heart is soft and squishy."

"Because I didn't yell at a three-year-old?" he challenged.

"You not only didn't yell," she pointed out. "You melted. That little girl looked at you with those big blue eyes and said, 'I so-wee, Unca Josh,' and it was as if you completely forgot she destroyed an eight hundred dollar phone."

"It's just a phone," he said, conveniently ignoring the monetary value.

"Well, at least now I know why you didn't answer any of my calls, text messages or emails today," she noted.

He was still crowding her, standing so close that she could feel the heat emanating from his body. So close she had only to lean forward to touch her mouth to his strong square jaw. Her lips tingled with anticipation; her body whispered "yes, please." She clamped her lips firmly together and pressed herself back against the wall.

"Were you worried about me, Tris?" he asked, the silky tone of his voice sliding over her like a caress.

"No," she denied. Lied. "I was annoyed that I had to give Dave Barkov the tour of GSR."

"I never doubted that you could handle it," he told her.

"That's not the point," she said, ducking under his arm and walking away.

He, naturally, followed. "Do you want an apology? Okay—I'm sorry I was out of touch for a few hours."

She shook her head as she returned to the kitchen to resume the task she'd abandoned earlier. "You don't get it, do you? It's not just that you didn't tell anyone you wouldn't be at work today—you didn't even tell your friends what was going on here."

He held her gaze for a long moment. "Is that what we are, Tris…friends?" he asked, in that same silky voice that could make any woman go weak in the knees.

Any woman but her, of course, because she was immune to the considerable charms of Josh Slater.

"Maybe not," she finally said, determined not to give any hint of the feelings churning inside her. "A friend probably would have known you have three nieces."

"It's not something that often comes up in conversation," he pointed out. "And since my sister moved to Seattle when Charlotte was a baby, I don't get to see them very often."

"That's why you go to Washington every Christmas," she realized.

"Not every Christmas." He picked up the soapy cloth to wipe down the stovetop. "But I go when I can."

She finished unloading the clean dishes and began to load the dirty ones. "So why are they here now?"

"Lucinda's manager decided, at the last minute, to send her to Spain. The company she works for is setting up a new distribution center there and her pregnant boss, who was supposed to supervise the setup and train the staff, was recently put on bed rest by her doctor, so the company tapped Lucy to go."

"Why did I always think your sister worked at Slater Industries?"

"My older sister, Miranda, does," he told her. "She lives in London with her husband and their kids and manages the office there."

Which meant that he probably didn't get to see them very often, either, and perhaps explained why he was always hanging out at Garrett family events. Something to think about.

"How did you end up with so many dishes from two meals?" she asked, as she continued to fill the dishwasher.

"Each of the girls wanted something different for breakfast," he admitted.

"And you indulged them," she guessed.

"Well, Emily was up first and she asked for dippy eggs with toast sticks, so I figured I would make eggs for everyone. Then Charlotte woke up and informed me she doesn't eat eggs—except if they're in pancake batter. So while Emily was eating her eggs, I found a recipe for pancakes and started making those for Charlotte. By this time, Hanna was awake, too. But she just wanted cereal and seemed perfectly happy with the Cheerios I put on the table in front of her—until I made the mistake of pouring milk into the bowl."

Tristyn's lips curved as she pictured the scene he'd described. "Did she scream like a banshee?"

"I thought the neighbors would be knocking on my door—or Family Services," he admitted.

"Kylie went through a dry cereal stage," she told him. "Except for Rice Krispies, because they 'talk' when you put milk on them."

"And this—" he said, scraping the remnants of a pot into the garbage can "—is what's left of the mac and cheese they all had for lunch."

"Well, that's a score," she noted. "Pleasing all three of them with the same food."

"Except that Charlotte likes hers with ketchup mixed into it, Emily doesn't like it with ketchup at all and Hanna's ketchup has to be squirted on top of the pasta in the shape of a smiley face."

Tristyn smiled at that image, too. "And how long are they staying?"

"Eight to ten weeks."

Her brows winged up. "What are you going to do with them for two months?"

He wiped his hands on a towel, then folded it over the

handle of the oven door. "I'm thinking I should talk to my grandparents, to see if they're willing to take them for the summer."

"Didn't your grandmother just celebrate her eightieth birthday a few weeks back?"

He nodded.

"And your grandfather's a couple of years older than she is," Tristyn pointed out.

"Yeah," he admitted. "But they both play golf several times a week."

"Which is impressive," she acknowledged, "but still not as physically demanding as chasing after three kids. And considering that your sister entrusted *you* with the care of her children, I don't think she'd be too happy to learn that you dumped them on someone else."

"So what am I supposed to do? Hire a sitter to take care of them when I'm not here? Which is most of the time during race season," he reminded her.

She shook her head. "That's not an ideal situation, either."

"Do you have a better idea?"

"Not off the top of my head," she admitted, closing the dishwasher.

"Well, let me know if you think of something," he said. "They've hardly been here twenty-four hours, and I'm desperate enough to consider almost anything."

As Tristyn watched the last half hour of the movie with Josh's nieces, she tried not to think about the fact that she was in Josh's bed. *On* Josh's bed, she hastily amended. As if that clarification made any difference.

She wondered how many women had passed through that same doorway, laid on this same bed. Then pushed the question aside, deciding she didn't want to know. Still, she felt as if she shouldn't be here. She knew now why he hadn't shown up at work today, and why he would be juggling his schedule for the rest of the week—and possibly the rest of the summer. And now that her questions were answered, there was no reason for her to stay.

No reason except that she'd made an impulsive promise to a little girl. A little girl who was even now pressed against her side, her face turned away from the screen as the Shadow Man's spirit was taken away by the demons. But truthfully, her promise to Emily was only part of it. She was also intrigued by the opportunity to glimpse a corner of Josh's personal life and curious to see him interact with the little girls.

She vaguely remembered Lucy Slater from Hillfield Academy. Josh's younger sister had been two years behind Tristyn—a popular girl who liked to party more than study. She got kicked out midway through her sophomore year and wound up pregnant a couple years after that. By that time, Tristyn was mostly keeping her distance from Josh, so any information she had was secondhand from her cousin Daniel. There had apparently been a hasty wedding, and an even hastier divorce.

Obviously Lucy had gone on to have two more children and was now the mother of three beautiful girls. Three beautiful girls who were in Josh's care for the summer. Tristyn smiled a little at the thought of how the responsibilities would put a crimp in his usually active social life. Maybe she could offer to help with the girls, because it might be fun to have a front-row seat to the fireworks while he figured out how to mesh his life with the needs and demands of his three nieces.

Except that spending too much time in close proximity to Josh was a risk. Sure, they were friends—or at least friendly—most of the time, but there was also that uncomfortable friction that occasionally reared up between them—seemingly more frequently in recent years.

As Daniel's best friend and business partner, Josh was almost an honorary Garrett. Because his parents traveled a lot to oversee the various offices and interests of Slater Industries—a multinational investment company—he was often on his own for national holidays, and Daniel's mom, Jane, always included him in whatever plans the Garretts made. As a result, Tristyn had spent a lot more time with him over the past two decades than she'd sometimes wanted to.

In many ways, Josh had been like another cousin, and almost as bossy and annoying as most of her cousins were—at least from the perspective of a ten-year-old girl who hated to be excluded from their activities because of her age and her gender. She didn't look at him any differently than she looked at Daniel or Justin or Nathan or Ryan. Not until the summer after she'd turned thirteen, when suddenly being around him made her heart beat just a little bit faster. And she would blush and stutter in response whenever he spoke to her.

Her sisters teased her about her crush on Daniel's best friend, which she vehemently denied. He was just an idiot boy like the rest of their idiot cousins and all the other idiot boys she knew. Of course, Lauryn and Jordyn didn't believe her denials. And when Tristyn saw Josh making out with Missy Harlowe (aka Missy Harlot) beneath the bleachers of the football field, she felt as if she'd been stabbed in the heart. This unexpectedly fierce reaction forced her to acknowledge the truth of her feelings, if only to herself. She was in love with Josh Slater.

Later, she'd realized that what she'd thought was love was only an infatuation. Regardless of what she called it, there was no denying that he'd been her first real crush. And seeing him with other girls—and there were *a lot* of other girls—had broken her heart each and every time. She cried when he graduated from Hillfield Academy, because she would no longer see him at school every day. And she cried again when he went away to college, certain that her broken heart would never heal.

By the time Josh came home with Daniel for Thanksgiving, she had a boyfriend. Mitch Harlowe—Missy's younger brother—was a varsity athlete and an honor roll student with curly brown hair and eyes the color of melted chocolate. And he looked at her in a way that Josh never had—as if she was the most beautiful girl in the world and he was the luckiest boy in the world just to be with her.

She dated Mitch for more than a year and a half, but they never went "all the way." She was tempted, but she didn't want to be one of "those girls." They did a lot of other things, and Mitch was mostly patient with her—and undeniably relieved when she suggested that, maybe, after prom, they could finally "do it." He was first in line the day prom tickets went on sale.

She smiled a little at the memory, but her smile faded when her thoughts skipped ahead to that night—and an ending that neither of them had planned.

"You were right," Emily said, drawing Tristyn's attention back to the screen where the human-again couple were sealing their wedding vows with a kiss. "It does have a happy ending."

"It's not over yet," Charlotte told her sister. "It's not over until they show all the names of the people in the movie."

But a few minutes later, it was over.

"Okay, girls," Josh said from the doorway. "Time to get your shoes on."

"That's my cue to head out," Tristyn said to them.

Josh looked slightly panicked as she made her way toward the door. "Do you have to go?"

"You're leaving, too," she pointed out.

"But I was thinking—hoping," he admitted, "that you might come with us."

She didn't delude herself into thinking that he wanted her company. The simple and obvious truth was that he had no clue what to do with the three little girls left in his care and he was desperate for help with them. And yet she couldn't resist turning his own words around on him.

"Why is that?" she asked, blatantly fluttering her eyelashes. "Does keeping up with three females require more stamina than you possess?"

Chapter Three

Josh slid an arm around her back and drew her closer. So close that her breasts rubbed against his chest. Even through the layers of clothing that separated them, she felt her nipples tighten and strain against the lace of her bra. She lifted her eyes to his, and the intensity in his gray gaze nearly made her shiver.

"Do you want a demonstration of my stamina?" he asked.

She wanted to push him away, but she wouldn't give him the satisfaction of knowing that his touch affected her. Instead, she rolled her eyes. "Not even in your dreams."

His lips curved into a slow, dangerous smile. "You have no control over my dreams."

"Then definitely not in any version of reality," she amended.

"Are you sure about that?" he asked, finally releasing her.

"Positive," she said, taking just a half step back so that she could breathe without his proximity short-circuiting her brain.

And clearly her brain had short-circuited or she wouldn't have baited him in such a way. Because even if she was no longer a teenager experiencing her first infatuation, compared to Josh Slater she was still a novice when it came to the games that men and women played.

"In that case, there's no reason you would object to accompanying me and the girls," he suggested.

He was right. For the past dozen years, most of their public interactions had been civil—if occasionally adversarial. It was only when they were alone together—which she tried to avoid, if at all possible—that they tiptoed around one another. But if she went along, they would have the barrier of three little girls to prevent them from rubbing one another the wrong way and creating a familiar and dangerously tempting friction.

"Let's go get you a phone," she agreed.

As soon as they stepped through the doors of the electronics store, Charlotte and Emily made a beeline toward the video games on display. Josh opened his mouth to call them back just as a young salesman stepped up and Hanna announced, "I has to go potty."

With an apologetic glance toward the store employee, he shifted his attention to his youngest niece. "Why didn't you go before we left home?"

"I didn't has to go before," she said with unerring logic. "I has to go now."

He looked at the salesman, who shook his head. "Sorry, we don't have any public restrooms here."

"There's a coffee shop next door," Tristyn pointed out. "I'll take her there."

"Thank you," Josh said.

As they turned around and went back out the door, he caught up with Charlotte and Emily. "You can stay here to look at the games or whatever," he told them. "But stay together."

"Okay," they agreed, each already with a controller in hand and attention fixed on the demo game system.

The hopeful employee was still hovering beside him—no doubt working on commission. "Can I help you find something, sir?"

"I need a new phone," he admitted, and handed over his dead—albeit squeaky clean—iPhone 7.

Tristyn returned with Hanna just as the tech guy—who had been attempting to work magic on Josh's SIM card—gave him the bad news: none of the information could be salvaged. Which wasn't really a surprise but a disappointment nonetheless.

"All of those names and numbers…gone?" Tristyn asked, feigning horror. "The cute little messages with kissy-face emojis from all of your girlfriends…gone? Your electronic little black book…gone?"

He slid her a look. "No worries—I have a real little black book for all of the important names and numbers."

"I have no doubt," she said.

Josh passed his credit card to the salesman. A few minutes later, he walked out of the store with his new phone, which indicated the time to be 5:26 p.m.

"I'm hungry, Uncle Josh," Emily said.

"It's not even five thirty," he noted. "What time do you guys usually eat?"

"Five thirty," Charlotte told him.

"I guess that means it's dinnertime," he acknowledged, mentally inventorying the contents of his refrigerator to determine if he had anything left to feed them. "What do you like to eat?"

"Pizza," Emily announced.

"Chicken fingers," Charlotte countered.

"S'ghetti," Hanna chimed in.

"Well, at least we have a consensus," he said drily.

"What's a sen-sus?" Emily asked.

"It means agreement," he told her.

Her little brow furrowed.

"He was being sarcastic," her older sister explained.

"Oh," Emily said. Then, "What's scar-tas-tic?"

"Sarcastic." Tristyn enunciated the word for her. "And it's your uncle Josh's way of trying to be funny, but he's not."

"S'ghetti," Hanna said again.

"You had pasta for lunch," Josh reminded her.

"Not s'ghetti," she argued.

"What's your vote, Tristyn?"

A peek at her watch made her grimace. "Actually, I—" she glanced at the girls' hopeful expressions "—I think going out to eat would allow everyone to choose what they wanted."

"And it would give my kitchen a reprieve," he agreed.

"I just need to make a quick call first," Tristyn said.

He offered his new phone.

"I've got my own," she reminded him, tapping the screen as she stepped away.

"Can we go eat now?" Emily implored. "I'm hungry."

"Me, too," Charlotte said.

"As soon as Tristyn's finished with her phone call, we'll go." He didn't pretend he wasn't eavesdropping on her call, and though he heard only bits and pieces of one side of the conversation, it was enough pieces to put together and figure out she was canceling plans for dinner with someone else.

"You had a date," he said, when she'd disconnected the call.

She nodded.

"You didn't have to cancel," he told her, though he was secretly pleased that she'd done so. And grateful that she would be sticking around to help him out with the girls for a little while longer.

"Well, my car's still at your place, and by the time we drove back there and then I drove home to change, I would have been late, anyway."

"I'm sure your date wouldn't mind waiting...especially if you promised to make it up to him later."

"So what's the plan for dinner?" she asked, deliberately ignoring his comment.

The question was answered with renewed calls for "pizza," "chicken fingers" and "s'ghetti."

"All of those are on the menu at Valentino's," Tristyn pointed out.

"But what do you want to eat?" he asked her, as he led the girls back to his truck.

"Are you buying?"

"It seems the least I can do to thank you for your help today," he told her.

"Then I want steak," she decided. "A nice thick juicy steak."

He buckled Hanna into her booster seat, then stepped back so that Emily could climb into hers while Tristyn opened the door on the other side for Charlotte. "From Valentino's?"

"No, from The Grille. So I'll have the seven-layer lasagna tonight and take an IOU for the steak."

He lifted a brow. "You're trying to wrangle a date, aren't you?"

"Ha!"

"Is that where you were supposed to go for dinner tonight?" he asked, settling behind the wheel and securing his own seat belt.

"I'm not discussing my plans with you," she told him.

"Who was your date with?"

"Refer to previous answer."

He should let it go. It really was none of his business, but he was curious. "Was it a first date?"

"Refer to previous answer," she said again.

"Because I haven't heard you mention that you were dating anyone."

"Should I add my social engagements to the itinerary of GSR's monthly meetings?"

"That would be helpful," he agreed.

"Well, it's not happening," she told him.

Her response didn't surprise him. What surprised him was how much he sincerely wanted answers to his questions. But for now, he decided to be satisfied with the knowledge that she'd canceled her date to have dinner with him.

The waitress introduced herself as Sydney, recited the daily specials as she handed out menus and filled their water glasses, then left them alone to peruse the offerings.

Valentino's didn't specifically have a children's menu, but they did offer child-sized portions of any of their entrées.

Charlotte frowned as she scanned the options. "There's no chicken fingers on the menu."

"The cook will make them," Tristyn assured her.

"How do you know?"

"Because he's made them for my niece before."

"I want pizza," Emily reminded them all.

Tristyn pointed to the section of the menu that listed the various options and toppings, but Emily wanted only cheese.

"Pep-ro-ni," Hanna said.

"You said you wanted spaghetti," Josh reminded her.

His youngest niece shook her head. "P'za."

"Pizza with pepperoni?" he asked, seeking clarification.

She nodded, and then said, "I has to go potty."

"You just went when we were at the store," he reminded her.

"I has to go agin," she insisted.

He looked at Tristyn, who sighed. "This is the real reason you offered to buy me dinner, isn't it? So that you could escape bathroom duty."

"Well, I can't take her into the men's room, and there's no way I'm walking into the women's," he pointed out.

"I hafta go, too," Emily said.

"Charlotte?" Tristyn prompted.

She shook her head.

"Why don't you come, anyway, to wash up before dinner?" Tristyn suggested.

So she herded the three girls off to the ladies' room, leaving Josh alone at a table for five. Thankfully, he knew what everyone wanted, so when Sydney passed by the table again, he was able to place their order.

Charlotte and Hanna returned first, and Josh was settling his youngest niece into the booster seat again when Tristyn's sister Jordyn came over. Jordyn was married to Marco Palermo, whose grandparents had started serving pasta in the original downtown location of Valentino's almost fifty years earlier. Recently, Marco had spearheaded the expansion of their business with Valentino's II. He and his wife had also recently expanded their family with the addition of twin boys, who were now about nine months old.

"Gemma told me that Josh Slater had come in with four gorgeous females, which I thought was a little excessive—even for you." Jordyn winked at him before turning her focus to the girls.

"These are my nieces Charlotte and Hanna," he told her. "Emily must still be in the bathroom."

"She stuck her hands up under the faucet and sprayed water all over her shirt," Charlotte explained. "Tristyn's drying it off under the hand dryer."

Jordyn's brows lifted as she turned back to Josh. "My sister Tristyn?"

"She's the only Tristyn I know," he acknowledged.

"She was supposed to have a date with Rafe tonight." Then she shook her head. "Apparently her plans changed."

"That might be my fault," he acknowledged. "She saw that I was overwhelmed by the prospect of cooking another meal for three fussy kids and obviously took pity on me."

"We're not fussy," Charlotte interjected. "We just like what we like and don't like what we don't."

"Which is exactly what their mother used to say when she refused to eat what was put on the table," he acknowledged.

"How long have you been staying with Uncle Josh?" Jordyn asked Charlotte.

"We got here yesterday, and we're supposed to stay for the whole summer," she said, her glum tone clearly indicating her displeasure.

Josh wasn't overjoyed, either, but he couldn't see a way out of the situation for any of them. "My sister's in Spain on business for the next eight to ten weeks."

"The whole summer with Uncle Josh," Jordyn mused. "That should be…interesting."

"For all of us, I'm sure," he remarked drily.

But Charlotte was shaking her head. "He doesn't have any cool stuff *and* I had to sleep with Emily."

"In *my* bed," he pointed out. "While I slept on the sofa."

Jordyn chuckled softly. "Oh, yes, it will be an interesting summer."

"How are Henry and Liam?" he asked.

"If I had my phone handy, I'd bore you with a thousand pictures," she said, her deep green eyes—so similar to her sister's—suddenly going soft and dreamy. "They are the lights of my life."

"Along with your darling and devoted husband," Marco said from behind her.

Jordyn grinned as she glanced over her shoulder. "Along

with my darling and devoted husband," she dutifully intoned.

The aforementioned spouse slid an arm across her shoulders. "You said you wanted to have a quick word with Gemma while I went to the kitchen to grab a tray of lasagna for the potluck tomorrow, and when I came out of the kitchen, you were gone."

"Gemma told me that Josh was here, so I came over to say hi. And now I've met his nieces Charlotte and Hanna—and this must be Emily," she said, as his third niece and Tristyn made their way back to the table.

"And now we really have to go," Marco urged. "We've already been away longer than we planned and your mom has a ton of things to do before the picnic tomorrow, none of which she is getting done with Henry and Liam underfoot."

"You're right, we have to go," she agreed. But she gave her sister a quick hug before she turned to Josh again. "Are you taking the girls to the parade tomorrow?"

"I hadn't really thought about it," he admitted. But if he had, he would have answered with a resounding no. He'd barely been able to keep track of them in an electronics store; he didn't want to imagine the nightmare of trying to keep them together in the midst of the crowds that gathered to celebrate the Fourth of July.

"What parade?" Charlotte asked.

"The Independence Parade is part of Charisma's 'Food, Fun & Fireworks' celebration," Jordyn explained.

"I wanna see the fireworks," Charlotte told Josh.

"I wanna see the fun," Emily chimed in.

"I wanna see some food," Tristyn interjected. "Tonight. I'm starving."

"I starvin', too," Hanna said, clearly not wanting to be left out of the conversation.

"And Sydney's on her way with your food right now," Marco said, gently nudging his wife away from the table.

"See you at the park tomorrow," Jordyn called back over her shoulder, though Josh wasn't sure if she was talking to him or—more likely—her sister.

Charlotte polished off her chicken fingers and ate most of the fries on her plate; Emily ate two slices of the individual cheese pizza she'd wanted; and Hanna ate one slice of her pepperoni pizza—but only after picking off all the pepperoni—and half of Tristyn's garlic bread. Josh offered her some of the spaghetti that came with his chicken parmesan, which was what she'd originally wanted, but she wrinkled her nose and shook her head.

He was waiting for the check when Tristyn noticed that Hanna had fallen asleep at the table.

"Because she didn't have her nap at two o'clock," Charlotte said matter-of-factly. "And now she's going to be awake until midnight."

"How was I supposed to know that she should have a nap at two o'clock?" he wondered.

"It's in the book," his eldest niece informed him.

"And when did I have time to read the book?" he asked.

Charlotte just shrugged.

"The book?" Tristyn said.

"Is actually a binder," he told her. "Filled with about four hundred pages of instructions from my sister on what her daughters like and don't like, dosages for medications, if required, and apparently nap times."

"Only Hanna has a nap," Charlotte said. "Emily and me are too big for naps."

He looked at his youngest niece, her head flopped back against the chair. "What do you think the odds are of me getting her home and into bed without waking her up?" he asked Tristyn.

"Not anything that I'd wager on," she told him.

But when they got back to his condo, she guided Charlotte and Emily into the elevator while he carried Hanna. He laid her carefully on the narrow cot his sister had brought along with all their other paraphernalia, then helped Tristyn supervise while Emily and Charlotte had their baths and got ready for bed. By the time their teeth were brushed, it was almost eight o'clock—and he was ready for bed, too.

And then, as soon as the other girls were tucked in, Hanna woke up, and he got to go through the whole routine again with her. But being ready for bed didn't mean that she was ready to sleep. In fact, she seemed completely revived after her "nap" and ready to play.

"I'm thinking Charlotte was right," Tristyn told him. "She's going to be awake now until midnight."

"Lucky me." He sighed. "And the other two will probably be awake at the crack of dawn, like they were this morning."

"You should take them to the parade tomorrow," she said.

"Why?"

"Because I think they'll enjoy it, and you know the whole Garrett clan will be at the park to help you keep an eye on them afterward."

"I almost forgot tomorrow was the Fourth of July," he admitted.

"It follows the third every year," she pointed out.

He laughed softly. "That's assuming I knew today was the third. I'm not even sure what day of the week it is."

"Monday," she said, heading toward the door.

"Thanks for all of your help," he said.

"You're welcome."

"I hope canceling your date tonight wasn't a problem."

She shook her head. "I'll see him tomorrow."

That revelation surprised him. "You guys must be pretty serious if you're introducing Rafe to your family," he commented.

"He's already met my family," she said, then she frowned. "Wait a minute—I never told you his name."

"Your sister mentioned it."

"What else did she mention?"

He shrugged. "She didn't tell me how long you've been dating him...or if you're sleeping with him."

Tristyn rolled her eyes. "You really don't understand the concept of boundaries, do you?"

"I'm guessing that's a 'no,'" Josh continued. "If your relationship was at that stage, you wouldn't have bailed on him tonight."

She frowned. "What kind of logic is that?"

"The undisputable kind. Because if you were sleeping with him—and he was able to satisfy you in the bedroom—you wouldn't have let anything interfere with your plans to be with him," he said.

"Of course, the other possibility is that you *are* sleeping with him but he's lousy in bed." Then he shook his head. "But no, I can't imagine you would still be with a man who wasn't able to meet your needs."

"You do realize this whole conversation could be categorized as sexual harassment," she noted.

"Are you feeling harassed?"

No, she was feeling...aroused, she realized uneasily.

Which, she was certain, had absolutely nothing to do with Josh but was simply a result of the topic of their conversation—and the fact that she hadn't had sex in almost two years. A sexual hiatus that she'd considered ending tonight.

She wondered what it said about her relationship with Rafe that she hadn't hesitated to break their plans—that she had, perhaps, even been a little relieved to have an ex-

cuse not to take that next step right now. She liked Rafe—
she really did. He was handsome and sweet and kind, and
she always had a good time with him. But for some inexplicable reason, she wasn't eager to get naked with him.

Or maybe the reason wasn't inexplicable at all.

Maybe the reason was standing right in front of her.

She pushed that unwarranted and unwelcome thought to
the back of her mind. "I'm going home now," she told Josh.

"And if you were sleeping with him," he continued, as
if she hadn't spoken, "you'd probably be stopping by his
place on your way home to—"

"Good night, Josh." And with those final words, she
opened the door and made her escape.

Unfortunately, it wasn't as easy to escape her own
thoughts and feelings. Because the truth was, simply being
in the same room with Josh stirred her up far more than
being in Rafe's arms ever did.

Chapter Four

The Independence Parade was always the opening event of Charisma's Fourth of July celebration. Although Josh enjoyed the festivities at Arbor Park, where the processional ended, he didn't usually seek out a spot on the parade route to watch the various groups and floats go by. Of course, he didn't usually have three little girls with him, but as soon as Jordyn had mentioned the parade and fireworks at the restaurant the night before, his nieces had been clamoring to attend. On the plus side, because they were in a hurry to get out of the house, they didn't grumble too much about having sandwiches for lunch.

Shortly before one o'clock, Josh was piling the girls into his truck again because he knew that all the best viewing spots would be gone at least an hour before the parade started. It was a beautiful, clear day, which meant that the sun was in full force. Thankfully, Charlotte had reminded him about the bottle of sunscreen that her mom had packed, and he'd rubbed them all down before they left his condo and brought the bottle along to reapply as necessary. They were all wearing hats, too, but he still worried that they were likely to bake in the North Carolina sunshine.

There were some trees along the parade route, but those

coveted spots were all occupied by the time he'd parked and herded the girls toward the end of the route, where they would be closer to the park for the other festivities when the processional ended. He hadn't gone too far before he found Tristyn's other sister, Lauryn, with her husband, Ryder, and their kids, Kylie and Zachary. Lauryn and Ryder rearranged their grouping to make room for Josh and his nieces to join them. Charlotte and Emily sat on the curb with Kylie, while Zach and Hanna perched on top of the chest cooler behind them.

He saw the speculation in Lauryn's gaze as she looked at the three girls, so before she could ask, he turned to Ryder and questioned him about the restoration he'd recently completed in Watkinsville, Georgia. That topic kept the conversation going for a while, then Ryder said, "But we've got an even bigger project under construction right now."

"What's that?" he asked, at the same time Lauryn rolled her eyes at her husband.

"We were going to wait awhile before we told the whole world," she reminded him.

"Josh isn't the whole world—he's practically a Garrett," Ryder argued. "And since we've told the rest of the family—" he turned back to Josh "—he should know that we're going to have another baby."

"Congratulations," Josh said, offering his hand to the handyman.

Though technically the baby that Lauryn was expecting would be her first with Ryder, her new husband had formally adopted the children from her previous marriage on the same day he'd married her, so that they officially became a family.

Josh couldn't resist teasing Lauryn, asking, "One baby or two?"

"One," she said quickly, firmly. "I have them one at a

time. Jordyn's the overachiever—and the twin gene came from Marco's family."

"One at a time works for me," Ryder said. "Because making them is half the fun."

"Yeah, we'll see how much fun you think it is when you don't get to sleep through the night for the first three months," his wife quipped.

He snaked an arm around her waist and drew her close to his side. "You won't be doing it on your own this time," he told her.

She looked up at him, her expression filled with love and gratitude. "I know," she admitted. "But I still think your plan to fill our house with six kids is a little over the top."

"Six?" Josh echoed, stunned. Because six was twice as many as he was responsible for now, and after three days, he was beginning to doubt whether he would make it through the summer with his sanity intact.

"I think he just wants an excuse to build a really big house," Lauryn confided.

"Actually, I've been thinking about an extension—" Ryder stopped abruptly when his wife held up a hand.

"I think I hear something," she said.

"Is it starting?" Kylie asked.

"I think it might be," her mom said.

Josh could hear it now, too—the drums and pipes that indicated the approach of a band from somewhere in the distance.

"I can't see," Hanna said.

"There's nothing to see right now," he told her.

But as the parade drew nearer, so did the crowd, edging ever closer to the curb. As a result, the little ones had trouble seeing past the bigger bodies, so Ryder lifted Zachary onto his shoulders and Josh did the same—a little uneasily—with Hanna.

The firm grip his youngest niece had on his hair suggested that she was as uneasy as he was—at least in the beginning. But she giggled when the fire department squirted the hot crowd with a hose and clapped when the majorettes paused in front of them to twirl and spin.

After the parade, he thanked Lauryn and Ryder for sharing their curb space, then directed the girls toward the park—where they spent almost an hour in line to have their faces painted before they went to get ice cream. As they made their way toward a cluster of picnic tables, his gaze avidly searched the crowd for a familiar face. He saw plenty of people he knew, but not the one person he most wanted to see.

They succeeded in snagging a picnic table in the shade—a minor miracle—and Charlotte and Emily mostly managed to finish their snacks before they melted. Hanna wasn't nearly as successful, and by the time she'd given up on the soggy remnants of her cone, she was covered nose to chin with chocolate ice cream.

"Apparently you've got a lot to learn," Tristyn teased as she set her cousin Andrew's youngest daughter, Lilly, onto the bench with her ice-cream cone and offered Josh a container of wet wipes.

He hadn't seen her approach, but his initial jolt of surprise was quickly supplanted by pleasure. And the pleasure grew as his gaze skimmed over her, from the ponytail on top of her head to the skimpy tank top that molded to her curves and short shorts that highlighted her mile-long legs.

"The first rule of child care," she continued, "is never go anywhere without wet wipes."

"I'll keep that in mind," he promised, gratefully removing a disposable cloth from the container and clumsily attempting to remove the sticky residue from his niece's face and hands. He glanced up at Tristyn. "Where's your boyfriend?"

He was hoping she would object to the label, but she only said, "He's helping set up the tables."

Then, in a not-so-subtle attempt to change the topic of conversation, she turned her attention to his nieces to ask, "Did you guys see the parade?"

They responded enthusiastically and in great detail, their words spilling over one another so that he wondered how Tristyn could understand anything they were saying. As he continued to clean up Hanna, out of the corner of his eye, he saw that Emily had stood up on the bench and was wiggling around.

"What are you doing?" he asked, horror dawning along with comprehension.

"I got ice cream on my shorts," she told him, attempting to push the offending garment over her hips.

"Well, you can't just take them off," he admonished.

"But they're sticky."

The glint of amusement in Tristyn's deep green eyes had him fighting to contain his own smile.

"Let's see if I can help you get rid of the sticky," Tristyn offered, taking a wipe from the container and scrubbing at the drip on Emily's shorts.

Josh appreciated her help. He'd quickly discovered that taking care of three little girls was a lot more work than he'd anticipated—and gave him a whole new respect for his sister. He'd also realized that sharing the responsibility with someone else—with Tristyn—made it not just easier but more enjoyable. He continued to wipe ice cream from Hanna's hands and face while Tristyn cleaned Emily's shorts and Lilly sat quietly eating her ice cream.

"There you go," Tristyn told Emily.

The little girl frowned at the wet spot.

"They'll dry in just a few minutes," Josh promised, anticipating her complaint. "Probably less in this heat."

"Look, Unca Josh," Hanna implored. "Bawoons!"

He turned to follow the direction her finger was pointing and saw a couple of clowns making balloon animals
for the kids who had gathered around.

With a sigh of resignation, he returned the container
of wipes to Tristyn. "When are the fireworks?" he asked
wearily.

She laughed softly. "Not for hours and hours yet."

"Do you want to come with us to get balloon animals?"

"Sorry," she said, not sounding sorry at all. "But I promised Rachel I would bring Lilly right back after she had
her ice cream."

"I guess I'll see you later then," he said, letting Hanna
tug him away from the bench.

"No doubt," she agreed.

After the girls each had a balloon animal in hand, Josh
steered them toward the Garretts' usual picnic spot.

His best friend's family had expanded over the past
several years, as Daniel and his brothers and cousins all
got married and started families of their own. Now there
were kids ranging in age from nine months to twelve years,
and his nieces were immediately accepted into the fold.

Although Charlotte was a few years younger than Maura
and Dylan, they were letting her hang out with them; Emily
was playing on a nearby climbing structure with Kylie and
Oliver; and Hanna had apparently become new best friends
with Jacob and Zachary. The family wasn't finished expanding yet, either. Ryan's wife, Harper, was about six
weeks away from her due date and, as he'd learned a few
hours earlier, Tristyn's sister Lauryn was scheduled to add
to her family around Christmas.

In fact, looking around at the various couples and
groups, he realized that Tristyn was the only one of Daniel's cousins who wasn't yet married—and he wondered
if the guy she was with planned to change that.

Marco had introduced Josh to Rafe when he arrived,

which was how he'd learned that Tristyn's date was also
Marco's cousin and the head chef at Valentino's II.

"So you're the reason that Tristyn canceled our plans
last night," Rafe commented, as he shook Josh's hand.

"Yeah, sorry about that," he said, as Marco moved away
to help his wife set up a portable play yard for their boys.

"No need to be," the other man assured him. "She explained the situation, and I know she'd never walk away
from a friend in need of help."

Though Josh couldn't deny the accuracy of the description, it still grated on his nerves that Rafe was so dismis-
sive of the time Tristyn had spent with him. It was as if
the guy was so secure in his relationship with her, he had
no worries about his girlfriend hanging out with another
man. Admittedly, she'd been hanging out with another
man and three kids, but still.

"There you are," Tristyn said, a smile lighting her face
as she made her way toward them. And for just a second, Josh thought she was talking to him. Then she linked
her arm through Rafe's, effectively dispelling that notion.
"Your nonna's looking for you."

"And I'm hiding from her," Rafe admitted. "It's my day
off and I don't want to talk about tweaking any of my reci-
pes or any other restaurant business today."

"Then let's take a walk before dinner," she suggested,
leading him away. "I saw your aunt brought cannoli, which
means that I need to get a head start on burning off the
extra calories."

Not wanting to watch them wander off together, Josh
purposely turned in the other direction.

Josh spent some time hanging out with Daniel and
Kenna and their kids; chatted with Harper about her return to WNCC—the local television station for which she
now produced the morning show—and her plans for jug-

gling her promotion with a new baby; and congratulated Braden and Cassie on their recent engagement. All the while, he kept a close eye on his three nieces, who were more than happy with their new friends. When the food was finally set out—the selection covering most of two picnic tables—everyone dropped what they were doing to get in line. Since Josh hadn't brought anything to contribute to the potluck, he bought a couple platters of burgers and sausages from the Fireman's Picnic—another Fourth of July tradition, which brought together the local ladder companies to cook up various offerings, with the proceeds going to support the children's wing of Mercy Hospital.

"I haven't seen you eat anything," Jane Garrett said, handing him a plate piled high with a double-decker cheeseburger, potato wedges, pasta salad and baked beans.

"I wasn't going to go hungry," he assured her. "I just wanted to make sure the girls were taken care of first."

"Tristyn helped the little one with her plate, but the other two managed to take care of themselves."

"The little one's Hanna," he said. "Emily is playing with Kylie, and Charlotte is with Maura and Dylan."

Jane smiled. "They're beautiful girls."

"Those Slater genes always come out on top," he teased.

"And still, you don't have any of your own running around here."

"And still, I somehow ended up responsible for three kids," he noted wryly.

"Your sister obviously trusted you to take care of her daughters."

"My sister obviously had no other options," he countered.

His friend's mother shook her head. "Don't go selling yourself short."

He chuckled. "No one's ever accused me of doing that before."

"I've known you a lot of years," she reminded him. "And I've admittedly known you to coast if you thought you could get away with it. High school English class, for example, when you decided to watch a movie rather than read the book it was based on in order to write a report."

Josh took a bite of the burger, so that he'd be too busy chewing to be able to respond to her allegation.

"I've also known you to show an incredible amount of focus and determination when something matters to you," she continued. "The success of GSR in such a short period of time is proof of that."

He swallowed. "Thank you," he said cautiously.

"Now I'm wondering when you're going to show that same level of commitment in a personal relationship."

"You don't need to worry about me," he assured her. "I'm perfectly happy with my life just the way it is."

"I do need to worry about you," she countered. "My other boys are all married now and have wives to take care of them. You're the only holdout."

He smiled. "You do realize I'm not actually your fourth son?"

"Of course I do. And lucky for you that you're not, or the thoughts you have when you look at my youngest niece would be highly inappropriate."

He nearly choked on a potato wedge. He coughed, cleared his throat. "You think you can read my mind now?"

"I don't need to be a mind reader to recognize lust in a man's eye," she told him.

"Jesu— Jeez," he hastily amended. "I don't— I mean—" He blew out a breath. "Okay, this is incredibly awkward."

Jane just chuckled. "I've watched you watch her for years," she admitted. "And I've been wondering when you're going to stop watching and actually do something to get the girl."

"I'm not," he told her. Reminded himself.

"Why not?" she demanded.

"Because Tristyn's a keeper," he answered honestly. "And I'm not the kind of guy who's looking to keep a woman."

She smiled knowingly. "It's been my experience that most guys think they're not that kind of guy—until the right woman comes along."

Tristyn was pleased to see that Josh had brought his nieces to the Fourth of July celebration. She wasn't pleased to realize how often her attention wandered in their direction throughout the afternoon. She told herself that she was just making sure the girls were having a good time, because she could imagine how difficult it was for them to be away from everything and everyone that was familiar for the summer. But after some initial hesitation, they appeared to have found their niche with the other kids. And the truth was, she spent a lot of time watching Josh watch the girls.

"Has your friend figured out what he's going to do with his nieces for the summer?" Rafe asked, proving that he was aware of the focus of her attention.

"I don't think so," she said. "But they were only dropped on his doorstep a few days ago."

"You mentioned that when you called last night."

She tipped her head back to look at him. "I'm really sorry I bailed on you at the last minute."

"It's okay," he said. "If I had three kids dumped on me, I'd be grateful for an extra set of hands."

"If you had three kids dumped on you, your mother and nonna would both be there in a heartbeat. Josh's family is…scattered. His other sister is in London, his parents are in France—or maybe Germany. His grandparents are local, but I don't know that they'd be able to keep up with three kids."

"Then he's lucky he has you," Rafe said.

Though his tone was casual, his word choice seemed deliberately odd to her. "He doesn't *have* me," Tristyn replied.

"Are you sure about that?" he probed.

She felt her cheeks flush. "Of course I'm sure."

"Because while you're doing a pretty good job of pretending that you're not looking at him, he's not even trying to hide the fact that he's watching you," Rafe said.

"Josh is Daniel's best friend and business partner, which means he's like another cousin to me—as if I didn't already have enough," she said lightly.

"One of the things I've always liked about you is that you're forthright and honest," he told her. "So I'm going to assume that you're not being deliberately deceitful now but are in denial of his feelings and your own."

She frowned, not finding either of those options particularly appealing.

He took both her hands. "When I first met you, at Marco and Jordyn's wedding, you completely took my breath away. After I spent some time with you, I was pleased to discover that a woman so incredibly beautiful could also be warm and witty and fun. And while it's been frustrating—for both of us, I think—to try to mesh our schedules to spend time together, I always suspected that wasn't the only obstacle between us."

"Rafe," she began, not sure what else she planned to say, just certain that she didn't like the direction she could see this conversation headed.

But he didn't seem to expect her to say anything else. He only dipped his head to kiss her. On the forehead.

"I have to go to the restaurant to do the prep for tomorrow," he said.

"I thought you'd decided to stay for the fireworks and save the prep for the morning," she reminded him.

"I think I'd rather get it done tonight," he decided.

Tristyn watched him walk away, feeling guilty and remorseful—and maybe just a little bit relieved.

The girls were tuckered out long before dark, but they didn't want to leave before the fireworks. So Josh, with Hanna snuggled in his lap, settled in where he could keep an eye on Charlotte and Emily, who were sprawled on the blankets spread out on the grass for the remaining children. Several of the couples with little ones had gone: Jordyn and Marco had taken Henry and Liam home after dinner; Daniel and Kenna had followed a short while later with Jacob and Logan; and Braden and Cassie had slipped away with Saige soon after that.

There was still a sizable group remaining when darkness fell—albeit not a big enough crowd that he failed to notice that, about an hour after Tristyn disappeared with Rafe, she returned to the gathering without him. Apparently he wasn't the only one with questions about their relationship, as he caught their names mentioned in a conversation from somewhere behind him.

"So…Tristyn and Rafe," he heard Rachel say. "How long has that been going on?"

Of course, he didn't know who she was talking to until he heard Lauryn respond, "I'm not sure anything's really going on. They've only been out three times in the past three months. Four times, I guess, if you count today as a date."

Then Justin's wife, Avery, joined the conversation. "It can be hard to sustain a relationship when people are on different schedules," she noted.

"Maybe they'll figure it out," Lauryn said, though she sounded dubious. "But watching them together—there just seems to be something missing."

"There's no sizzle," Rachel decided.

"I used to think sizzle was overrated," Avery admitted. "Until I met Justin."

"Still, a relationship needs more than chemistry to work," Lauryn pointed out.

"Says the woman who got knocked up by 'America's Hottest Handyman,'" Rachel teased.

It occurred to Josh that he should move away so he wasn't eavesdropping on their conversation, but the window of opportunity for doing so had passed when Hanna fell asleep in his arms.

"I'm not saying that chemistry isn't important," Lauryn said, and though he couldn't see her face, he could hear the blush in her voice. "I just think that it's not a complete foundation for a relationship."

"But without it, there's no foundation," Avery argued.

"I like Rafe," Rachel said. "But I'm not sure he's the right guy for Tristyn."

"No one thinks he's the right guy for Tristyn, because everyone's waiting for her to hook up with Josh," Avery said matter-of-factly.

Now Josh was really wishing he'd moved away when he had had the chance. It was bad enough that Daniel's mom had picked up on his never-to-be-acted-upon attraction to her niece, but to discover that the rest of the family was aware of the chemistry between him and Tristyn was more than a little unnerving.

"I'm not sure that's ever going to happen," Rachel said in response to Avery's comment. "I mean, the guy's had plenty of time and opportunities, and he's never made a move."

There was a beep and then, "Oh, that's Justin wondering where I wandered off to," Avery said.

"I should track down Andrew before the fireworks start,

too," Rachel said. "And that looks like Ryder heading this way—no doubt looking for you."

And with that, the women went their separate ways, leaving Josh in the dark—both figuratively and literally.

Chapter Five

Since Josh hadn't yet been able to make any long-term plans for his nieces, he took them with him to the office on Wednesday. He packed up some of their DVDs with the intention of settling them in front of the TV in the conference room while he caught up on the emails and phone calls that he'd missed while he was away and couldn't seem to focus on at home with the girls running around. He also saved himself more kitchen chaos by taking the girls to The Morning Glory for breakfast rather than attempting to cook for them. Confident that they were adequately fueled and content with their movie, he settled behind his desk and got to work.

About an hour later, he got up to refill his mug of coffee from the seemingly always full carafe in the reception area and spotted an RV parked in front of the offices.

"Why is there a fifth wheel outside?" Josh asked, when Daniel walked past with a handful of papers.

"Oh, I didn't realize he was here already," his partner said, dropping the papers onto Stephanie's desk.

"Who?" Josh prompted.

"Eric Voss," Daniel said, naming the team's former

crew chief, who had retired at the end of the previous season to take care of his ailing wife.

"Is he living in his RV now?" Josh wondered.

"No. I ran into him at Arbor Park yesterday and he told me that he's thinking of selling it—or possibly renting it out for the summer. And I realized it would be a convenient way to travel with a family."

Josh swallowed a mouthful of coffee. "Are you planning on taking Kenna and the kids on the road this summer?"

"For part of it, maybe," Daniel said. "But Eric's RV is probably bigger than what we'd need. On the other hand, it would be perfect for you and the girls."

Josh immediately shook his head. "I don't think so."

"Have you figured out what you're going to do with them this summer?" his friend pressed.

"No," he admitted, watching as the side of the RV slid out to expand the interior space. "I've looked at some summer camps, but Hanna is too young for most of them and those that would be appropriate for Emily and Charlotte are already at capacity."

"We could manage without you, if you needed to take some time off," Daniel assured him.

"I know," he agreed. "But I don't see how a couple of weeks of vacation is going to alter the situation when my sister expects to be gone for eight to ten."

His business partner whistled. "That long, huh?"

"She said she would try to wrap up as quickly as possible, but she warned me that it could be the beginning of September before she's back."

"Do you really plan to sit out eight to ten weeks of the season?"

Josh understood his friend's skepticism. Although it wasn't a requirement for team owners to be at the track, he'd always considered attending races as one of the perks of the position. He loved the energy and atmosphere of race day and rarely missed an event. "I'd rather not," he admitted now.

"Then maybe you should check out the RV," his friend suggested, as their former crew chief walked into the reception area.

"Unless the RV is equipped with a full-time babysitter, I'm not sure it will solve my dilemma," Josh told him.

"I'd say it comes with everything but the kitchen sink," Eric said. "However, it *has* the kitchen sink, just no babysitter."

The retired crew chief grinned as he shook hands with each of his former employers. "Team GSR has had some good results already this season—congratulations."

"There are still a lot of races to be run," Daniel pointed out.

Eric nodded. "A lot of potential for D'Alesio to move even further up in the standings if he continues to drive the way he's been driving."

Out of the corner of his eye, Josh saw Charlotte look around as she exited the conference room, then make her way toward him. "Hanna wants to know…" Her words trailed off as she spotted the RV. "What's that?"

"It's a house on wheels," Eric responded.

Her expression was skeptical. "It doesn't look much like a house."

"Inside it does," he assured her. "Do you want to see?"

She looked from Eric to the RV and back again. "Can I?"

"Sure," he said.

"You were saying something about Hanna," Josh reminded her.

"Oh, right." She suddenly remembered. "She wants to know where the bathroom is."

"I'll be right back," Josh told the other men, then hurried to the conference room.

When Hanna was finished in the bathroom, he saw that Emily had joined the group gathered in the lobby and heard Charlotte inviting her sister to "look at the house on wheels." Although Josh had barely had a chance to get his head around his friend's suggestion of taking the girls on the road with him, he figured there was no harm in looking at the RV.

At Eric's urging, Daniel led the girls up the steps and into the living area, while Josh walked around the outside with the vehicle's owner.

"You've got a similar truck to mine," Josh commented.

The other man nodded. "You don't need anything bigger for this size RV."

"But I bet hauling an extra twelve-to-fifteen-thousand pounds would wreak havoc on my gas mileage."

Eric shook his head. "You won't get me to take that kind of sucker bet," he said. "On the other hand, the nightly rate at an RV park is a heck of a lot less than a hotel. With the added benefit of having a full kitchen to do your own cooking."

"How is doing my own cooking a benefit?" Josh wondered, as he stepped inside to check out the interior.

"Well, my wife did the cooking," Eric admitted, gesturing for Josh to check out the interior. "So it was a benefit to my wallet. And my stomach—Lainie was a helluva cook."

But Josh wasn't, and remembering the disaster of his kitchen when he'd tried to keep up with the numerous and various demands of feeding three little girls made him shudder. On the other hand, logic dictated that a disaster in a kitchen half the size of his own would also be half the size.

"Feel free to poke around," Eric said. "Open doors and drawers, sit at the dinette, bounce on the beds."

At those words, Charlotte, Emily and Hanna all glanced up.

"No," Josh said firmly, looking at each one in turn. "No bouncing on the beds."

The matching hopeful expressions on their faces instantly faded.

Eric chuckled. "Okay, I'll leave you to explore while I go into the shop to see what modifications the crew is making for the next race."

"There's more space than you would guess, once the living area and master bedroom are opened up," Daniel commented.

"But only one bathroom," Josh noted. Not that he'd expected there would be more than that, but he did wonder about the logistics of sharing limited facilities with three little girls—especially when one of them seemed to be going to the bathroom every five minutes.

"And bunk beds, Uncle Josh," Emily chimed in excitedly.

"Bunk beds, huh?"

She nodded. "Can I sleep on the top?"

"No, I want the top," Charlotte said.

"Whoa!" Josh said. "What makes you think anyone will be sleeping in here?"

"Mr. Daniel said we might get to live in this for the summer," his eldest niece told him.

Josh slanted a look at his friend.

"Might," Daniel emphasized. "I said *might.*"

"Can we, Uncle Josh?" Charlotte asked.

"Please," Emily added.

"P'ease," Hanna echoed.

"Knock knock," Tristyn said, climbing into the RV, Kenna on her heels.

Daniel's face immediately lit up at the sight of his wife. "What are you doing here?" he asked, sliding his arm around her and drawing her close for a kiss.

"I thought I'd see if I could steal my husband away for a lunch break," she told him.

"You shouldn't steal," Emily said solemnly. "Stealing's bad."

"You're right," Kenna confirmed. "Stealing is very bad. But in this case, it's just an expression."

"Okay," Emily said, but she still looked uncertain.

"Where are the boys?" Daniel asked.

"Having a teddy bear picnic with their cousins at your parents' place." She glanced around. "This looks like a fun way to travel."

Emily tugged on Tristyn's hand. "It has bunk beds," she said again.

"Wow, bunk beds are pretty cool," Tristyn acknowledged. Then, to Josh, "Are you really thinking of doing this?"

"I haven't come up with any other options," he admitted. "But I'm not sure this one is viable."

"The girls seem to like it," Daniel pointed out.

"But managing the vehicle and three kids on my own is—"

"Tristyn could come with us," Charlotte interjected.

"What?" Tristyn said, obviously taken aback by the suggestion.

"Yay!" Emily said, clapping her hands together in obvious agreement with her sister's plan.

It was Josh's immediate instinct to nix the suggestion, but no sooner had the words come out of Charlotte's mouth than the idea began to take root in his mind.

"It would certainly help to have an extra set of hands— and eyes—on three kids," he agreed.

But Tristyn was already shaking her head. "Sorry," she said to the girls. "But I have to stay here to work."

"Actually, you've often said that as long as you have

Wi-Fi, you could work almost anywhere," Daniel reminded her.

"Except that someone needs to cover reception while Stephanie is in Michigan for six weeks," she pointed out.

"My friend Laurel was supposed to teach a summer school course, but it was canceled," Kenna chimed in. "She's a huge racing fan and I know she'd love to have something to do for the summer."

Tristyn frowned. "Didn't Laurel and Ren have a…" She trailed off and glanced at the girls, obviously trying to censor her words in their presence.

"Orgy?" Emily piped up, completely *un*censored.

Kenna's brows rose; Daniel coughed to hide a chuckle.

Josh closed his eyes. "Kill me now and save my sister from doing it when she comes home and hears that word coming out of the mouth of her five-year-old."

"Where did she hear that word?" Kenna wondered.

"It was my fault," Tristyn admitted, her cheeks flushing. "And it's a bad word that I should never have used," she said, addressing Emily now. "So please don't say it again or your mommy will be very mad at me."

"Okay," Emily agreed easily. "So will you come with us?"

"I'm not sure your uncle has made any final decisions yet," she hedged, looking to Josh for help.

"Don't wait too long to decide," Daniel advised his friend. "Eric's ad just went up on craigslist this morning, and he's already had a dozen inquiries."

Josh nodded.

"Why don't we take the girls back so you and Tristyn can talk about this?" Kenna suggested, already ushering his nieces toward the exit.

"You're actually thinking about it, aren't you?" Tristyn mused when they'd gone.

"Are you thinking I'm crazy to even consider it?" he asked her.

"No," she said, wandering through the RV. "In fact, I think it's a good idea."

"Really?"

She nodded. "It will give you the opportunity to spend some quality time with them, something more than the few days you usually have a couple of times a year."

"You can't honestly think that spending the better part of the summer in a tiny house on wheels with me is the best option for three little girls."

"It's hardly tiny," she chided. "In fact, this RV is bigger than my first apartment. And actually, I do think spending the summer in this with you is the best option for your nieces."

"Really? Because just last week you referred to me as—" he tapped a finger to the dimple in his chin "—just a minute, I want to get the words exactly right. I think you said I was 'an immature and unreliable jackass.'"

"I said you were *behaving* like an immature and unreliable jackass," she acknowledged. "But I believe you have the potential to be so much more."

"Thank you for that vote of confidence," he said drily.

"And spending the summer with your nieces would prove it."

"If it doesn't drive me insane in the process."

"Eric Voss used to travel in this RV with his wife and four kids," she said, pointedly ignoring his remark.

"Okay, I'll do it," he decided. "If you come with us."

Tristyn laughed. "You can't honestly think *that's* a good idea."

"It's the only way I can imagine this working."

"Really? Because when I think about spending my summer in an RV with you, I imagine having to call my sisters to bail me out of jail after the police find your body."

He lifted a brow, his expression more amused than worried. "I don't think there's as much animosity between us as you like to pretend there is."

"We can hardly be in the same room together for ten minutes without snapping at one another."

"You spent four and a half hours with me the other night with no bloodshed," he pointed out to her.

"Because your three nieces were there to act as a buffer."

"And they'll be there every mile of the road trip."

She shook her head. "There's a huge difference between a few hours and several weeks."

He deliberately stepped in front of her. "I don't think it's the possibility of conflict that worries you," he said. "I think it's the attraction."

She snorted. "Get over yourself, Slater."

His lips curved, just a little. "I think you're the one who needs to get over me."

"I did that. A long time ago."

"Did you?" he asked softly.

"Twelve years ago," she assured him.

Twelve years ago, she'd been a senior at Hillfield Academy, eagerly getting ready for the Spring Fling, when she got the call from Mitch, her steady boyfriend of almost eighteen months. Actually, it was Mitch's mom who had called because Mitch was in bed with the stomach flu and a bucket.

Tristyn had felt bad for Mitch, and selfishly disappointed for herself. Because the senior prom was *the* biggest social event at Hillfield Academy and she'd been looking forward to this day since her freshman year. To miss it would be unthinkable. To show up without a date only slightly less mortifying.

Enter Josh Slater—best friend of her cousin Daniel—who rode to her rescue like the proverbial white knight. Josh had also graduated from Hillfield, where he'd been an honor roll student and quarterback of the varsity football team in his junior and senior years. He'd been one of the popular kids—genuinely liked by all the guys and wanted by all the girls. So when Tristyn Garrett showed up to her senior prom on the arm of Josh Slater, there were whispers. She told everyone that she and Josh were just friends, but sometime during that night, she was the one who forgot that basic fact.

She'd been seventeen years old—a naive and hopeless romantic who had, over the course of several months, built the night up in her mind to be something truly special. And when Josh asked her to dance, her knees had trembled. When he'd taken her in his arms, her breasts had tingled. At twenty, his lean, youthful frame had started to fill out, setting him apart as a man in a room filled with boys. They'd danced a few more times throughout the evening, and then they'd walked hand in hand in the moonlight.

When he finally took her home at the end of the night, she'd tipped her head back to look at him, silently urging him to kiss her. His gaze had dropped to her lips, lingered. But when he made no move to breach that distance, she'd decided that she would—and nearly fell off the porch when he took a deliberate step back and walked away from her.

She pushed the humiliating memory to the back of her mind.

"Then spending a few weeks in a motor home with me and my nieces shouldn't be a problem for you." His statement drew her attention back to the present—and the present dilemma.

"You're just trying to get a free babysitter," she accused.

"Not at all," he denied. "I'm acknowledging that I'm

going to need help with the kids—and I'm willing to pay for your help."

She was annoyed that he would offer, because then she couldn't be mad at him for trying to take advantage of her. And because she would never accept money for doing a favor for a friend. Which was the trump card he played next.

"You also said," he continued, "that I should reach out to my friends for help."

"And you questioned whether we were, in fact, friends," she reminded him.

"That was before you came through for me the other night."

"I didn't really do anything," she pointed out.

"You canceled your date to help me out. Or is that the real reason for your hesitation now?" he asked. "Are you worried that Rafe will disapprove?"

She shook her head. No, far more worrying to Tristyn was the fact that she hadn't once considered how the other man might respond when he learned of her plans. Even if her relationship status with Rafe was unclear, she should have at least considered how he might feel. "I can't imagine why he would have any objections," she finally said.

"Can't you?" Josh asked. "Because I promise that if I was dating you, I wouldn't be happy to hear that you were making plans to spend the better part of the summer in the company of another man."

"Well, you're not dating me, and Rafe isn't you."

"Does that mean you'll come with us?"

She stood in the middle of the living area and looked around, then slowly nodded. "On one condition."

"Anything," he promised.

"I get the master bedroom."

Chapter Six

"Anything but that," Josh said in response to Tristyn's suggestion.

"That's my only condition," she said. "And it's non-negotiable."

"Why should you get the bedroom?" he challenged.

"Because I'm doing you a favor," she reminded him.

"You can do me another one by giving me the bed."

She shook her head. "I don't think so."

"Come on, Tris—I'm about a foot taller than you."

She lifted her gaze from his chin, which was at her eye level, to meet his. "If you think that's a foot, then your concept of six inches is probably equally exaggerated."

He narrowed his gaze. "Let's just agree that I'm a lot taller than you."

"And that sofa bed is probably seventy-six inches long when it's opened up."

"And not even the width of a double bed."

"Since you won't be entertaining any female friends while you're taking care of your nieces, I'm sure that won't be a problem."

"Okay, I have another idea," he told her.

"No."

"You haven't even heard my idea."

"I don't need to hear it," she said.

"A king-size bed is the equivalent of two double beds," he pointed out. "So two people sharing a king is almost the same as each of them having a double."

"No," she said again.

"Let's be logical about this," he urged. "Since I'm the only male, it will afford everyone more privacy if my sleeping area is separate and apart from all of the females."

"You want logical? Consider this—I get the bedroom or I stay home," she said.

He sighed. "I guess you get the bedroom."

Because in the brief time that she'd been around his nieces, he'd finally grasped how much he needed her. Not just because she was a woman, but because she had a lot more experience with kids than he did. She was "Auntie Tristyn" not only to her sisters' kids but to the offspring of her numerous cousins, and she was obviously comfortable surrounded by little ones of all ages—as she inevitably was whenever the Garrett family gathered.

He still had reservations about the trip—he'd have to be crazy not to—but he was confident Charlotte, Emily and Hanna would enjoy the experience a lot more with Tristyn around. Unfortunately, he didn't expect to enjoy the experience at all. Because he knew that being with Tristyn 24/7 would be more than a challenge—it would require him to continue to ignore his true feelings for her.

On the plus side, he had a lot of practice with that—he'd been doing it for twelve years already.

When Tristyn got home from work that afternoon, she called her sisters and invited them to come over. Because Marco was at Valentino's, Jordyn brought the twins with her, and Lauryn brought Kylie and Zachary, too, so the kids could all "play" together. Not that Henry and Liam did much playing yet, but Kylie certainly liked playing "mommy" to the little ones.

When the children were settled with their toys and the adults with their wine—except for Lauryn, who was drinking herbal tea—Tristyn said, "I need some advice."

"About what?" her oldest sister asked.

"Something I agreed to do that now I'm thinking I shouldn't have."

"Sounds intriguing," Jordyn said. "What did you agree to do?"

"Help Josh look after his nieces for the summer."

"That doesn't sound like any cause for concern," Jordyn said.

"You're great with kids," Lauryn pointed out. "And it was apparent at the Fourth of July picnic that Josh's nieces are already taken with you."

"It's not the kids I'm worried about," Tristyn admitted.

"Ahh." Jordyn nodded. "Now we're getting somewhere."

"And the first somewhere is Kentucky."

"Now you've lost me," Lauryn admitted.

"We're going to spend the next few weeks—or eight to ten—on the road together in an RV."

Jordyn's lips curved. "Now this is getting *really* interesting. You and Josh…in close proximity to a bedroom."

"Me and Josh *and* the three girls."

"Who are—if I remember correctly—about seven, five and three?" Lauryn said.

She nodded.

"So I wouldn't count on them being very effective chaperones," her oldest sister warned. "Even Charlotte will probably be lights out by eight o'clock and asleep by nine. Which means that you and Josh will have to find something else to occupy your time together during those evening hours."

"Have you both forgotten that I've been dating Rafe?"

Jordyn snorted. "You talked about dating more than you actually did."

"Although it would be courteous to tell him that you're shacking up with another man for the next couple of months," Lauryn suggested.

"I'm not shacking up with anyone," Tristyn retorted. "And Rafe—" she blew out a breath "—he left the picnic early last night because of Josh. He said it was because he had prep to do at the restaurant, but it was right after he decided that Josh was an obstacle to our relationship."

"Obviously he's more intuitive than most guys," Lauryn noted.

"And he's right," Jordyn said. "You've been with Rafe for three months and you still haven't slept with him."

"We only managed to sync our schedules for three dates in those three months," Tristyn reminded her sisters. "And how do you know I haven't slept with him?"

"There's not a sense of intimacy between you."

She frowned. "What does that even mean?"

"She's talking about the casual, easy touches and shared glances that communicate without a word being spoken," Lauryn explained.

"Anyway, I do think this trip could be a good opportunity for you," Jordyn said.

"An opportunity for what?" Tristyn asked warily.

"To finally get over your teenage crush on Josh."

"I stopped being a teenager a lot of years ago," she reminded her sisters.

"That doesn't mean you ever resolved your feelings for him," Lauryn pointed out.

"Trust me, those feelings were resolved," Tristyn said firmly.

She didn't know if her sisters believed her claim, because as confident as she'd tried to sound, she wasn't sure she believed it herself.

* * *

Josh offered to do the grocery shopping, to stock up the RV, while Tristyn stayed with the girls. She declined the offer, because although she suspected that dragging three kids around the grocery store wasn't likely to be fun for any of them, she wanted to ensure that he purchased foods and snacks that his nieces would actually eat.

Tristyn didn't usually do major shopping. She tended to pick up a few things here and there, because as much as she liked to cook, she never knew what she wanted to eat from one day to the next. Obviously cooking for three kids—and Josh—was going to require a little more planning.

When she'd asked the girls what they liked to eat, she got the usual responses: chicken fingers, macaroni and cheese, and hot dogs. When she asked specifically about vegetables, she learned that Charlotte liked corn and carrots but not peas; Emily liked broccoli and carrots but not corn; Hanna hated anything yellow but would eat almost anything else. Fruit was more of the same. Charlotte liked red grapes and bananas; Emily liked apples, but only if they were cut into wedges, and oranges; Hanna liked grapes, bananas—because apparently the ban on yellow applied only to vegetables—and apples. But they hit the jackpot in the freezer aisle when they discovered that the girls unanimously loved ice cream and ice-cream sandwiches.

The cashier—Nikki, according to her employee ID tag—looked from Josh to the three girls and back again. "I haven't seen you in a while," she said. "But I didn't think it had been *that* long."

He looked at her blankly.

"Nikki Bishop," she told him. "You dated my sister, Katie, a few years back."

He nodded, as if he suddenly remembered. And maybe he did. On the other hand, Josh had dated so many women,

Tristyn suspected he had trouble keeping all their names straight. "And the kids aren't mine," he explained. "They're my sister's."

"They're pretty girls," the woman remarked, as she began to scan and bag the groceries.

He nodded again but said nothing to explain Tristyn's presence.

"I'm the babysitter," she piped up, continuing to transfer the contents of the cart to the conveyor belt. "So if you wanted to write your number on the receipt for him, I'm not going to be offended."

Nikki looked at Josh again, a speculative gleam in her eye.

Tristyn held back a smile as Josh slid her a look.

"Although the reason I'm buying all these groceries is that I'm heading out of town on a road trip," he explained to Nikki. "I'll be gone most of the summer."

She processed his payment, then tore the register receipt off and scrawled on the back of it. "Since I have no plans to move out of town, you can give me a call whenever you get back."

"Thanks," Josh said, taking the receipt and stuffing it into the last bag.

When they got back to his condo, the girls went into the living room to play Candyland—one of the many games their mother had sent to keep them busy while they were at Uncle Josh's—and Tristyn helped Josh unpack the groceries.

"Whoops! I almost threw this away," she said, folding the receipt and tucking it under the edge of his coffeemaker so that Nikki's name and phone number were prominently displayed.

Josh grabbed the piece of paper and crumpled it in his fist, then dropped it into the garbage can under the sink.

Tristyn tsked. "Eventually you'll make your way through the legions of women who line up at your door and might need that number," she warned.

He didn't respond to her provocative comment.

"Such are the charms of Josh Slater that not even the presence of three children dissuades the ladies," she mused, unable to resist needling him a little more.

"I thought, when you agreed to come on this trip, it was a sign that you had my back," he grumbled.

"I do," Tristyn assured him.

"Then why did you just throw me to the wolves?"

"That pretty little blonde didn't look anything like a wolf," she argued. "More like a…bunny."

"If bunnies were bloodthirsty predators," he grumbled as he began packing dry goods into the boxes they would be taking in the RV. "Why did you tell her that you're the babysitter?"

"Isn't that what I am?" she queried. "Besides, I didn't want to interfere in any way, shape or form with your romantic prospects."

"No worries," he said, shaking his head. "She's not my type."

"You have a type?"

"As a matter of fact, I do."

"Let me guess…female, naked and willing?"

"And *not* seventeen," he told her.

Her gaze narrowed in response to the direct hit.

"But you're not seventeen anymore, are you, Tris?" he asked, his tone speculative now.

"No, I'm not," she acknowledged. "And you lost your chance to take advantage of an infatuated schoolgirl a long time ago."

"Because it would have been taking advantage," he acknowledged. "But now we're both adults, standing on equal ground."

"Now we need to stop standing around and get the ice-cream sandwiches in the freezer before they melt."

"You keep insisting that you're over what happened that night, but you refuse to talk to me about it."

"There's nothing to talk about. *Nothing* happened."

"And you still haven't forgiven me for that," he noted.

She opened the refrigerator door and began putting the fruits and vegetables away.

Josh found the ice-cream sandwiches, tossed the box in the freezer, then closed the door and turned back to her. "You were seventeen," he said again. "And you had a boyfriend. Remember? That's why I ended up taking you to the prom—because your boyfriend was sick."

"I remember," she said tightly. "And I don't really think this is the appropriate time or place to take this conversation any further."

"You might be right," he admitted. "But in twelve years, you haven't been willing to talk about it…"

"It was my prom, I tried to kiss you good-night, you weren't interested," she acknowledged. "End of story."

"You had a boyfriend," he said again.

"And you've *never* kissed a girl who had a boyfriend?"

"Not if I knew about the boyfriend."

"Really?" she asked skeptically.

"Really," he confirmed. "But even if you didn't have a boyfriend—even if you'd needed a date that night because you'd broken up with him—I wouldn't have kissed you."

"Thanks for that clarification."

"Not because I didn't want to," he told her. "But because I couldn't be sure that I'd be able to stop after one kiss."

"I would have stopped you after one kiss," she assured him.

"Would you?" he asked softly. "Maybe you don't remember the way you looked at me that night, but I do. You were young and beautiful and curious. I could see it in your eyes—the way you looked at me when we walked along the path under the magnolia trees—the wanting and the wondering. And there was no way in hell I was going to be the man who took your innocence."

Except that he had taken a part of it. Even without touching her body, he'd taken the innocence of Tristyn's heart.

It was almost midnight by the time Tristyn finished packing. Though her body was exhausted when she fell into bed, she couldn't sleep. She couldn't stop thinking about what Josh had said about the night of her prom.

He was right about her feelings. She *had* wanted him. But only because she'd allowed herself to get caught up in the romantic ambience of the evening. And Josh had been so incredibly handsome in his tux.

When she saw him standing in the foyer of her parents' home, waiting for her with a corsage box in his hand, her heart had fluttered wildly inside her chest. She'd had to hold on to the railing as she descended the stairs, because her knees were trembling so much she was afraid they would buckle.

Her stomach had been so tied up in knots, she'd barely been able to eat. And when his thigh inadvertently brushed against hers beneath the table, heat had rushed through her veins. She'd been relieved when their plates were taken away and the DJ took the stage. But dancing with Josh had been another new and incredible experience. She'd danced with other boys, of course, but Josh was no longer a boy. And being held close to his body had stirred her own in ways she'd never before imagined.

If he'd kissed her beneath those magnolia trees—and oh, how she'd wanted him to kiss her beneath those magnolia trees—she might have suggested that they go for a drive instead of him taking her directly home.

But he hadn't kissed her then—or later.

And it wasn't just the recollection of that night that kept her awake—it was the memory of the way he'd looked at her tonight. That night, his rejection had been sharp and brutal, cruelly cutting. His eyes had been cold, leaving her with absolutely no doubt that he didn't want any of what she was offering. Tonight, there had been nothing but heat.

Maybe she was tempted. Maybe there was a part of her that still wondered what it would be like to be kissed by Josh, touched by Josh, loved by Josh.

That part wasn't invited on their road trip, she decided.

Instead, she would be the babysitter that she'd told Nikki she was. She would focus on the girls to the exclusion of all else. She would not succumb to Josh's considerable charms, and she definitely wouldn't give him an opportunity to reject her again.

Chapter Seven

It turned out that Josh's plan to be on the road by 10:00 a.m. was a little optimistic. By the time the girls were all dressed and had eaten breakfast—he made a mental note to ensure they ate *before* getting dressed in the future, since Hanna required a complete change of clothes after spilling juice down her front, and Charlotte needed a new shirt because she leaned over her plate as she reached for the bottle of syrup—it was almost that time already.

Tristyn showed up at nine forty-five, fresh and well rested and so beautiful it made him ache just to look at her. She quickly surveyed the situation and took charge of the chaos, instructing Josh to finish packing the RV while she cleaned up. As a result, they were only half an hour late pulling away from his building.

They'd been driving for just over an hour when Emily suddenly put down the beginner book she'd been reading and said, "I don't feel so good, Uncle Josh."

"What's the matter, Em?"

"My tummy feels icky."

"We're going to be stopping in about thirty miles," he told her.

"It hurts now," she insisted.

"Well, there's nowhere for me to stop right now, so you'll just have to wait."

"But—"

Tristyn, quickly assessing the situation, dumped the snacks and juice boxes out of the small cooler at her feet and shoved it into the backseat—just as Emily threw up her breakfast. Mostly into the cooler.

"Eww!" Charlotte said. "She barfed on the back of your seat, Uncle Josh."

"Eww!" Hanna echoed.

Emily started to cry.

"It's okay," Tristyn soothed, reaching back to rub the girl's knee. "As soon as Uncle Josh can pull over, we'll get it cleaned up."

"Lucky I've got leather," he muttered.

"It stinks," Charlotte grumbled.

Josh didn't disagree.

Tristyn uncapped a bottle of water and passed it back to Emily. "Small sips," she instructed.

It seemed to take forever to travel those thirty miles to the next rest stop. Tristyn opened Emily's window in the hope that the flow of air would help her feel better, but his middle niece continued to cry softly, Charlotte complained that there was too much noise with the window open and Hanna kept kicking the side of his seat.

When he finally pulled over, Tristyn found a change of clothes for Emily and took her into the restroom to wash up.

"Emily always gets carsick," Charlotte said, as Josh attempted to clean the now-dried spots of vomit off the back of his seat with the wet wipes he'd stocked up on, pursuant to Tristyn's advice on the Fourth of July.

He continued to scrub the leather. "And you didn't think to tell me this earlier?"

His eldest niece shrugged. "I didn't think about it earlier, but it's probably in the book."

When he finally got the last remnants of vomit cleaned up, he pulled out the damn book his eldest niece kept referencing. Sure enough, it was noted that Emily had a tendency toward motion sickness when she was in a car for an extended period of time and recommended that she be seated in the middle of the backseat with an unobstructed view out the front windshield.

"'If planning any extended trips, be sure to give her children's Dramamine beforehand,'" he read aloud.

Charlotte nodded approvingly. "I told you it would be in the book."

There was also a parenthetical reference to the fact that Emily had no problem with roller coasters, probably because the air flow that accompanied the motion ensured that she didn't feel nauseated.

When Tristyn came back with Emily, he crossed his fingers and went into the convenience store attached to the fast-food options and restrooms. Perhaps car sickness was more common than he suspected, because he found what he was looking for on a shelf with Tylenol, cough syrup and Band-Aids.

"I got the Dramamine," he told Emily, triumphantly holding up the box for her inspection.

But she shook her head. "That's not the medicine Mommy gives me."

"It's in the book," he told her, since the girls seemed to believe all the important information had been duly noted in the book.

Emily shook her head again. "The one Mommy gives me is purple."

"And it says 'children' on the label," Charlotte offered.

"They didn't have one specifically for children," Josh explained. "They only had this one, but it says right on the label, 'for children two-to-six, give half of a chew-able tablet.'"

"I like purple," Emily said.

"When we get to a town with a real pharmacy, we'll try to find the purple one," he promised. "But right now, I need you to eat the orange one."

Emily still looked wary, but she took the half tablet from his hand and put it on her tongue. As soon as her taste buds registered the unfamiliar flavor, she spat it out on the ground. "I don't like it."

"I'm sorry that you don't like it," Tristyn said gently. "But you have to take it so that your tummy won't feel icky while we're riding in the truck."

The little girl's eyes filled with tears. "I don't wanna take it."

Desperate to figure out a solution to the dilemma and get back on the road, Josh asked, "What's your favorite treat?"

Emily blinked, seeming surprised by—and perhaps a little wary of—the abrupt change of topic. "What?"

"If your mom lets you pick a favorite treat, what would you choose?" he prompted.

"Skittles."

"Gummy bears," Hanna chimed in.

"What do you like?" he asked Charlotte.

"Kit Kat."

"Okay—let's make a deal," he suggested. "I'll go back into the store to get some Skittles, gummy bears and a Kit Kat bar if Emily chews and swallows the other half of the pill."

"Maybe you should get the Skittles first," Emily bargained, after considering his plan. "Then I can put the candy in my mouth right away to get rid of the taste of the medicine."

"Alright," he relented. "I'll go get the candy first."

When Emily had finally taken the medicine and the kids were settled back in the truck with their candy—Emily in the middle seat now, as per his sister's suggestion—he glanced over at Tristyn and saw her looking at him.

"You just bribed a five-year-old," she commented.

"And you disapprove," he guessed.

"Actually I don't," she said. "In fact, I'm impressed with your quick thinking."

He shrugged as he pulled back out onto the highway. "Isn't there some saying about sugar helping the medicine go down?"

"Look at you—quoting Mary Poppins," she teased. "Although the recommended dosage is a spoonful and I don't want to think about how many spoonfuls of sugar are in that candy."

"The candy got the job done," he pointed out. "Now, fingers crossed, we won't have any more mishaps between here and Sparta."

"Fingers crossed," she agreed.

The Dramamine didn't just help settle Emily's tummy, it made her sleepy. Before they'd driven another half hour, she was conked out. A short while later, Hanna was asleep, too. Charlotte, on the other hand, was wide-awake and growing increasingly impatient with the journey. Her steady and repeated requests of "How much longer?" had Josh clenching his jaw and his hands strangling the steering wheel. Still, he answered patiently every time. Tristyn tried to distract her with word games and stories, but Charlotte was nothing if not focused.

Then Hanna woke up and had to go to the bathroom. Again, they were nowhere near a rest stop and Josh's entreaties for her to "hold it just a little longer" were met by Hanna's increasingly frantic assertions that she had to go "now." He finally gave up on making it to a rest stop and pulled onto the shoulder of the highway so that she could use the toilet in the RV, but by then, it was too late. So Tristyn found a change of clothes for Hanna and put her dirty clothes in the bag with Emily's.

"Looks like our plan for once-a-week laundry is going to need to be tweaked," she commented.

Josh nodded as he pulled the vehicle back onto the road. "I'm thinking a lot of this plan needs tweaking—if not outright scrapping."

"It's only day one," she said.

"Are you trying to reassure or discourage me?"

"There's always a steep learning curve with kids."

"Maybe too steep," he said.

"And you should be prepared for the possibility that they'll test you a little bit," she warned.

"Are you saying that the last few hours haven't been a test?"

She shook her head. "Not a deliberate one, anyway," she clarified. "Motion sickness and bladder limits are just facts of life."

"Facts I never considered before I agreed to make this trip," he admitted.

When he finally saw the sign for Halliday RV Park & Campground, he wanted to exhale a grateful sigh of relief—but he knew there was a lot of work still to be done. First he had to check in, then follow the map he was given to their allocated hookup spot, which was partly shaded by a stand of evergreen trees and had its own picnic table and fire pit.

"I didn't think we were ever going to make it," Josh said, when he'd finally parked the vehicle.

"We probably should have done today's trip over two days," she acknowledged. "But then we wouldn't have made it in time for the race."

"We're here now," he said.

"Finally," Charlotte said emphatically.

"I saw on the map that there are toilets and shower facilities over by the playground and pool," Tristyn told him. "Why don't I take the girls there to wash up while you take care of the hookup?"

It wasn't a quick process, but by the time Tristyn got back with the girls, he was done and ready to put his feet up and relax with a cold beer. But apparently that wasn't an option. As she explained, the girls had been cooped up in the truck for hours and needed to burn off some energy, so she gave him the choice of taking them to explore the campground or make dinner while she went exploring with them. They both knew there wasn't a choice to be made, since Josh was a pretty lousy cook.

Tristyn made spaghetti for dinner, because it was easy and all the kids liked pasta. Of course, Charlotte wanted meatballs, Emily wanted meat sauce and Hanna didn't want any sauce. She served the spaghetti with a garden salad and garlic bread. Charlotte picked the cucumbers out of her salad, Emily pushed aside the cherry tomatoes and Hanna ate only the cucumbers and tomatoes. Josh, at least, cleared his plate—and a second.

They'd made a deal that Tristyn would do the cooking and Josh would take care of the cleanup, but since he'd spent most of the day driving, she volunteered to handle his chores—just this once. He suggested that one of them could wash and the other dry, but she immediately nixed that idea. The kitchen, though beautifully designed and well-equipped, was still small—too small for two adults to navigate without bumping into one another.

By the time she'd finished, it was nearly eight o'clock. Josh reported that both Hanna and Emily were almost asleep in their respective bunks, while Charlotte was settled into hers with a reading light and a book, but even she was struggling to keep her eyes open. Tristyn folded the dish towel over the handle of the oven and went to say good-night to the girls.

When she returned to the kitchen, she saw that Josh had opened a bottle of wine and poured two glasses. He held one out to her. Tristyn eyed the offering warily.

"I haven't poisoned it," he assured her. "If nothing else, today's adventures confirmed that there is no way I'd be able to do this without you."

"If that's a thank-you, you're welcome," she said.

"To the conclusion of day one," he said, and touched the rim of his glass to hers.

"And the power of Dramamine," Tristyn added.

Josh sipped his wine. "I just wish Charlotte had thought to mention the car sickness thing before we left Charisma this morning."

"She's seven," she reminded him. "She didn't withhold the information on purpose—she probably didn't even think about it until Emily said that her tummy hurt."

"Well, I'll definitely find a pharmacy and get some of the children's Dramamine before we have to hit the road again."

"Or at least another bag of Skittles," she said.

"Why don't we go outside so our conversation doesn't keep the girls awake?" Josh suggested.

She nodded and followed him, closing the door quietly behind her.

They sat side by side on the top of the picnic table, with their feet on the bench. It was the height of tourist season and the camp was almost filled to capacity, so there were plenty of other people around—some sitting around fires, roasting marshmallows and singing camp songs. But though it wasn't quiet, it was peaceful, and the display of stars winking against the black night was absolutely breathtaking.

Except that Josh was having trouble focusing on the

stars in the sky with Tristyn sitting so close, her enticing feminine scent clouding his brain and stirring other parts of his body.

"Can you see the Big Dipper?" she asked.

He tipped his head back to search for the constellation, then nodded.

"Do you see anything else you recognize?" she asked him.

"Orion's Belt," he suggested. Although he didn't know much more than that it was a line of three stars, there were so many stars he figured those three had to be up there somewhere.

But Tristyn shook her head. "You can only see Orion's Belt in the northern hemisphere between November and February."

"How do you know so much about the constellations?" he asked her.

"I took a few courses in astronomy and astrology in college, just for fun."

His idea of fun at college had obviously been a lot different than hers, and he suspected that mentioning that now would destroy the tentative peace they'd established. "What else do you see?" he asked instead.

"The Little Dipper, with Polaris at the tip of the handle. Then there's Cassiopeia, Cepheus and Draco—all circumpolar constellations."

"How do I know you're not just making all these names up?"

She laughed softly. "I guess you don't," she admitted. "But you don't need to know the names of the constellations or what stars they're comprised of to appreciate the view."

"You're right about that," he agreed, watching her watch the sky.

I've been wondering when you're going to stop watch-

ing and actually do something to get the girl. The echo of Jane Garrett's words both taunted and tempted him. But making a move on his best friend's cousin would be crazy. Especially as Tristyn was the type of woman a man could really fall for—and Josh had no intention of falling.

She lifted her glass to her lips and sipped her wine. "I know this view isn't all that different from my backyard at home," she admitted, "but it feels like a different world—to be surrounded by nature instead of the city."

"I'm really glad Charlotte suggested that you come with us," he confided.

"It's only day one," she reminded him.

"True," he said. Then, after another minute had passed, "I have to admit that I've been wondering about something."

"What's that?"

"Why you agreed to this trip."

"I've been wondering the same thing myself," she acknowledged.

"It could be that you couldn't resist the opportunity to spend some time with me."

"I spend more time with you than I want to at GSR," she noted.

"But we're rarely alone at the office," he pointed out.

"And we're not alone now."

"For all intents and purposes we are."

"I'm not interested in your intents or purposes," she said.

"You're interested," he said. "You're just pretending not to be."

"You're delusional," she countered.

"What did Rafe say when you told him you were coming on this trip with me? Or didn't you tell him?"

"I told you, I'm not discussing my relationship with Rafe with you."

"But a few dates isn't really a relationship, is it?"

"What do you know about relationships?" she challenged.

"Not a lot," he admitted. "In fact, probably about as much as I know about kids."

"You did okay today."

He shook his head. "I couldn't even get them out of the condo without your help this morning."

"You were managing," she said generously. "You were just a little behind schedule."

"And you managed to get us back on schedule—or very near," he noted.

"Aren't my organizational skills one of the reasons you and Daniel hired me at GSR?"

"They're why Daniel wanted to hire you," Josh admitted. "I added my vote because I like the way you look."

She shook her head, but she was smiling a little.

"Seriously, though, you handled Emily like a pro today. I was happier cleaning up puke than trying to soothe a distressed little girl."

"I've got a lot of experience soothing distressed kids," she reminded him.

"The number of little Garretts running around seems to increase at every holiday," he agreed.

She nodded. "There were fourteen at the Fourth of July celebration," she told him. "Harper and Ryan's baby will be number fifteen, and Lauryn and Ryder's will be sixteen. My cousins in Pinehurst have eight more between them, but they don't visit very often."

"Do you have any thoughts of adding to that number?" he asked.

"Someday," she said lightly. "I'd never thought of marriage and motherhood as life goals—there were so many other things I wanted to see and do. But recently, I've started to see the appeal of sharing my life with someone."

"Do you think Rafe is that someone?"

"You don't take a hint, do you?"

"I'm just curious if he's the type of guy you see yourself settling down with someday."

"I don't know," she admitted. "He's a really great guy—and a fabulous cook."

"But?" Josh prompted.

She shrugged. "Maybe there is no 'but.' Maybe he's perfect for me and we'll get married and have half a dozen kids and live happily-ever-after."

"There is a 'but,'" he insisted. "If you really believed Rafe was perfect, you wouldn't be here with me now."

"I'm not *with* you," she argued.

"And the 'but' is chemistry," he continued, as if she hadn't spoken.

"What?"

"There's no chemistry between you and Rafe."

She frowned. "How can you make a statement like that?"

"Because I saw the two of you together."

"For all of about five minutes," she pointed out.

"And it was obvious to me in the first two of those five minutes," he told her. "And confirmed when he left the picnic and you stayed to watch the fireworks with your sisters."

"The fireworks are the best part of the Fourth of July."

"If you and Rafe had chemistry, you would have been happy to make your own fireworks."

She shook her head. "Not everything has to be about sex."

"Maybe not," he allowed. "But I don't see that there's much hope for the future of a relationship if you don't want to get naked with your partner."

"Forgive me if I choose not to take relationship advice

from a man who's never had a relationship that lasted more than a few weeks."

"Maybe I haven't had a long-term relationship," he acknowledged. "But I've had a lot of great sex along the way."

She stood up, shaking her head. "You truly are a Neanderthal."

"Anytime you want me to drag you back to my cave to show you what you're missing, just let me know."

"A charming invitation, to be sure," she said drily, "but I think I'll pass."

He shrugged. "Your call."

She turned and walked back into the RV without even saying good-night.

He couldn't blame her for being annoyed with him—not when he'd deliberately antagonized her. But it had been a matter of self-preservation. Sitting under the stars and chatting about family and future plans with a woman should have sent him into a panic. Instead, because that woman was Tristyn, it had felt comfortable and easy.

And feeling comfortable and easy about those kinds of things could lead a man down a dangerous path.

Chapter Eight

"It's not right," Josh grumbled from beneath the pillow he'd pulled over his face, "that the person with a private bedroom should get to invade the public space where someone else is sleeping."

"Wake up, Grumpy Bear," Tristyn said.

"Grumpy Bear?"

"It's what Lauryn calls Zachary when he's in a mood."

"I'm not in a mood," he denied . "Unless sleeping is a mood. In which case, I'm definitely in a sleeping mood, and you're ruining that mood by banging around in the kitchen."

"I made coffee," she said.

He reluctantly moved the pillow aside and sat up to take the proffered mug. He sipped the strong, hot brew and blinked, attempting to focus. "What the hell are you wearing?"

"They're called pajamas," she said drily.

His gaze skimmed over her—from the notched collar of the long-sleeved, button-front shirt to the matching full-length pants. Aside from the fact that they were pink with a subtle white stripe, they looked more like a man's pajamas. Or an old lady's. "You sleep in granny jammies?"

She frowned. "These aren't granny jammies."

"They are so granny jammies." He lifted the mug to his lips again.

"Well, I thought—since I would be sleeping in close proximity to three impressionable young girls—that I should wear something…modest." She returned to the stove and dropped a slice of egg-soaked bread into one of two pans already on the burners.

Now that the first jolt of caffeine had hit his brain, he could hear sizzling. He sniffed the air and sighed happily. "Where are the girls?"

"They were up early, so I let them go into my room to watch the TV there so they wouldn't wake you."

"Then you came in here to bang around in the kitchen and do that yourself," he noted, shoving back the covers.

"I'm making breakfast," she pointed out. "If that's too noisy for you, I'll let you go hungry tomorrow."

"The scent of bacon is making me forget my annoyance," he admitted, moving to the pot to refill his mug of coffee. "But not my curiosity."

She flipped the bread in the pan. "I'm sure I'm going to regret asking, but what are you curious about?"

"What you usually wear to bed," he admitted.

"Not granny jammies," she told him.

He swallowed another mouthful of coffee, and though he knew it was a dangerous road for his mind to travel, he couldn't resist. He leaned closer and dropped his voice to a seductive whisper, "What do you prefer to sleep in? Whisper-thin silk? Peekaboo lace? Maybe a cute little baby doll with a ruffled hem that barely covers your—"

"No," she interjected firmly, pointing at him with the spatula in her hand.

"No baby doll?" he pressed.

"No to all of the above."

Which didn't, as far as he could see, leave any other options. "Ha! You do sleep in granny jammies."

She shook her head as she added the slice of French toast to a platter warming in the oven, then dipped another slice of bread in the egg mixture before transferring it to the pan. Finally she turned to face him. "Do you really want to know?"

"Yes, I really want to know."

"Nothing."

"Nothing," he echoed, his brain not comprehending—or maybe not wanting to comprehend—her response.

Her lips curved, just a little. "I usually sleep in the nude."

It wasn't often that Tristyn had the pleasure of seeing Josh Slater at a loss for words, but he was apparently speechless now. She read the shock in his eyes—and maybe a hint of arousal, too, and decided to play with him a little.

"I like nice clothes," she said, lifting the bacon out of the pan and setting it on paper towels to drain the grease. "But after wearing them for ten or twelve hours, it feels good to finally strip them away and slide naked between the sheets. There's nothing like the sensation of Egyptian cotton against my body."

She hummed with pleasure as she added two more slices of toast to the stack in the oven. "Except maybe the touch of a man…the slide of strong hands over my silky skin… lingering in all the right places."

"I would suggest you not casually throw around mention of your lovers," he warned.

"Why not?"

"Because I might be tempted to take you to my bed and make you forget the names of everyone else you've ever been with."

"And here I thought there wasn't anything about me that ever tempted you," she mused.

"You could tempt a saint," he told her. "And we both know that's one thing I'm not."

"Then I guess I have nothing to worry about."

He reached past her to snag a piece of bacon. "You're feeling pretty brave this morning—after running away last night," he remarked.

"I didn't run away," she denied. "I was tired."

"You were scared."

"You don't scare me, Josh."

"I know—it's your own feelings that you're afraid of."

"You might be right," she acknowledged, her tone a seductive whisper that awakened his body more effectively than the caffeine he'd consumed.

"In fact, there are times—" she looked up at him, then dropped her gaze, deliberately fluttered her lashes "—I'm not sure I can control the overwhelming urge—" she fluttered her lashes again "—to brain you with a frying pan."

He grinned and tugged on the end of her ponytail. "Please try—at least until after you've finished cooking breakfast."

"I'd be more successful if you'd give me some space," she told him.

"Okay." He snagged another piece of bacon. "I'm going to grab a quick shower while you're finishing up."

Tristyn silently cursed Josh as she tossed two pieces of burned toast into the sink and dipped new slices of bread. Making French toast was a simple task—but he'd managed to unnerve her so completely that she hadn't realized the bread was burning. Yeah, a lot of years had passed since she was a seventeen-year-old girl with a crush on her cousin's best friend. Unfortunately, her visceral response to his nearness was unchanged, but no way was she going to let him know it.

It's your own feelings that you're afraid of.

Maybe she wasn't as adept at hiding her emotions as she wanted to believe. Or maybe he was just being Josh—teasing and flirting because that was his natural response when he was in the company of anyone female. And she teased and flirted back, because it helped preserve the illusion that she was unaffected by him. Except that the burned toast in the sink and the quivers in her belly proved otherwise.

When the bread in the pan was cooked, she added it to the platter in the oven along with the bacon and began to set the table for breakfast. She was pouring juice for the girls when Hanna came into the kitchen, holding the front of her shorts.

"I has to go potty."

"Your uncle Josh is in the shower, so you're going to have to wait a few minutes," she warned the little girl.

"I has to go now," Hanna insisted. Which, based on their experience the day before, meant that Tristyn didn't have time to walk the girl halfway across the camp to the public facilities.

"Pee pee or poop?" she asked, thinking it wouldn't be a big deal to take the little girl outside and let her squat behind a tree.

"Poop!" Hanna told her, then giggled.

Tristyn sighed. "Okay—just a sec." She went to the narrow door and knocked. "Hanna needs the toilet."

"Can she wait five minutes?" Josh replied through the door.

She looked at the little girl, who was still holding the front of her shorts and shifting impatiently from one foot to the other. "I doubt it."

He responded by shutting off the water. Thirty seconds

later, the door opened and he stepped out with only a towel wrapped around his exquisitely muscled and dripping-wet torso.

Hanna immediately pushed past him and into the bathroom.

Tristyn stood where she was, her feet rooted to the floor, her gaze riveted on the droplets of water that were sliding over Josh's taut and tanned skin. She curled her fingers into her palms to resist the urge to touch him. Because she did want to touch him. She wanted to run her hands over all his body, tracing the contours of those rippling muscles. She wanted to step closer and breathe in his clean, masculine scent, to press her lips to his skin and—

"Tristyn," Josh said.

She lifted her eyes and saw the hunger she felt reflected in his.

"I go pee pee," Hanna announced from inside the bathroom.

Tristyn shifted her attention from Josh and stepped toward the door. "You said you had to poop," she reminded the little girl.

"Poop," Hanna echoed, and giggled again.

"I think she just likes saying the word," Josh remarked.

Unbidden, Tristyn's gaze slid in his direction again, lingering on the shampoo lather that had dripped from his hair to his broad shoulders…to his wide chest…the six-pack abs…and lower.

"You're staring," he said softly, amusement mingled with the heat in his tone.

She tore her gaze away, and reached into the bathroom to grab the little girl's arm and turn her toward the door.

"I has to wash up," Hanna protested.

"You can do that in the kitchen."

Josh moved past them into the bathroom to resume his shower. She heard the door latch, then the water start again.

He would be discarding the towel now, exposing the rest of his hard, lean body—

She shoved the tantalizing image firmly to the back of her mind and focused her attention on serving up breakfast.

The girls had never been to a stock car race, so the whole experience was a little overwhelming to them. Hanna, in particular, was terrified by the crowds and the noise, and she wrapped her arms around one of Josh's legs as if she wouldn't ever let go. Even Emily and Charlotte dutifully stuck close when he bought them Ren D'Alesio T-shirts and hats at the souvenir hauler so they would be appropriately attired for the race.

Charlotte wrinkled her nose when he handed her the goodies. "Why can't I have a purple T-shirt like that one?" she asked, pointing to a girl wearing the colors of a rival team.

"Because then you'd be showing your support for Scott Peterson's car. Our car is green and gold."

"Who picked those colors?"

"They match the Archer Glass logo," he explained, naming the major sponsor of the GSR team.

Though she still didn't look thrilled, she dutifully put on the shirt when Tristyn escorted them to the bathroom to change. Of course, it probably helped that Tristyn was wearing her GSR polo shirt in the same colors. After ensuring they were settled in the owners' suite, she'd disappeared for a meeting with Ren's PA, leaving Josh with the three girls.

"Why are there so many people?" Emily asked, leaning forward in her seat and craning her neck to survey through the glass the crowd that packed the grandstands.

"They're here to meet the drivers and watch the race."

She seemed satisfied with that answer—at least for the

moment. After about ten minutes had passed, she looked at him again. "They just go round and round in a circle?"

"Well, it's a little more complicated than that," he said, though he couldn't think of an explanation that would make sense to or satisfy an inquisitive five-year-old girl.

"How do you know who's in front?" Charlotte asked, since the cars were spread out around the track.

"The blue-and-white car—number 535—is leading right now."

"How do you know?"

"Because I've been watching the race. But also because the numbers of the leaders are posted on that tower," he said, pointing it out to her.

"Oh," she said.

Hanna was paying more attention to her frayed shoe-lace than the action on the track, but at least she was sitting quietly.

"I'm hungry," Emily told him.

Hanna looked up. "I tirsty."

He glanced at Charlotte, who shrugged.

So he got them set up with food and drinks and was just replying to a text message from his business partner when the door opened and Paris Smythe, a stock car fan and racing blogger, slipped into the room. Over the past few months, she'd made it clear to Josh that she would be happy to give his team some extra coverage—if he got under the covers with her. She was a beautiful woman and he couldn't deny that he'd been tempted, but so far he'd managed to resist her overtures.

He hit Send, then tucked his phone away again.

"I missed you in Daytona," Paris said to him.

"I wasn't at the race," he admitted. "I had to go back to Charisma early to deal with a family situation."

"Well, you can make it up to me tonight," she suggested, shifting closer and tipping her head back to brush her lips over his. "I'm at the Courtland Hotel—room 722." She slid a key card into his pocket. "I figured you'd be able to remember that number."

He took the card out of his pocket and put it back in her hand. "I'm sorry," he lied. "But I won't be able to make it tonight."

The teasing glint in her eye faded. "Why not?"

"Because I'm still dealing with the family situation I mentioned," he said.

"What family situation?" she finally asked.

He turned her to face the front of the box, where Charlotte, Emily and Hanna were seated. "You see those three little girls?"

Her eyes went wide. "They're not yours."

"No," he acknowledged. "They're my sister's—but they're my responsibility for the summer."

"Jeez, you had me worried there for a minute," she said, and laughed weakly. Then she looked at him again. "Three kids? For the whole summer?"

He nodded.

She traced one of the buttons on his shirt with a fingernail. "Well, can't you find someone to watch them for at least one night?" she implored.

"Not tonight," he told her. "They've only been with me for a couple of days and we're still getting accustomed to roles and routines. On the other hand, if you wanted—"

"No," she cut him off abruptly. "Kids aren't really my thing—not even with a man as handsome as you as the potential reward." She trailed her fingers down his shirt, hooked a finger in his belt and tugged playfully. "But if you find yourself free, you know where to find me."

He nodded. "Enjoy the race."

"I always do," she said.

Then she was gone.

"Who was that?"

He jolted at the question, then turned to find his eldest niece standing behind him. "Who?"

"The lady who just left."

"Oh, um, that was Paris Smythe. She's writes about racing."

"Paris is a place not a name," she informed him.

"Charlotte is also a place," he pointed out to her.

"No, it's not," she denied.

"Sure it is. In fact, it's the largest city in North Carolina."

She frowned at that for a minute, before she asked, "Is Paris your girlfriend?"

"What? No."

"Then why was she kissing you?" she pressed.

"I don't know what you think you saw—"

"I saw her kissing you," Charlotte said. "And your lips are pink now."

He wiped a hand over his mouth to erase the remnants of Paris's lipstick. "She was just being friendly."

"Mommy says that a girl should never kiss a boy unless she means it."

"Means what?" Josh wondered.

Charlotte shrugged. "How should I know? I'm only seven."

He fought against a smile as he attempted to redirect the conversation. "What do you think of the race so far?"

"It's okay," she said, then, "Is Tristyn your girlfriend?"

"No, she's just a friend."

"Does she kiss you like that?"

"No," he said. "What's with all the kissing questions?"

"I'm just trying to figure things out."

"Let's try to figure out if our car is going to win this race," he suggested, guiding her back to the seat beside her sisters—including one who was now topless.

He closed his eyes as he drew in a slow, steadying breath. "Emily, where's your shirt?"

She pointed to the floor.

He picked up the discarded garment and tried again. "*Why* is your shirt on the floor?"

"'Cuz it's scratchy."

He hunkered down beside her chair. "Sweetie, you can't just take off your clothes in a public place."

"I only taked off my shirt," she told him.

"Please put it back on."

"It's scratchy," she said again.

He looked around. "Where's the backpack with your other shirt?"

Then he remembered that Tristyn had it and that she'd gone to Ren's hauler for the meeting.

"You're going to have to put this one back on until we can find Tristyn," he told Emily.

"Can we find her now?"

"Not right now," he said, tugging the shirt over her head. "She's in a meeting."

"When can we go back to the trailer?" Charlotte asked.

"When the race is over," he promised.

"When's it gonna be over?" Emily asked. "They've gone round and round lotsa times."

He glanced at the tower to check the lap number. "They've gone around sixty-two times," he told her.

Which meant there were only 205 laps left to go.

And it was definitely time to find Tristyn.

Chapter Nine

Tristyn didn't say much on the return trip, but Josh suspected that might have been because the girls were chattering nonstop and it would have been difficult to get a word in edgewise. Although he was preoccupied with his own thoughts about the race—grateful that the top-ten finish would help both D'Alesio and GSR in the overall standings—he sensed that her mind was focused on something else.

It was dinnertime when they got back to the RV, but the girls had eaten so much at the track—hot dogs and popcorn and ice cream—that they weren't really hungry. Tristyn claimed that she wasn't, either, although she'd had almost continuous meetings while they were at the track, and even during the race, so he didn't know when she would have managed to grab a bite. He made himself a grilled-cheese sandwich while she took Charlotte, Emily and Hanna to the playground so that they could burn off their excess energy.

When they came back, Tristyn instructed them to get their pajamas on. Of course, that was when they decided they needed a snack, so she fixed them each a bowl of cereal. After the girls were finished eating and had brushed their teeth and were tucked into bed, she busied herself with wiping the table and washing the dishes.

"You're going to wash the stripes right off that bowl," he said, when she'd swiped the cloth over it for the fifth time.

"What?"

He looked pointedly at the bowl in her hands.

"Oh." She rinsed the soap off and set it in the dish drainer to dry.

"Are you going to tell me what I did to piss you off?"

She was silent for a minute, as if considering how to answer the question, but she didn't deny that she was pissed off.

"Charlotte told me that she saw you kissing Paris," she finally said.

"I didn't kiss her," he said. "*She* kissed *me*."

"I don't really care who was kissing whom," Tristyn said. "I'm just asking you to remember that you have three impressionable little girls watching your every move this summer."

"I'm well aware of that," he told her.

"Which means you're not going to be able to…socialize to the extent you're accustomed to."

"Socialize?" he echoed.

She rolled her eyes. "Are you really going to make me spell it out?"

"I think that would be good."

"Okay," she relented. "You're going to have to leave the fence bunnies at the fence."

Josh knew there was as much action to be found away from the track as on it. And while he couldn't deny that he got a kick out of the attention that came from owning a race team, he'd never—not once—said yes to any of the frequent and explicit offers that had been whispered in his ear by eager groupies. Sure, he sometimes partied with fans in celebration of a victory, but he'd never spent the night with one of them.

There were other women involved with the sport who he'd crossed paths with on a regular basis. Sometimes they hung out together, sometimes it was more than hanging out. But those women knew the circuit, they knew the rules and they didn't want anything more than he did. And he'd be damned if he would apologize to Tristyn for indiscretions that didn't exist anywhere outside of her own mind.

Instead, he only nodded. "No worries. As you know, girls who throw themselves at me aren't my style."

Twin spots of color appeared high on her cheeks. "Touché."

Dammit. He closed his eyes and silently cursed himself for lashing out. Yeah, she'd pissed him off, but he shouldn't have hit back at her. He shouldn't have hurt her. Again.

Not that she would ever admit to feeling hurt. She kept her chin up and her gaze level, but he saw the truth in those deep green eyes. And for that he would apologize. "I'm sorry, Tris."

She shook her head. "Don't ever apologize for being honest about your feelings."

Which sounded like good advice, except that he'd never been honest with her about his feelings. He was barely capable of being honest with himself.

His nieces had crashed a long time ago and Tristyn had firmly closed the door of her bedroom more than an hour earlier, but Josh still couldn't sleep. He thought about the key card Paris had slipped into his pocket earlier—the key card he hadn't hesitated to give back. The explanation he'd given was a valid one—he was responsible for his nieces and had no intention of abandoning them for the pursuit of personal pleasure. But it wasn't the complete truth, which was that he knew a few hours of fun in another woman's bed wouldn't make him forget the one woman he wanted. The one woman he couldn't have.

The woman who was sleeping less than fifteen feet away, snuggled beneath the covers of a king-size bed in granny jammies despite her alleged preference for sleeping in the nude. Fact or fiction? He wasn't entirely convinced she'd been telling him the truth. More likely, she'd made it up for the sole purpose of keeping him awake at night. Which it was.

Because as much as he'd made fun of the shapeless boxy pj's, Tristyn had looked sexy even in those, and the buttons that ran down the front of the top started low enough to reveal a tantalizing hint of cleavage. Which he definitely should not be thinking about when he was trying to sleep, because now his body was wide-awake and ready for action.

He never should have agreed to do this road trip. And as far as bad ideas went, inviting Tristyn to come along with them ranked right up there with the worst of them. They were at the end of only their second day together, and he couldn't sleep for wanting her.

Though Josh would never admit it to anyone, she'd haunted his dreams for years. Twelve years, in fact. Since the night of her senior prom, when he'd decided to be a nice guy and save Tristyn—and Daniel—the humiliation of her being escorted to the event by a relative. That was the solution her mother had originally proposed, when Tristyn's boyfriend came down with the flu and was unable to attend, and Josh had stepped up as a favor to his friend. He'd certainly never expected to feel anything for his best friend's cousin.

Tristyn had been done up for the big event as if the Spring Fling was a royal wedding. Her dress had even been white, though that wasn't the first thing he'd noticed about it. No, what he'd noticed was that the tight, elaborately

beaded bodice of the strapless gown drew his attention—
and probably that of every other guy in the room—to her
no-longer-flat chest.

In that moment, Josh had realized his best friend's little
cousin wasn't so little anymore and that this "favor" wasn't
going to be nearly as effortless as he'd anticipated. That
was when he'd begun to sweat inside his tuxedo jacket.

Her long dark hair had been done up in some fancy
twist with sparkly pins artfully arranged in it. Stunningly
beautiful even without any cosmetic enhancement, a subtle
touch of makeup had made her eyes look bigger and darker,
her lips glossy and kissable. She'd been the embodiment
of temptation, and when he'd taken her arm and led her to
his car, he hadn't been certain that he'd be able to resist.

It had taken an extreme force of will—and consider-
ation of how Daniel might react if Josh made a move on
his best friend's cousin—but he'd delivered her home at
the end of the night as untouched as she'd been at the beginning. After eight torturous hours with Tristyn being
close enough to touch—and not being allowed to touch her.

He'd barely survived those eight hours—and now he'd
signed up for eight weeks in close proximity to her.

What had he been thinking?

When Charlotte had impulsively invited Tristyn to join
them, he should have said no, firmly and unequivocally.
That he'd implored her to say yes was proof he hadn't
been thinking—at least not with his brain. Now he was
trapped in less than three hundred square feet of living
space with a beautiful woman who turned him inside out
just by breathing.

He was pretty sure the attraction he felt wasn't entirely
one-sided. He'd caught her staring at him when he stepped
out of the shower, and the look in her eyes had not been that
of a disinterested woman. And since they were both unat-
tached adults—because he didn't believe that her claims

of a relationship with Rafe were anything more than a smoke screen—why shouldn't they explore the attraction between them?

The primary reason, of course, was that she was still his best friend's cousin. And if Daniel had any idea that Josh was even thinking about getting Tristyn naked—well, he didn't want to imagine what his friend might say or do, how it would affect not just their friendship but their business partnership.

Still, he suspected that one night with Tristyn might be worth the fallout. His fear was that one night would not be enough.

The following morning, Josh didn't wake up to the sounds of Tristyn banging around in the kitchen. He woke up to whispers.

It took him a minute for the words to register, and another few seconds for him to be able to identify the individual speakers.

"We're not s'posed to wake him up," Charlotte admonished.

"But how long is he gonna sleep?" Emily asked.

"Maybe he's jus' 'tendin' to s'eep," Hanna suggested.

"Adults don't pretend to sleep," Charlotte informed her.

"How d'you know?" her youngest sister pressed.

"Because no one would get mad at them for not being asleep when they're supposed to be."

"Do you think he'll be mad if we wake him?" Emily asked.

"Tristyn told us not to," Charlotte reminded her.

"We could poke him. Pokin's not wakin'."

"No—don't poke him!"

"Mommy usually wakes up when we stand by her bed."

"Because she's got 'tuition," Emily said. "Uncle Josh doesn't got kids so he doesn't got that."

"He does have ears, though," Josh said softly. "So maybe if you keep talking, he'll hear you."

"He's awake," Emily announced, clearly pleased by the discovery.

"But his eyes is c'osed," Hanna protested.

He finally, reluctantly, lifted one eyelid, then the other.

Hanna rewarded him with a beaming smile. "*Now* he's awake."

He scrubbed a hand over his face. "What time is it?"

"Seven thirty-seven," Charlotte told him.

Which wasn't insanely early—it only felt insanely early because he'd slept so poorly the night before.

He glanced toward the closed door of the master bedroom. "I guess Tristyn's still sleeping."

The three girls all shook their heads. "She went for a walk," Emily said.

"To get buttermilk," Charlotte added.

"Fo' pancakes!" Hanna chimed in.

He wondered where she could have walked to for buttermilk at such an early hour. Connected to the campground office was a small store with basic groceries and other essentials, but he doubted she would find buttermilk there.

"So you didn't wake me up to make your breakfast," he guessed.

"We wanna go swimmin'," Hanna announced.

Only then did he notice that they were all wearing their swimsuits and holding beach towels.

"At seven thirty-seven in the morning?"

They nodded enthusiastically.

"It's seven forty now," Charlotte pointed out.

"And the splash pad and pool don't open until ten," he told them.

"Oh."

But he got out of bed now and stumbled toward the coffeemaker, which—thanks to Tristyn—had already brewed a fresh pot of coffee. He poured the hot liquid into a mug and sipped carefully.

"Why do you drink coffee?" Emily asked.

"Because I like it," he told her.

"Caffeine's not good for you," Charlotte informed him. "It will stunt your growth."

"Since I'm pretty sure I'm finished growing, that's not really a concern," he said.

Tristyn returned just as he was starting on his second cup of coffee. She wished him a good morning and immediately set about making breakfast.

Charlotte looked at the container she'd brought back from the store.

"That's not milk, it's yogurt," Charlotte said.

"I like yogurt," Emily said. "Especially the kind with blueberries."

"This is plain yogurt," Tristyn explained. "They didn't have buttermilk, so I'm going to improvise."

"What's improvise?" Emily asked.

"It means to make something from what's available."

"Are we still gonna have pancakes?" she wondered.

"Yes, we're still going to have pancakes."

"And then we can go swimming?"

"Then we can go swimming," Tristyn confirmed, then she looked pointedly at Josh. "And that 'we' includes you."

He could think of few things less appealing than a public pool crowded with screaming kids and weary parents. But then he added something to the picture in his mind: Tristyn in a bathing suit. A teeny, tiny bikini. And that prospect silenced any remaining protest. Lucy called just as the girls were finishing up their breakfast. Because of her work schedule and the time difference, she hadn't been able to talk to the girls every day, although Josh did send her regular updates and occasional pictures of them.

When each of the girls had talked to her for a few minutes and Lucy finally said goodbye, Hanna started to cry. "I miss Mommy."

"Don't be a baby," Charlotte snapped at her.

Emily's eyes filled with tears, too, but she valiantly held them in check.

Hanna's fell freely down her cheeks as she climbed into her uncle's lap. "When's she comin' home, Unca Josh?"

"She's hoping to be back by the twenty-ninth of August, but she's doing a very important job in Spain and it might take longer than that," he cautioned.

Emily was already looking at the calendar Tristyn had hung up on the fridge, counting the days. "The twenty-ninth isn't so long," she said.

"That's the twenty-ninth of July, dummy," Charlotte told her.

"Oh." Emily's face fell.

"Don't call your sister names," Josh admonished.

"Your mom will be home as soon as she can, because she misses you guys as much as you miss her," Tristyn assured them.

"How do you know?" Charlotte challenged.

"Because she's your mom—and there's nothing harder for a mom than to be away from her children."

"How do you know?" Charlotte asked again. "You don't have any kids."

"No, I don't," Tristyn acknowledged. "But I have two sisters and they both have kids, and I know they don't like to be away from them for more than a few hours."

"Why don't you have kids?" Emily asked curiously.

"Um…" She glanced at Josh, who was fighting a smile, clearly amused by her interrogation at the hands of two little girls. "Because I'm not married," she finally responded.

"You don't have to be married to have kids," Charlotte pointed out matter-of-factly. "Our mom wasn't married when she had Emily and Hanna."

"That's true," she acknowledged cautiously. "But I guess I always hoped to get married before I had kids."

"When are you gonna get married?" Emily asked her.

"I have no idea," Tristyn admitted.

"You could may-wee Unca Josh," Hanna piped up.

The amusement on Josh's face vanished and a slightly panicked expression took its place.

Tristyn shook her head. "I don't see that happening."

"Why not?" Charlotte asked. "You wouldn't have agreed to come on this trip if you didn't like Uncle Josh."

"Of course, I like your uncle Josh," she agreed. "But the real reason I decided to come on this trip is that I didn't know if he could cook, and I wanted to be sure you guys wouldn't starve."

Emily giggled at that.

Charlotte rolled her eyes. "He wouldn't let us starve."

"Living on fast food is almost as bad," Tristyn said.

"I fed them fast food twice," he pointed out.

"Twice in two days."

"And you're trying to distract us from talking about your wedding plans," he chided.

"Why don't we talk about *your* wedding plans?" she countered. "Oh, right—because you don't plan to *ever* get married."

"Why not?" Emily asked, shifting her attention to her uncle.

Josh's narrowed gaze promised retribution for Tristyn.

"Because he wants to…date…a different girl every night," she said.

"Maybe I'd change my mind if I met a woman who could convince me that the advantages of spending my life with her outweighed the disadvantages of marriage."

Tristyn was surprised by his response, until she realized he was simply attempting to appease his nieces.

"Can we go to the pool now?" Charlotte asked, clearly bored with the topic of conversation.

"As soon as your uncle gets his bathing suit on," she agreed, grateful for the reprieve.

He went to put on his bathing suit.

Tristyn was spraying sunscreen on the girls when he came out of the bathroom. Unfortunately, he couldn't tell if she was wearing a teeny, tiny bikini because she was wearing one of those cover-up things on top of her bathing suit. Even when they got to the pool, she stayed in the shallow end with Hanna—and kept the cover-up on.

Though both Charlotte and Emily claimed that they'd had swimming lessons, Josh bought them inflatable armbands to provide some extra peace of mind—probably for him more than the girls.

After almost two hours in the pool, they went back to the RV for lunch.

"When I was at the store this morning, I talked to Mrs. Halliday about extending our reservation," Tristyn said, as she buttered slices of bread to make sandwiches.

"We can't extend our reservation," he argued. "Not if we're going to make it to New Hampshire by next weekend."

"I don't think the girls are eager to head to another racetrack, especially not one that's more than nine hundred miles away."

"Wasn't that the whole point of getting the RV?" he asked. "So that we could travel with the girls?"

"It was," she confirmed. "And we will. I just think that it will be easier on all of us if we stay here and you fly to New Hampshire for the weekend."

"The girls are my responsibility," he reminded her. "And I'm sure how I'd feel about being so far away from them when their mother is in another country."

"I'll be with them every minute of every day that you're gone," she told him.

"That's a lot of minutes," he warned.

"We'll be fine. The girls have wanted to play mini-putt and I'm sure we'll spend some more time at the pool and the playground. And if it rains, we've got a bin full of games, puzzles and books. Plus there's an activity room in the community center with more games and dress-up clothes and craft supplies." She assembled the sandwiches, cut them in halves—and Hanna's in quarters—then set them on plates. "Besides," she said, "Paris will most likely be in New Hampshire."

"How is she a factor in any of this?"

Tristyn shrugged. "I understand the value of maintaining good relationships with the media."

"You're not suggesting I seduce a writer to get GSR mentioned on some racing blog?"

"Of course not," she said quickly, her cheeks flushing. "Although that blog has twenty-two thousand subscribers."

"Including you?" he guessed.

"She's a good writer and does a nice job showing fans the human side of the sport." She was also blonde, beautiful and built, but Tristyn tried not to hold that against her.

"Even so, I have no interest in extracurricular activities with Paris Smythe," he told her.

"It's none of my business," she said. "I realize I might have come down a little hard because of what Charlotte saw at the track, but that was more about your lack of discretion than Paris."

His brows lifted. "So now you're sending me off to New Hampshire on my own so I can be…discreet? Or are you trying to get rid of me in the hope that some distance might lessen the…tension…between us?"

Chapter Ten

Though she didn't look at him, Josh saw Tristyn's cheeks flush with guilty color, confirming his suspicions. Living in close proximity was making it increasingly difficult—for both of them—to deny the attraction that simmered beneath the surface. And it was only a matter of time before the heat between them turned that simmer to a full boil.

"I'm just trying to come up with a plan that works for everyone," she told him now.

"We had a plan," he reminded her. "And it was for the girls to come with me on the road."

"I'm only suggesting a minor amendment to that plan—to spare them another nine hundred miles on the road, which we'd then have to do all over again to make the trip from New Hampshire to Indiana the following weekend. But if we stay here, we're only a two-hour drive from Indianapolis."

"Okay," he relented. "If they want to stay here, I won't object."

He wasn't really surprised when Charlotte, Emily and Hanna unanimously voted to skip the journey to Loudon. Day one of their road trip hadn't been a lot of fun for any of them—especially Emily. And Hanna. But while he could understand that they weren't eager to get on the road again—and maybe sitting out the longest leg of the journey was a good idea—they would have to get back on the road eventually. But at least they were equipped with Dramamine now.

Not having to drive nine hundred miles gave Josh more free time with the girls before he left. He was surprised to discover that he really enjoyed hanging out with them—swimming in the pool, playing Candyland, patiently, and repeatedly, explaining the basics of stock car racing in an effort to foster some appreciation of the sport.

It was the time he spent alone with Tristyn, after the girls had gone to bed at night, that was much more of a challenge for him. The RV was spacious, as far as RVs were concerned. But after only a week of sharing that space with a gorgeous, sexy woman, the temptation was proving stronger than his will to resist.

The night before his flight, Tristyn was in the kitchen, making muffins. He'd noticed that she didn't seem to spend much time sitting still, and he didn't know if she had a constant need to be busy or if she didn't want to sit down because there was nowhere to sit that wouldn't be close to him. Whatever the reason, she was in the kitchen while he was watching a ball game on TV.

During the seventh-inning stretch, he got up to grab a beer from the fridge and, as he turned with the bottle in hand, Tristyn leaned over to put the batter in the oven. Their movements coincided in a way that caused the sexy curve of her behind to brush the front of his shorts. The inadvertent contact nearly made him groan.

Tristyn did gasp as she straightened up again and turned. "You're in my space."

"Yeah," he agreed, making no effort to move away.

A tiny furrow appeared between her brows. "Could you please get *out* of my space?"

"I could," he agreed, taking a moment to give her idea some thought. "In fact, I'd say we've done a pretty good job of maintaining our separate spaces over the past week."

"Until now," she said pointedly.

"Uh huh."

She looked at him, her gorgeous green eyes filled with wariness—and maybe a little bit of desire.

She was so damn beautiful. But her beauty was only part of the appeal for Josh. She was also warm and sweet and funny and smart. And that whole package was pretty close to irresistible.

"Twelve years," he murmured.

"Josh," she said.

A warning or request?

"It's a long time to wonder, don't you think?" he asked softly.

"I guess that depends on what you're wondering." Her tone was deliberately neutral, but the slight breathlessness gave her away.

"The same thing you are," he told her.

The way he was looking at her was making everything inside of her tremble. Not with fear, Tristyn realized, but desire. But going down that path with Josh—especially now—would be dangerous.

"Whether Ren will get the pole in Loudon?" she suggested, desperately trying to shift the conversation to safer ground.

Amusement flickered in his eyes for just a moment before the heat took over, sizzling between them.

"I'm not thinking about the race," he said. "And neither are you."

Before she could argue the point, because she had no intention of admitting that he was right, his mouth was on hers. And with the first brush of contact, any thought of resistance—any thought at all—fizzled away.

In that moment, there was nothing but Josh.

Nothing but Josh and the exquisite, intoxicating sensation of his kiss.

The pressure of his mouth on hers was every bit as glorious as she'd imagined—and yes, she'd spent a lot of time imagining his kiss since she'd seen him making out with Missy Harlowe when she was thirteen. More time than she was willing to admit.

Except for the finger and thumb that held her chin immobile, he touched her only with his lips. That was all he needed to hold her under his spell, simultaneously captivating and mesmerizing her. He kissed like a man who knew how to kiss a woman, who could take her to the edge with just the masterful seduction of his mouth on hers.

He didn't just taste, he savored. And she savored his flavor in return. Twelve years ago, she would have given almost anything to experience his kiss. Twelve years ago, she'd been totally unprepared for something like this. Even now, she wasn't sure what to do with the desire that spread through her veins, the desperate need that clawed at her belly.

She curled her fingers into her palms, digging her nails into the soft flesh to prevent herself from reaching for him. Because she was afraid that if she touched him now, she wouldn't be able to stop. She wouldn't want to stop.

It was Josh who finally, eventually, ended the kiss, easing his lips from hers with obvious reluctance.

She exhaled, a slow, unsteady breath, and finally dared to look at him. He rubbed a thumb over her bottom lip, swollen from his kiss. The sensual caress made her shiver.

"And that," he said, his gaze lingering on her mouth, "is why I didn't kiss you twelve years ago."

She swallowed, but she didn't respond to his comment.

There was nothing really to say, no way to avoid the truth that had been revealed by the meeting of their lips.

That kiss was only the beginning.

Josh's flight was delayed because of a storm, and he'd just arrived at the track when his cell phone rang. A quick glance at the display had him cringing—and considering letting the call go to voice mail. Unfortunately, that would only delay the inevitable argument that probably could have been avoided if he'd thought to call his sister and advise her of the change of plans in advance of changing them.

"Hey, Luce—how is Madrid?"

"Right now, it's raining," she told him.

"Here, too," he said, as thunder rumbled overhead. "How are my girls?"

"Great," he said. "They're having a lot of fun in the pool at the campground."

"They do love the water," she confirmed. "What are they doing now?"

"Oh, um, I'm not actually sure," he admitted. "They're with Tristyn."

"And where are you?" she asked.

"New Hampshire."

There was silence on the other end of the line.

"Luce?" he prompted.

"I'm here," she admitted. "I'm just trying to figure out what to say in response to discovering that my brother—who I entrusted with my three daughters for the summer—has abandoned them with a babysitter in another state."

"First of all, you didn't 'entrust' me with your daughters—you dumped them on me," he pointed out.

"Because there was no one else that I trusted to take care of them."

"Second, you know that Tristyn isn't a babysitter."

"Excuse me—your girlfriend-of-the-week," his sister amended.

"She's a friend who's helping me out because I was overwhelmed by the prospect of taking care of three girls on my own all summer."

"Those three girls are your nieces," she reminded him.

"Who barely know me because, for the past six years, you've refused to come to Charisma for a visit."

"You're supposed to be getting to know them now. Instead, you're in New Hampshire."

"I'll be back in Kentucky tomorrow night," he promised her.

"I have to go," she said. "I've got another call coming through."

"I'll text you Tristyn's number," he said.

But she'd already hung up.

Tristyn and the girls kept busy while Josh was in New Hampshire. They played mini-putt, spent some time at the splash pad and swimming pool, made friends with the neighbors and even went to a movie. She also watched the race on TV, pleased to see that Ren and his team put in a solid performance, consistently in the top twenty, sometimes even breaking the top ten. GSR's driver seemed poised for another strong finish until the third turn of lap 296, and her heart nearly stopped as she witnessed the 722 car get clipped by the 416 and then, seemingly in slow motion, spin into the wall.

Accidents weren't an uncommon occurrence on the track, but even the commentators noted that it didn't look much like an accident and speculated that Curtis Bond, the driver of the 416, was still mad at D'Alesio for sneaking past him on the outside and taking the checkered flag in Kansas City a few weeks earlier. The race officials would review the tapes and decide what—if any—disciplinary measures to take against the driver, but Tristyn knew that was little consolation for Ren and his team, who worked hard to prepare for every race.

As the damaged cars were moved off the track, Hanna climbed into Tristyn's lap, dropped her head back and slid her thumb into her mouth—a telltale sign that she was sleepy. Tristyn lifted a hand and brushed her soft, wispy bangs away from her face. Cuddling with the little girl, she felt a tug of longing deep inside. She'd always assumed that motherhood was in her future somewhere, but she hadn't been in any rush to head in that direction. Recently, she'd started to feel differently.

She blamed Lauryn and Jordyn for that. She'd been perfectly happy with her life—she had a great house and a fabulous job and a wonderful family. But the recent marriages of both of her sisters had made her realize that she wanted more. That she wanted to meet someone to share her life and raise a family with, too.

Tristyn had been only twenty-four when Kylie was born—thrilled to be an aunt but definitely not ready to even think about being a mother. Two years later, she'd had a much more hands-on role for Zachary's birth and was actually in the delivery room with her sister, coaching Lauryn in place of her deadbeat husband, who had already left town with the yoga instructor.

Tristyn had felt the first twinges of longing then, not just because she was the first to hold the baby—after his mom, of course—but because it had been such an awesome and amazing experience to play even a small part in the process of bringing a new life into the world. In addition to having a front-row seat for the birth, she'd had a front-row seat to the chaos that was her sister's life at the time. Sure, Lauryn had a beautiful toddler daughter and an adorable newborn son, but she also had a mountain of debt and a broken heart. Tristyn had no desire to experience that kind of upheaval and turmoil. Now Lauryn had a new husband and another baby on the way, and Tristyn was thrilled for her.

A few months after Lauryn and Ryder's wedding, Jordyn had given birth to her twin sons. Marco had been right there, holding his wife's hand and breathing with her through every contraction, so Tristyn didn't have the same front-row seat for that event—thank God for small favors—but the pure and sweet love that filled her heart when she held those tiny babies for the first time was the same. Yet it was more than just the babies that had changed her focus. It was seeing Jordyn and Marco cuddling the precious lives they'd created and brought into the world together. That was the moment when it had hit her, when she'd realized that she wanted what they had—the partnership, the commitment, the love.

Someday, she promised herself, as she tucked Hanna into her bunk.

As a result of Ren's DNF—Did Not Finish—Josh was in a lousy mood when he got on the plane in New Hampshire, and his disposition hadn't changed at all by the time he landed in Kentucky. He arrived at the campground just as Tristyn and the girls were returning from the splash pad. His nieces seemed happy to see him and chattered away about everything he'd missed while he was away. Tristyn, sensing his mood, gave him a wider berth.

She'd just finished helping Hanna dress as a knock sounded.

Josh's scowl deepened when he saw a man standing on the other side of the door, holding a square glass pan.

"Hey, is Tristyn around?" he asked.

"I'm right here, Sean," she immediately responded from behind him.

The other guy's—*Sean's*—eyes lit up when he saw her.

Josh stepped away from the door but not out of earshot.

"I just wanted to return your pan," Sean said. "And to thank you again for the brownies."

"They're gone already?"

"They were gone the first night," he admitted. "It just took us two days to get around to doing the dishes."

Tristyn laughed, a warm, seductive sound that stirred Josh's blood—and likely had the same effect on the guy who was staring at her with adoring eyes.

"The girls and I are going to make chocolate chip cookies later," she told him. "I'll bring some over when we're done."

"You don't have to do that," Sean said. "But we'll certainly enjoy them if you do."

"I'll see you later," she promised.

"I'll look forward to it."

Josh watched through the kitchen window as the other man walked away—a whole twenty-five feet to the RV parked directly beside theirs.

"Who was that?" he asked, as Tristyn moved past him to put the pan in the cupboard.

"Sean."

"Yeah, I caught the name," he admitted. "I was looking for a little more detail than that."

"He's an electrician from West Virginia. He and Blake and Owen grew up together and they still take a few days to get away together every summer. It used to be a week, but since Owen got married a couple of years ago, they cut it back to a few days."

"Do Sean and Blake have wives?"

She shook her head. "Blake's engaged, though, and getting married in the fall."

"And how did you meet these guys?" he wondered.

"They rescued our dinner Friday night," she told him. "I'd just put the burgers on the grill when the flames sputtered and died. Blake saw me attempting to unhook the tank and offered to throw our burgers on their grill. After we ate, he switched out the tanks for me, so I made them some brownies to say thanks."

Which was, Josh knew, exactly the kind of thing she would do and absolutely no reason for the petty jealousy gnawing at the pit of his belly.

"And when I took the brownies over, they asked me to be their fourth for euchre, so I spent a few hours playing cards with them."

"While the girls were…where?" he prompted.

"At the pool," she said, picking up the wet towels they'd dumped on the table when they came back from swimming.

He frowned at that.

Tristyn shook her head, clearly exasperated with him. "Honestly, Josh—where do you *think* they were?"

"With you," he guessed.

"Of course, they were with me." She pushed open the door and headed outside to hang up the towels.

He followed. "Playing euchre?"

"PlayStation," she corrected. "Because apparently 'roughing it' does not mean living without video games for some people."

"I hope you had Hanna in bed at her usual bedtime."

"She fell asleep on their sofa."

"How late were you there?"

"Since I was unaware that I had a curfew, I didn't actually make note of the time when we left," she told him.

"Lucy said it's important for the girls to have a consistent schedule."

"A couple of late nights isn't a big deal."

"A couple of nights?" he echoed.

"Yes, Josh. We were over there last night, too. While you were banging Paris Smythe into next week, I was corrupting your three young nieces with euchre and video games."

"I wasn't banging Paris Smythe—or anyone else, for that matter," he retorted.

"Well, that might explain your lousy mood," she acknowledged.

"Did you really think I'd kiss you on Thursday and sleep with another woman on Friday?"

"Truthfully, I didn't think about that kiss at all."

The words might have stung his pride except that the flush in her cheeks and the rapid beating of the pulse point below her ear told a different story. He took a step closer, forcing her to tip her head back to meet his gaze. "Liar," he said softly.

She put her hands on his chest and shoved. Though her effort was ineffectual, he took a deliberate step back. He wasn't in the habit of intimidating women, but he'd never known a woman like Tristyn. She had an uncanny ability to make him crazy without even trying, to make him want her just by breathing.

"I waited twelve years to kiss you," he reminded her. "I won't wait that long to kiss you again—or take you to my bed."

She lifted her chin. "Nobody takes me anywhere I don't want to go."

"Lucky for me, you want me as much as I want you."

"Lucky for you, you've got that enormous ego to fill your bed, so you won't be lonely without me in it."

And with that parting remark, she walked away.

Chapter Eleven

Tristyn knew that she could walk all the way back to Charisma and not walk off her frustration with Josh. So she went only as far as the end of the lane before she pulled her phone out of her pocket. She knew that she could count on either of her sisters to commiserate with her, and dialed Jordyn's number because she was first in her alphabetical list of contacts.

"The man is driving me insane," she said without preamble when her sister had connected the call.

"Hold on a sec," Jordyn said. "Lauryn's here, so I'm going to put you on speakerphone so we both know what's happening."

She heard a click, then her oldest sister's voice. "Hi, Tris. What's happening?"

"He's driving me crazy."

"Josh?"

She huffed out a breath. "Of course, Josh."

"What's he done now?"

"Nothing new, really," she admitted. "He's just being his usual arrogant, annoying self."

"Something must have happened to prompt this call," Lauryn remarked.

"Yeah—he got back from Loudon and started criticizing how I spent my time with his nieces while he was away."

"He was probably upset that Ren crashed with only five laps left," Jordyn said, revealing that she'd watched the race, too—or at least the highlights.

"There's no excuse for being a jerk," Tristyn said.

"I'm guessing his behavior is a sign that you haven't gotten naked with him yet," Lauryn mused.

"What? Of course not."

"It's not completely outside the realm of possibility," Jordyn noted.

"I'm *not* going to get naked with Josh," she said firmly. But, because she had no secrets from her sisters, she confided, "He did kiss me, though."

"Finally," Lauryn said.

"And then?" Jordyn prompted.

Tristyn frowned. "Isn't that enough?"

"Not if it was a good kiss," Jordyn said.

"And Josh Slater looks like a man who would know how to kiss," Lauryn chimed in.

"He does know how to kiss," she acknowledged.

"And then?" Jordyn said again.

"And then I remembered what happened the last time I let myself fall under the spell of Josh Slater."

"That was twelve years ago," Lauryn reminded her. "Neither of you are the same people now."

"I know I'm not the same naive girl I was then, but I'm not sure Josh has changed at all." She sighed. "I never should have agreed to this road trip. There's no way I can spend another six weeks in that RV with him without killing him."

"You could try jumping his bones instead," Jordyn suggested.

Tristyn choked on a laugh. "I guess that is another possibility—except that I'm not giving him another chance to push me away."

"He's not going to push you away," Lauryn assured her.

"How do you know?"

"Because we've seen the way he looks at you when he thinks no one else is looking," Jordyn said.

"Well, it's not likely I'd have an opportunity to jump his bones with three kids around, anyway."

"I have two babies at home, but I can assure you, I jump Marco's bones every chance I get."

"Please," Lauryn interrupted. "Even between sisters, there's such a thing as too much information."

"As if you're not riding Ryder every night."

"La-la-la," Tristyn sang, attempting to drown them out as she'd done when they were kids and she didn't want to hear what they were saying.

"My point," Jordyn said, speaking loudly enough to be heard over the singing, "is that the bedroom door has a lock."

"Can we talk about something else?" Tristyn suggested, because the more she talked about the possibility of getting naked with Josh, the more tempted she was—despite the fact that he was acting like an idiot.

"Uh uh," Jordyn said. "You called to talk about Josh, so that's what we're doing."

"I called so that you could agree he's being an idiot."

"He's being an idiot," Lauryn said loyally.

"Probably because the memory of that kiss is keeping him up at night—and I don't just mean awake," Jordyn added.

"Not helpful," Tristyn said.

"Okay, let's forget about what Josh wants for a minute," Lauryn said.

"Thank you."

But her sister's next words made her realize that her expression of gratitude was premature.

"What do *you* want?" Lauryn asked gently. "Honestly. Because if you're really unhappy or uncomfortable with the situation, you can leave. You don't owe Josh any favors."

She thought about her sister's question for a moment before responding, "I want to not have the feelings I'm feeling."

"Will those feelings go away if you come home?" Lauryn asked.

She sighed. "Probably not."

"Then try to forgive him for being an idiot, enjoy being with him and see what happens."

Talking to her sisters helped a little; walking around the campground helped some more. When she got back to the RV, Josh was on the phone with Daniel, giving what sounded like a play-by-play of every adjustment made to Ren's car for the previous day's race. The girls were anxious to do something, so she got out the ingredients for chocolate chip cookies, then enlisted their help with the measuring and mixing.

She'd planned to make a pot of chili for dinner, but she'd forgotten to pick up chili powder at the grocery store and decided on meat loaf instead. When she served it up, Emily eyed the slice on her plate skeptically.

"What is it?"

"Meat loaf," Josh answered.

His niece poked it with her fork. "What kind of meat?"

"Ground beef."

"That's cow," Charlotte informed her sister. "Moooo!"

"Charlotte," her uncle said, a warning in his tone.

"I don't like ground beef," Emily announced.

"It's the same kind of meat we had the other night in the form of a hamburger," Tristyn told her.

"So this is like a hamburger?" Emily asked skeptically.

"Sort of," she agreed.

"Can I have it on a bun?"

"It's like a hamburger but it's not a hamburger," Josh tried to explain. "It's meat loaf, and you eat it with a fork."

"I wanna eat it on a bun," Emily insisted.

Josh looked at Tristyn.

She shrugged. "I guess it doesn't matter how she eats it as long as she eats it."

He found the leftover bag of buns and opened one up, then put the slice of meat from Emily's plate on it.

"I wanna bun, too," Hanna decided. "An' ketchup."

He looked at Charlotte, who was nibbling tentatively on a tiny piece of meat. She nodded.

So the girls ate their meat loaf as if it was a hamburger. Emily even put her mashed potatoes and corn on top of the meat, as if the vegetables were condiments.

"Well, I think we can take meat loaf off the menu for next week," Tristyn decided, as the girls cleared their plates from the table.

"I thought it was delicious," he told her.

"Your nieces weren't exactly thrilled with it."

"You've read the book," he reminded her. "According to Lucy, they eat what's put in front of them or they don't eat."

"Still, if I'm going to cook, I'd rather cook something that's going to be eaten—and enjoyed—by everyone."

"Well, the chocolate chip cookies were a hit."

"Who doesn't love chocolate chip cookies?"

"I like brownies, too," he said, nudging her away from the sink. "But I guess there were none of those left."

"You guessed right," she said. "What are you doing?"

"Dishes. That's my job," he reminded her.

"Can we go to the playground?" Charlotte asked.

Tristyn glanced at the clock. "I guess we can go for an hour, and then it will be time for your showers and pajamas."

Although it was undoubtedly convenient to have a bathroom in the RV, the narrowness of the shower stall and the limited capacity of the hot water tank made it awkward to get the girls cleaned up and ready for bed. After scoping out the public facilities, Tristyn had decided that they should shower and get ready for bed there. The first night, Charlotte had been embarrassed to walk across the campground in her pajamas—until she saw several other kids, some even older than her, doing the same thing. Now they were all accustomed to the bedtime routine, which was much more efficient than taking turns in the trailer.

By the time they returned, Josh had the dishes washed, dried and put away, and was watching a baseball game on TV.

"It's sto-wee time, Unca Josh," Hanna announced, as soon as she stepped into the RV.

Josh didn't know how or why he'd become the resident storyteller, but he found he enjoyed the time with Hanna before she went to bed at night. And although Charlotte and Emily could both read age-appropriate books, they sometimes listened in to story time with their little sister, too.

He muted the sound on the television. "Okay, go pick out a book to read."

When he came back to the living area after story time, Tristyn was sitting on one end of the sofa with her iPad in hand. "Are the girls tucked in?"

He nodded and lowered himself onto the sofa, facing her instead of the television.

"I owe you an apology," he said.

"Yes, you do," she agreed.

"I was in a lousy mood earlier and I took it out on you."

"That's an explanation, not an apology."

"I'm sorry," he said.

She nodded, her attention still on the iPad screen. "I accept your apology."

"That's it? You're not going to make me grovel?"

She sent him a sideways glance. "Would you?"

"Probably," he admitted.

"Well, I appreciate the thought," she said, her gaze back on the article she was reading, "but it's really not necessary."

He took the iPad from her, closed the cover and set it aside. "We need to talk about this."

She frowned. "I thought we just did."

"Not about what happened earlier," he said.

"About what?" she asked warily.

"The fact that you make me crazy."

"*I* make *you* crazy?" she said incredulously.

He nodded. "You were right—Paris was at Loudon, and she invited me to spend the night with her. And I wasn't the least bit tempted, because even when I was more than nine hundred miles away from you, I couldn't stop thinking about you. I couldn't stop wanting you."

He kissed her then—a kiss full of frustration and need. And she kissed him back, because she was just as frustrated and needy as he. And because this was Josh, and she'd wanted him for too long to deny herself now. His tongue swept along the seam of her lips, parting them so that he could deepen the kiss. She hooked her hands over his shoulders, holding on to him as the world spun around her.

It was just a kiss, and not even their first. But that kiss had been a tentative exploration. Now, she was more than ready to surrender to the passion that pulsed in her veins.

Except that he pulled back and raked a hand through his hair, already disheveled from her fingers. "See what you—"

She silenced him with her lips.

If Josh was surprised by her initiative, he didn't show it. He certainly didn't protest. And while his mouth was busy with hers, he slid his hands beneath the hem of her T-shirt. His fingertips glided over her stomach and his thumbs traced the underside of her breasts through the lace of her bra.

It was barely a graze, but her body immediately responded. Her nipples grew taut as heat pulsed in her veins. His hands shifted a little higher, and his thumbs brushed the peaks of her nipples this time. She gasped softly.

"Yes?" He whispered the question against her mouth.

She could say no.

She *should* say no.

This was her chance to put on the brakes, to take a step back. But she didn't want to put on the brakes. She didn't want to step back. She wanted Josh.

After an almost imperceptible hesitation, she replied, "Yes."

He unhooked the front fastening of her bra and pushed the cups aside. Then his hands were on her breasts, cradling their weight in his palms as his thumbs continued to trace and tease her nipples. It had been a long time since she'd had a man's hands on her, and the exquisite sensation of Josh's hands on her now nearly made her whimper.

Desperate to touch him, too, she tugged his T-shirt out of his shorts and slid her hands beneath the hem to explore the rippling muscles of his abdomen and chest. He pushed her shirt up and lowered his head to capture one turgid nipple in his mouth, suckling deeply. She gasped again as arrows of sensation shot toward her center.

He eased her back on the sofa and settled himself between her thighs. Even through her shorts and his, she could feel the rigid length of his erection. She instinctively lifted her pelvis to rub provocatively against him.

He grasped her hips in his hands. "You're killing me, Tris."

"I warned you that might happen if I came on this trip with you."

He chuckled softly. "Do you have any—"

She put a hand to his lips. "Shh."

He immediately stilled.

"I thought I heard something," she whispered to him. "What?"

"A click. Like the latch of a door."

The words were barely out of her mouth when the toilet flushed—a definite and timely reminder that they weren't alone.

She pushed him away and scrambled up off the sofa. She fumbled in her efforts to refasten her bra with unsteady hands, but finally got it done. She tugged her shirt back into place while the bathroom taps turned on, then off again. Her breathing was unsteady; her knees were trembling. Thankfully, it was almost dark now, so he probably couldn't see the hot color that filled her cheeks.

The bathroom door opened, then Charlotte turned back to her bedroom, giving no indication that she'd seen or heard anything.

Tristyn exhaled a shaky sigh.

"Tristyn—"

She shook her head. "Don't."

"Don't what?"

"Don't say anything."

"All I was going to say is that I'm sorry we're not alone," he told her.

She was sorry, too.

And grateful.

And unbearably aroused and incredibly confused.

She wanted him—she could no longer deny that simple fact.

But she didn't want to want him.

She especially didn't want to end up nursing a broken heart, and she knew that getting involved with Josh could only end in heartache.

She'd been so certain that she was in control of her emotions. That she could spend the better part of the summer with Josh and not be affected by his proximity. She'd managed to hold out for all of ten days.

She lifted her hands to her face, appalled by her own wanton behavior. If she hadn't heard Charlotte go into the bathroom—if they hadn't been reminded that they weren't alone—how far would they have gone?

She was ashamed to admit that she didn't know. That she couldn't be sure she would have put on the brakes. She'd been so incredibly aroused by his kiss and his touch, almost desperate for more.

"On the other hand, your bedroom door has a lock," he noted.

She shook her head. "You just want to sleep in my bed," she said lightly, attempting to shift the conversation back to safer ground.

He was silent for a moment, then he nodded, taking her cue. "Can't blame a guy for trying."

Josh went to bed alone.

After Tristyn retreated into her room, he pulled open the sofa bed and stretched out on top of the mattress. He tried to focus his thoughts on anything but Tristyn, but his efforts were futile. He didn't need to wonder about what might have happened if Charlotte hadn't woken up to go to the bathroom. There was no mistaking the fact that Tristyn had been as hot for him as he was for her. And if they hadn't been disturbed, they would have stripped their clothes away and finally given in to the passion that had burned between them for so long.

He didn't know whether to be grateful or annoyed that they'd been interrupted before that could happen. He did know that he was still aroused—rock hard and aching for her. Only her.

It took him a long time to fall asleep, and it seemed like only moments later that he felt something jab into his shoulder. And then again.

He opened one eye to find Hanna standing beside his bed, her favorite teddy bear clutched in one hand. "I had a bad dweam, Unca Josh."

He sat up and scrubbed his hands over his face, resigned to the fact that he wasn't going to get much sleep at all tonight. "What was your bad dream about?"

"I don't 'member," she told him.

"Then how do you know it was a bad dream?"

"'Cuz I woke up wif my tummy hurtin'."

"Do you need a drink?"

She shook her head.

"Do you want me to tuck you back into your bed?"

She shook her head again.

"What do you want?" he asked, unable to think of any other options.

"I wanna s'eep wif you."

"With me?"

She nodded. "P'ease."

He shifted over so Hanna had room to climb up. She was asleep again within two minutes—on his pillow.

Women, he mused, settling back on the edge of the mattress with his hands clasped behind his head and trying not to think about the woman who was sleeping on the other side of a very thin wall.

The only woman he wanted.

Chapter Twelve

Tristyn was awake first, as she usually was. Following her morning routine, she tiptoed into the kitchen to start the coffee brewing, then moved past the sofa bed where Josh was sprawled out, still sleeping, to the back bedroom, where the girls slept in their bunks.

As usual, Charlotte was on her tummy, her covers bunched up at her feet, her pillow on the floor. Emily was spread out like a starfish, using every inch of her mattress. Seeing the way she slept, Tristyn could understand why Charlotte had been unhappy about having to share a bed with her at Uncle Josh's condo. Hanna was…not in her bed.

Tristyn's breath caught in her throat and her heart started to race. She bent down to pull back the covers, in case the little girl was so tangled up inside she couldn't see her. She found four plush animals but not Hanna—and her favorite teddy bear was missing, too.

She rushed back to the living area—no longer worried about tiptoeing, not thinking about anything except that Josh's youngest niece was gone.

"Josh." She choked out his name as she shoved at his shoulder to wake him. "Josh—wake up. Hanna's gone."

"What?" He immediately bolted upright. "Where?"

"I don't know," she admitted, trying to quell the panic rising inside of her. "I went to check on the girls, like I do every morning, and—oh." Relief flooded her system and tears filled her eyes as she spotted his youngest niece curled up under the covers on the other side of the mattress. Tristyn smacked him again then, even harder this time.

"Ow." He rubbed his shoulder. "What was that for?"

"For letting me think that I'd lost your niece."

"I didn't let you think anything," he protested. "I didn't know what you were thinking until you came in here and started yelling—"

"I wasn't yelling," she retorted.

"You weren't whispering."

Of course, his voice was raised now, too, and Hanna shifted restlessly in the bed, her little brow furrowed.

Tristyn turned on her heel and retreated to the kitchen area. Though her heart hadn't yet settled back into its usual place inside her chest, the rhythm wasn't quite as fast and frantic as it had been a few minutes earlier.

She didn't realize Josh had followed until she turned around and nearly ran right into his chest. His broad, tanned and naked chest. She immediately stepped back—and bumped into the stove. He caught her shoulders to help steady her, except that she could feel the imprint of each and every finger through the thin fabric of her pajama top, and the effect was anything but steadying.

"I'm sorry you were worried," he murmured. "She had a bad dream and wanted to sleep with me."

"It wasn't your fault," she acknowledged, blinking back the tears that had filled her eyes. And maybe, if she hadn't been so deliberately averting her gaze from the tempting image of those broad shoulders, she might have noticed the little girl was tucked in beside him. "A bad dream, huh?"

He nodded and lifted a hand to brush away a tear that trembled on her lashes.

The unexpected gentleness of his touch sent a shiver down her spine. "And she went to Unca Josh to slay her dragons," she said, managing a weak smile.

"I'm no one's hero," he said, the words an unmistakable warning.

"Last night you were Hanna's," she pointed out.

"All I did was share my pillow."

"Sometimes a little kindness is all it takes."

He took two mugs from the cupboard and filled them with coffee from the pot, sliding one across the counter to her. "Do you ever have bad dreams?" he asked.

"Not bad enough to entice me to climb into your bed for comfort," she assured him.

"When you climb into my bed, it won't be for comfort," he said.

She wanted to take issue with his arrogant tone as much as his words, but she suspected that challenging his assertion would lead them down a dangerous path. A path that her mind warned could lead to heartache even as her body urged her to follow wherever he wanted to go.

"I need to get dressed," she said, and headed for the sanctuary of her bedroom instead.

Daniel and Kenna decided to bring their boys to the race at Indianapolis. They arrived on the Thursday night, so that Daniel could be at the track for qualifying on Friday, and came to the campground to visit with Josh and Tristyn and the girls. After spending some time at the playground—a much bigger park than at Sparta but which the girls agreed did not make up for the lack of a swimming pool—they went back to the RV, where Josh was going to barbecue chicken and ribs for dinner.

Over the past few days, Tristyn and Josh had gone back to tiptoeing around one another while the attraction between them continued to simmer just below the surface.

Thankfully, Josh's nieces were unaware of the tension between the adults, but Tristyn worried that her cousin and his wife wouldn't be. A worry that proved founded when Daniel caught Tristyn alone in the RV as she was putting together some snacks.

"So—how have things been going?" he asked.

"Good," she said, but kept her attention focused on the vegetable platter she was making.

"Do you think you could expand on that response a little?"

"What else do you want to know?"

He slid the platter away from her, forcing her to look up at him. "Do I need to beat up my business partner?"

She shook her head. "Absolutely not."

He held her gaze for another few seconds, then shook his head. "I should have discouraged you from doing this."

"Putting out snacks?" she asked, deliberately misunderstanding him.

"Spending your summer in close quarters with Josh."

"It was your idea," she reminded him.

"For Josh and his nieces," he agreed. "I didn't know he was going to ask you to go with them."

"It was actually Charlotte who asked. And while I wouldn't say it seemed like a good idea at the time, I wanted to help Josh—to help Charlotte, Emily and Hanna."

"And now?" he prompted.

She shrugged. "You know me and Josh are like oil and water much of the time, but we're managing."

Daniel pinned her with his gaze. "Do you still have feelings for him?"

She turned her focus back to her task. "I was infatuated with him for a short while when I was seventeen," she said. "I'm a lot older and a lot wiser now."

"And living with him," her cousin pointed out.

"A temporary arrangement."

Daniel nodded, but he still looked worried. "What if I said I needed you back at the office?"

Tristyn spooned dip into the bowl she'd set in the center of the platter. "Is Laurel struggling with things?"

"No, she's doing a great job," he admitted. "The only problem is that I don't like the way Josh has been looking at you."

"How has he been looking at me?"

"Like he wants to see you naked."

She felt her cheeks flame as she remembered how close they'd come to that actually happening, but for the grace of a seven-year-old's bladder. "I'm sure you're mistaken."

"I'm sure I'm not," he told her.

"Can we maybe switch to a less awkward topic of conversation?"

"I've known Josh a long time," Daniel continued, ignoring her request. "He's not just my business partner, he's my best friend."

"I know all of that," she reminded him.

"He's kind and generous and sincere—the type of guy who wouldn't hesitate to give the shirt off his back to help someone else."

"Is there a point to this?"

"The point is that he's generally a really great guy, but he doesn't have a clue when it comes to romantic relationships."

"No worries," she assured him. "Because we don't have a relationship—romantic or otherwise."

"And you're not just my cousin, but a valued member of our team. I don't want to lose you at GSR because Josh steps out of line."

"Stop worrying," she said again. "I can handle Josh."

"I hope so," Daniel said. "Because Kenna had the bright idea of inviting the girls for a slumber party in our hotel suite tomorrow night."

That gave her pause, but she was careful not to let Daniel know it. "You have two kids of your own already—why would you want to add three more?" she asked.

"Well, she suggested it to give you and Josh a break, and I agreed because she's been making noises about having another baby and this seemed like a good opportunity to see what a house full of kids would be like."

"You're counting on Josh's nieces to make your case in favor of birth control?" she guessed.

He shrugged. "I realize the plan may very well backfire. Kenna's always wanted a big family, and I think she'd really like to try for a girl."

"And if your plan does backfire?" Tristyn prompted.

"Then I guess we'll be talking to Ryder about an addition for our house."

Tristyn smiled, because the resignation in his tone was tempered by the overwhelming love that she knew her cousin had found with his wife. Four years earlier, Daniel had married Kenna for the sole purpose of gaining access to his trust fund and with the intention of divorcing her at the end of twelve months. Long before that deadline, they'd fallen in love.

Daniel's willingness to agree to anything his wife asked was proof of his love for her, and warmed Tristyn's heart. The prospect of spending a night in the RV alone with Josh heated the rest of her body.

And that was exactly what made her apprehensive about an evening without their pint-size chaperones.

While Daniel was catching up with Tristyn, Kenna was sharing her proposed plan with Josh.

"A slumber party?" he said dubiously.

"Kids love sleepovers," Kenna assured him.

"I'm not sure it's a good idea."

"You don't trust me with your nieces?" she asked, sounding hurt.

"You know that's not it," he told her.

"Then what is it?" she demanded.

"I just think you'll be pulling your hair out with five kids underfoot—and it's really pretty hair."

She smiled. "Always the charmer, aren't you?"

His gaze automatically shifted to the RV, with Tristyn inside. "Not everyone would agree with that assessment."

"A woman who's had her heart bruised is understandably going to be wary," Kenna told him. "Especially around the man who did the bruising."

Josh said nothing.

"I know why you did it," she said gently. "You deliberately hurt her a little because you were afraid of hurting her a lot."

"I didn't want to hurt her at all," he said.

"Have you explained that to Tristyn?"

"I've tried," he admitted. "But she won't listen. And maybe it's better that way—because nothing has really changed."

"Really?" Kenna looked at him skeptically. "Nothing has changed? Your feelings for her are exactly the same now as they were twelve years ago?"

"Well, I'm no longer denying that I want to get into her pants," he said.

Kenna merely lifted a brow. "I grew up on the south side," she reminded him. "I'm not shocked by a few crude words—and I'm not convinced, either."

"You don't believe I want to get into her pants?"

"I don't believe that's all you want," she said. "And if you do believe it, you're kidding yourself."

* * *

The next day, Josh dropped the girls off at the hotel with Kenna—as per her suggestion—so they didn't have to hang out at the track all day. While Josh and Daniel met with Ren and his crew chief, Tristyn was dealing with various administrative tasks. After the first round of qualifying was finished, Ren had the fastest time and was awarded the pole for Saturday's race.

"I guess the slumber party is a go," Josh said, when Tristyn came out of a meeting with Ren's personal assistant.

Tristyn shook her head. "Kenna is a brave woman."

"What about Daniel—doesn't he get any credit for agreeing to the plan?"

"No, because he had ulterior motives," she said, and went on to explain her cousin's rationale.

"So I guess they'll be having another kid," Josh said.

Tristyn laughed. "I guess they will."

"While Daniel and I were growing up, it was always our dream to be surrounded by fast cars and faster—" He glanced at her and abruptly closed his mouth.

"Women?" she guessed, and laughed again.

He shrugged. "My point is, I never would have pictured my best friend as a devoted husband and doting father, but there's no doubt those roles look good on him."

"They lucked out," Tristyn agreed. "They might have got married for the wrong reasons, but they decided to stay married for all the right ones."

"Yeah," Josh admitted. "But I didn't come in here to talk about Daniel and Kenna—aside from the fact that their offer to keep the girls overnight made me wonder if you'd want to go out for dinner tonight."

She raised an eyebrow. "Really? You're asking me to go out for dinner...with you?"

He shrugged. "I thought it might be a nice change for both of us."

"We've eaten dinner together almost every night for the past three weeks. How would this be a change?"

"For starters, you won't have to cook it," he told her.

"That would be a plus," she agreed.

"And since we won't have to worry about the dangers of children around an open flame, we could even dine by candlelight."

"That sounds…romantic," she said, her tone tinged with suspicion.

"Do you have something against romance?"

"No," she admitted. "But don't make the mistake of thinking that I'm going to let you share my bed just because you buy me a romantic dinner."

He didn't deny that he wanted to share her bed but only said, "What's your answer, Tristyn? Yes or no?"

She knew that he was asking about more than dinner. And if she said yes, she would be saying yes to more than dinner. She wanted to say yes, because the prospect of a night out, with wine and candlelight and adult conversation, was incredibly appealing.

The prospect of a night out with Josh—and taking their relationship to the next level—was undeniably unnerving. It had taken only one kiss for her to accept that there was some potent chemistry between them. The second kiss, which had very nearly led to a lot more, proved that any attempt to deny her attraction would be futile. But was she ready to give in to that attraction? Was she willing to be yet one more woman in a long line who had succumbed to the seductive charms of Josh Slater?

"Yes or no?" he asked again.

After a long moment during which she waged an internal battle over her decision, Josh nodded.

"It's okay," he said. "I understand."

"What do you understand?" she asked warily.

"You're afraid that, without the kids to act as a buffer, you won't be able to keep your hands off me," he said.

Tristyn rolled her eyes. "Maybe I'm afraid you won't be able to keep your hands off *me*," she countered.

"You shouldn't be," he told her. "If I find myself tempted, all I have to do is picture you in your granny jammies and the temptation will pass."

She knew she was being played—just as he knew she wouldn't be able to resist the challenge he'd issued.

"In that case, and because you do owe me a steak, my answer is yes," she said, and secretly vowed to make him eat his words before dinner was served.

Since Tristyn had mentioned wanting steak, Josh made a few inquiries, then a reservation at The Chophouse for seven o'clock. The restaurant was about a fifteen minute drive from the campground, so at six forty, he knocked on her bedroom door.

"Just a sec," Tristyn said.

Josh turned away to scoop up his keys and cell phone from the counter. He was occupied for no more than a second, and when he turned back, she was exiting the bedroom, as promised.

He expected her to be punctual. He didn't expect his tongue to nearly fall out of his mouth when he saw her.

It was his own fault. He realized that now. He'd issued the challenge and she'd responded—with devastating effectiveness.

Though he'd been joking about her granny jammies—mostly—at the moment, he couldn't even remember what they looked like. Because the dress she was wearing right now wrapped around her curves like a second skin. The skirt fell just a few inches above her knees, and the neckline dipped low between her breasts, revealing a shadowy hint of cleavage. Her long, shapely legs were bare, her feet tucked into sexy sandals with four-inch heels. Her usually smooth and sleek hair was teased and tousled as if she'd just crawled out of bed—an image that made him want to march her back through the door and topple onto the king-size mattress with her.

On any given day, she was beautiful. Sexy. Tempting. Tonight, she was stunning. Scorching. Irresistible.

He vaguely registered the movement of her lips—painted the same scarlet color as her dress—but he couldn't hear what she said over the roar of blood through his veins. "What?"

Those lips curved into a smile that was a lot sexy—and just a little bit smug. "I said I was ready to go."

He was ready to go, too, directly to her bedroom—

"Dinner," she prompted.

"Dinner. Right."

He looked around for his keys, then remembered he had them in his hand.

He put his other hand—without the keys—on the small of her back to guide her toward his truck. She sucked in a breath, a response that assured him she wasn't as unaffected by his touch as she pretended to be.

He opened the passenger-side door for her and she eyed the distance between the ground and the seat doubtfully. "Clearly I wasn't thinking about our mode of transportation when I bought this dress."

"What were you thinking about?" he asked, as he lifted her onto the seat.

"Making you drool," she admitted.

His gaze raked over her again. "Mission accomplished."

Chapter Thirteen

The hostess seated them at a table for two and handed them menus in embossed leather folders. The ivory linen tablecloth was pristine, the silverware gleamed, the crystal sparkled. The overhead lighting was subdued, supplemented by the flame of a votive candle that flickered behind a hurricane shade.

Tristyn had just started to peruse the menu when a waitress came by to deliver warm bread and offer drinks. After they'd ordered, they shared a few minutes of easy, casual conversation before Josh looked at her across the table and said, "You're going to make me admit it, aren't you?"

She folded her arms on the table and leaned forward, well aware that the posture pushed her breasts up to the neckline of her dress. "What is it that you don't want to admit?"

To his credit, he kept his eyes locked on hers. Mostly.

"That the way you look in that dress is enough to make me forget about your granny jammies."

"That almost sounds like a compliment," she mused.

"You've probably been told that you're beautiful more times than you can count."

"Maybe," she acknowledged. "But I've never heard *you* say those words."

"Do you need me to say them?"

"Only if you believe them."

His gaze held steady on hers. "You, Tristyn Garrett, are the most beautiful woman I've ever known."

"Hmm…that sounded like the well-rehearsed line of a man who's hoping to end the evening in a woman's bed."

"I'm not going to deny that I'm hoping, but that doesn't make the words any less true," he told her. "And if they sounded rehearsed, it's only because I've thought them a thousand times in my mind."

And when he looked at her the way he was looking at her now, she almost believed him. Then she reminded herself that this was Josh—and Josh had probably charmed more females out of their panties than she wanted to count. Thankfully, the arrival of the servers with their plates saved her from having to respond, because she was afraid that anything she said would reveal the effect his words had on her.

She'd opted for a thick, juicy rib eye, and it was prepared just the way she liked it, served with a fully loaded baked potato and broccoli florets. Josh had the prime rib with mashed potatoes and baby carrots. While they ate their food and sipped a delicious Cabernet Sauvignon, they chatted about various current events and shared news from home.

Thinking about her sisters and her cousins, she was reminded of her promise to herself that she would never settle for anything less than the forever-after kind of love each of them had found with their respective partners. So why had she agreed to this date with Josh tonight when she knew that he wasn't the man to give her what she wanted?

Okay, he could give her some of what she wanted— because she also really wanted to get naked with him and discover if he lived up to his reputation. But getting involved with him, even temporarily, could screw up a lot of things. Not just because they had to work together when they went back to Charisma, but because he was practically a member of her family.

"What are you thinking about?" Tristyn asked, when she realized that Josh had also been silent for several minutes. Then she shook her head. "That's a silly question to ask the night before a race—of course you're thinking about Ren's chances tomorrow."

"Actually, I wasn't thinking about the race," he admitted. "In fact, I haven't thought about the race or the team or anything related to GSR since you walked out of your bedroom in that killer dress."

"Then I guess it was worth every penny that I paid for it," she mused.

"Except it's not only the dress."

"You're one of those guys who likes a woman in high heels, aren't you?"

"Well, yes," he agreed, lifting the wine bottle to top up her glass. "But that wasn't what I meant, either."

"What did you mean?"

"It's the woman inside the dress—and the shoes—who continues to intrigue me," he told her. "I've known you for almost twenty years. I spend more holidays with your family than my own. And for the past three years, I've seen you almost every day at work."

She picked up her glass, sipped.

"After all that time, you'd think I'd know everything about you," he continued. "That we'd run out of things to talk about. But you continue to fascinate me, and I'm never bored in your company."

"So why do you look as if you're worried about something?" she asked.

"Because you worry me," he confided. "I look at you and I know you could be the perfect woman for me.

"But I'm not looking for the perfect woman," he hastened to add. "What you said to the girls about me was true—I'm not looking to settle down. I don't want to give up my lifestyle for a ring on my finger, rug rats at home and a woman in my bed—not even a woman as beautiful and tempting as you."

"Well, you can stop worrying," she told him. "Because I'm not looking to be your perfect woman. I do want what each of my sisters has found with her husband—someday. But I'm not looking to settle down right now, either." Okay, that was a little white lie, but she decided it was a forgivable one under the circumstances. "And I promise you, even if I was, I know better than to look in your direction."

"So what are you looking for now?" he asked her.

She thought about his question for a minute before answering, "To satisfy my curiosity."

He reached across the table and stroked the back of her hand. "I can satisfy more than your curiosity."

The way her body responded to his casual touch, she had no doubt that he could. But admitting as much would be a boost that his ego didn't need.

"Give me a chance to prove it," he urged.

"I'm thinking about it," she admitted.

His eyes lit with wicked promise, but before he could say anything, the waitress came by with dessert menus.

"I'm not sure I could eat another bite," Tristyn said, even as she skimmed the offerings. "Oh, but they have a tiramisu cake."

"You do have a sweet tooth, don't you?"

"I do," she agreed. "But the cake probably wouldn't be as good as Rafe's tiramisu."

Josh's jaw tightened perceptibly at the mention of the other man's name. "Are you still seeing him?"

"I've been on the road with you for the past three weeks. When would I have seen him?"

He nodded in acknowledgment of her point. "Okay, maybe what I should have asked is—are you planning to see him again when you get back to Charisma?"

"I don't know," she admitted. "We kind of left things open-ended."

"We're going to close that opening," he told her. "You and me—tonight."

A quick thrill of anticipation raced through her veins, but Tristyn refused to let him see it. Instead, she lifted her wineglass, sipped.

"Have you decided on dessert?" the waitress returned to their table to ask.

"Yes," Tristyn said. "I'll have the tiramisu cake."

"To go," Josh said firmly.

"Yes, sir." The server nodded and slipped away again.

Tristyn lifted a brow. "What if I want to eat my dessert here?"

The heat in his gaze practically melted her bones. "Finish your wine, Tristyn."

Though it wasn't in her nature to blindly follow orders, she picked up her glass and finished her wine.

Josh ignored the speed limit as he drove to the campground. Tristyn didn't object, because the truth was, she was just as eager as he was to get back to the RV. By the time he pulled up beside the fifth wheel, her heart was pounding so loudly she was certain he must be able to hear it.

Tonight, she thought, with almost giddy relief.

Finally, tonight, she was going to experience the bliss of making love with Josh. And the way her body responded to his kiss, his touch, she didn't doubt for a minute that it would be bliss.

He came around to open her door and helped her out of the truck. When he set her down, he took her hand, his thumb brushing the inside of her wrist, where her pulse was racing. He unlocked the RV and gestured for her to enter.

"You're having second thoughts," he guessed, when she hesitated inside the door.

"Not about tonight," she told him.

"About what?"

"Tomorrow," she admitted. "I don't want things to be awkward and weird in the morning."

"So don't act awkward and weird in the morning," he advised.

A smile tugged at her lips as she shook her head. "Is it really that simple for you?"

"I'm a guy," he reminded her. "It's not in my nature to overthink things."

"You don't have *any* concerns about how this will affect our working relationship?"

"My only worry right now is that you might change your mind. But it's your choice, Tristyn. If you tell me you don't want me, don't want this, I'll walk away."

Of course, she couldn't do it. Maybe she did have some reservations, but she knew that if she backed out now, she'd regret it for the rest of her life. Still, she couldn't resist teasing him, just a little.

She tipped her head back and kept her gaze steady on his as she said, "I don't want…"

His eyes narrowed when she paused.

"…to waste any more time talking."

His only response was to draw her into his arms and cover her lips with his own.

Her physical reaction was immediate and intense. If this was the chemistry he'd referred to, she'd never experienced it—not to the same extent—with anyone else. She willingly parted her lips as he deepened the kiss, and the erotic stroke of his tongue stirred a new hunger inside her.

She lifted her arms to link them behind his neck as she pressed herself closer to him. His hands skimmed down her back, to the hem of her dress, then dipped beneath it to slide up her thighs to her buttocks. He groaned, a sound of pure male appreciation. "You're wearing a thong."

"I don't like panty lines."

"I don't care why—I'm just grateful," he told her, his hands kneading her bare flesh. Then he pushed her skirt up and dropped to his knees in front of her.

Her stomach quivered; her thighs trembled. "Josh."

He glanced up, his eyes hot and intent. "Do you have any objections?"

She could only shake her head.

"Good," he said, and pressed his mouth to the triangle of lace at the apex of her thighs.

She reached behind to grab hold of the edge of the counter for balance as he explored her intimately with his tongue and his teeth. The barrier of lace was hardly that, but he paused long enough to yank it away and gain unfettered access. He drove her quickly toward the verge of climax…then ruthlessly pushed her over the edge.

The orgasm ripped through her body, so fierce and strong her knees actually buckled, and she would have crumpled to the floor if Josh hadn't been holding her up. With a satisfied grin, he rose to his feet and scooped her into his arms and carried her to the bedroom. He set her on her feet beside the bed and ripped back the covers.

"The first time is going to be fast," he warned.

"Not fast enough," she said, tugging at his tie, then immediately going to work on the buttons of his shirt.

"And I thought I was impatient," he teased, kicking off his shoes and socks.

"I feel as if I've been waiting for you forever," she admitted, pushing his shirt over his shoulders and running her hands over the smooth, hard muscles of his chest.

"Not much longer," he promised, unfastening the buckle of his belt, then quickly discarding his pants and knit boxers.

She reached for him then, wrapping her fingers around the velvety length of him. He sucked in a breath.

"It's going to be too fast if you keep that up," he warned.

She opened the drawer of the night table and pulled out a little square packet, because there had never been any doubt in her mind about how this night would end and she'd wanted to be prepared. She carefully tore the wrapper and removed the condom, then deftly unrolled the latex over his rigid shaft.

"Now," she told him.

At any other time, Josh might have been amused by her bossy tone. Right now, he was too aroused to do anything but obey. He dumped her unceremoniously onto the bed and spread her legs, then finally positioned himself between them.

He was rock hard and aching for her, desperate to take what she was offering. He drove into her, groaning in satisfaction as he was enveloped by her wet heat. She cried out his name as another series of tremors rippled through her body—and his. The clenching of her inner muscles around him was almost more than he could stand. He fisted his hands in the bedsheet and counted his ragged breaths while he waited out her climax.

When the tremors began to abate, he slowly withdrew, then pushed in again, steady strokes that increased in speed and had her breath coming in shallow gasps.

"I don't... I can't... Oh...my...oh...yes... Josh."

When the next waves of pleasure began to roll through her, he let himself ride along with her until they were dragged under together.

* * *

It was a long time later before Josh managed to catch his breath again, before he rolled away from Tristyn and went to discard the condom. When he came back from the bathroom, she still hadn't moved. Her hair was spread out on her pillow, her skirt was bunched around her waist and one strap of her dress had fallen down to her elbow, exposing the luscious curve of one creamy breast. She looked like she'd just been ravished, and the smile that curved her lips assured him that she'd thoroughly enjoyed the experience.

"I didn't even take your dress off you."

"You can take it off me now," she suggested.

He reached for her hand and helped her up off the bed.

"I really do like the way you look in this dress," he told her, nudging the other strap from her shoulder. "But I think I'm going to like you naked even more."

He found the zipper hidden at the side, then peeled the garment slowly down her body. Undressing Tristyn was like unwrapping a coveted birthday present, and he sincerely regretted skipping this step earlier. Especially when he discovered that she was wearing a lace demi-cup bra that matched the thong he'd dispensed with much earlier. There was something about the contrast of the sexy black lingerie against the creamy silk of her skin that had an immediate and predictable effect on him.

His body's reaction did not go unnoticed. "Apparently the rumors about your stamina were not exaggerated," Tristyn said.

Over the years, he'd done nothing to dispel the rumors he knew she would hear, because he'd trusted that his reputation would be an effective barrier between them. And it had worked—maybe too well. Because now that he finally had her where he'd wanted her for so long, he didn't want any obstacles in the way. But he wasn't quite ready to bare his heart and soul and admit that, for the past twelve years, she was the only one he'd wanted, so he only said, "Let's see if you can keep up."

He hooked his fingers in the straps of her bra and tugged them down, then dipped his head to kiss the curve of her breasts. First one, then the other. Her nipples strained against the fabric, a silent request that he couldn't ignore. He took one of the turgid peaks in his mouth and suckled gently. A low sound of pleasure hummed deep in her throat as her fingers slid into his hair.

"This time isn't going to be fast," he told her. "This time, I'm going to take my time exploring every inch of your delectable body."

And he did. He traced every dip and curve with his hands and his lips, pausing only to turn her onto her stomach so he could continue his exploration on her backside.

"You have a tattoo on your butt."

She glanced at him over her shoulder. "Do you have a problem with tattoos?"

"No," he assured her. "I guess I'm just…surprised." He traced the outline of the tat with his thumb. "Is it Celtic?"

She nodded. "It's a quaternary knot. Some people believe the four sides represent the four seasons, others claim that they're representative of the four cardinal directions."

"Why did you choose to get a quaternary knot tattooed on your butt?" he asked.

"I like the symbolism of it. The unending paths illustrate continuity and eternity, and the weaving together of the different strands suggests unity."

"I like it, too," he said, then slid down her body and kissed the inked flesh.

"Now I can tell everyone that Josh Slater kissed my butt," she teased.

His lips curved as he tore open another condom. "You've told me to often enough—although I think you used a word other than *butt*."

"That's because you're often a pain in my...butt."

"Yeah, we do have a tendency to rub one another the wrong way," he acknowledged, as he covered himself to protect both of them.

"I like the way you're rubbing against me now," she told him.

"Let's see what else you like," he said, and slid into her.

Her eyes closed on a sigh. "That," she said. "I really like that."

"And this?" he asked, and began to move.

"Oh, yeah," she agreed.

Later, Josh fell asleep with Tristyn in his arms. But they came together again and again in the night, unable to get enough of one another. When he woke up in the morning, he automatically reached for her and was disappointed to discover that he was alone.

He glanced at the clock just as she walked through the door carrying two mugs.

"I know you can't function in the morning without your caffeine," she said, offering coffee to him.

He took the mug and set it on the table beside the bed, then reached for hers and put it down, too.

She frowned. "What are you doing?"

"Apparently, I need to show you that my function is just fine in the morning."

She laughed softly. "I wasn't disparaging your manhood," she assured him. "I just thought you'd want coffee."

What he wanted, what he couldn't seem to get enough of, was Tristyn. But he wasn't going to think about that now. Because if he thought about it, he'd worry about it, and he didn't want to waste any of the time they had together worrying.

As he'd told her the night before, he didn't like to overthink things. *Keep it simple*, he reminded himself.

"There are some things that are even better than coffee in the morning," he said, tugging her down onto the mattress and rolling on top of her to prove it.

Chapter Fourteen

A long time later, while Josh was in the shower, Tristyn reheated the coffee that had gone cold while they'd lingered in bed. She had no complaints. In fact, she thought she might be able to give up coffee completely if she could wake up with him in her bed every morning—but that was dangerous thinking.

Because as spectacular as it had been to make love with Josh, she knew she couldn't let it happen again. She'd wanted to satisfy her curiosity; he'd done that and more. Expecting, or even allowing, one night to become two would be a mistake.

"We need to get to the track," she said, when he was showered and dressed.

"Yeah, we do," he agreed, though he slid his arms around her and drew her close.

"And Ren has the pole today," she said, though it was unlikely he needed a reminder.

"I have a pole, too," he said, rubbing against her.

A laugh bubbled up inside her even as her body began to respond to his. "Unfortunately, we don't have time to deal with your...pole—again," she said.

"Maybe later?" he asked hopefully.

She shook her head. "I don't think so."

Josh frowned at her response, no doubt unaccustomed to a woman saying no to him—especially a woman who had already said yes. But it was important to Tristyn to put their relationship back on the friendship track. It was the only way she could be sure she wouldn't fall for him again.

"So this was a one-night stand?" he asked.

"Well, technically one night and one morning," she said lightly.

"What if one night and one morning wasn't enough?"

She couldn't let his question sway her. Even if he wanted more nights and more mornings now, he would eventually decide that there had been enough, and she'd be the one left nursing a broken heart.

"Last night was incredible," she admitted. "But pretending it was anything more than a night of really great sex would be a mistake."

He didn't dispute her characterization, but he did ask, "Why is one night of really great sex okay, but two nights— or two weeks or two months—would be a mistake?"

"Because our lives are too closely entwined," she pointed out. "You're not just my boss and my cousin's best friend, you're practically an honorary member of my family."

"So this is it? We just go back to the way things were, as if last night never happened?"

"I'm not likely to forget it—and I don't want to," she admitted. "But it can't happen again."

"I said that it was your choice, and I meant it," he said. "But I can't pretend I'm not disappointed."

"Better to be disappointed now than heartbroken later," she said lightly.

"Maybe you're right," he finally agreed.

Josh wasn't happy with Tristyn's unilateral decision to put on the brakes. He wasn't looking for a long-term relationship, but he had hoped that they could continue to enjoy being together throughout the summer. Before they'd made love, being around her and not being able to touch her had almost been impossible. Now that he knew how she responded to his touch, not being able to touch her was going to be torturous.

Pretending it was anything more than a night of really great sex would be a mistake.

Maybe she was right. Maybe he was trying to make it into something more because he felt guilty about getting naked with his best friend's cousin. But he'd had one-night stands before without obsessing about any of the women afterward. So why was he obsessing about Tristyn now?

He'd walked away from her twelve years earlier, not because he wanted to but because he knew it was necessary. Somehow, even then, he'd known that if he touched her, if he tasted her, he'd never want to let her go.

For so long, he'd wanted no one but her. But he'd ignored the truth and he'd turned his attention to other women, certain that they could satisfy the aching need inside him. He'd been wrong.

He hadn't expected making love with Tristyn to change anything—except maybe to alleviate the sexual tension they'd been living with. He didn't expect to feel any differently about her or their situation. Now that he'd experienced the thrill of making love with Tristyn, he wondered if he could ever be satisfied with anyone else, anything less than her hungry kisses, eager touches and unbridled passion.

And he wanted more than one night, dammit. He wanted more conversations under the stars, more lazy mornings, even more games of mini-putt and arguments over laundry duty. He especially wanted more opportunities to make love with her all through the night until the sun began to rise.

Wanting those things should have created a full-scale panic. He wasn't supposed to want those things. He'd never wanted them before.

But the wanting didn't scare him. What scared him was the realization that if he let her go, he might forever lose his chance to have everything he'd ever wanted. And Tristyn was that everything.

Tristyn had worried that there would be tension between her and Josh when they went back to the RV, but the presence of his nieces—and their incessant chatter—ensured otherwise, allowing them to fall back into the routines they'd already established.

After the first day, she was relieved to note that Josh didn't seem inclined to challenge her "one night" directive. But sometimes when she was in the kitchen, he'd come in to get a drink or a snack and make a point of squeezing past her in the narrow space, ensuring that his body brushed against hers. If she asked him to pass her something at the dinner table, he'd let his fingers graze hers in the transfer, and linger longer than was necessary.

It all had the appearance of innocence, but she knew better. There wasn't an innocent bone in Josh's body and he was deliberately attempting to stir up her hormones. What he didn't know, what she wouldn't admit, was that his actions were unnecessary. Because she hadn't stopped wanting him, and being in close proximity to him day after day—even without his deliberately provocative touches—was quietly but steadily driving her insane.

Every once in a while, she'd catch him looking at her with undisguised hunger in his eyes. It was admittedly thrilling—and arousing—to know that he still desired her. Though none of her reasons for not wanting to get involved with him had changed, ultimately none of them proved strong enough to counter her own desire.

After Indianapolis they headed to Pocono, breaking up the six hundred plus mile journey into two parts. When they got to their scheduled stop after the first part, it was right in the middle of a torrential downpour. By the time Josh finished the hookups—having rejected Tristyn's suggestion that he wait to see if the storm would pass—he was soaked and the girls were cranky from being cooped up in the truck for six hours.

Searching online, Tristyn found a family fun center not too far away. After Josh had dried off and changed, they headed out so the kids could climb and jump at the indoor jungle gym. Then Tristyn slipped away while Josh and his nieces were bumper bowling to do a little personal shopping. When she returned, everyone was "starving," so they went next door for pizza.

The rain had stopped by the time they got back to the RV, and soon after that the girls were snuggled into their respective bunks and fast asleep. Josh took some time then to catch up on emails and phone messages while Tristyn debated with herself the wisdom of changing the rules in the middle of a game.

Josh was on the phone with Daniel when Tristyn came out of her bedroom. And she wasn't wearing the familiar pink-striped pajamas he liked to tease her about. He felt his body stir as his gaze skimmed over her—from the top of her head to the tips of her toes, lingering on the fantasy of silk and lace that barely covered up all his favorite parts in between.

He heard a voice in his ear, but he was no longer following the conversation. As if of its own volition, his thumb tapped the screen, disconnecting the call.

Tristyn arched a brow, her green eyes dancing with amusement. "Did you just hang up on your business partner and best friend?"

"I think I did."

"And how are you going to explain that to him?" she asked.

Josh couldn't tear his eyes away from the feminine curves showcased in fantasy lingerie. "Bad cell phone coverage in this area." He cleared his throat. "Um…what happened to your granny jammies?"

"They're in the laundry."

He swallowed. "Oh."

Her lips curved then. "You're not going to comment on what I'm wearing instead?"

"No," he said, then changed his mind. "Except that maybe you should put on a robe. You look…cold."

"I'm not cold," she assured him, stepping forward to stand directly in front of him.

"Okay," he said.

"I saw this when I was shopping today, and I thought it fit your description of peekaboo lace."

The delicate lace panels did provide tantalizing glimpses of her skin. And the silky fabric seemed to caress her shapely curves. "You were thinking of me when you bought this?"

"Actually…I was thinking about how much I'd like you to take it off me."

He swallowed again. "What about your one-night rule?"

She lifted the hem of her silky slip, exposing several inches of shapely thigh, then bracketed his hips with her knees. As she settled onto his lap, all of the blood from his brain did, too.

"I've decided that it requires a minor amendment," she told him.

"An amendment?" he echoed, because he didn't seem capable of finding words of his own.

"Mmm hmm." She tugged his T-shirt out of his shorts and slid her palms beneath it.

He cleared his throat. "What kind of, uh, amendment?"

"That so long as we're together this summer, we should have as much sex as often as possible."

"That's a…major…amendment," he noted, struggling to maintain his train of thought as she raked her nails lightly down his chest.

"I was concerned that having sex again would complicate our relationship," she admitted, leaning forward to press her lips to his jaw. "But not having sex these last four nights hasn't done anything to simplify our relationship, has it?"

"That's true," he agreed, in a strangled tone.

"And if we both want the same thing—" she nipped lightly at his chin "—why are we denying ourselves?"

"I have no idea."

She looked at him now, and he saw that there was a hint of uncertainty in her desire-clouded eyes. "Do we both want the same thing?"

He wondered how she could possibly question the effect she had on him, and he silently vowed to eliminate the last of her doubts here and now. "If the same thing is me buried deep inside you, then I'd say yes."

Her lips curved. "Do you want to discuss this some more or do you want to take me to bed?"

"I want to take you—right here, right now," he told her, his gaze hot and hungry. "But considering that there are three little girls sleeping less than thirty feet away, your bed is probably a better idea."

"Probably," she agreed.

He wrapped his arms around her and lifted her with him as he stood. She hooked her legs behind his back so that their bodies were aligned from chest to hip and all the erogenous points in between. He carried her like that to the bedroom, pausing only to ensure the door was closed and locked before he tumbled on top of the mattress with her.

* * *

The first night they'd spent together had been an introduction to the exquisite joy of sex with Josh Slater. This time, Tristyn thought she knew what to expect. She was wrong.

Every time she believed that he'd taken her to the limit, he showed her that there was more. It was as if he knew her body better than she did. He certainly knew where to touch, when to linger, to enhance her sensual pleasure.

"I didn't expect it to be as good this time," she admitted.

Josh lifted a brow as he leisurely stroked a hand down her back.

"I figured part of the rush was the realization of long-term anticipation, and that once that mystery was gone, the intensity would fade."

"You were wrong."

She nodded. "You could become an addiction."

"You already are," he said, drawing her close.

He kissed her again, and Tristyn realized it had never been like this with anyone else. Probably because she'd never before had a lover of Josh's caliber and experience, and she wasn't going to delude herself into thinking that a shocking number of orgasms was indicative of anything other than that.

"Hey," he said, drawing her attention back to him. "Where'd you go?"

"Sorry, I guess my thoughts wandered."

"Wherever they wandered, they put a line between your brows," he observed, touching a finger to the crease. "Do you want to tell me about it?"

"Not really."

He waited patiently.

She sighed. "I was just thinking about how you acquired your intimate and extensive knowledge of the female body," she admitted.

"I haven't lived like a monk," he acknowledged. "But the stories you heard me tell may have been exaggerated a little—for your benefit."

"For *my* benefit? Why?"

"Because I wanted to give you a reason to stay far away from me," he confessed. "But I haven't been with as many women as you think."

"The number doesn't matter," she decided. "As long as the number of women you're involved with right now is one."

"You are the only one," he assured her. "The only one I'm with—the only one I want."

"For now but not forever," she reminded him.

"You do like your rules," he mused.

"And another of those rules is no overnight guests."

"You're trying to kick me out of your bed, aren't you?"

"It wouldn't look right if one of the girls woke up and found you were in my bed instead of your own," she told him.

"Alright," he finally relented, unable to dispute her point. "Do I at least get a good-night kiss?"

"I think you've already had more than a few good-night kisses," she said, nudging him toward the edge of the mattress.

"Uh uh," he denied. "Those were precoital, midcoital and postcoital kisses."

She was smiling as she shook her head. "It will probably be quicker for me to give you a good-night kiss than to debate your categorizations, won't it?"

"Probably," he agreed.

So she kissed him good-night, and by the time she eased her lips from his, she was tempted to break her own rule and invite him to spend the night in her bed. But she was afraid that breaking one rule would set a precedent that encouraged her to disregard others. And if she did that, she might foolishly open up her heart and fall in love with him—and that was a risk she wasn't willing to take.

Chapter Fifteen

Of the three sisters, Emily was usually the first awake. In the mornings, while Tristyn sat outside enjoying a cup of coffee, the five-year-old was often there to keep her company. The first morning in Pennsylvania, she'd barely taken a sip from her cup when the little girl said, "Look, Tristyn—my tooth is really wiggly now."

"Wow," she said, trying to sound more impressed than repulsed when Emily managed to push the tooth with her tongue so that it was practically horizontal in her mouth. "I don't think it's going to be much longer before that comes out."

"An' then the tooth fairy comes," the little girl announced.

"Does she?" Tristyn said, wondering if there were guidelines as to what the tooth fairy was supposed to give in exchange for a tooth. "And what does the tooth fairy do?"

"She gives money!"

"Like an ATM?"

Emily giggled. "Not that much money. Just a dollar."

"Still, a dollar for a tooth—that seems like a pretty good deal to me."

The child's smile slipped. "Do you think the tooth fairy will be able to find me here?"

"I'm sure she'll be able to find you, wherever you are," Tristyn assured her.

Emily's tooth came out when she was brushing her teeth before bed that night. The gentle pressure of her brush was all it took to set it free. As a result, there was hardly any blood, for which Tristyn was extremely grateful.

"Do you have a dollar for the tooth fairy?" she asked Josh, after the girls had all fallen asleep.

"Isn't she supposed to leave the money?"

Tristyn rolled her eyes as Josh opened his wallet.

"The smallest bill I have is a ten," he said.

"You can't give her ten dollars for losing a tooth," Tristyn protested. "Or Charlotte and Hanna will be trying to pull out their teeth, too."

"I'm guessing you don't have a dollar?"

She nipped the ten out of his fingers as she shook her head. "I used the last of my cash to buy ice-cream cones for the girls this afternoon."

"So what are you going to do with that?"

"I'll go to the little store beside registration and ask for change."

She came back less than ten minutes later with a package of candy in her hand.

He shook his head, as if disappointed. "You traded the cow for magic beans?"

"You read *Jack and the Beanstalk* to Hanna tonight, didn't you?" she guessed.

"Last night," he admitted.

"Gummy bears not magic beans," she said, showing him the package.

He made a face. "Gummy bears?"

"You have something against gummy bears?"

"The last time I had gummy bears, they got stuck in my braces," he told her.

"I knew that perfect smile had to have orthodontic help," she mused.

"You didn't have braces?"

She shook her head and leaned close to whisper, "Everything about me is au naturel."

"Except the tattoo," he said, pulling her down into his lap. "Did you get a dollar for the tooth fairy?"

She drew the change out of her pocket and set it on the table, then tore open her package of candy. "Do you want to share my gummy bears?"

"No, thanks. I'll have my treat later—in accordance with the amended agreement."

She nibbled on a piece of candy. "When I said as much sex as often as possible, I didn't realize you were insatiable," she teased.

"Are you growing bored with me already?"

"Not quite yet," she said. But the truth was just the opposite. The more time she spent with Josh, the more she wanted to be with him. As phenomenal as the sex was, it wasn't all about the sex. They would often snuggle together in her bed for hours afterward, talking about all manner of things and nothing in particular. She'd known Josh for a lot of years, but there were a lot of things she still didn't know about him and she was enjoying the discovery process. She definitely wasn't bored, and she suspected that she could spend a lifetime with him and not tire of his company and companionship.

For now, not forever, she reminded herself.

And focused on enjoying the now.

Emily woke up in the morning, panicked and crying. "It's gone! It's gone!"

Tristyn rushed into her room, wondering what could

have put the little girl into such a state of distress. "What's gone?"

Tears streamed down the child's face. "My tooth."

She exhaled a slow breath, confident the crisis would pass when Emily found the payment she'd received in exchange for the tooth. "Well, the tooth fairy must have come to get it," she said, attempting to soothe her. "Is there any money in its place?"

Emily nodded and held up the crumpled bill, but the tears continued to fall. "The tooth fairy isn't s'posed to take it."

Josh—standing in the doorway after being awakened by the little girl's cries along with everyone else—exchanged a look with Tristyn. "She's not?"

The distraught child shook her head. "Not the first one. Only the ones that come after."

The adults exchanged another look.

"That's a new one to me," Tristyn admitted.

"Maybe the tooth fairy didn't realize it was your first one," Josh said, as Charlotte looked at the adults suspiciously.

"Mommy kept Charlotte's first tooth in a special box," Emily said. "An' she has boxes for me an' Hanna, too. An' now my box is always gonna be empty."

Desperate for a solution to the dilemma, Tristyn impulsively said, "Maybe we can get your tooth back."

Emily sniffled. "How?"

"We can write a note to the tooth fairy."

Charlotte immediately shook her head. "That won't work—the tooth fairy only comes when someone loses a tooth, so she wouldn't be here to see the note."

Emily started to cry harder.

"There's got to be some way we can get her attention," Tristyn said, looking desperately at Josh for help.

"Smoke signals," he suggested.

Emily lifted her head and wiped her tear-streaked cheeks.

"What are smoke signals?" Charlotte asked suspiciously.

"It's an ancient way of communicating over great distances, developed long before cell phones."

His eldest niece still looked skeptical.

"That's a great idea," Tristyn declared, though she wasn't at all convinced that his plan would satisfy the girls—or that Josh knew the first thing about creating smoke signals.

"How do you make smoke signals?" Charlotte asked.

"First, you build a fire," he said.

Emily stopped sniffling long enough to ask, "Can we make s'mores at the fire?"

He glanced at Tristyn. She nodded, mentally adding the necessary ingredients to her shopping list.

"Sure," he said. "But only after we summon the tooth fairy."

"How will we know if she got the message?" Emily asked worriedly.

"We won't know for sure until tomorrow," Josh admitted. "But if it doesn't work tonight, we'll try again and again until it does."

Worried that he might set the camp on fire in his effort to generate smoke signals, Tristyn offered an alternate suggestion. "Maybe the tooth fairy's on Twitter."

"That would certainly be easier," he agreed.

"Why don't you come into the kitchen and we'll see if we can figure this out after we've had breakfast?" Tristyn suggested.

The girls immediately complied, and when everyone had eaten, Tristyn opened her tablet and linked to the social media site, then searched for "tooth fairy." The screen filled with potential matches.

Emily, sitting up on her knees now, peered at the screen, her brow furrowed. "But which one's the *real* tooth fairy?"

"The real tooth fairy will find our message," Tristyn assured her.

"What should we say?"

"Maybe something like 'recall requested hashtag tooth fairy'?" she suggested.

"But that doesn't tell her who or where," Charlotte pointed out.

Which was true, because Tristyn had hoped to keep the message deliberately vague. "What if we add 'by Emily at Pocono Mountain RV Park'?"

Emily nodded her approval; her older sister still looked dubious.

"Let's give it a shot," Tristyn urged. "If it doesn't work, we can try the smoke signals tomorrow, okay?"

"Can we still have s'mores tonight?" Emily asked.

"We can still have s'mores tonight," she confirmed. "*If* you all get washed up and dressed and come shopping with me."

"But you haven't hit Send," Charlotte pointed out.

"Oh, right." With the three girls and their uncle looking on, Tristyn tapped the button and the message went out into the world.

Lucy called while Tristyn was out shopping with the girls, which gave Josh an opportunity to fill her in on the tooth fairy fiasco. She laughed when he told her about the tweet, then she sighed wistfully.

"I didn't realize she had a loose tooth, or I would have told you about the tooth fairy."

"That would have been good," Josh agreed. "I'm just glad that I actually did keep the tooth for you rather than tossing it in the trash."

"Her first tooth," Lucy said, with a little sniffle.

"She'll lose a lot more before she's through," he pointed out.

"I know," she admitted.

"How are things going there?" he asked, in an effort to divert a complete meltdown.

"Good," she said. "We're actually a little bit ahead of schedule."

"I guess that means you haven't taken much time to see the sights."

"There's nothing here that I want to see as much as my girls," his sister said.

"It won't be too long before you're home again," he soothed. "And then I'll finally get my life back."

Except that the life he had before embarking on this road trip with Tristyn didn't hold the same appeal anymore. Because in that life, he crossed paths with Tristyn at the office and Garrett family events, but he didn't have the right to drag her into a corner to steal a kiss, or sneak into her bedroom at night, or even just sit out under the stars and talk about anything and everything.

"I know I didn't really give you a choice about any of this," Lucy admitted, drawing his attention back to their conversation. "But I appreciate everything you're doing."

"I'm enjoying spending time with them," he admitted, no longer surprised to realize it was true.

"And how are things going with Tristyn?" she prompted.

"Even from another country and across an ocean, you can't resist meddling in my life, can you?" he muttered.

"I just want you to find someone and be happy."

"Why don't you focus on your own life?" he suggested.

She sighed. "You're right—I have no business telling you how to live your life when I've screwed up mine."

"You haven't screwed up anything," he denied. "You're a wonderful mother to three fabulous kids."

"It's hard to believe that when I'm almost four thousand miles away from them," she acknowledged.

"Then get back to work so you can come home," he advised.

"I'll do that," she agreed. "Give my girls big hugs and kisses from me and tell them that I love them."

"Every day," he promised.

Tristyn could recall listening to her aunt Ellen and aunt Jane talk about how much food teenage boys could put away at a meal. Over the past few weeks, she'd begun to suspect that active little girls could probably give teenage boys a run for their money.

When they got back to the RV after shopping, Josh was there to help them carry the bags inside and put the groceries away. Though she wouldn't ever comment aloud, she couldn't help but notice that Josh had stepped up in a big way—not just with the girls, but tackling his share of the domestic chores. And though she knew it was sometimes difficult for him to juggle the responsibilities of his job with the demands of his nieces, he never balked at spending time with them. And Charlotte, Emily and Hanna had all thrived as a result of his attention.

"We're gonna make s'mores, Unca Josh."

"It looks like you're going to make a lot of s'mores," he noted, holding an enormous bag of marshmallows.

"The big bag was on sale," Charlotte told him.

"And then, of course, we needed enough chocolate and graham crackers to go with the marshmallows," Tristyn said.

"Of course," he agreed drily, as he continued to unpack. "You even bought sticks?"

She nodded. "They were conveniently located beside the other ingredients."

He shook his head. "Real s'mores are made with marshmallows toasted on the end of sticks hunted up in the woods and sharpened with a knife."

"I wanna make *real* s'mores," Emily announced.

"Me, too," Hanna chimed in.

"They will be real s'mores," Charlotte assured her sisters. "They just won't have real bugs in them that might crawl out of sticks picked up off the ground."

Hanna wrinkled her nose. "I don' 'ike bugs."

"There are no bugs in these sticks," Tristyn promised. "Plus, there are two prongs, so you can roast two marshmallows at the same time—or cook hot dogs."

"But we're havin' s'ghetti tonight," Emily reminded her.

"I meant we could use them to cook hot dogs at another time," Tristyn clarified.

"Are we having meatballs or meat sauce?" Charlotte asked, more interested in what they would be eating today than in the future.

Tristyn had taken the meat out of the freezer but hadn't decided what she was going to do with it, so she was surprised when Josh responded to his niece's question.

"Both," he said. In response to Tristyn's questioning look, he shrugged. "You were out with the girls, so I thought I'd take care of dinner tonight."

"Mom usually just throws the meat into the sauce," Charlotte said. "She says it's too much trouble to make both."

"Well, since I don't have to do it all the time, I don't mind," he said.

"Are we gonna have garlic bread, too?" Emily asked.

"Yes, we'll have garlic bread, too," he confirmed.

"With or without cheese?"

"Half with and half without," he said, because over the past few weeks he'd learned that they had very different preferences about such things.

Tristyn held back a smile.

When it was time for dinner, he dished up Charlotte's pasta, added sauce and meatballs, and a slice of plain garlic bread; Emily got pasta and meat sauce and garlic bread with cheese; Hanna had her noodles with butter and parmesan and plain garlic bread.

"What do you prefer?" Josh asked Tristyn. "Meatballs or meat sauce?"

"I'll let the chef decide," she told him.

He served up a plate of pasta with meatballs and a side of garlic bread with cheese for her, then took his own to his seat at the table.

"This is really good, Uncle Josh," Charlotte said.

"Contrary to popular belief, I don't live on frozen dinners and fast food," he said.

"What can you make besides spaghetti?" Tristyn asked.

"Penne, rigatoni, ravioli, tortellini—basically anything that cooks in boiling water."

Charlotte and Emily giggled. Hanna probably didn't understand why her sisters were laughing, but she joined in.

"You make hamburgers, too," Emily pointed out.

"Well, yes, I can grill," he acknowledged. "But most women don't consider that cooking."

"Anything that puts food on the table is cooking in my book," Tristyn assured him.

Emily finished her pasta and reached for another slice of garlic bread. She nibbled on the corner, then looked at Tristyn and tentatively asked, "Do you think the tooth fairy got your message?"

"I think she probably did," Tristyn told her.

"But how do you know?" she persisted, obviously worried that her first tooth might be lost forever.

"Because the tweet Tristyn sent out has been retweeted two hundred and eighteen times," Josh said.

Tristyn looked at him, stunned. "No kidding?"

"No kidding," he confirmed. "Of course, that's probably because Ren D'Alesio was one of the first to retweet the message, with a plea to his fans to spread it far and wide. Which they've apparently done." Josh ruffled Emily's hair.

"So I think the odds are pretty good that the tooth fairy got your message."

"But what if she doesn't still have the tooth?" Charlotte wondered.

Tristyn groaned inwardly. "Let's deal with one issue at a time," she suggested.

"I'm just saying—no one knows what the tooth fairy actually *does* with the teeth. And if she picked up a lot of teeth last night, how will she know which one to give back?"

Emily's brow furrowed as she mulled over the dilemmas her sister presented.

"Let's not borrow trouble," Josh said to her.

Charlotte frowned. "What does that even mean?"

"It means that we should wait and see what happens tonight before we worry about all kinds of other possibilities."

Emily apparently agreed with his philosophy, because her next question was, "Can we have s'mores now?"

Chapter Sixteen

Tristyn cleaned up the kitchen while Josh assembled a tower of kindling and wood and started the fire. When everything was ready, Tristyn sat with Hanna on her lap and let the little girl help her turn the stick with the marshmallow on the end. Both Charlotte and Emily insisted that they were big enough to do their own, so Josh let them, though he was seated between the two girls to keep a close eye on both of them.

Charlotte was very precise and methodical, and her marshmallows were always evenly toasted and golden brown. Emily was a little more impatient and held her stick closer to the flame to cook the marshmallow more quickly. As a result, hers were often dark on one side and uncooked on the other, but she didn't seem to mind. By the time the older girls had each eaten two s'mores, Josh had consumed at least three, while Tristyn and Hanna had shared one—which was still more sugar than she thought the three-year-old should have right before bed.

And it was apparent that Josh's youngest niece was ready for bed, so she lifted the sleepy girl into her arms and took her inside to get her washed up and changed into her pajamas. Hanna's eyes were drifting shut even before

Tristyn tucked her favorite teddy bear under her arm and pulled up the covers.

"You're next, Emily," Tristyn said, when she returned to the campfire. "It's already past your bedtime."

"Can I make one more? Please?" she asked.

"Me, too," Charlotte implored.

Tristyn looked to Josh, who could hardly say no when he'd just put another marshmallow on his stick.

"If you have another one, you have to brush your teeth twice," he told them.

Both girls nodded their agreement, already reaching into the bag for more marshmallows.

But Tristyn suspected they didn't really want any more s'mores as much as they wanted to delay bedtime a little longer. A suspicion that was confirmed when she saw Charlotte's attention had waned from her task, the marshmallow at the end of her stick hovering dangerously close to the fire.

"Charlotte, your marshmallow is smoking," Tristyn said.

Before the girl could pull her stick away, the spongy sugar confection burst into flame.

"It's on fire. It's on fire," Charlotte said. "What do I do?"

"Gently shake the stick to—"

Before Josh could finish issuing his instructions, his panicked niece jerked the stick so hard that the flaming marshmallow flew right off the end and landed on the back of Josh's hand. He swore and shook his arm in an attempt to dislodge the marshmallow, but melted sugar was sticky and a fair amount of it remained on his skin. Tristyn instinctively dumped her glass of water onto his hand.

Charlotte looked up at him with wide eyes filled with horror and tears. "I'm so sorry, Uncle Josh."

"S'okay," he said, through gritted teeth.

Emily had dropped her stick, with the marshmallow still attached, to the ground, her request for one last s'more forgotten. Her eyes were worried, too, as she looked at her uncle, who was obviously in more pain than he wanted them to know.

"Go put some ice on that while I help the girls get ready for bed," Tristyn suggested.

He nodded tersely.

"He didn't stop, drop and roll," Emily said worriedly.

She fought against the smile that wanted to curve her lips. "It was just the marshmallow that was on fire, not Uncle Josh."

"Is he going to be okay?" Charlotte asked.

"His hand might be a little swollen and red for a while— and he'll probably use it as an excuse to get out of doing dishes—but he's going to be fine," Tristyn assured her.

"I'll do his dishes," she immediately offered.

Tristyn brushed a hand over Charlotte's hair. "It was an accident. There's no need for you to do penance."

Emily giggled. "She said dishes, not pens-itch." Then she tilted her head, as if trying to figure something out. "What is pens-itch?"

This time, Tristyn let the smile come. *"Penance,"* she clarified. "It's kind of like punishment you give to yourself—a way of showing that you're sorry."

"But I am sorry," Charlotte said, her voice tearful.

"I know," Tristyn agreed. "And Uncle Josh knows, too. So why don't you go give him a hug, then get washed up and brush your teeth?"

After the girls were tucked into bed, she dug the first-aid kit out of the bathroom cabinet.

"How is it?" she asked Josh.

"It feels a lot better already," he said, lifting the bag of ice away so that she could see for herself.

She winced when she saw the skin, angrily red and already blistered. "It doesn't look like it feels too good."

He made a fist, stretching the skin. "I just hope it doesn't scar."

"Are you worried that a permanent mark will detract from your masculine beauty?"

"Of course not," he replied. "Scars add character and intrigue—except when they're caused by flaming marshmallow, which is not a story I'd ever want to share."

She smiled as she opened the first aid box. "Let's get you bandaged up so that we can reduce the likelihood of that being necessary."

She applied some antibiotic cream to a square of sterile gauze, then gently set the gauze on his wound and wrapped it with medical tape.

"Aren't you a regular Florence Nightingale," he mused. "Any chance you have a nurse's uniform tucked in your closet?"

"Is that one of your fantasies—to play disciplinary doctor and naughty nurse?"

"My only fantasies are about playing with you," he told her.

"Well, right now you should go in and say good-night to the girls," she suggested. "And reassure Charlotte that you're not going to die."

"I'm sure she doesn't think I'm going to die," he chided.

"She's worried—and feeling guilty," Tristyn told him. "And she probably won't sleep until she sees for herself that you're going to be okay."

While he was doing that, she went back outside to put out the fire and retrieve the sticks that had been discarded.

"Everything okay?" she asked, when Josh came out of the girls' bedroom.

He nodded, then sniffed. "You smell like smoke."

"I put out the fire."

"Thank you." He lifted his uninjured hand to her mouth, rubbed his thumb gently over the bottom curve of her lip. "You scarfed some more chocolate, too, didn't you?"

"Guilty," she admitted, her tongue instinctively swiping over her lip where his finger had touched.

He lowered his head and brushed his lips over hers. "Mmm, you taste sweet."

"That would be the chocolate and marshmallow."

But he shook his head. "It's you," he insisted. "It's always been you."

Her heart swelled with hope and joy, until her brain cautioned it not to read too much into a few simple words. Josh was a master at saying and doing all the right things to make a woman feel good. She refused to believe that his offhand remark meant anything more than that he was focused on her now, and for now, that would be enough.

"Is your hand really okay?" she asked instead.

"It would feel a lot better if it was on your naked skin."

She smiled. "I think that can be arranged...*after* the tooth fairy puts Emily's tooth back under her pillow."

When that task had been completed, he took her to bed and proved that—even with an injury—his hands were capable of working magic. After, while their bodies were still joined together, she found herself thinking back on everything that had happened over the past several weeks, and she couldn't help being impressed at how willingly and competently he'd handled almost anything that came up.

"You surprise me sometimes," she said to him now.

"That's what all the girls say."

She narrowed her gaze. "Do you really want to remind me of 'all the girls' when my knee is positioned where it could jeopardize your future romantic pursuits?"

"Of course, the only girl who really matters is the one in my arms right now."

"Nice save," she told him.

He grinned and pressed his mouth to hers. "I do some of my best work under pressure."

"Such as your suggestion to summon the tooth fairy with smoke signals?"

"And sometimes desperate men say stupid things," he acknowledged.

"Aside from the fact that dropping a wet blanket over a fire is potentially much more dangerous than a flying, flaming marshmallow, you would have looked ridiculous."

"Maybe," he acknowledged.

"But you would have done it, anyway, for Emily, wouldn't you?"

"Sure," he agreed without hesitation.

"I'm starting to suspect that you might make a half-decent father someday," she mused.

The hand that was stroking down her back faltered for the space of a single heartbeat. "Are you making an observation or offering to bear my children?" he asked.

"Just an observation," she said immediately, emphatically.

"Well, that was certainly an unequivocal response," he noted. "No worries about my ego inflating around you."

"I didn't mean to sound so horrified," she told him. "I just meant to reassure you that I'm not looking for any kind of happily-ever-after with two kids and a dog and a white picket fence."

"You don't want what everyone else in your family has? What each of your sisters has?" he pressed.

"Well, sure. Someday," she admitted.

"Just not with me."

"I thought you would be relieved," she said, wondering at the hint of anger—and maybe even hurt—in his tone. "We agreed that whatever happened between us when we were on the road this summer would end when we returned to Charisma."

"You're right," he said, in that same clipped tone.

"So why are you acting all pissy because I'm abiding by the terms of our agreement?"

That was a good question—and not one that Josh had a ready answer for, so he opted for denial. "I'm not."

Tristyn looked skeptical.

"Okay, maybe I was," he acknowledged. "And I shouldn't have been. Because you're right—we have an agreement. And that agreement is for as much sex as often as possible, right?"

He didn't wait for a response but crushed his mouth down on hers.

He was hurt and angry and punishing her for nothing more than being honest with him. Which he knew was irrational, and that knowledge only pissed him off more as his hands moved over her body, not coaxing a response but demanding it. He was trying to pick a fight, but Tristyn wasn't interested in fighting back. She didn't balk at the pressure of his mouth or the roughness of his hands, but responded willingly, even eagerly, with a passion that, even after more than two weeks together, never failed to take his breath away.

She was so open and warm and giving, and as her hands moved over him, stroking and soothing, his own touch gentled. Because this was Tristyn. The most beautiful, sweet and loving woman he'd ever known. She was the kind of woman a man might think about settling down with, if he was a settling kind of man. Which Josh wasn't.

He should be glad she'd reminded him of that before he did something stupid—like fall in love with her.

Order was restored in Emily's world when she awakened the following morning and discovered that the tooth fairy had, in fact, returned sometime during the night and put her tooth back under the pillow. A few hours later, they were on their way to the track. The number 722 car experienced some engine problems that held it back early in the race, and Ren finished twenty-second in the field.

When they got back to the RV, they started to pack up in anticipation of the journey back to North Carolina. A two-week break in the race schedule meant that they would be able to spend a chunk of time in Charisma before they had to focus on the next race in Tennessee.

Tristyn had plotted out all their driving routes, noting food options and rest stops available along the way, but she generally didn't pay too much attention to anything but the scenery while Josh was driving. She trusted that he could follow the directions given to him by his GPS, until she watched him drive past the turn she'd expected him to take.

"Where are you going?" she asked.

"We're making a slight detour," he told her.

"Why?"

"Because I have a surprise for the girls."

"What kind of surprise?" Charlotte asked, proving that though she usually had a book in front of her face, she was listening to every word of their conversation in the front seat.

"If I told you, it wouldn't be a surprise," he pointed out.

Which meant that he wouldn't be able to tell Tristyn, either, without potentially ruining the surprise.

"I like s'prises," Emily said—awake because the children's Dramamine didn't seem to have the same sedative effect on her as even a child dose of the adult medication.

"S'prise!" Hanna agreed.

Another half an hour passed before they arrived at their destination—thirty minutes during which all three girls, excited about the unknown surprise, entertained the adults with an unending chorus of "Are we there yet?"

There, when they did arrive, turned out to be Hersheypark.

The girls were speechless when they discovered what their uncle had planned—for all of about three seconds. Then the questions started, their words rushing over one another: "How long can we stay?"

"Where's the biggest roller coaster?"

"I has to go potty."

They stayed three days, and it turned out that Emily—who couldn't ride in the backseat of a car without feeling sick—loved the roller coasters. The bigger the better. Charlotte seemed a little more apprehensive, but she had too much competitive spirit to let herself be outdone by her younger sister. Tristyn and Josh traded off between the older girls and the thrill rides and Hanna and the family-rated attractions.

At the beginning of the summer, if anyone had dared to suggest that Josh would choose to spend three days at an amusement park with his young nieces, Tristyn would have laughed out loud. It was amazing how five weeks on the road with him and the girls had made her see him differently—*want* to see him differently.

"This was a wonderful surprise," she said, as they exited the gates after their last day at the park, the girls each carrying a bag filled with souvenirs and treats. Well, Charlotte and Emily were carrying theirs, Tristyn was carrying Hanna's, and Josh was carrying Hanna—who had protested, after three days of running on excitement supplemented by candy, that her legs couldn't possibly walk another step—on his shoulders.

"They've been pretty good sports about being dragged around from racetrack to racetrack, so I thought they deserved a break from that routine."

"You definitely delivered," she told him. "No doubt these last few days are going to be the highlight of their summer."

He nudged her shoulder as they headed toward the RV parked in the adjacent campground. "What's been the highlight of yours?"

She knew what he wanted to hear, and the truth was, every day with Josh had been a highlight surpassed only by every night he'd shared her bed. "Actually, I'm not sure mine has happened yet, but I've got a bottle of chocolate syrup in this bag that has definite potential."

He lifted his brows. "Chocolate syrup?"

She smiled at him then. "I didn't buy it as a topping for ice cream."

The closer they got to Charisma, the more excited and apprehensive Tristyn was. She had missed her family while she was away, but returning to North Carolina meant returning to the real world—and in the real world, she and Josh were colleagues and friends, not lovers. Josh seemed to have mixed feelings about their return, too, though neither of them seemed inclined to talk about what was going to happen next.

They'd made an early start that morning, and the girls—still tired out from three days of excitement at the park—had quickly fallen asleep again when they were on the road. It was only when they'd crossed the border into North Carolina that Josh remarked, "I'm finally going to be back in my own place tonight, but I'm still not going to get to sleep in a real bed."

"I don't think you have any cause for complaint. You've spent a lot of time in a real bed over the past two-and-a-half weeks."

"I have absolutely no complaints about the time I spent

in that bed," he assured her. "But very little of it was sleeping."

"It's not my fault you're insatiable."

"But you're the one who kicked me out whenever I started to fall asleep."

"Because I'd rather your nieces not go home at the end of the summer and tell their mom that Uncle Josh was sleeping in Tristyn's bed."

"Better than Emily telling her that we had an orgy," he teased.

Tristyn shook her head. "I think she's finally forgotten that word."

"You better hope so," he said. "Because I won't hesitate to lay the blame for that one at your feet."

"I would never have said it if you hadn't baited me with your comments about three females keeping you up," she reminded him.

"Lately it's only been one female keeping me up," he commented, reaching across the console to take her hand and link their fingers together. "And I'm going to miss her tonight."

It was hardly a declaration of undying love, but the sincerity in his tone tugged at her heart. "I'll be thinking of you trying not to fall off your sofa while I'm stretched out between the crisp, cool sheets of my own bed...naked," she teased, attempting to lighten the tenor of their conversation.

"You're a cruel woman," he said. Then, curiously, "You really do sleep in the nude?"

"I really do," she confirmed.

"Damn, I'm going to miss you tonight," he said. "Unless—"

"No," she said.

"You don't even know what I was going to say," he protested.

"Yes, I do. And yes, I have a three-bedroom house, but there are only beds in two of them and there would be a lot of questions from a lot of people if your truck was parked outside my house overnight."

He sighed, because that was a truth he couldn't deny.

When they got back to his condo, where Tristyn had left her car parked, he felt like he should kiss her goodbye. Except that this wasn't really goodbye, only a temporary break in their schedule. After six days in Charisma, they would pack up again and head toward Tennessee.

He didn't make any plans to see her during those six days, because he suspected that after five weeks away, her family would claim every minute of her time. Besides, it was only six days, and he decided spending that time apart would provide him with the perfect opportunity to get his head on straight again. Because some of the crazy thoughts and outrageous ideas that had nudged at his mind recently proved to Josh that his head was skewed.

Crazy thoughts of a future with Tristyn, not just for the last few weeks of summer, but always. The outrageous idea that she might actually want him, not just for now, but forever.

Yeah, a few days apart from Tristyn would definitely help him get his head on straight.

Really good sex could become addictive, and that's what he'd shared with Tristyn over the past two-and-a-half weeks. Sure, they also shared a lot of common interests. And maybe he even enjoyed talking to her about topics on which they disagreed, because she challenged his opinions and ideas and listened when he challenged hers. Plus, living in close proximity to someone for a period of time was bound to create a feeling of connection. Add in the fact that he'd known not just Tristyn but her whole family a long time, and a guy could be forgiven for thinking he might fit into that close-knit circle.

None of that was cause for panic—was it?

Chapter Seventeen

When Tristyn told her sisters that she would be home on Saturday, Lauryn and Jordyn immediately cleared their schedules, left the children in the care of their grandparents and booked an afternoon at the spa. After seaweed wraps and hot stone massages, the sisters reunited in the pedicure room.

"So…five weeks on the road with Josh and you both came back alive," Jordyn mused, as their feet were soaking in adjacent tubs of bubbling scented water.

"There were a few moments, especially in the beginning, when I wasn't sure we would," she admitted.

"What changed?" Lauryn asked.

"We learned to…coexist."

Jordyn snorted. "Is that what the kids are calling it now?"

Tristyn felt a smile tug at her lips. "And yes, having lots of scorching-hot sex probably helped ease some of the tension, too."

Lauryn grinned. "Good for you."

"It's been amazing," she admitted.

"So why are you chewing on your bottom lip like you do when you're worried about something?" Jordyn asked.

"Because it's been amazing," she said again. "So amazing I almost wish this summer would never end."

"You've fallen in love with him," Jordyn realized.

"No," she immediately denied. "Maybe." She blew out a frustrated breath. "I don't know."

"You do know," Lauryn said gently. "You're just scared."

"There are days—or at least brief moments—when I wish I'd never agreed to go on this road trip."

"Why would you say that?"

"Because being with Josh, helping to take care of his nieces and spending time with him—in and out of the bedroom—it's almost felt like we were a family."

"Why is that a bad thing?" Jordyn asked.

"Because this time that we've had together is like an alternate reality—definitely a fantasy. And I know that. But, every once in a while, I find myself wishing that the fantasy could become reality."

"Of course it can," Lauryn insisted.

But Tristyn shook her head. "If there's one thing Josh isn't, it's a family man."

"Well, he's done a pretty good imitation over the past few weeks," Jordyn pointed out.

"He is great with his nieces," she agreed. "Because they're his nieces and he knows that, as soon as his sister comes back from Spain, they'll go back to Seattle with their mom again."

"And then his life will feel empty and lonely and he'll finally realize that he wants a family of his own, but only if you agree to be the mother of his children."

Tristyn smiled at the fanciful picture her sister was painting, but she shook her head again. "Not likely. Besides, we talked about this, in the beginning, and we both agreed that whatever happened between us while we were away would end when we got back to Charisma."

"So when this road trip is over, you'll go back to working at GSR, seeing him every day, and you won't want to jump his bones?" Jordyn asked skeptically.

"I can't promise that I won't want to," she acknowledged. "Only that I won't actually do it."

Her sisters exchanged looks.

"She won't last a week," Lauryn declared.

"Five days, tops," Jordyn voted.

Tristyn rolled her eyes. "Thank you both for your overwhelming confidence and support."

"We do have confidence in you," Lauryn assured her.

"Which is why we're confident you won't give up on the only man you've ever loved," Jordyn added.

After Tristyn said goodbye to her sisters and left the spa, she impulsively stopped at the grocery store and picked up what she needed to make the chicken-and-broccoli casserole that had been a big hit with Josh and the girls. She didn't expect a woman to answer when she knocked on the door of his condo, and she was so surprised that it took her a minute to recognize the woman as his sister.

"Lucy—when did you get back?"

"Just a few hours ago," she said.

"Does this mean your project in Madrid is finished?"

Lucy nodded. "I had to burn the midnight oil every day, but I didn't want to be away from the girls any longer than absolutely necessary. And I'm jet-lagged, so I've forgotten my manners," she apologized, opening the door wider. "Please, come in."

"I don't want to intrude on your reunion," Tristyn said.

"It's not much of a reunion right now," Lucy said, tugging on Tristyn's arm to draw her inside. "Josh popped out for a minute and the girls are playing with the castanets I brought back for them."

She could hear them now, although the sound—not

quite of a caliber that could be called music—was distant and muted.

"The instruments seemed like a good idea when I was in Spain—not so much now that the girls are clicking away with them," she admitted. "Which is why Josh shut them in the bedroom."

Tristyn smiled. "They must have been so thrilled to see you."

"I think they were," Lucy agreed. "And thank you for helping Josh with the girls while I was away."

"It was a pleasure."

Lucy chuckled. "I'm sure it was at times—and other times, not so much."

"My sisters and cousins all have kids," Tristyn told her. "So I was prepared for almost anything—except the tooth fairy fiasco."

"Which, I understand, you handled very creatively."

"Well, tweeting seemed a little less dangerous than your brother's idea of sending smoke signals."

"Ohmygod—he didn't actually suggest that?"

"He did."

"I think he learned how to send smoke signals in Boy Scouts, about twenty years ago."

"He really was a Boy Scout?" Tristyn asked dubiously.

Lucy nodded. "He really was."

"Well, that former Boy Scout was really great with your daughters."

"I knew he would be. Although he did warn me that he thinks my middle child might have a future as a stripper due to her penchant of taking off her clothes wherever and whenever."

"It only happened three—or maybe four—times," Tristyn said, smiling a little at the memory of how shocked and embarrassed he was each of those times. "He's going to miss them when you go back to Washington."

"And they'll miss him, too," Josh's sister acknowledged. "Which is why we've already decided to come and visit more often."

"That's great," Tristyn said. "Are you planning to stay for a few days now?"

"I'm eager to get home and get the girls settled back into their normal routines, but we might hang out for a while first."

"Speaking of routines, I really should…" Her words trailed away when Josh walked through the door with three flat boxes in his hands.

His lips curved when he saw her standing just inside the doorway. "Tristyn—hi."

"I'm just on my way out," she told him.

"Why?"

"Because I didn't realize Lucy was back."

"And I'm going to go tell the girls that dinner is here," Lucy said, slipping out of the room.

"I should have called to tell you," he said. "But I thought you were probably busy with your family and enjoying a much-needed break from all of us."

"I had breakfast with my parents, then spent the after-noon with my sisters, but they both had other plans for dinner, so I picked up a few groceries and took a chance that you guys might be hungry, too."

"You've spent the past five weeks with us—you know we're always hungry."

"But you obviously had a different dinner plan."

"Stay and eat with us," he urged. "There's more than enough pizza to go around."

Tristyn shook her head. "Thanks, but your sister's been away for a long time and I'm sure you have a lot to catch up on."

He touched a hand to her arm. "I'll give you a call later."

"Sure," she agreed. But she knew it would be foolish to count on it.

She took her groceries home and cooked the chicken and broccoli, anyway. She even opened the bottle of wine she found in the fridge and drank two glasses while she was cooking, then a third while she picked unenthusiastically at her meal.

Since Jordyn had married Marco, Tristyn had lived alone in the house they used to share, and she was generally content with her own company. But after spending the past five weeks with Josh and his nieces in the RV, her house seemed too big and too empty.

Which was crazy, especially considering that she'd been so excited about coming home and having a little bit of breathing room. But now that Lucy was back, it was the end of the road for her and Josh—literally. She blinked away the tears that stung her eyes. She absolutely would *not* cry over the end of a relationship that was never intended to be anything more than a summer fling.

But she hadn't expected it to end so soon.

And she hadn't expected to miss Josh so much already.

Tristyn had just finished putting her dishes in the dishwasher when the doorbell rang. Wiping her hands on a towel, she went to peek through the sidelight, her heart immediately pounding harder and faster when she saw Josh standing on her porch. She drew in a long, deep breath and turned the knob.

"There's a distinct shortage of beds in my condo, especially with Lucy there now, too," he said, in lieu of a greeting.

"And you thought I'd take pity on you and let you share mine?" she guessed.

"Actually, I hoped that you wouldn't want to sleep without me—because I don't want to sleep without you."

How was a woman supposed to resist a man who told her exactly what she wanted to hear?

Tristyn didn't know that she could, but she felt compelled to at least make an effort to protect her heart. "This is a violation of the rule," she pointed out.

"Yeah, I was hoping you might consider another minor amendment," he said.

And then he kissed her, and the illusion of any resistance melted away under the seductive pressure of his mouth on hers.

She'd lost count of the number of times they'd made love over the past two-and-a-half weeks, but somehow, this felt different. Being on the road with Josh had supported the illusion that this wasn't real, that whatever feelings she had for him were a product of the situation and circumstances. Allowing Josh to be here, in her house, in her bed, made her feel more exposed and vulnerable.

Twelve years earlier, she'd been a naive and innocent girl with a huge crush on her cousin's best friend. She was neither naive nor innocent anymore. She'd had a handful of lovers and she wasn't ashamed of the fact, because she'd never fallen into bed with a man without at least feeling some affection for him. But she'd never made love with a man she loved…until now.

When Tristyn woke up in the morning, he was gone.

She couldn't deny that she was disappointed, but she understood that he needed to get back to his own place, to spend some time with his sister and the girls before Lucy headed back to Seattle with her family.

She took a quick shower, then headed to the kitchen for a much-needed cup of coffee—and found Josh standing at her stove, cooking eggs.

"You're still here."

He looked up from the pan, his brows raised. "Did you think I'd leave without saying goodbye?"

"I had no expectations," she said.

"Sometimes I think that's the problem," he said.

She poured a mug of the coffee he'd already brewed. "What's that supposed to mean?"

"Did you really expect that we would spend the better part of the summer together and then just go our separate ways?"

"That was the agreement."

"Screw the agreement," he said. "I'm not ready for this to end."

They were almost the words she wanted to hear him say, and probably the closest to a declaration of affection that she would get from him. Unfortunately, they weren't enough to change her mind.

They were good together—on so many levels. She knew their connection was about more than just sex; she also knew that they ultimately wanted different things. She wanted to get married and have a family someday—and Josh didn't. He'd been clear about that from the beginning.

So when he said he wasn't ready for their relationship to be over, she knew he wasn't thinking of a forever-after future for them together but a few more weeks—maybe even a couple months. And Tristyn couldn't do it. Because the more time she spent with Josh, the more completely she would fall in love, and she needed to get over him so she could move on with her life.

"Being with you over the last few weeks has been... amazing," she admitted. "But it was easy when we were on the road."

He divided the eggs onto two plates, added a couple slices of toast to each. "Were we on the same trip? Because there are a lot of words I might use to describe the last five of weeks, and *easy* isn't one of them."

She smiled at that. "The you and me part was easy," she amended. "Once you stopped acting like an idiot, I mean."

He smiled, clearly unoffended by her remark, as he set her plate in front of her. "It can still be easy."

But Tristyn shook her head. "Not here. Not in a town where I have not just my parents and sisters, but aunts, uncles and cousins ready to offer commentary on everything I do. And especially not with both of us working at GSR."

"You think your family would disapprove of our relationship?"

"No, Josh. I think my family would read too much into the relationship, and when we eventually parted ways, it would be awkward for everyone."

"How do you know that we'd eventually part ways?"

She pushed her eggs around on her plate. "Because you told me—in clear and unequivocal terms—that you're not looking to settle down."

He was quiet for a minute before he finally said, "Maybe that could change."

A tentative blossom of hope bloomed in her heart as she bit into a piece of toast, because she knew he was trying to make this work for her. And from a man who had eschewed personal commitment for so long, his words were a major concession. If he'd said, "My feelings have changed," she would have thrown all the rules out the window and gone for it. But "could change" was too much like a consolation prize—and it wasn't enough. Giving him her heart in the hope that he might someday reciprocate her feelings was too big a risk.

"I've still got the RV," he said, when she remained silent. "Let's take it to Bristol like we'd originally planned."

She wanted to say yes, to extend this magical summer a little bit longer. But she knew that going with him to Tennessee would only prolong the inevitable. Not to mention that Daniel would surely wonder why she was still road-tripping with his business partner when Josh's nieces—her explanation for being with him in the first place—would not be with them.

"I don't think that's a good idea," she finally said.

"You don't think *we're* a good idea," he accused, pushing away his half-eaten breakfast.

She stood up to clear away their plates. "I think, if we try to make this into something more than it is, it could mess up our working relationship, our friendship and your partnership with Daniel."

"You might be right," he finally decided.

But if she was wrong, she might have just let her best chance at happiness walk out the door.

On Monday, Lucy brought the girls to GSR before heading home to Seattle, and Tristyn teared up when she hugged each of them goodbye. On Tuesday, she reconsidered Josh's invitation to go with him to Bristol. On Wednesday, she affirmed her decision to stay home, concluding that she needed some time away from him to rebuild the shields around her heart.

She almost changed her mind again when she learned that Ren won the pole. She'd actually started to look for flights and was about to input her credit card data when she stopped herself.

Was she really eager to be there in case Ren won?

Or was it just an excuse to be with Josh?

She'd long ago promised herself that she would never be the type of woman who became so infatuated with a man that she would follow him to the ends of the earth, and she was certain now that her feelings for Josh were nothing more than infatuation. Being with him, she'd deluded herself into thinking it was love. But that was crazy.

Probably spending time with her sisters and their husbands had made her believe in fairy tales and happy endings—and she was pleased that both of them had found theirs. But she wasn't unhappy with her life. She didn't need a man to complete her. Sure, she'd love to have kids someday and she'd had a lot of fun hanging out with Josh's nieces, but she'd known going in that it was only temporary.

So why did she feel like her heart was breaking every morning that she woke up without him? Why did she think she was going to have to walk away from a job she loved at GSR because she didn't know if she could stand seeing him every day and not be with him?

Worse than not being with him would be seeing him with someone else. Or numerous someone elses. Daniel used to be the same way—a serial monogamist who dated countless beautiful women. Until he fell in love with Kenna. But just because Daniel had altered his ways didn't mean that Josh could—especially since he'd shown no indication that he wanted to. And a vague "maybe that could change" wasn't a guarantee of anything but heartache.

So she stayed home and watched the race on TV. And she was thrilled to see Ren take the checkered flag at Bristol. It was his fourth win of the season—a new record for the young driver and a definite reason to celebrate. Social media showed him out and about, with most of the guys from his pit crew and a few fans, doing just that. And in the background of one of the most widely circulated photos, Tristyn recognized Paris Smythe—with her arms around Josh.

Chapter Eighteen

Jordyn stopped by Sunday afternoon to drop off Gryffindor, because Tristyn had offered to take care of the cat when she heard that her sister and brother-in-law were planning to sneak away for a few days to Braden's house on Ocracoke. She set the cat's pillow in the corner of the living room, where it had always been when he'd lived there.

"Not a lot of treats," Jordyn cautioned, turning to her sister. "The vet said…" Her words trailed off. "Tristyn—what's wrong?"

Tristyn shook her head as she blinked back the tears. "Nothing."

"Then why does it look as if you're trying not to cry?"

"Allergies," she decided.

Jordyn narrowed her gaze. "You don't have allergies."

"Allergies can be acquired," she pointed out.

"What are you allergic to?"

"Cats," she said.

Jordyn fisted her hands on her hips. "Do I need to go and kick Josh Slater's butt?"

"No." Tristyn sighed. "It's really not his fault."

"What's not his fault?" her sister pressed.

She swiped at an errant tear that spilled onto her cheek. "That I fell in love and he didn't."

"Oh, honey," Jordyn said, and enfolded Tristyn in her embrace.

The dam cracked. Tristyn thought she'd done a pretty good job holding it together, but suddenly the tears broke through. Anguished sobs, wrenched from the bottom of her bruised and battered heart, burned her throat as she finally gave in to the storm of emotion that had been building inside her. She didn't know how long she cried, just that the tears seemed endless. Jordyn didn't offer any useless platitudes, only strong and familiar comfort.

A short while later, Lauryn showed up with a bottle of Pinot Noir and a box of dark chocolate covered cherries. Somehow, in the midst of the back rubbing and tissue passing, Jordyn had managed to text their other sister.

So Tristyn told them what had happened, because she needed to tell someone. But she felt like an idiot, blubbering to her sisters who had each endured much worse heartache than simply being dumped. In comparison to the death of a fiancé and a cheating husband, watching Josh walk away was nothing.

"Except that it doesn't sound like it was his choice to walk away," Lauryn pointed out.

"But he did," she insisted.

Jordyn shook her head. "Only after he asked you to go to Bristol with him."

"You can't get mad at him for being with someone else when you told him you didn't want to be with him," Lauryn admonished gently.

"I agree with that, with the added proviso that you have no reason to believe Josh is actually *with* Paris," Jordyn said.

Tristyn shoved her iPad toward her sister. "This clinch

that's circulating all over social media looks pretty real to me."

"I'm not saying that Paris wasn't there with him. But without knowing the details of how or why, you can't be mad at Josh."

"Yes, I can," she insisted. "This picture was taken six days after he walked out of my house. Six days after he spent the night in my bed, making love with me, he was with someone else."

"I don't believe for a minute that Josh was with her," Jordyn said.

Tristyn dabbed at her eyes with a tissue. "I wanted him to fight for me," she admitted softly. "I wanted to believe our relationship was worth fighting for—that *I* was worth fighting for."

"Where is this coming from?" Lauryn asked.

"Brett Taylor," Jordyn said.

Lauryn looked blank. "Who?"

"You were already married," Jordyn remembered. "Tristyn was in her second year at Duke, he was in his third. They were going to build houses together in Costa Rica that summer, but at the last minute, he decided to go to Europe instead."

"But that would have been…what—ten years ago?" Lauryn asked.

Tristyn nodded. "And then there was Kevin Wakefield, the second baseman for the Durham Bulls."

Lauryn smiled. "*Him* I remember."

"Do you also remember that he asked for a trade—to Pawtucket?"

"As I recall, he thought he had a better chance of being called up to Boston than Tampa Bay."

She nodded again. "But he never considered that the trade would signify the end of our relationship. I wasn't even a factor in his decision."

"Because he was an idiot," Lauryn said gently.

"And Josh went to Bristol without me," she pointed out to her sisters.

"You told him to go," Jordyn reminded her.

"Because I wanted him to say that he didn't want to go without me. And if I didn't want to go, he would stay with me. I wanted him to want me more than he wanted to be in Bristol."

"That's not really fair, Tris. You know that he feels obligated, as an owner of the team, to represent GSR."

She swiped at the tears that spilled onto her cheeks. "I know," she admitted. "But the fact that he went out to celebrate with Paris proves that I never mattered to him any more than any other woman he's ever been with."

She wasn't the type to wallow—at least not for very long. Talking to her sisters, along with the wine and the chocolate, helped her put things into perspective a little.

She'd given her heart to the wrong man and it had ended up in pieces. Now she had to put those pieces back together—and she had to do it before Monday morning, when she would be back behind her desk at GSR. Because she was determined not to let anyone—especially Josh—see that she was hurting.

Ren D'Alesio was having the season of his career, and Josh was thrilled to be a part of it. The only thing that dampened his enthusiasm when he watched his driver take the checkered flag at Bristol was that Tristyn wasn't there to witness the victory. But that had been her choice, and he wasn't going to skip the celebration just to sit around his hotel room and wish she was there.

So he went out with the team. In the past couple years, Ren had steadily moved up the ranks, showing not just skill but smarts in his racing, and the other drivers—and the media—had begun to pay attention. As a result, there were reporters shoving microphones in his face and photographers snapping pictures everywhere he went—especially on race day. Josh had never craved the spotlight and was happy to hover in the background when fans or media asked for photos. So he didn't see the picture that was circulating on social media until the next day, when his sister sent him a copy attached to an email with "WTF" in the subject line.

WTF, indeed.

He didn't know what to say to Tristyn when he saw her in the office Monday morning. He wanted to explain, but she'd made it clear that whatever they'd shared was over and done. As it turned out, she was on the phone when he walked by her desk and she never even glanced in his direction. It wasn't until he returned from lunch that she called him over.

"What's up?" he asked, attempting to match her easy tone.

"Phone messages," she said, handing him a pile of pink slips. "Apparently your voice mail is full."

"I turned off my ringer during my meeting with Daniel and Archie this morning," he said, using the nickname of Calvin Archer, the owner of Archer Glass. "I guess I forgot to turn it back on." He glanced at the message on top, and winced inwardly when he saw Paris Smythe's name and number in Tristyn's familiar handwriting.

"You should call her," she said, finally looking up at him.

"Why?"

"Because you're not the kind of guy who doesn't call."

"I didn't spend the weekend with her in Bristol," he said, wanting to be clear about that.

"It's none of my business if you did or didn't," Tristyn said.

"I didn't," he said again, holding her gaze.

She nodded. "You should call her, anyway."

"Tristyn—"

"I saw Rafe last night."

She blurted the words out before he could say anything else, and the impact of her statement made him feel as if he'd been kicked in the chest. When he'd managed to draw air into his lungs, he asked, "Is this your way of telling me that you've moved on and I should, too?"

She nodded.

He took the messages and retreated to his office.

It was just his luck that Tristyn's sister Jordyn was at the restaurant when Josh stopped by later that afternoon. "Is Rafe working tonight?"

"Yes," she admitted warily. "Why?"

"I need to talk to him."

"Why?" she asked again.

"Because I'm in love with your sister."

Her lips curved into a smile so reminiscent of Tristyn's, it actually made his heart ache. And the possibility that he might never again be the focus of Tristyn's smile was one that he refused to consider. Whatever it took, he was going to win her back.

"We were beginning to think you would never figure it out," Jordyn said to him now.

"We?" he asked, though he wasn't sure he wanted to know.

"Me and Lauryn. And Kenna," she admitted.

He shook his head. "I shouldn't have asked."

"Now I'm asking—what does any of this have to do with Rafe?"

"Tristyn told me that she was with him last night," he finally confided.

"So you came here to—what? Fight for her?"

"If that's what it takes."

"Against a man who has an impressive assortment of

knives capable of chopping, dicing and carving within arm's reach?"

He answered without hesitation. "There isn't anything I wouldn't do for her."

Jordyn touched a hand to his arm. "Then before you go storming into the kitchen and making a fool of yourself, you should know that Tristyn only saw Rafe last night because she was here for dinner."

He took a moment to absorb the implications of her words. "She wasn't out on a date with him?"

Jordyn shook her head. "She wasn't out on a date with him."

He frowned. "She deliberately misled me."

"Or maybe you misinterpreted what she said," she countered.

"No," he stated. "She deliberately misled me because she wanted me to think that she'd already moved on. And the only reason she'd want me to think that was if it wasn't true."

"While I'm not entirely sure I followed all of that, I'd like to make a suggestion," Jordyn said.

"Okay," he agreed, the realization that Tristyn still had feelings for him already making his heart lighter.

"Go have this conversation with my sister. Tell *her* how you feel."

"I will," he promised.

But there was one more stop he had to make first.

Tristyn had just settled on the sofa with a bowl of popcorn in her lap and a glass of Pinot Noir beside her, intending to spend the night binge-watching *Game of Thrones*, when a knock sounded at the door. She hadn't been expecting any company and was comfortably dressed in a pair of denim cutoffs and an old Duke T-shirt. She decided to ignore the summons. If it was either or both of her sisters, they had keys they could use. If it was anyone else, she wasn't in the mood for company.

"Come on, Tris—open up."

She immediately recognized Josh's voice. What she didn't know was why he was here.

"I know you're in there," he continued, when she failed to respond. "I can hear the *Game of Thrones* theme playing."

Inwardly cursing the single-pane windows as an ineffective sound barrier, she finally, reluctantly, pushed herself off the sofa and went to the door. She opened it with the intention of sending him away, but the words slid back down her throat when her gaze landed on him.

He was wearing a tuxedo.

And holding a corsage box in his hand.

Her heart thudded against her ribs.

Of course, any woman would probably have the same reaction. Josh always looked good, but in black tie, the man was absolutely devastating.

Without waiting for an invitation, he stepped past her and into the foyer.

She finally found her voice to ask, "Why are you here, Josh?"

Instead of answering her question, he opened the plastic box and removed the corsage. "This is for you."

"I'm a little underdressed for orchids," she protested, as he took her hand to slide the band onto her wrist.

"You're beautiful," he assured her. "Even in cutoff shorts and an old T-shirt—even in granny jammies—you're the most beautiful woman I've ever known."

She swallowed around the tightness in her throat. She didn't know what game he was playing, but she didn't want to be involved. She couldn't do this anymore. She couldn't be with him and continue to pretend that she didn't love him with her whole heart. "You shouldn't be here," she said.

But the protest sounded weak, even to her own ears.

Josh gently squeezed the hand he was still holding. "Yes, I should," he said. "Because I don't want to be anywhere else."

Then he led her into her own living room, where he immediately began to rearrange her furniture—pushing back the sofa and moving aside the coffee table to clear the center of the room.

"What are you doing?" she asked, sincerely baffled.

He didn't reply until he'd finished his task. "Rewriting history," he finally said. "*Our* history. I want to show you how I wish the night of your prom could have ended twelve years ago."

Then he tapped the screen of his iPhone a few times and the first notes of a familiar Savage Garden tune spilled out of the tiny speaker. He set it on the table and held out his hand. "Will you dance with me?"

She didn't think she'd made a move, but somehow her hand found its way to his. The way her knees were trembling, she wasn't sure she'd be able to dance, though. Then his arm, warm and strong, was at her back, drawing her closer, and she let herself relax into his embrace and move with him to the music.

"Do you remember this song?" he asked.

She nodded. "'Truly Madly Deeply.'"

"It's the song that was playing the first time we ever danced together," he reminded her.

"I didn't think you remembered," she admitted.

"I remember every second of that first dance," he assured her. "Of our first kiss, and the first time we made love."

He kissed her then—a soft and surprisingly sweet kiss, the kind of kiss that she'd yearned for the night of her prom. But she wasn't a naive seventeen-year-old girl anymore, and her yearnings weren't nearly as innocent as they'd been twelve years earlier.

"I didn't call Paris," he told her now.

"Why?"

"Because even if you're okay with me dating other women, I'm not. I don't want any woman but you."

Her heart swelled inside her chest, but her brain continued to urge caution.

"For twelve years, every other woman I've dated has been a pale substitute for the one woman I really wanted but didn't believe I'd ever have—you. And I don't want to spend the next twelve years doing the same thing in a futile effort to get over you, because I know it won't ever happen."

"It's only been two weeks," she pointed out.

He tipped her chin up so that she could see the truth of his feelings in his eyes. "Two weeks, two months, two years—it doesn't matter," he told her. "It's always been you for me. Only you."

And those words, spoken from his heart, began to heal the broken pieces of her own.

"It's always been you for me," she admitted, as she led him to her bedroom. "Only you."

He framed her face in his hands and kissed her again.

"I've missed you." He whispered the confession against her lips. "I was going crazy, wondering if I'd ever be here with you like this again. If I'd ever have the chance to hold you, touch you, love you."

"Love me now," she suggested.

"I will." He kissed her once. "I am." Then again. "I do."

They quickly dispensed with their clothing, then fell together on top of her bed, a tangle of limbs and needs. Their mouths collided, clung; hands stroked, seduced; bodies merged, mated. The rhythm of their lovemaking was familiar—and somehow different. This time, all the illusions and pretensions had been stripped away by the acknowledgment of their feelings for one another, discarded like the garments that littered the floor. Now they were just a man and a woman, loving one another—and it was all either of them wanted or needed.

"I love you, Tristyn," he said.

To hear the words now, to know they were true, filled her heart to overflowing. "I love you, too," she admitted. "I tried not to—but I couldn't seem to help myself."

"I'm not sorry about that," he said. "I think I started to fall for you twelve years ago, but I wasn't nearly ready to acknowledge the depth of my feelings for you then." His lips curved in a wry smile. "Who am I kidding? I wasn't ready to acknowledge the depth of my feelings for you even a few weeks ago. Because I knew that you were the perfect woman for the rest of my life—and I was having too much fun in the moment to think about the rest of my life.

"And then, you were no longer with me in the moment. And I realized that I didn't want anything else as much as I wanted to be with you. Not just for the moment, but for always."

"Really?"

"Really," he assured her. "Over the past few weeks, I realized something else, too."

"What's that?"

"I think I'd like to have one or two kids of my own someday—if I could have them with you."

"I really like the sound of that," she told him.

"But while I was thinking about what I wanted for our future together, it occurred to me that your family—especially your cousin, my business partner and best friend—might not approve of us making plans to start a family before I put a ring on your finger."

"Well, I didn't think we were going to try to make a baby just yet," she noted.

"Not just yet," he confirmed, reaching into the pocket of his discarded jacket for the small velvet box. "But still—I'd like to do things in their proper order."

Then he flipped open the lid to reveal the three-carat, emerald-cut diamond centered on a platinum band set with pavé diamonds.

Tristyn gasped. "Oh, Josh."

"Daniel said that you'd have to be dazzled to ever agree to marry me."

And she was dazzled—as much by his revelation as the ring. "You told Daniel you were planning to propose?"

"I needed to make sure my best friend would be my best man," he told her. "So what do you say, Tristyn Garrett—will you marry me and turn 'for now' into 'forever'?"

She threw her arms around his neck and drew his mouth down to hers. "There isn't anything I want more."

Epilogue

Over the past six years, nine of Tristyn's cousins and both her sisters had married. Now, *finally*, it was her turn.

Once Josh had put his ring on her finger, he'd been eager to move from "engaged" to "married" as quickly as possible. Tristyn was excited about starting their life together, too, but she wanted to share the happy occasion with all their family and friends. They decided on an early spring date—on a non-race weekend, of course—at Trinity Church in downtown Charisma, with a bridal party reminiscent of a royal wedding.

Both Tristyn's sisters stood up with her, and Charlotte, Emily, Kylie and Hanna were all flower girls. On the groom's side, Josh had Daniel as his best man, champion race-car driver Ren D'Alesio as an usher, and though there were only two rings to be exchanged, there were five ring bearers: Jacob, Zachary, Logan, Henry and Liam.

"Afraid she's going to be a no-show and leave you standing at the altar?" Daniel asked the question under his breath, as they watched the procession of flower girls make their way toward the front of the church.

"No," Josh denied, unfazed by his friend's teasing.

He didn't believe for a minute that Tristyn would bail

on him—on them. It might have taken them a long time to find their way to one another, but there was no doubt in either of their minds that this was it for both of them.

And when she finally appeared at the back of the church, the sight of her made his heart race like the number 722 car on the straightaway at Talladega. He didn't know that the dress she was wearing was a tulle ball gown with a sweetheart neckline, back corset, chapel train and lace appliqués on the bodice and hem. He only knew that she took his breath away.

The ceremony did not go off without a hitch. Of course, with so many little ones in the wedding party, no one expected that it would. In the middle of the vows, Emily piped up to complain that her dress was scratchy and Henry pushed Liam off the dais, but through it all, Tristyn and Josh remained focused only on one another.

When the minister pronounced they were husband and wife, it was the end of the ceremony but only the beginning of the celebration. Hundreds of pictures were taken of the bride and the groom—alone and with various members of the wedding party, then more with other family members who were in attendance, including all the Garrett cousins from Pinehurst who had traveled to Charisma with their spouses and children for the occasion.

"How long do we have to stick around and make conversation with all these people?" Josh asked Tristyn.

"Considering that 'all these people' are our wedding guests—and many of them are family—a little while longer," she told him.

"I'm eager to get my wife back to the honeymoon suite so that I can peel that gorgeous wedding dress off her gorgeous body and we can consummate our marriage—and maybe get started on a family of our own."

"You don't want to take some time to get used to being husband and wife before we become daddy and mommy?"

"I'm ready." He pulled her into his arms. "I'm ready for anything with you by my side."

"And that's where I'm going to be," she promised him. "For now and forever."

He kissed her then—not at the direction of the minister or for the benefit of their wedding guests, but simply because she was his wife now and he could kiss her anywhere and anytime that he wanted to. When he released her, he caught a flutter of movement out of the corner of his eye.

Tristyn laughed, obviously having noticed Ren waving the checkered flag, too. "I bet you've been looking for an opportunity to do that all day."

"I have," the driver agreed, then winked at her before passing the flag to the groom. "Because he's obviously the big winner today."

"He's right," Josh agreed as Ren moved away. "Today, I am the luckiest man in the world."

"I think I got pretty lucky today, too," his bride said.

"What do you think about saying goodbye to our guests and going somewhere that we can get luckier?" he asked.

She smiled. "That idea gets a definite green flag from me."

And that's what they did.

* * * * *

MILLS & BOON®

Cherish™

EXPERIENCE THE ULTIMATE RUSH OF FALLING IN LOVE

MILLS & BOON®

EXCLUSIVE EXTRACT

Miranda Marlowe has just discovered
she's pregnant with her boss's baby…

Read on for a sneak preview of
HER PREGNANCY BOMBSHELL

Tomorrow she would go down to the beach, feel the
sand beneath her feet, let the cold water of the
Mediterranean run over her toes. Then, like an old lady,
she would go and lie up to her neck in a rock pool heated
by the hot spring and let its warmth melt away the
confused mix of feelings; the desperate hope that she
would turn around, Cleve would be there and, somehow,
everything would be back to normal.

It wasn't going to happen and she wasn't going to
burden Cleve with this.

She'd known what she was doing when she'd chosen
to see him through a crisis in the only way she knew
how.

She'd seen him at his weakest, broken, weeping for
all that he'd lost, and she'd left before he woke so that
he wouldn't have to face her. Struggle to find something
to talk about over breakfast.

She'd known that there was only ever going to be
one end to the night they'd spent together. One of them
would have to walk away and it couldn't be Cleve.

Four weeks ago she was an experienced pilot working

for Goldfinch Air Services, a rapidly expanding air charter and freight company. She could have called any number of contacts and walked into another job.

Three weeks and six days ago she'd spent a night with the boss and she was about to become a cliché. Pregnant, single and grounded.

She'd told the border official that she was running away and she was, but not from a future in which there would be two of them. The baby she was carrying was a gift. She was running away from telling Cleve that she was pregnant.

She needed to sort out exactly what she was going to do before, have a plan firmly in place, everything settled, so that when she told him the news he understood that she expected nothing. That he need do nothing…

Don't miss
HER PREGNANCY BOMBSHELL
by Liz Fielding

Available June 2017
www.millsandboon.co.uk

Copyright ©2017 Liz Fielding

MILLS & BOON®
are delighted to support
World Book Night

Georgie Lee

The Secret
Marriage Pact

World Book Night is run by The Reading Agency and is a national celebration of reading and books which takes place on 23 April every year. To find out more visit worldbooknight.org.

THE
READING
AGENCY

www.millsandboon.co.uk